The Penny Falls

Mark Bastable

Eleanor Grace Publishing Ltd

All names, characters, places, and incidents in this publication are fictitious or are used fictitiously. Any resemblance to real persons, living or dead, events or locales is entirely coincidental.

© 2013 by Mark Bastable

All rights reserved under International and Pan-American "CopyRight" Conventions. By payment of the required fees, you have been granted the non-exclusive, non-transferable right to access and read the text of this e-book on-screen. No part of this text may be reproduced, transmitted, down-loaded, decompiled, reverse engineered, or stored in or introduced into any information storage and retrieval system, in any form or by any means, whether electronic or mechanical, now known or hereinafter invented, without the express written permission of the author.

Cover design by Rachel Cole, Littera Designs

Eleanor Grace Publishing Ltd
ISBN: 9798669302528

Lovers and madmen have such seething brains,
Such shaping fantasies, that apprehend
More than cool reason ever comprehends.
The lunatic, the lover, and the poet
Are of imagination all compact.

William Shakespeare, *A Midsummer Night's Dream*

Contents

Chapter One	Given The Circumstances
Chapter Two	Turn Over This Coal
Chapter Three	Ghosts and Expiation
Chapter Four	A Yolky Stain
Chapter Five	Tinsel Elvis Twirls
Chapter Six	A Record of Accidents
Chapter Seven	The Kid with the Haunted Head
Chapter Eight	Posthumous Encouragement
Chapter Nine	Days Burning in Our Wake
Chapter Ten	A Mere Bag of Blood
Chapter Eleven	Dumb Luck and Cigarettes
Chapter Twelve	Unalloyed
Chapter Thirteen	Flame without a Candle
Chapter Fourteen	Dragging Hector
Chapter Fifteen	All That Made-Up Crap
Chapter Sixteen	In the Soft Hot Red
Chapter Seventeen	A Walk in the Garden
Chapter Eighteen	Are You Staying with Us Today?

Chapter One
Given the Circumstances

Carrying a plastic bag and soaked from head to toe in viscous blood, Pablo Lyne strode along Old Compton Street, past restaurants and sex shops, oblivious to the stalled traffic and the horrified pedestrians stepping aside to let him pass.

He paused at the junction with Wardour Street, and then he crossed the road and walked into the Golden Goose Amusement Arcade. He pushed a fifty-pound-note across the counter of the change-booth and asked for two-pence pieces. The lady handed over fistfuls of coins without counting them, her eyes never leaving Pablo's gore-streaked face. Pablo scooped the coppers into his plastic bag and wandered towards the back of the arcade where the old-fashioned penny-games were to be found.

The woman in the booth picked up the phone and called the police.

I watched all this, unseen, unnoticed. For the first time ever I was at a distance. I was independent of Pablo – tethered, but floating above him, carried on a tide of noise and colour; the panicky electronic shrieks of the video games, the promiscuous lights of the pinball tables, the neon tarantella paced out above the slot machines. I felt very alive – which was unexpected, given the circumstances.

Patrol cars pulled up outside the Golden Goose, blues flashing, and four policemen pushed through the crowd that had coagulated at the arcade entrance. The lady in the booth pointed at Pablo who was methodically and disinterestedly feeding coins into his chosen machine. The officers approached cautiously. One of them put a hand on Pablo's arm.

"You all right, mate? Why don't you come with us?"

"Okay," Pablo murmured. He nodded towards the machine he was playing. "I think I've won."

"Good for you. We'll bring your money – don't worry."

Pablo allowed himself to be led to the street and I tagged along after him. I didn't know what else to do.

As the policemen steered Pablo to the squad car, the crowd pressed towards him. Cameras flashed and journalists called out questions.

"What's your name? What have you done? Whose blood is that?"

One of the cops opened the door of the car and told Pablo to get in.

"Did you kill someone? Who did you kill?" a journalist shouted.

Pablo paused. He turned and looked at the crowd.

"My brother," he said. "Myself."

Chapter Two
Turn Over This Coal

One springtime evening in the centre of London, my twin brother confessed to murdering me.

I wasn't particularly put out. Having endured forty years of Pablo I was used to his attention-seeking stunts – and, anyway, I had quite enough on my plate. A month earlier, my sister's announcement of planned nuptials in New Zealand had focussed the family's attention on my terror of air travel. I'd tried to avoid the issue, but daily phone calls from my mother and dozens of bullying sororial e-mails eventually convinced me to sign up for a course of treatment. Ten days prior to Pablo's arrest I attended my first therapy session at the Camden Holistic Wellness Centre, which occupied three vanilla-scented rooms above a falafel shop in Chalk Farm.

"Tom Lyne? I'm Alice Brett."

My psychotherapist was a bespectacled, greying woman of about fifty, wearing a mauve blouse and wooden beads. Twenty years earlier she might have been the aunt you quite fancied as a teenager. She led me to a windowless room lit by a black-chrome uplighter over which a diaphanous scarlet scarf had been draped. I sat in an armchair and Alice settled herself opposite me, a notebook on her knee.

"This is cosy," I said, twisting the top off my mineral water. "Is it supposed to be womblike?"

"Is that how you see it?"

"My memory of the original isn't that clear."

Our subsequent conversation was supposed to be about me, of course, but as soon as I mentioned to Alice that I was a twin, her eyes lit up. If there's one thing guaranteed to get a psychologist going, it's repetitive siblings – a *tabula rasa* test-group for experiments in nature and nurture.

"Tell me about your brother," she said.

I've had to put up with this kind of eager fascination my entire life and it irks me. I resent the implication that the most interesting thing about me is that I'm nearly someone else.

"What's the relevance of my brother?"

"Maybe none. I don't know."

I sighed. "Okay – here's a quirky detail. I was born in a different year and a different country to my twin."

"How so?"

As this was all on the clock, I gave her the abridged version. "I was born at two o'clock in the morning on the first of January, 1963, in the Solomon Islands. In the airport, in fact. I was three weeks early and I had come into the world just as a spectacular typhoon was about to hit. My father, God knows how, persuaded an American air force plane to take my mother and me – still bloody and blue – out of the path of the weather. No one had any idea that mum's labour wasn't over. The plane flew east to Samoa, where my brother Pablo was born."

"Amazing."

"But the plane had crossed the international dateline into the previous day. So Pablo was born on the thirty-first of December, 1962 – after me, but the day before me."

Alice clapped her hands, laughing. "Oh, I love that."

"It breaks the ice at parties." I took another gulp of water. "Incidentally, if you suggest to me that my fear of flying springs from the neo-natal experience of storms over the Pacific, I shall laugh haha and terminate this course of treatment. Life is not that easily explained."

"I'd be out of a job if it were," Alice said.

*　　　　　*　　　　　*　　　　　*

Whether Tom likes it or not, it's true that we are all very nearly someone else. I am very nearly someone who was loved, who breathed, who was carried downstairs in a warm blanket and indulged. I am very nearly a drinker of wine and a seducer of women, a creator of art and a juggler of funds. And Pablo and Tom are very nearly someone blameless and abandoned, rotted away in the hot soil of a distant island.

Very nearly – that's my story in two words. Forty years ago, the billion-sided dice of genetic proteins were rolled and they came up a double – as they do sometimes – so I very nearly won back then. Instead, I am expunged, cut out. I always have been.

It seems to me that the living are made of moments forgotten. You no more recall the events that shaped you than the fired pot remembers the furnace. I squat amongst the warm embers of what forged Tom, and I know that if I were to blow on them they'd flare up and he'd be consumed by an incendiary flash of memory. But he's unaware of the heat he carries with him.

I'll turn over this coal of his past that burned long before I was coddled in the soft, hot red.

The carnal twins are a few months old – able to sit up, but not yet crawling. Their mother is trying to bathe them. She crouches on the green mat beside the bath-tub, one hand supporting Pablo, the other ready to catch Tom if he slips. Tom won't slip. He's confident and in possession of himself. Pablo won't slip either, because the Condesa is holding him up.

Tom slaps his little hands on the surface of the shallow, tepid water, splashing Pablo.

"No, no, Tomàs," the Condesa says in Catalan. "Be careful of Pablito."

Tom splashes again. Pablo laughs and shifts on his backside excitedly. He loses his balance and the Condesa has to keep him upright.

"James! Come and take Tomàs out, please. He's upsetting Pablo."

Dad strides into the bathroom. "Out you get, little man," he says, lifting Tom up in a warm towel from the rail. "Are you all clean and lovely?"

"He's fine," my mother says. She's patting Pablo's back with one soapy hand, gingerly, as if she's afraid she might open the welted crimson scar that runs parallel to his spine, from shoulder to hip. "Mother of Christ, James. Do you think it will always look like that?"

"I'm sure it'll fade," Dad says.

The Condesa cries silently as she washes Pablo. Every night she cries washing him. And Dad, powerless to prevent his wife's tears, stands there, looking at the baby in the bath and feeling that he, the patriarch, has failed somehow by allowing unhappiness in. He will spend his whole life trying to shield Pablo and the Condesa from unhappiness.

Both Dad and Mum gaze forlornly at scarred little Pablo while Tom, disregarded, falls asleep against Dad's shoulder. Dad puts him to bed alone, then goes downstairs where he and the Condesa watch TV with tireless Pablo sitting between them on the sofa, gurgling, until midnight.

Tom doesn't remember any of that, though the coal still burns, as do a hundred more that baked hard the clay of who he is. Bodies forget almost everything.

I don't. I remember everything that has ever happened to my brothers. I live on what they've chosen to discard. I clothe myself in hand-me-downs, but I find coins in the linings of these cast-offs; scribbled notes in coat pockets; train tickets and restaurant receipts; beach sand in summer shoes; strands of hair, lipstick stains, flecks of blood, smears of shit.

I construct our history from the traces that Tom and Pablo leave. I build the case against them. I prepare my claim.

*   *   *   *

Alice said, "Let's talk a little about what brings you to the Centre."

"Ah, the eternal human question – what brings you to the centre?" It was intended as joke but she didn't seem to get it, which was disappointing. I like people who can take a little gentle mockery. "It's simple. I'm nervous about aeroplanes."

"Nervous about them doing what? Looping the loop? Waking you in the night? Forgetting to land?"

I tipped my head to one side. "Are you making fun of me? I'm serious about this."

"Good. How would you prefer to feel about aeroplanes?"

"I suppose what I'd prefer," I said, noticing the way the light threw streaky crimson shadows across the ceiling, "is to see flying as merely dull." I looked back at Alice. "That must be a first – how many people come in here asking you to make their lives duller?"

"Most of them."

She asked me about previous occasions when I'd flown. My mother is Spanish, so when I was a child we flew regularly to Bilbao – my mum and dad, me and Pablo and our big sister Jacinta – so I must have been okay with it back then. To be honest, I can't recall my childhood in the way that other people seem to. My memories are reconstructed from my mother's anecdotes about me, as if it were someone else.

"Can you remember what it was like to *be* a child?" Alice asked.

"Not really. If I think about childhood, what I get is an overwhelming feeling of injustice. Life isn't fair when you're a kid. You get told off for things you didn't do. Promised treats fail to materialise."

"Do you think Pablo would feel the same way about his childhood?"

"What? What's it got to do with Pablo?"

"I just wondered whether you felt that life was unfair for all children – or just you."

I took a swig of my mineral water. "Pablo's childhood was one long, indulgent compensation for his birth," I said.

When Pablo was born, in an American military hospital in Samoa, he was hustled away from my mother before she could see him. My father, remember, was still stranded on the typhoon-tossed Solomon Islands, clinging to a palm tree with Jacinta strapped to his chest. Mother was alone, disorientated and hardly *compos mentis*. In the previous twenty-four hours, she'd undergone a lengthy labour delivering me, she'd been flown through a tropical storm in a USAF aircraft and she'd suffered a second labour to give birth to Pablo.

This was in the days before ultrasound, of course – she hadn't even been aware that she was carrying more than one baby. What's more, she barely spoke English at all. So when a midwife whisked the newborn away before she could even hold it, the Condesa became forgivably agitated. They knocked her out with a syringeful of something, and when she woke up I was in a crib beside her.

She assumed, understandably, that I was the infant she had most recently given birth to, and that somehow she had mislaid the one she had brought with her from the Solomon Islands. She tried to explain this to a nurse using a combination of mime and fractured English. She was holding me in the crook of one elbow, but she stretched out the other arm like an aeroplane wing, and then made baby-rocking motions. "Where baby? Two baby! Where baby?"

The gesture with the stiff, extended arm was unfortunate, because it led the nurse to believe that my mother had been told about Pablo. She brought him from the nursery and handed him over. Unlike me, he was not snugly dressed in a hospital all-in-one sleepsuit. He was loosely wrapped in a woollen blanket. My mother put me in the crib so that she could swaddle Pablo more cosily. She pulled the blanket off him – and screamed. She screamed as only an emotionally-exhausted Iberian mother can scream.

Protruding from the baby's back, slightly to the left of the spine, was an underdeveloped but perfectly recognisable arm complete with tiny hand and tinier fingers. The rest of the foetus, it turned out, was enclosed within the newborn's body – a separate being, but undeniably part of Pablo. One child consumed by the other within the womb.

"So, strictly speaking, you and Pablo are not twins at all," Alice said.

"No. We're surviving triplets."

*   *   *   *

Three days after Pablo was born, a nurse brought a telephone to the Condesa's room and plugged it in to a socket on the wall.

"Isabel?" my father said. "How are you?"

"Are you on your way?" my mother asked. "You said you'd be here tonight."

"I can't get a flight till tomorrow. Just not possible." He paused. The next sentence would have been difficult even in his native tongue. In clunky Castilian, it was nerve-wracking. "So – have they done, you know, the procedure? With the baby?"

The Condesa swallowed. "They're doing it now. That poor little thing. He's just a tiny scrap. I can't bear to think of it."

The tiny scrap was not me, of course – it was my brother. He was a 'poor little thing' because he had smothered me in the womb.

"He'll be fine – I'm sure he will. Is that Tomàs I hear crying?"

The Condesa looked at Tomàs in his crib beside her bed. She leaned across to pull his blanket up to his trembling chin.

"He cries all the time. I don't know what to do." She swapped the phone to the other ear. "Do you think it was the diving? If we hadn't gone out in the boat so often…"

"Izzy, it wasn't the diving. You didn't do anything wrong."

"Please get here soon, James. No one speaks any kind of Spanish in this place. I don't know what they're saying about us. I don't know what's going on."

"They're in touch with me all the time. Don't worry." He took a deep breath. *"Izzy – they're asking about names. For both of them."*

"Both of them?" She glanced at the baby in the crib. *"But we've already decided on Tomàs."*

"No – both the...the other two. We need to give them names in case – you know – in case things don't go well."

Difficult to see how things could possibly have gone well for me. It was a bit late for that. What my father meant was that they needed a name to bury me with. The Condesa was distraught at the implication, and it was several minutes before Dad calmed her down sufficiently to discuss it.

"I hadn't thought beyond 'Tomàs'," she said. *"But I like 'Pau'."*

"Pow?"

"It's Catalan. Like the saint. The road to Damascus."

"Oh, I see. No – 'Pau' won't work in Britain. Though 'Pablo' I don't mind at all."

They pushed back and forth, but the Condesa was too tired to fight her corner, and Dad's suggested compromise prevailed. Then they turned to the problem of naming a dead child – me.

"I was thinking perhaps Jordi, after your father," Dad said.

"You want me to tell my father that we named a dead baby in his honour?"

"No – I meant..."

"I can't talk about this. Not now."

"Izz, we have to decide before..."

...before they could dispose of me. Once I'd been cut from Pablo's body, I had to be given a name so they could forget it.

"You decide, James. I don't want to know. You decide."

There was a silence on the telephone line. Tomàs whimpered. He was hungry.

"James?" my mother said. "It'll all be all right, won't it?"

"I'll be there the day after tomorrow. It'll all be all right."

"How's Jacinta?"

"She's fine. Missing you."

They exchanged reassurances and, in tears, they ended the call.

The nurse returned, accompanied by a grubby and discomfited young man who made a half-bow to the Condesa.

"I'm Xavi, the gardener. They want me to translate for you," he said in Castilian. He glanced at Tomàs, wide-eyed in his crib. "The other baby is out of the operating theatre."

The nurse spoke in English and the young man nodded. He turned back to my mother.

"He's weak but he seems to be stable. As long as he stays clear of infection, he should be okay."

"I want to see him," the Condesa said.

They helped her out of bed and off she went to look at Pablo, wired up, tube-stuck, bandaged and wounded. The Condesa wept, shredded by the guilt of having done such terrible damage to a little baby. She would *spend the rest of her life attempting to make up for it whilst simultaneously trying to pretend it never happened. The sustenance of that paradox was an exhausting and time-consuming obligation. And hopeless, of course.*

Back in the room, Tomàs lay in his crib and stared up at the rotating ceiling fan, hungry but past crying – just waiting for his mother to return from fretting over Pablo.

*　　　*　　　*　　　*

Jacinta was asleep on the sofa in the hotel room in the Solomon Islands. The phone rang and Dad turned the TV off to take the call. The surgeon in Samoa reported that the baby was going to be fine. The anomaly – me, me! – had been successfully excised. The surgeon said that I was recognisably a foetus – hair, limbs, face – but that I had never been, in any real sense, alive. Dad put down the phone and went out to the balcony. He lit a cigarette which he smoked slowly, gazing at the sun subsiding into the Pacific.

He went back inside, draped a blanket over Jacinta and picked up the telephone. It took him an hour to organise a connection. At last he got through to the hospital chaplain in Samoa.

"I've talked to my wife about names."

"Good, good. I have the forms right here."

"We've decided on Pablo Jordi Vivas." He spelled it out and Father Cahill read it back.

"Yes. Perfect," Dad said. He lit another cigarette, merely to create time to think. He still hadn't come up with a name for me. He understood why the Condesa refused to participate, but he didn't want to bear the responsibility alone. It seemed to him more delicate a matter to choose a name for a dead baby than for a healthy one. It would have enormous evocative power that could never be diminished. Being so seldom voiced, it would retain all the potency of a curse. A mother calling to her kid in the supermarket, a character on a TV soap – the very sound of it would drag down the day or punch a hole through an evening.

"And for the lost boy?" the chaplain prompted.

Dad registered the euphemism – 'the lost boy.' It gave the impression of a temporary misplacement, as if James and Isabel's third twin was bound to turn up in a minute, announced over the fairground PA system, found sheepish in the admin office. As was his habit, Dad tried it in Spanish. El hijo perdido. He liked it. He had taught scuba to a girl called Perdita. Presumably the masculine equivalent would be 'Perdito'. The lost boy. It worked.

"Perdito," Dad told the chaplain. "Perdito James Vivas Lyne."

"Can you spell it please?"

Dad did so.

"And then 'James', like you?" Father Cahill said.

"Yes."

When my mother found out, she was tearfully furious.

"Perdito? That's not a name! It's not even a word! Are you out of your mind?"

But it was too late. The name was on the birth certificate and it was the one with which my anomalous flesh was buried. Distorted and repulsive abomination that I was, I had quite properly been saddled with a malformed and nonexistent name.

Though she acknowledges its use by her family, the Condesa has never accepted it. Not once has she said my name aloud. If ever she's obliged to refer to me, she calls me 'Pedrito' – little Peter.

My mother has convinced herself that her lost baby was a misprint.

*   *   *   *

As I was dead at the time, one might wonder how I know all this.

Flesh retains everything, though it remembers so little. Every noise, every movement, every colour and texture, noticed or otherwise – all of it is held in the synapses forever.

I wasn't there, but three-day-old Tomàs was. His blank little brain was being inscribed already with experience. Many years later, in hiding, lying in wait, I filled the days by gorging myself on Tom's memory.

But I have my own memories too. I even remember when I became conscious of flesh. It happened five years after my brothers were born and I was discarded. In those intervening years of limbo, there had been only a gluey, unfocussed awareness of sensation – not even a specific nameable sense of colour or sound or texture. I existed in a miasma that had no temperature or light or lack of light, and I was surrounded by a shifting flavourless hum.

Still – as time passed I was learning. I understood that I was not solitary, not independent. And I believed that I was called Pablo, although I felt that I shouldn't be. I knew that there was Tomàs and that Tomàs was not me, but part of me.

I had no notion of where these convictions came from, but they were there – and at one time they had not been. Apart from knowledge, nothing was.

And then, suddenly, there was everything.

"Pablo – are you alright? Pablo? Look at me! How many fingers?"

Unblinding light. And fingers – the palm of the hand towards me, the thumb folded across. My father – I knew he was my father – was looking at me, concerned and panicky. His eyes were blue as shiver. I remember that blue, despite being instantaneously assaulted by the mob-handed spectrum into which I'd been thrust. Behind my father an ecstatic violence of colours – pinching, stroking, slapping, bear-hugging, smooching colours – dumbfounded me like a scald.

"Mare de Deu – what happened?"

"He got a shock from the Christmas lights," my father said, his eyes on me. "He's breathing. It's okay."

"Pablito! What did you do?" My mother appeared behind my pale, grave father, blocking my view of the rainbow eruptions in the background. "He's not speaking, James!" Her hair was long and golden like July. "What's wrong with his eyes? Can he see? James – oh, God – he can't see! Pablo – look at Mummy!"

"My head hurts," someone said. I heard it said, and I knew that I'd said it. And I understood it when I heard it. Close by, my head hurt.

I sat up, helped by my father. My mother pushed him aside and pulled me to her, wrapping her arms around me. The smell of her was bright and smooth, something that undulated. "Thank God you're all right. Thank God, thank God."

I began to cry. I could tell it was me crying, but I didn't know how I was doing it. The pain was close to me, and the crying was further away, but still part of me. My mother and father were more distant still – outside me. Not me.

"I don't think he's quite conscious yet," my father said. "Give him a chance to breath, Izz."

My mother let go and I sat cross-legged on the carpet looking at my bare knees and my green shorts and my hands resting on my thighs.

"Is something burning in the kitchen?" my father asked.

"Oh, God – the birthday cakes!" my mother said, and scurried out through the door.

My father put his hand under my chin and lifted my head. My eyes looked at him – and I could feel him receding.

"Perhaps you'll pay a bit more attention when I tell you not to touch things now, eh? You scared the living daylights out of me, you little bugger." He lifted up the body I was in, resting its head on his shoulder.

Again I could see the insanity of colours and shapes that had so shocked me a few minutes before, but they were further away now. They stroked and tickled and prodded without any real force. I longed for their joyous violence.

"For a moment there I thought I'd lost you, Pablo," my father whispered huskily.

The body I was in pressed against my father's chest. The arms of the body I was in wrapped themselves around his neck, and I felt distanced. "It's okay, Daddy," *said the voice that was not me.* "I'm all right now."

"You're still shaking," my father said. "But you'll be back to yourself in no time."

And once again, nothing was.

Time passed, and I knew it passed only because knowledge seeped into me like rising damp into an unlit cellar. I found I knew I was Perdito. I was not Pablo. Pablo was someone else. But not in the way that my parents were someone else. Pablo was not-me not in the way that my father was not me.

I was Perdito. I was not Tomàs. Tomàs was someone else. But Tomàs was not someone else in the way that Pablo was someone else. Tomàs was someone else in a way that no one else was not me.

Then, in the not-there, came a dancing vein – skipping and wavering across nothing, red as nettle and warm. It scooted up and slid down. It waved. It weaved. It climbed towards me and teased away. The darkness loosened and I could feel Pablo there.

"Pablo? Hello?"

The world opened up to me – and it was Pablo's world.

Chapter Three
Ghosts and Expiation

My name is Stephen Richmond, and I first became aware of Pablo Lyne at a crucifixion in Covent Garden.

It was Ash Wednesday. I was on my way to see a publisher for lunch, and my path across the Piazza was blocked by a gawking crowd. A cross had been set up – perhaps eight feet high – and convincingly nailed to it was a gaunt man wearing a loincloth. I would have taken this spectacle to be part of a Passion Play were it not for a flashing purple neon sign above the Christ-figure's head, that read "Happy Easter!" As I watched, the crucified man began to sing *There is a Green Hill Far Away*, in a childish falsetto that was both eerie and mocking. The entire performance was merrily blasphemous, but also rather intriguing.

As the hymn concluded the police arrived, and I departed for my lunch appointment. That evening, the 'disturbance' – as the newsreader termed it – featured as a short item on the local BBC radio station. I wondered with what exactly the police had charged the pseudo-Christ.

Almost a year later, I turned on the television to see a shot of the same man. His face was haggard and streaked with blood as he gazed out of the window of a police car. Pablo Lyne, 40, of no fixed address, had confessed – falsely, as it turned out - to the murder of his brother.

The police could not, of course, give me any direct information about Pablo Lyne, but they did tell me the name of the firm of solicitors representing him. It was that in which my old friend George Sandham was a senior partner. He arranged a meeting at their chambers in Holborn.

"Good to see you, Stephen," George said, ushering me into his office. "So you sense some profit in our Mr Lyne?"

"Perhaps, yes," I said, taking a seat. "I may be wrong."

"I thought you agent chaps barricaded yourself in and listened to the scribblers scratching at the door."

I accepted a cup of tea from George's assistant and allowed myself a biscuit.

"I indulge a hunch from time to time." The truth was that I was tired of pedestrian thrillers and celebrity cookbooks. I'd recently sold a footballer's autobiography, and the advance I secured on those two hundred pages of callow reminiscence was three times greater than any other I've negotiated. "It's a form of expiation, I suppose. An offering to the literary idealist in me. My instinct is that your client has a worthwhile story to tell – though I may have to bring in a ghost to write it."

"Ghosts and expiation – the story of both our lives," George said. He and I had been friends for forty years and there was little we didn't know about each other. "I can imagine, of course, precisely why Mr Lyne's circumstances are of interest to you."

"You're overanalysing, George. What do you make of him?"

"He's an odd bird, to be honest." George steepled his fingers and let out a long breath. "It's as if he sees the world in different colours to the rest of us."

"He's unintelligible? Impossible to communicate with?"

"No, no. He's very lucid and forthcoming. But sometimes he seems to be operating with an alternative spectrum."

I was pleased that George was perplexed. It was partial confirmation of my instinct that Pablo Lyne was an unusual individual.

Though he didn't look it. In an office at the end of the corridor, I was introduced to a thin man of forty – collar-length light brown hair greying around the high widow's peak, chill-blue eyes like a Christmas sky, a weak chin and a wide mouth. He was wearing a white t-shirt, narrow blue jeans and white canvas shoes stained with what I suspected was blood. The implications of that macabre detail apart, he was not a remarkable man, but not an unattractive one either.

I held out my hand. "Mr Lyne – I am Stephen Richmond. It's nice to meet you."

Pablo nodded. "I'm told you're a literary agent."

"I am, yes."

"Is there any chance of you buying me lunch in an attempt to persuade me to do whatever it is you want me to do?"

"I think I can manage that."

He was hardly dressed to dine at my club, so we went to an Italian restaurant on the Strand. Over a bottle of Chianti we chatted about his recent encounter with the law, which had occupied the newspapers for a day or two. The coverage harked back to the crucifixion I'd happened upon in Covent Garden and one or two similar stunts.

"So I take it you are a conceptual artist. A situationist, perhaps?"

"Christ, no," he laughed, running his fingers through his hair and tugging the curls at the nape of his neck. This was a gesture that I'd get to know well. Pablo had many of them. He would take a cigarette from the pack and toss it into his mouth with a flick of his palm, catching it neatly on his jutted lower lip – I rarely saw him miss. When he was thinking an idea through, he would lean his head back, mouth open, flicking his eyes from side to side for several seconds, before dropping his chin and saying, "Right. I think it works like this…"

"Then what would you call your appearances?" I asked him.

He tapped a cigarette out.

"Conversation," he said.

"With whom?"

"I tend to talk to people who are about at the time. If you talk to people who aren't there, you get some very funny looks."

I smiled. "Fair enough. Though writing gives you the chance to talk to people who aren't there."

"It gives you the chance to talk *at* people who aren't there," he said. "which is a very different thing." He flipped the cigarette and caught it.

"And can you write? I mean, have you ever written anything for publication?"

"No. But I expect I could."

Perhaps I should have been impressed by his confidence, but I rarely meet anyone who doesn't believe they have a book in them. Taxi drivers, waiters, accountants, barristers. I wish I had the commission on an advance for every time I've heard, 'I should write a book about this job. It'd make a fortune.'

"There's more to it than simply being literate, you know."

Pablo glanced at the menu. "I'll have the Bolognese," he said. "Have you got any paper in your briefcase?" I found a yellow legal pad and a pen, which I handed to him. He lit the cigarette and topped up his wine glass. "Give me a subject."

"Something about your childhood."

"Okay."

I watched him as he wrote, never pausing, never appearing to consider the next sentence. He was scribbling right-handed – but then he swapped the pen to his other hand so that he could pick up his cigarette from the ashtray, and he continued writing with his left hand, apparently unaware of what he'd done. Our food arrived and he forked pasta into his mouth with his right hand whilst continuing to write with his left, breaking off only long enough to take large gulps of wine and drags on the cigarette.

As I was finishing my ravioli, he handed the pad back to me.

"There you go," he said.

His handwriting was large and loopy, the hoops of each *y* and *g* tangling with the upstrokes of the letters on the line below. The concept of paragraphs was one that Pablo eschewed. He began at the top left-hand corner of the legal pad, and wrote in an unbroken stream to the bottom right, each line filled to the edges of the paper, ignoring the ruled margins. Apart from that adjustment for the sake of legibility, I present Pablo's first piece of prose unedited.

When I was a child I read all the time. All I wanted, really, was to be left alone to wander in the world of fiction. My favourite book was Alf's Button *– a tatty hardcover with nicotine-coloured pages that smelled of a time before plastic, television aerials and natural gas.*

I loved stories about the wondrous amidst the mundane, and Alf's Button *delivered. A soldier in the Great War is polishing the buttons on his tunic when a genie appears and offers him three wishes.*

Alf makes a total comic mess of it, as I was sure he would. I'd thought about this a lot. I knew that genies were slippery bastards, but when mine turned up he was going to discover that Pablo Lyne had prepared wishes that pre-empted all weaselly over-literal interpretations of wording and any obtuse misunderstanding of intention. I'd considered the problems of commanding a genie or adopting a Neanderthal or chumming around with the ghost of a Victorian schoolgirl walled-up in our basement, and I was prepared.

My literary interests readied me, I guess, for what happened on the London train and after.

"Well, that's really not bad at all," I said, laying the pad on the table. I was pleasantly surprised. At the very least Pablo could express himself on the page.

"Thank you. Any chance of another bottle?"

"Of course." I ordered more wine.

"So what do you want me to write?" Pablo said.

"I want to read the story that ends with a man in an amusement arcade on Wardour Street, soaked from head to foot in blood and claiming to have killed his brother."

Pablo laughed. "Yeah. I'd quite like to get that straight myself."

"I'm told you're homeless," I said. "Where did you spend last night?"

"At the Ritz."

I nodded. "Fair enough. It was an impertinent question and it deserved a fatuous answer. Let me put it differently. Where do you plan to spend tonight?"

"I might go to the Savoy. The Ritz is a bit stuffy for my tastes."

"Would it help if I were to offer you a place to stay? I have plenty of room at my house."

Had anyone asked me at that moment why I was inviting Pablo into my home, I would have said that I was a good judge of character and I had a fine instinct for a tale. Now – after all that's happened – I believe that I sensed my own salvation in Pablo. Over the following months, as his narrative unfolded before me, I became able to understand my own story. And not before time.

"I get my own room, I take it?" Pablo said, grinning.

"I suppose it would be naïve of me to protest that the question is unnecessary – but, yes. Of course."

"Okay," Pablo said. "Yes. Why not?"

We took the train back to Aylesbury, and my new house-guest embarked dauntlessly on the task of emptying the wine cellar whilst churning out pages of handwritten prose.

*   *   *   *

I awoke this morning from uneasy dreams to find myself transformed in my bed into a gigantic insect. That's a great first line. Everything I've ever read about writing says you've got to have a grabby opening sentence, and that's the one I want.

But actually, I awoke this morning from a dreamless sleep to find myself alone, which still feels so strange to me that transformation into a cockroach would be less of a shock. I lit a cigarette and lay there looking at the ceiling and listening to the lack of another voice.

I wandered down to the kitchen where my host was making breakfast. Stephen asked me how I'd slept, and I told him that I'd slept fine, thanks. He indicated the newspaper folded on the table.

"Trouble in Israel," he said, sighing. "I don't know, I'm sure."

I ground pepper onto the eggs. "I refuse to feel guilty about it," I said. "I've only just forgiven myself for the slave trade and the East India Company."

He gave the indulgent, half-amused grin that he uses when he's not sure whether I'm serious.

"I'm off to town today," he said. "Will you be alright?"

I assured him I would.

After breakfast I went back to bed and snoozed until I heard the crunchy swoosh of Bentley wheels on gravel as Stephen headed off down the drive. I got up and padded through to the bathroom. I like this bathroom. It has hinged full-length mirrors facing each other, which means that by angling them just so, I can study my own back. You don't get to see your own back very often. I stood there naked, and looked at the pink scar that follows the motorway of my spine like an A-road – from a little below my shoulder blades to just above my buttocks, where it ends in an untidy squiggle.

"I'm sorry," I told it, as I always do. "Dumb luck."

I checked out my cock. It's a terrible piece of design, the male member. It looks like it was stuck on afterwards, lazily. "Oh, shit," you can imagine God saying, "What about reproduction?" And he reached for some clay, which he rolled between his palms, looking up and down the model. He slapped it on about halfway up, smoothing the base in with his fingers. "Bugger it – that'll do."

Having showered, I pulled on my jeans and t-shirt and wandered downstairs – through the dining room to the French doors leading to the terrace that overlooks the garden. It was a beautiful morning – spring sunshine and glinting dew. I strolled towards the flowerbeds and got down on all fours as I approached the crocuses and daffodils. I crawled up to them, eye-level. I let them awe my vision – cheek-spasming yellow and drunken purple. I extended my tongue and touched the sticky dust in them, like a bee. I turned over on my back and looked up at the trumpet of a narcissus – so definedly crinkled and terribly fragile – so close to being not what it was. It could have been different, but it remained what it was supposed to be. That's a neat trick.

I lay there under the trumpet of the narcissus for the duration of a cigarette. And then I got up and came back in here to the room that Stephen has designated as my workspace. This is the bargain – the price I pay for the breakfasts and the care and the run of the grounds. I must write my story for Stephen.

Not that I mind. I have a few months to kill before the next big fluke in my life is due.

...*of Nuns*

A tightness, a fiddle, a floe, or a harmony
A habit or matin, devotion or rosary,
A notion, conversion, susurration or vesper,
A prayer book, a patience, a purse or a whisper.

Last night I complained to Stephen that I had no idea how to write my story. He's given me a structure. I have it taped to the left-hand speaker of the PC in front of me.

Childhood
Adolescence
Academic Education
Emotional Education
Profession/Jobs
Recent Activities

It's pretty much chronological, evidently. But I'm not sure that I think of my life in that way. Life's simply a series of random events that happen to be studded across time like peanuts in a chocolate bar. You might get to them in a specific order as you chomp your way along it, but the relative position of any given peanut to the others has no real significance. Everything is down to luck. Dumb luck.

Take, for instance, how my dad died. He was a rugby fan. He used to follow Harlequins. One bleak and showery spring Saturday, he was standing, as he always did, on the terrace behind the posts, in his long grey mackintosh and wonderfully anachronistic homburg. The rain had let up and he was poaching gently in the sudden spring sunshine, when the ball was kicked, hard and direct, into the crowd. Dad saw it coming and ducked. It hit the bloke behind him full in the face. The bloke staggered forward and pushed Dad, still crouched, down the terrace. The guy in front was holding a furled umbrella over his shoulder like a rifle, and the point went straight through Dad's left eye and into his brain.

No one to blame. No irony and no plot. Just dumb luck.

*   *   *   *

I read it before dinner as we sat on the terrace, Pablo smoking ceaseless cigarettes and topping up his glass of claret after every sip.

"What do you think?" he asked, when I put the sheaf on the table and stood the bottle on top to stop it blowing away in the light breeze.

I reached for my glass. "Why did you write it all longhand?"

"I like the smell of ink."

"Fair enough. I'll get it typed up." I tapped the sheets of paper with my forefinger. "I like the tone and the detail. The problem is structure. It hasn't got one."

"It has. It's the structure of me. My thoughts go that way and that's how I write. It's valid."

I have often been confronted by authors making this argument. It's a variation on the idea that self-expression is, by definition, interesting and consequential – a philosophy that was the bane of every twentieth-century art form, as if 'honest' self-expression obviated the need for the presumably mendacious application of technique, style, structure or even talent.

"Pablo, if you made tea-pots and you came up with one that had the handle on the bottom, and a spout eight feet long, and the whole thing made of chicken-wire, would you still say that that was how you made teapots, and that therefore it was a 'valid' teapot?"

"Probably, yes," he said, flipping a cigarette into his mouth.

"And you have the right to, I suppose. But you would have made a teapot that never fulfilled the function of containing and pouring tea. One, in fact, that *couldn't* fulfil that function. So it would not be, in any observable sense, a teapot, would it?"

"I thought the whole idea was that we're after my story, as told by me."

"But comprehensible to other people."

Pablo sighed and picked up the empty claret bottle. "All right. I'll try." He stood and walked into the house, then paused, sniffing the air. "Something's burning," he said.

"Oh, bother," I said, getting to my feet. "The goulash."

As I brushed past Pablo on my way to the kitchen, he said, "If it's burnt, congealed and inedible, it doesn't in any observable sense fulfil the function of a goulash, does it?"

*   *   *   *

Stephen's house, huge though it is, must have been very inexpensive to wallpaper. Every foot of wall that's not window is covered with bookshelves. Here in the drawing room there are bookshelves from the parquet to the cornice. One wall of the kitchen is given over to books; there are books ranked on the working surfaces and piled on the windowsill above the sink. The long drop of the stairwell is lined with books, and bookshelves follow the landing, allowing begrudged gaps for the doors to the bedrooms. There is a bookcase in each of the bathrooms and when you use the downstairs toilet, your knees brush against the books on either side. It's discouraging. As I sit here with my pad and pen, I can't see that the world really needs another book.

"I've been looking at your books," I told Stephen last night after dinner. We were sitting out on the terrace with a bottle of wine. "They're not in any real order, are they? Fiction's mixed in with biography. Gardening books turn up in the middle of a run of fine art. How do you ever find anything?"

He got to his feet and picked up the empty wine bottle. "Oh, I manage. Excuse me while I nip to the cellar for another."

While he was down there I made a quick tour of the house with my legal pad. As Stephen was opening the wine I said, "What's the Portuguese for corkscrew?"

He raised an eyebrow. "I've no idea. I have an English-Portuguese dictionary somewhere. Hold on." He popped the cork, poured me a glass and left the room. Within five minutes he was back with the dictionary, flicking through it. He'd got it from the second-to-top shelf on the right-hand wall in the dining-room – which is where I had noticed it a few minutes before.

"*Saca-rolhas,* apparently," he said, looking up from the page. "Why do you ask?"

I told him that I had a surreal idea for an episode to write. It was based on a Philip K. Dick short story I'd read as a teenager. Actually, I mused, I could do with looking over that story again.

It took him seven minutes to find a volume of Dick's short stories, which was in a bookcase behind the door of the box room.

I paged through it, tutting. "No. Maybe I'm wrong. Maybe it was Asimov. Sorry to make you run around like this."

"No problem," he said, scurrying off again. Two minutes. Bottom shelf on the half-landing.

I like this lack of organisation in the storing of Stephen's books. And I like the way he copes with it – developing a technique for handling randomness rather than putting effort into imposing order. That's what life is, really.

Most people spend their whole lives pretending that the universe acts predictably when it evidently doesn't. It's as if we want a world in which the only permitted colour is blue. When it proves impossible to squint or blink in such a way that no red or yellow or green impinges on our vision, we put on blue-filter sunglasses that cut out any other hue.

Look – blue sky, blue sea, blue clouds, beautifully counterpointed by black roses and black grass. Everything that's not blue is no colour at all. Blue boiled potatoes, blue cod fillet with some black spinach and black sweetcorn, washed down with a nice glass of blue wine. Lovely.

It's understandable. The full spectrum of uncontrolled possibility is a scary thing. Falling piano, terrorist attack, drunken bus driver, a rugby ball punted into the crowd – you don't want to think about the innumerable shades of happenstance that could black you out. A million trillion things might occur, and you'd probably emerge alive from about ten of them. Human beings can't cope with the implication of their own insignificance that arises from the maths. But – hey – you're already ahead of the game just by being here at all. There are two hundred and fifty million spermatozoa in the average consignment, so the chances of you existing were pretty slim from the start.

My mother has spent her life in blue glasses, though chromatically-flawed ones. They let her see all sorts of colours she'd rather not know about –

and once she's seen them, she can't stop herself mixing them on the palette of her imagination into a terrifying psychedelic abstract.

One Wednesday in the early summer of 1972, my sister Jazz was taken ill after my father left for work. Mum was supposed to accompany me to Moorfields Eye Hospital for an appointment that had taken six months to arrange. She called Dad at the office.

"No, James," she was saying as I wandered through the hallway. "He's only a baby. I don't put him on train by himself. God alone knows what happens."

"Just shovel him on. All he has to do is sit there until it terminates at Waterloo and I'll meet him. He's nine years old, Isabel."

"He maybe gets off the wrong place! Or you don't find him in Waterloo!"

"He won't and I will. He can read a station sign, can't he?"

The Condesa was unconvinced. What if the train was unexpectedly terminated at an earlier stop? What if I lost my ticket and there was an inspection? What if there was a nationwide power cut or my father's cab wrapped itself around a lamppost and he was killed?

Dad knew that there was no point in soothing the Condesa's fears – you had to trump them. "What if Pablo has a serious eye condition and he loses his sight before we can get another slot with the quack?"

Eventually my mother called a taxi to take us both to the station – she has never learned to drive. As she bustled me out of the front door, she forbade Jazz to move from the sofa. "Don't touch anything! No kettle, no lights! You like this programme? Okay – so no need to touch TV, understand? I come home in twenty minutes only."

At the station she reluctantly ushered me aboard, patting my hand through the open window as if I were off to the Somme. I sat there with Stig of the Dump in one pocket and a Mars bar in the other. The train began to move and my mother released her grip, calling "You don't move out this seat before Waterloo, Pablito! Understand? Close the window!" I *nodded and waved, and as soon as the station had fallen away I got up and strolled along the carriage.*

It was one o'clock on a midweek afternoon – too late for people going up to town to shop, but too early for those travelling to the West End for dinner. I was nine years old and I had never been out in the world on my own. In fact I'd very rarely been alone at all – twins don't get a lot of privacy. But now I had an entire train carriage to myself.

I ate the Mars bar and gazed out of the window as the train sped past lumber yards, churches, suburban back gardens, treasured allotments. Between the flitting trunks of trees I saw freeze-frames of an old man bending in a flower border; a little girl hesitating at the top of a slide; a farmer in a red shirt opening a five-bar gate. Every so often a greenhouse would flash sunshine at me. For a tiny fraction of a second as the train rushed towards London I was at exactly the right spot in the universe to receive the reflected light of the sun bounced from one angled pane of glass. No other human being would ever catch that dazzle of light exactly as I had caught it. No one had ever seen and no one would ever see the bending old man or the hesitating little girl or the red-shirted farmer as I saw them.

It was a hot day and the train wasn't air-conditioned. I pressed my forehead to the glass, feeling the sun on my cheek. A red cable ran alongside the track. I watched it undulating towards me and then drifting further away; slinking tight in by the carriage for a few seconds before diving out towards the cutting. As the train roared through stations the cable adroitly dodged close to the track. It skipped around pylons and climbed the wall when we entered a tunnel. I went into a mild trance. I was thinking of nothing, focussed on the red cable in such a way that it occupied my eyes without engaging my brain.

And I heard a voice close to me say, "Pablo. Hello, Pablo?"

I turned, startled – but there was no one there. The rattle and roar of the train suddenly seemed deafening, and the sunlight through the window was wincingly bright. I was aware of the texture of the covered seat against the palm of my hand, plush and warm, and as I looked down, its plaid pattern was three dimensional, the green stripe hovering above the blue background, the yellow thread weaving between my fingers as if my hand were cats-cradled into the fabric. The smell of the carriage crowded me – I could taste the oily tang of the print on a discarded newspaper at my feet; the heavy mustiness of baked travel-dust; spilt coffee.

"Pablo?"

Again, close to me, behind me. I was frightened, and I felt faint. I whimpered and closed my eyes. The smells of the carriage made me nauseous and my arms were goosefleshed. I started to shiver. Even with my eyes shut I could see the red cable, swooping, retreating, coming in tight – and humming now. Singing. I could smell cinnamon and nettles. I felt I was falling backwards but not moving at all.

"Pablo? Hey, wake up, you dozy bugger."

The train was stationary and there were passengers in the other seats. My father was lifting me up, his hand under my bum and my head on his shoulder. He carried me off the train on to the platform and I heard slamming doors and a guard's whistle.

My dad chuckled. "That was close. I wouldn't have fancied phoning your mother to say I'd missed you." He leaned me back from his shoulder so that he could look me in the face as he strode towards the barrier. He was dressed for work – dark suit and bright red tie. "You look a bit flushed, mate. Are you all right?" Eyes fixed on the tie, I seemed to feel the intensity of the colour as a physical sensation – a fingertip stroked against the back of my throat. I gulped weakly and Dad frowned. "Pablo? What's wrong?"

There was a roaring in my head, and my eyeballs ached. I opened my mouth to speak and threw up all over my father's chest.

My puke-spattered father cleaned us both up somewhat in the public lavatories and we travelled home in the guard's van to avoid offending other commuters. I suspect Dad slipped the guard a few pounds. He was always of the opinion that a well-placed fiver could solve most everyday problems, and his unfettered application of this philosophy used to drive my parsimonious mother insane.

The Condesa put me to bed with an orange plastic bucket and a dose of Dr Collis Brown's patent elixir. I don't know whether they still sell the stuff, but if they do I bet it contains less morphine now than it did when I was nine. I loved it. My mother rather carelessly left the bottle on the bedside table, and every time I woke from my opiate-addled sleep I took another swig and dozed off again. I think I was out for a couple of days – and during that blissful vacation, everything changed.

"Pablo? Hello?"

I could feel the pillow against my face and the covers pulled up around my ears; I could hear myself snoring softly.

"Pablo – here I am."

"Hello?" I said – perhaps aloud.

"I'm here."

"Who are you?"

There was a pause and I could feel something in me – but not me – contemplating the question.

"I think I'm Perdito. But I don't know who Perdito is."

I knew who Perdito was. Since we were very young, Tomàs, Jazz and I had known that my mother had had a baby who died. It wasn't mentioned often – in fact, I can't remember it ever being mentioned at all, so I don't know how I was aware of it. I imagine we'd been told when we were too small to be other than blasé about the idea.

"You must be a ghost," I said.

"But I'm not dead."

He had a point. He didn't sound like a ghost. In fact he sounded just like me.

"Where are you?" I asked.

Again I could feel puzzlement and confusion that was separate from me but somehow attached to me – as you might feel a shoelace come loose as you walk.

"I'm where you are. I'm in bed," Perdito said eventually.

I sat up – or I dreamt I sat up – and I looked from side to side.

"Where?" *I said.*

There was a sudden lurch of panic, like an unexpected dip in the road. "Don't wake up! Please – sleep!"

"I'm already awake."

Perdito sounded perplexed. "You can't be." *He was thinking again.* "Can you see the orange bucket?"

I was looking straight at it. "Yeah."

"We can see the orange bucket. Both of us." *Another pause.* "Move a finger."

I don't think this conversation could have taken place at any other time in my life. Much older than nine I would have put it down to the effects of the Collis Brown and, having scared myself sober, dismissed it. Any younger, I would have accepted that to chat with voices in your head was no more unusual than to take tea with teddy bears or to have one's nose stolen by a visiting uncle. I might not have sustained interest in it.

Under the covers, I wiggled the little finger of my left hand.

"Little finger left hand," *Perdito said immediately and his voice was triumphantly gleeful.* "We're both here!"

The door opened and my mother walked in.

"How you feeling, sweetie?" *she asked, laying a hand on my forehead.* "Sitting up so you're much better, hm?"

I doubt that any kid, however stoned, would have so little nous as to announce to their mother, even in a dream, that they were in conversation with the ghost of their dead brother.

"I don't feel sick anymore," I said.

The Condesa smiled. "So – you try a little egg, yes?"

I felt Perdito startle with excitement.

"Yes – let's eat!" he said.

"Yes," I told my mother, "Egg on toast, please."

She patted my cheek. "Good."

As she turned to leave, she picked the bottle of Dr Collis Browne's from the bedside table. She frowned and held it to the light.

"Pablito – you drink all this bottle? My God! When you drink all this?"

Appalled, she rushed out to phone the doctor. I lay back and listened for Perdito, who I sensed was still there. The next thing I knew my mother was shaking me awake and offering me a glass of salt water to make me vomit.

My eye condition, incidentally, turned out to be mundane. Apparently my pupils are naturally dilated. Light doesn't cause them to constrict as much as most people's. The specialist said that my brain had got used to adjusting for it, but I can't imagine how the hell he'd know. Maybe I just see a more dazzling world than everyone else.

    *   *   *   *

That night when Tom and I were in bed – him on the top bunk, me beneath – I said, "You know the dead baby Mum had?"

"Yeah."

"He's a ghost inside me."

"What?"

"He's a ghost in my brain. He talked to me."

Tom's head appeared upside down over the edge of his bunk. "What do you mean?"

"I heard him talking," I said, sitting up.

"You're nuts."

"No – it's true. It's not scary or anything."

Tom tutted and withdrew, settling back onto his pillows.

"Can't wait till you tell Mum and Dad," he said. "They'll have you locked up."

That seemed quite likely. I decided to keep Perdito to myself. It'd be fun.

Chapter Four
A Yolky Stain

The week leading up to Pablo's arrest was particularly fraught for me. I had a lot of work on, around which I had to fit two sessions with Alice, and on top of that my father's youngest brother had died, so I was obliged to drive out to Hook to take my mother to the funeral.

My mother lives on a road that is too well-ordered to be truly rural, but not sufficiently formal to be considered suburban. One could say much the same of her. Too exotic to be British, but too bourgeois to be truly Spanish. The Condesa, as my father used to refer to her, has lived in the Home Counties for forty years and she still dresses like a flamenco teacher in an unexpected cold snap. She has retained a strong accent, and she regards the rules of English grammar like speed limits – worthy of note but not necessarily applicable. Her two great passions are tapas and tulips. She's about the height of a tulip, actually.

I called her when I left home, and again from the motorway – but, as I'd anticipated, she was still in her housecoat when I arrived, not even close to being ready to go. However much time she has, however easy it would be to arrive relaxed and punctual, she always contrives to create a panic. When I was a child it drove me up the wall.

"Why aren't you dressed?" I asked, following her into the kitchen. "We've got to be there at two."

She shrugged as she pulled on her rubber gloves and filled a bucket at the sink. "I can't leave the kitchen floor this mess, Tomàs. It is five minutes only to put clothes on."

We missed the eulogy, but got there in time for the committal to the flames. I wondered how they prevent the smell of roasted flesh permeating the entire building. I couldn't avoid envisaging the specifics of the process

– the bubbling skin and erupting eyeballs; the white-hot bones. It's horrific. And yet everyone just stood there merely snivelling, as if something melancholy and rather gentle were going on.

We all trooped back to Auntie May's Victorian terrace with its bilious staircarpet and apple-and-pear motif on the wall-tiles in the kitchen. The women passed around anaemic sausage rolls that flaked like a skin condition, while the men opened cans of lager which – in deference to the solemnity of the occasion – they attempted to decant into petrol-station glasses, before discovering they were too small and swigging the rest from the can.

"Waste not want not, eh, Tom?" my Uncle Bob said, tossing an empty into the swing-top. "Here's to Alan, the old bastard. Two down, two to go." He took a long slug and smacked his lips. "Just me and Trevor left now. And Trev's not been well."

"I'm sorry to hear that," I said, glancing through the serving-hatch at Uncle Trevor who was trying to balance a plate on his arm whilst holding a beer and lighting a cigarette. "He looks all right."

Bob leaned forward. "Cancer," he said, in a carrying whisper. "It's his bowel. Nothing they can do for him. The ciggies can't hurt him now." There was a yolky stain on Bob's black tie. I imagine he had taken it off and tossed it drunkenly into the wardrobe after the last family funeral.

"Still in the will-writing business?" he asked. "Must get that sorted. Can't take it with you, can you?"

"We're working on it."

An hour or so later – and five crates of beer more relaxed – the inconsolable mourners put some music on and had a party. They would have referred to it, I suspect, as a *knees-up*. I exchanged glances with my mother, who was rigid with smiling embarrassment on the sofa. I tipped my head towards the door.

"Did you see them, Tomàs?" she hissed in the car. "Mother of God – they have no class! No class at all!"

"So where did Dad come by any class?" I asked her.

"In some people it is natural. Like painting." She opened her handbag and extracted a compact. "I can see it the first time I meet him. Peasant bones, but good class."

"Which makes me a peasant too."

"No! You have your father's good class, and noble Catalan blood. Anyone can see that. An idiot can see it."

This, incidentally, is another of my mother's recurring themes. She's not Spanish – she's Catalonian. It explains the blonde hair and her sense of beleaguered superiority. I'm sure there are Catalans who till the soil and herd pigs, but in the view of Isabel Maria Vivas Lyne every one of them, however humble, is part of a natural aristocracy.

"All of you – Pablo, Jacinta – all of you have good blood."

"Speaking of whom, was Pablo invited today?"

My mother put her make-up back in her bag and tutted.

"I don't know where he is. He's not call since my birthday. Where is he?"

"I have no idea," I told her. "I'm surprised he remembered your birthday."

"Remember my birthday? No – it was coincidence. 'Pablo – how nice you call me on my birthday,' I tell him. He says, 'Oh – it's your birthday?' He is not right in his head."

"He'll turn up when he needs some money," I told her.

"You find him and make sure he's okay, Tomàs."

As it happened, it wouldn't be necessary to find him because a few days later he'd be all over the ten o'clock news. But, as ever, my mother expected me to be the responsible one, the protective one, the dutiful one. Pablo was considered too delicate and unworldly to take care of himself.

As a kid, I couldn't understand it – how can you choose a favourite from twins, for God's sake?

That night I had dinner with a woman I'd met in Harrod's a few days previously. Angela was mid-forties, auburn with help, slightly overweight without being podgy, and married. As so many of them are. During whitebait and Pinot Grigio, I gave her every opportunity to shine, but she turned out to have no more wit than an escarpment. By the time we got to coffee I had given up hope completely and ordered a taxi for her, having offered all the usual assurances of follow-up phone calls.

I slept fitfully, troubled by the *puttanesca*.

*   *   *   *

Cooking was always too much for me. The chaotic overload of colour, scent, taste, sound and texture; eruptions of strawberry-bleed and muscular sizzle, aromatic drip and dough-squeezed warmth; carnal hiss, acid foam, pliable creamy sugared glisten.

Spices pummel me. Cinnamon – deafening, humming cinnamon – presses me to an ecstatic huddle. Anise shrieks laughing. The sudden slamming orchestral stabs of cayenne thump me backwards and mustard is a keening violin soar that lifts me up to where saffron twitters and chirrups.

Bodies are immersed daily in this scintillating tumult and I don't understand how you stay conscious or sane. Why are you not driven mad by colour? The nettle sting of paper-white, the tickle of crimson in the back of the throat, the puncturing stab of aquamarine, ochre's woolly smother – infinite shades and hues and tints constantly prodding, abrading, caressing, goosing you. Your world is an electric storm of confusion and derangement. If you didn't close your eyes you'd never be able to sleep at all.

And as if the sensory commotion of nature weren't enough, you add to the bewilderment with delicious racket of your own making. The language in your mouths still amazes me, delights me after all this time. The savour of particular words is breathtaking. Synonymous, *for instance – a blueberry-yoghurt tang that causes me nearly to swoon.* Interrogate *– saline, fishy and pungent.* Saskatchewan *– which always dumbfounds me* *with its meaty, pink, drooling ooze; as does the burnt bark crumbliness of* tanmateix.

The realm of the physical is so overwhelming, it's no wonder that flesh has so little time for the spiritual.

*   *   *   *

Alice gave me homework, in the form of a list of 'prompt phrases' each of which was supposed to nudge me towards a memory of my childhood.

New Year's Day
Sharing
Dad's Influence
Mum's Influence
Bedtime
School Days
I've Never Been So Embarrassed
My Favourite Toy
Travesty
Sunshine
Ouch

She insisted that I write short essays on three of them. If I hadn't paid in advance for the next counselling session, I'd have refused to take part in so pedestrian and tiresome an assignment. However, I've never shirked a chore in my life, so I wrote the damn essays.

Essay for Alice – New Year's Day

When I was a child, New Year was a busy time, what with Pablo's birthday on the 31st, and mine on the 1st. My parents always organised a New Year's bash that doubled – tripled, I suppose – as two birthday parties. Family and friends crammed into our house in the early evening and Pablo opened his presents and blew out his candles to much oohing and aahing from the guests, all of whom gathered around him to sing Happy Birthday. He'd sit there lapping it up.

Then the New Year's party would get underway – the drinking and the games-playing, kids running up and down the stairs, the record player blasting in the front room. Come midnight, everyone would watch Big Ben on the television, counting down the seconds to the first resounding strike of twelve. Champagne would be inexpertly opened; all the adults would embrace and smooch. The terrible dirge of *Auld Lang Syne* would be plodded through, with everyone mouthing words that they didn't actually know and wouldn't have understood even if they did. And then my mother would shout above the hubbub, "Now it's time for Tomàs's birthday!"

My presents were brought out and I would open them sitting on the sofa, ignored, hemmed in by adult backsides, the owners of which were still jabbering and quaffing their champagne. My mother would push through the melee with my cake and I would blow out the candles as Pablo and our cousins raced along the hallway, tired and over-excited, utterly uninterested in seeing me make a wish. My dad would cajole whoever happened to be in the room to join in a chorus of Happy Birthday to Tom, but some drunken uncle would belch a vulgar version of the words and everyone would hoot with laughter. And then it would be time for kids to go to bed.

Every December – actually, probably from the beginning of September until Christmas – I begged my mother for a party of my own, on my birthday, in the evening, with proper guests who were there only for me. But this was an impractical demand, apparently.

"It's such a busy day, after the party. You know how the state of the house is. And everyone so tired. No, no. It's nice to have big party at New Year. You like that."

None of which was either convincing or entirely true. The real reason I wasn't allowed a party was that my mother and father always disappeared on the afternoon of New Year's Day. My mother was uncharacteristically punctual about getting out of the door at the stipulated hour, and my father didn't station himself in the hall thirty minutes before it was time to leave, looking at his watch and huffing. A neighbour would come in to get us lunch, and off my parents would go in the car.

I was in my teens before I discovered where they went.

Five miles from our house there was a National Trust property called Pelham Grange – a Victorian mansion with grounds originally designed by Gertrude Jekyll. My paternal grandfather was head gardener there, and he spent twenty years restoring the beds and the woodlands, the walks and the arbours, to Jekyll's original plan. If I have any regard for the branch of my family tree from which the Lynes hairily swing, it's invested in Grandad, who remade the grounds of the Grange. They are beautiful.

At the eastern edge of the property there is gentle hill where a spring rises and feeds a brook that meanders through the various garden-rooms. And beside the spring, at the best vantage from which to overlook the grounds, there is a bench that Jekyll didn't include in her design. My grandfather had it installed at the request of my parents. Carved into the wood of the bench, in English and Catalan, is a quotation from Byron.

...you shall not kiss him; at least not now...

My parents went there every New Year's Day to honour the memory of Perdito.

You see? Even our dead brother's birthday was more important than mine. Not only was I less favoured than Pablo, I was shunted into third place by a child that never lived.

Chapter Five
Tinsel Elvis Twirls

I was amused by Pablo's observation about my books and his teasing me with testing errands. It was no less amusing for its complete wrong-headedness. But still his raw text demanded considerable rejigging. This is a small selection of what I excised.

Once, twice, thrice,
Force, fits, seize,
Severance, ace, nonce,
Tinsel, elvis, twirls.

I can see the gardener from here, planting perennials in Stephen's summer border. Beyond him there's a formal area of box hedges and gravel paths in which, apparently, white standard roses will bloom, underplanted with swathes of pink dianthus to tastefully contrast and accent. The spotless gardener tells me that one must avoid planting colours that clash. I hate that. When a poppyseed is windborne to a fertile little patch of soil, it doesn't look around and think, "Oops – purple foxgloves and blue cornflowers. My scarlet petals would look a fright here. I had better be careful not to germinate." One day I'm going to have a garden, and it'll look like Mother Nature at an impromptu rave.

I don't think all cigarettes cause lung cancer – any more than all aeroplanes crash. Any aeroplane might *crash, but most don't. I'm looking at a pack of Lights now. Eventually one of these fags will trigger insane cell-division, I expect. In fact – I think it's that one there. I've just crumbled it up in the ashtray. The others are quite safe, I can tell.*

Those are the most coherent extracts, and the easiest to cut. There were many other meanders that proved to be dead-ends. But I never had to ask Pablo to rewrite. Everything required was on the page – one just had to concentrate for a moment to see it, like those tests for colour-blindness in which the number 9 is picked out in pale green blobs amongst surrounding splats of pink.

I found the second sheaf of pages on the occasional table outside my bedroom door. As I ate my breakfast and read through the new work I could see Pablo sitting cross-legged on the lawn, smoking. I didn't know whether cigarette ash would harm grass, but I felt a rather small-minded tremor of anxiety.

"You're up early," I said, taking a cup of tea out to him. The dew soaked into the trouser-cuffs of my suit, which served me right for walking on the grass at all. It's not something I usually do.

"Late," he said.

"Well, you make your own hours, of course."

"Did you like the bit?"

"I did. It makes me want to know what happens next, which is always a good sign."

He shrugged and stared across the lawn at nothing. I couldn't tell whether he was distracted, exhausted or unhappy. Unhappiness worries me – particularly in my guests, for whom I feel responsible.

"Is everything all right?" I said. "Perhaps there's someone you want to call?"

Pablo flicked his burning cigarette stub across the smooth wet grass and laced his fingers behind his head. "Oh, Christ, yeah," he murmured.

I took a couple of paces and picked up the smoking fag-end. "You're welcome to use the phone, of course." I pinched out the glow-worm bud of the cigarette between finger and thumb.

"Thanks. But I think I'll maintain radio silence for a while." He stood up. The seat of his jeans was soaked through. "I need sleep. See you later."

Making a note to buy him some clothes while I was in town, I left for the station.

I had a lunch appointment with George Sandham. We would get together every couple of months, and we had since our thirties. Our conversations, which used to revolve around our plans and ambitions, more recently tended to focus on wistful reminiscence and reviews of obituary columns.

"How's it going with your waif?" he asked me towards the end of the meal.

"Can you be a waif at forty? I think there's an upper age limit on waifdom."

He swallowed the last mouthful of treacle pudding, put down his spoon and unbuttoned his waistcoat. "What leads you to believe that Mr Lyne has anything to say?"

"My instinct, I suppose. And my interest in his claim to have killed his brother. It smacks to me of something unresolved. Want of resolution is the starting point of all good stories."

"And you find the fraternal element particularly compelling, of course."

"Yes. Thank you for that insight."

He waved the waiter towards us and ordered coffee and a bottle of brandy. Then he grinned at me. "But – tell me – is it honestly just because you're intrigued by his story?"

I sighed. "Please don't start all that again."

"Fine, fine. I shall take your word for it. Though he is a fetching chap, in a winsome sort of way."

I smiled. "And I shall take your word for that." I accepted a glass of brandy. "What do we know about the twin?"

"I met him only briefly at the police station. From the conversation between the two of them, I don't think that the Messrs Lyne are close."

"But identical?"

"How do you tell?" he asked. "They look very alike, although the other one is rather better fed and certainly better groomed. But I don't know whether they're fraternal or…" He waved a hand in the air. "…whatever the other sort is. Monozygotic? You'd have to do a DNA test, I suppose."

"But the police did exactly that, didn't they?"

"Only on your one. No reason to test the other one as he turned out to be walking and talking. Talking a blue streak, actually." He belched and tapped his sternum with a clenched fist. "Christ – are we getting too old for this kind of lunch?"

"This kind of lunch is my only indulgence, so I hope not. Did Pablo leave with his brother?"

"I think so." He pushed his chair back and rested his hands on his stomach. "Do you think I'm getting fat? I mean, relatively. For a man of my age?"

"You're sylph-like. Though a sylph that's let herself go just a tad."

"At least I do let myself go now and then. You should try it."

"Oh, please, George."

It seems to me that there's something slightly distasteful about a sixty-five-year-old solicitor offering sexual counselling to a sixty-one-year-old literary agent – which is too frequently the direction in which George coaxes our conversation. It is a well-meant but unwelcome insistence fed by the zeal of a man who, having exorcised the demons from his own house, then seeks them haunting others' homes so that he can drive them out all over again.

In his forties, and to absolutely no one's surprise, George publicly professed his homosexuality. Overnight he was relieved of the burden of defensively declaring that, actually, he just wasn't particularly interested in sex, had more important things to think about, was sure that one day

Miss Right would happen by. "I frittered away so much time telling lies and betraying my true nature," he explained – often and at length. All George's friends agreed that this was indeed a tragic waste, but presumably he'd be getting on with being gay now, and it wouldn't be necessary to discuss it further, hm?

So it transpired. George doesn't talk about his sexuality except to parade his history as an exemplar of the terrible consequences of self-deceit. Exactly the sort of self-deceit, for instance, that he feels I am engaged in. Why do I have no wife? Well, George, because I'm just not particularly interested in sex. I have more important things to think about. Aha! That's what George said before he came out. The very words! Really – if only I would find the courage to face myself, to look myself in the eyes.

And so on and so forth. Drunk as we were, we blundered into this discussion again during our very long lunch. As ever, George refused to countenance my protestation that I am straightforwardly uninterested in sex, just as one might be uninterested in sport or food.

"Why should that not be so?" I said. I popped a *petit four* into my mouth.

"Your analogy is fallacious." George had that glowing intensity of focus that only alcohol can bring. "One might be uninterested in gourmet cooking – that's a choice to be made. But no one can go without food."

"Apparently I can," I said, squinting. My focus, unlike George's, was being pulled randomly to and fro.

"No, no – sex is a basic need. Do you masturbate?"

"I see no reason to answer a question so pim..pinpertinent, George." That told him. Unsteadily, I poured another brandy. "But, no. Not for years is the answer." That told him too, rather more specifically. Hadn't meant to say that.

"Not credible," George told me. "You'd lose a jury's sympathy with just that one assertion. No one would believe it."

But I was telling the truth as I always have. There's nothing Freudian about it except that a cigar is sometimes only a cigar.

"Well, have it your own way," George said. He grinned. "Which is not to have it at all, apparently."

*   *   *   *

At first I thought of Perdito as little more than an untypically autonomous secret companion – a version of myself who urged me to climb trees, jump over fences, take furtive sips from the vodka in my father's drinks cabinet. I didn't hear a voice any more, but thoughts came to me and I knew they weren't mine – they were his. He was a lobbying appetite

Eating, in fact, is what he encouraged most. My mother was most gratified by my sudden culinary adventurousness, which she compared favourably to Tom's implacable resistance to anything other than sausage and mash. And my father was delighted at my having apparently achieved a more healthy balance between bookishness and physical exertion.

"I see you were up on the roof of the treehouse today, Pablo." he said, grinding pepper on his paprika chicken. "Very enterprising. Good view from up there, eh?"

"On the roof of the treehouse?" my mother gasped, spooning out peas. "Mother of God – don't you go there any more, Pablito. You going to break your neck!"

Dad ruffled my hair. "He'll be fine. It's good to see him out and about."

"Has this got garlic in it?" Tom asked, poking at the chicken breast with his knife.

"Give it here if you don't want it," I said. "I've only got a tiny bit."

Jazz tutted. "Jesus Christ, you're such a pig."

"Never say the name of our Saviour like this, Jacinta! Where you learn this talk?"

"With all the running around he does these days, he can afford to eat as much as he likes," Dad said. "More spuds, Pablo?"

"Can't I just have a ham sandwich or something?" Tom said, forking the chicken portion and holding it out towards me.

"Don't drip sauce on table!"

"Put that back on your plate and eat it, Tom." Dad said. "It's very mild."

"Anaemic, actually," Jazz murmured.

"Anaemic?" the Condesa asked, eyes narrowed. "What is this word? Is not good word for the food I make, eh?"

"It means 'delicious'," my sister smiled, and Dad shot her a look that was a fifty-fifty combination of warning and amusement.

As I shovelled down the meal I could feel Perdito thrilling at each mouthful, impatient already for dessert. Afterwards he'd want me to go back to the treehouse. I'd sit on the roof reading my latest Silver Surfer magazine, and he'd luxuriate in the sensation of evening sunshine on the back of my neck, soaking up the Roman purple of the flowering clematis that scrambled through the branches of the cedar. I was used to having him there and I accepted it without concern or wonder. I no more agonised over the implications of having Perdito suggest adventures to me than I contemplated the conundrum of genies conjuring banquets amidst the squalor of the Somme. I didn't consider the what or how of Perdito.

But like a five-finger piano exercise practised in a room down the hall, the question began to play over and over in my head. It was hardly noticeable at first, plink-plinking at the edge of my attention, and before long I was humming it under my breath, hearing it in my sleep. One day I found myself putting words to it.

I was shivering in wet swimming trunks on the platform of a vertiginous water-flume in Orlando where the family was taking a late autumn holiday. Tom was standing behind me holding our rubber mat.

"Two more, then it's us," he said.

"You know Perdito?" I said.

"Don't talk about that. Everyone'll think you're nuts."

"How can he be a ghost? He died when he was a baby – and ghosts don't get older."

Ahead of us a two teenage girls were clambering onto their mat at the top of the chute. The young attendant – a wiry, tanned guy with hair to his waist and psychedelic shorts – stretched his arm in front of them, waiting for the red light above the tube to switch to green.

"Really – shut up about it," Tom said. "I've told you before."

He had. He hated any mention of Perdito – the idea scared him. But I wasn't really talking to Tom at all. I was just talking.

The light changed, the attendant lifted his hand and the two girls disappeared shrieking into the flume. *"Next up, guys,"* the attendant said, waving Tom and me forward.

"Come on!" Tom said, pushing past me. He flopped the mat onto the launch-pad and sat down. *"Me in front!"*

I clambered on behind him, my knees under his arms. The attendant told me to lean forward and clutch Tom around the chest, which I did. He was wearing a t-shirt and it was wet through, cold and clammy against my bare chest.

"If he's dead," I said, *"how did he die?"* I had never thought about it before.

The attendant raised his arm in front of Tom who was edging our mat towards the lip of the drop.

"Jeez," the attendant frowned, pointing at my back, *"that's one freakin' mother of a scar. How'd you get it?"*

"I dunno," I said. My mother's line was that I'd fallen off a wall when I was little, but I wasn't convinced.

The ready-light changed and I felt the attendant's hand between my shoulder blades giving just enough of a push to carry Tom and me over the edge of the platform.

In the brief moment of stasis before the mat plunged down the tube of the flume, Tom said, "Ask Dad." And suddenly we dropped into the dim blue, both screaming, plummeting through twists and turns towards the splash pool at the bottom where, behind the rail, the Condesa waited anxiously, clutching our locker keys on a knotted string and running her fingers up and down it like a rosary.

*   *   *   *

"Dad," I said as he paid for hotdogs at the stand, "what happened to Perdito?"

"Ketchup?" he said, squirting some on my dog. "Why do you ask?"

I didn't have an answer for that, and he didn't really want one. He was buying time. He asked the vendor for a tray to carry the food back to our table in the picnic area.

"Let's join the others and talk about it," he said, resting his hand on my shoulder.

"Put your shirt on, Pablito," my mother said as we sat down, "or you catch cold."

"Does anyone want a coke?" Dad asked. "I should have got some." He looked at Mum. "Izzy, come and help me with the drinks."

"No – already they drink lots of coke." She rummaged in her hold-all. "I bring some water. Here."

"Isabel," Dad said again. "Come and help me with the drinks." And then, "Te necesito aqui con las bebidas, querida."

Frowning, my mother got to her feet. My father's use of Castilian meant trouble. Jazz, whose Spanish was much better than mine or Tom's, leaned *across the picnic table as Mum followed Dad back towards the snack vendor.*

"What have you done now?" she demanded.

I bit my lip, unsure of what I'd done. I'd asked the question without any idea of what it might mean to my parents, but now, as I glanced at them in conversation by the hot dog stand – Dad calm and making soothing gestures, my mother agitated and evidently upset – I could see that I'd landed my boot hard in the ribs of a large sleeping dog. Mum's jumpy protectiveness of her children covered not only physical threats – busy roads, strangers with pear-drops, two-bar electric fires – but also anything that might prove emotionally disturbing. The Condesa had a rather romantic and Victorian view of childhood – sunshine innocence and twinkling Christmas trees – and she didn't want anything nasty or sordid to encroach. She was wearing blue glasses on our behalf.

After a few minutes, Mum and Dad came back to the picnic table, the Condesa dawdling behind and looking anywhere but at us, like someone heading up the street towards the dentist's surgery, hoping that a shop window will offer a few minutes' legitimate distraction.

"Cokes all round," Dad said as he sat down. My mother was ashen and – what really worried me – silent.

"Pablo asked about Perdito," Dad began, his hands clasped together on the table in front of him. He looked around at the three of us. "He wanted to know what happened to him. Do you other two want to know too?"

Jazz nodded gravely. Dad looked at Tom.

"You too, Tom?"

"Okay," he said, through a mouthful of fries.

"All right," Dad said. The Condesa was fiddling with her wedding ring, sliding it up and down her finger, eyes lowered. "You understand how twins come about – two babies growing in the mummy's tummy at the same time? Well, sometimes there are three babies."

"Triplets," Tom said, taking a bite of his hot dog.

"Exactly," Dad nodded. *"Very good."*

Tom smirked. It must have been all he could do not to raise his hand.

"Well, sometimes – very, very rarely – things get mixed up in there. One baby gets caught up with another baby and doesn't grow properly. That's what happened to Perdito. He got all caught up with Pablo and he couldn't grow properly. It was just terribly bad luck."

"Caught up?" Tom said. *"What does that mean?"*

I said nothing. My eyes were fixed on my father – and he was looking only at me now. I didn't fully understand what he was saying, but I felt that as long as he and I were looking at each other he'd make sure I was all right.

Jazz turned to Mum. *"There were three babies?"* she asked. *"All at the same time?"*

The Condesa, who was still staring at her hands, nodded her head slightly.

"And when you boys were born," Dad went on, his voice calm and even, *"the doctors had to unmix Pablo and Perdito. Poor Perdito hadn't grown properly and it was all very dangerous for you, Pablo. His little body was all confused with your body and..."*

"Was Perdito alive?" Tom asked.

Mum let out a sob and Dad put his hand over hers as he answered. *"No, Tom. Perdito was never really alive at all. He never even got to be a baby, really."*

"But he must have been alive in mummy's tummy," Tom insisted.

"Very early on, perhaps." Dad said. *"But we can't even be sure of that. He got mixed up with Pablo and..."*

"I don't get it," Jazz said, frowning. "Mixed up?"

My mother was weeping silently, one fist to her mouth as she chewed her wedding ring.

"Mixed up before he could properly be alive," my father said. He was desperately trying to avoid the macabre and gory truth of our birth, hoping we'd be so overwhelmed by the fundamental concept that we'd accept his skirting the specifics. But as I watched him fielding my siblings' questions, all the buzzing euphemisms swarmed together and clustered like bees on a dropped lolly, and suddenly I saw what they were about.

"Perdito was inside me, wasn't he?" I said quietly.

And the talking stopped. My father's eyes met mine again, and I felt a tear skitter down my cheek. I was shiveringly aware of the long pink scar on my back, as if it were new and itchy and unhealed. And Perdito, who always understood everything I understood, seemed to be welling up like a howl in my head – a lipless howl that drowned out the screeching of riders on the Raging Rapids and the thump of pop music from the sideshows.

"Oh, that's disgusting," Tom said, screwing up his face. "Really disgusting."

"Don't you dare say that!" Dad barked, lashing out at him, slapping him around the side of the head. "You shut up now!"

He'd never struck any of us in his life. Tom was amazed for a moment and then he burst into tears. Mum started crying aloud too, and Jazz just sat there, pale and serious, looking from one to another of us. Quickly, Dad reached across the table to take Tom's hand, saying, "I'm sorry, Tom. I'm so sorry.

And I blinked, immobile, listening to Perdito screaming in my ear.

"You killed me! You killed me! You killed me!"

    *   *   *   *

I was in London to attend a meeting of Sub Judice, of which I am the current Chair. We're an organisation that lobbies the Home Secretary to re-open criminal cases that may have been miscarriages, and I first became involved some thirty years ago when I had as a client a convicted rapist who had written a book about his trial. He'd been framed, clumsily and vindictively, but he served eighteen years before his innocence was acknowledged by the government of the day. Had he not been literate and determined, had Sub Judice not supported him, he would have died in prison.

The process of law, it occurred to me as I sat in the meeting, is our mechanism for imposing order. Even if Pablo was right about the arbitrary nature of existence – *especially* if he was right about it – human beings have a duty to be even-handed and systematically fair to each other. It would have been no comfort to my client's wife or to his daughter, in whose childhood he was denied any involvement at all, to be told that it was a chaotic and random Universe and that's just the way that dumb luck goes.

I nodded off on the train, and by the time I got home I was grumpy and I had a pulsing headache. Pablo was lying on the sofa watching television and drinking a bottle of port that I'd been saving for an occasion rather more special than the one he cheerfully toasted as I collapsed into an armchair.

"Bloody good day's writing," he said. "I'm getting the hang of it now." Scattering cigarette ash across the carpet, he leaned backwards to lift a pad of paper from the floor. He shooshed it across the coffee table towards me. "I'll get you a glass to wash it down."

I rubbed my eyes and started reading. Pablo came back with a tumbler, which was an optimistic choice given how much port was left. He poured me half an inch and topped up his own glass with the rest. Then he sprawled back on the sofa, grinning eagerly as I ploughed through his day's work.

He nodded towards the sheaf of paper. "Bowling along now, isn't it?"

"It's certainly better. Fewer flights of irrelevant fancy."

"Irrelevant to what?"

"To your story."

"How do you know yet what's irrelevant? I don't."

"No, all right – but there should be nothing on the page that doesn't contribute to either the thrust of the plot or the development of the characters."

Pablo tutted. "I'm not the Mayor of fucking Casterbridge. All this crap about structure and narrative flow just makes it look like there's some kind of sense to what happens. There ain't."

He flipped yet another cigarette into his mouth and lit it. Nobody had smoked in this house for years. I suppose that dinner guests and weekending friends smoked around the place in the days before it became impolite to light up indoors – yet the smell of Pablo's cigarette took me back not to any adult evening of wine and chatter, but to my adolescence. I felt that if I turned my head towards the doors, I would see Leo strolling across the lawn from the orchard, a cigarette hanging from the corner of his mouth, one eye screwed up against the smoke.

"I'm not saying you should make it novelistic, Pablo. Just that it must carry the reader along. You do want your book to be read, don't you?"

Pablo scraped his fingers through his hair and scratched the back of his neck. "Not particularly," he said.

"Then why are you writing it?"

"Because you asked me to. You asked and I said, why not?"

He was sitting forward with his elbows on his knees and his hair falling over his eyes. His expression was sullen – even sulky. The man was forty years old, but his demeanour was that of a teenager. And that was exactly how I'd been treating him – cooking his meals, helping him with his homework, tutting resignedly over his careless untidiness and his apparent inability to close the fridge door properly.

Perhaps that was all that was extraordinary about Pablo – he was an intelligent middle-aged man with teenage attitudes. In an adult, and out of their usual context, those attitudes appeared fascinatingly skewed, original, challenging. George had said that Pablo seemed to operate with an alternative spectrum – but maybe it was just that he saw the world in the garish colours of Marvel comics and urban graffiti. If that was the case, then Pablo was entertaining company, but no more likely to produce a saleable story than a hundred other convivial people I could name.

Then again, none of that hundred had been found on Wardour Street looking like the final scene of a Jacobean tragedy and claiming to have killed their twin brother. It was that, I reminded myself, that had made my professional antennae twitch.

"A story must have structure," I said. "That's all I'm saying."

"A real life story might not," he said. "In the real world, stuff just happens."

"Nothing 'just happens.' When you look at the world – the ecological balance that sustains all living things, the beauty of a flawless diamond, the sweep of the Alps – you don't see any creative hand behind any of it?"

Pablo laughed. "Why does the Almighty get such great reviews for landscapes? It might be that God gave us a really crap planet – a slum world with ex-display forests and cheap flat-pack mountains. How would we know?" He drained his glass. "But if you're going to give him credit for the Alps, then you should remember that snow-capped peaks are just the big-ticket item from the wonderful guy who brought us cancer of the palate and spina bifida. Me, I prefer his early funny stuff." He drained his glass and stood up. "Did you eat in town? Just I'm a tad peckish so I'll make myself a sandwich if you're not planning on cooking."

"Help yourself," I said distractedly, following him to the kitchen. The phone rang. Pablo picked it up and handed it to me. I tucked it under my chin as I filled a glass from the tap.

It was George.

"Sorry to call so late," he said. He was slurring somewhat. "I'm still in the office."

"You sound absolutely plastered."

"I am, I am. And I've done a very stupid thing, I'm afraid. Stupid drunken thing. Sorry."

I frowned and sipped my water. "What's the matter?"

"A Natalie Crowther called just now looking for your waif. Went on and on at me like a harpy." There was a pause and I heard the chink of a scotch tumbler against teeth. "I gave her your phone number. Stupid of me. I totally caved in. Terribly sorry. Not what a friend should do. Sorry."

I glanced at Pablo who was buttering a slice of bread with the back of a tablespoon that had been the first item of cutlery he'd happened upon. I sighed and opened a drawer for a butter knife, which I offered him. He waved it away.

"Oh, I wouldn't worry, George. Forget it. I'm sure it's not a problem."

He belched. "That's very decent of you, old man – but you don't know what she's like."

"I'll manage," I assured him. "I'd go home to bed now if I were you."

I was about to tell Pablo that Natalie might be in touch – although I had no way of knowing whether or not he'd consider that welcome news – but as soon as I hung up on George, the phone rang again. It was the wife of my gardener. He'd slipped a disc.

"Well, don't worry, Mrs Scott," I said as I returned to the drawing room. "No, no – I'll sort something out. Just tell him to get better soon."

"Trouble?" Pablo asked, settling on the sofa. He took a bite from his sandwich, shedding crumbs.

"The gardener has put his back out. I must remember to send flowers."

"It's probably flowers that caused it. Chocolates might be better."

I chuckled, happier now. I can't sustain grumpiness for long. "It's a busy time of year in the garden. I've just ordered a consignment of perennials to replenish the summer border. And autumn bulbs too. I shall have to get someone in for a week or two."

Pablo reached for his cigarettes, although his mouth was still full of sandwich.

"If you opened another bottle of plonk, you could probably talk me into doing it," he said. "I mean, I can only write for a few hours a day. I get fed up with it. But I like gardens. My granddad was a professional gardener. It's in the blood."

I was taken aback. "Well, I suppose so."

"I'd enjoy it. And it'd make me feel better about eating your food and drinking your wine." He waggled his empty glass at me. "Speaking of which…"

So I forgot to mention Natalie to him. I forgot her myself in fact. But I was soon to be reminded.

*   *   *   *

This is how it works.

For a start, there are three sorts of twins, not two. There's fraternal twins – two eggs, two sperm, producing conventional siblings who simply happen to occupy the womb simultaneously. Then there's monozygotic twins – one sperm and one egg that splits after fertilisation, leading to twins who are genetically identical. But there are also half-identical twins – two sperm but one egg that splits just before or at the moment of fertilisation, giving siblings who share DNA from the mother but have dissimilar DNA inherited from the father. It's possible that Tom and I are half-identical – we certainly look very alike, though not quite the same. The only way you could find out for sure is by DNA testing, and we've never had any real reason to do that.

But whatever the genetic relationship between me and Tom, it's pretty certain that Perdito and I are identical. In my mind's eye, when I imagine our conception, an egg splits as two sperm approach. One sperm connects with the left-hand blob and becomes Tom. The other sperm crash-lands in the other half of the egg, which then splits into the potential pair of me and Perdito.

A very young embryo is flat, and it rolls up like a scroll so that the sides meet to form the symmetry of the foetal body. I must have rolled up around Perdito, almost enclosing him, and he grew like that, within me. I permitted him to grow, but I prevented him from living.

Dumb luck.

*   *   *   *

"You killed me! You killed me!"

I sat motionless at the picnic table as Perdito screamed. Dad suggested that the Condesa take Tom and Jazz to see a stunt-show, and the three of them wandered off looking solemn.

"You all right, son?" Dad said.

I nodded. Perdito had fallen silent, but I could still feel him there, sulking.

"Shall we go and waste money in the arcade?" Dad said. "Just you and me?"

For half an hour we pushed coins into slots, deafened by bells and alarms, assaulted by flash and blink. I tried to look as if I was having fun – the arcade was a big treat and I wanted Dad to be pleased that I was enjoying it – but really I was waiting to be accused again.

Mindlessly, I fed the Penny Falls machine. I watched the coins drop, bouncing off the little nails, tipping onto the sliding shelves, shuffling towards the precipice.

"No, no, Pablo," Dad said, leaning down over my shoulder. "Your timing's all wrong. Wait! Wait! Now!"

I couldn't get it. I couldn't concentrate. There didn't seem to be any connection between my letting go of the coin and how it was shoved into the muddle of a thousand other pennies. But still I thumbed coppers in, smiling for my father's sake. I trusted Dad's generous coins to the gaudy indifference of the random, but not a single one fell as a reward into the hopper against which my thighs were pressed.

*   *   *   *

The following morning Pablo and I made a tour of the garden. It's an extensive space. My father, who was not a man given to irony, used to refer to it as 'the grounds'. These days such terminology, however appropriate, would sound either pretentious or anachronistic.

Had he been strolling alongside Pablo and me, my father would have noticed very little change since the Thirties when he'd restored the old pile – Twyborough Cross House, to give its formal title. The old man returned both the building and the grounds to their original Georgian design, which was considered an eccentric project at a time when aggressive modernism was in vogue. Like him, I regard the place with respect but also with nostalgic affection. I took my first infant steps on this lawn. On the far side of the lake there stands a Palladian folly that my brother and I defended against Sioux war-parties. We stalked mammoth in the Old Pasture and flew Spitfires along the clipped allées. From my bedroom window I can see, beyond the knot-garden, two red oaks planted sixty years ago by my parents – one for my brother and one for me.

When I walk alone in the garden these memories twine about my legs like persistent cats, welcome and loved though on the periphery of my attention. But as I strolled with Pablo – telling him where I wanted the autumn crocuses, asking him to prune the shrubs along the path to the folly – I reminisced aloud, and it was as if I were bending down to pick up my pets and stroke them, presenting them to my guest, inviting him to listen to them purr.

"You keep saying 'we'," Pablo said as we made our way back between the box hedges. "It's always, 'We played here. We swam there.' Who else?"

I hesitated. "My brother."

I left it at that, and we walked in silence to the terrace.

"I've noticed something about your house," Pablo said. "Your family has lived here for – what? – eighty years, but there are no family photographs. Lots of art, lots of antiques. Millions of books, obviously. But no photographs."

I chuckled. "That implies a very twentieth-century perspective – the idea that nothing is important unless it's recorded on film."

"Maybe. But you should have corrected me. There is *one* photograph, in your study above the desk."

"Ah."

"A young man on a motorbike outside this house. Is that your brother?"

Not for the first time Pablo had wrong-footed me.

"Yes, it is."

The twelfth of July, 1956. Leo's eighteenth birthday. The motorbike was a BSA 650 Goldflash. I know less about motorbikes than I know about cars, but I would recognize a BSA 650 just from its silhouette. I was fourteen when my father bought it for Leo and I thought it the most beautiful thing I would ever see.

"Leo," my father said as he led me and my brother out to the drive, "your mother appears convinced – and she has persuaded me – that you are sufficiently mature to behave responsibly with this machine. I would be most disappointed if you were to let us down."

"Absolutely. Got it." Leo said, straddling the seat. "Thank you." He kick-started it first time, and the bike seemed to gather itself and flex, like a gryphon waking.

"Leo – can I ride on the back?" I shouted over the growling revs.

"Hop on," he mouthed, jerking his thumb towards the pillion.

As I stepped forward, my father grabbed my bicep and gestured to Leo to turn off the engine.

"Leo, if I ever," he said when the engine had quietened, "*ever* see Stephen on this motorcycle, I shall confiscate it indefinitely. Is that clear?"

My brother nodded. "Of course. Quite right." He shrugged at me. "Sorry, half-pint. Wait till you get one of your own."

My mother emerged from the house with a camera. "Oh, it does suit you, Leo. Bring it round this way a bit so you're not squinting into the sun."

After breakfast, when father had left for work and mother had gone into the village, Leo took the bike out for a run around the countryside.

"Let's test the efficacy of our Brylcreem, shall we?" he suggested.

Pressed to his back, my arms around his waist, I blinked over Leo's shoulder into the wind to see that the speedo was touching a hundred. It seemed faster.

"Lean!" Leo yelled as we screamed into long curves between ripening fields. "Hold on tight!" he shouted as the BSA accelerated down deserted, poplar-lined avenues. I felt as if the bike would shoot away from beneath me, tumbling me along the hot, merciless surface of the road in its magnificent wake. I was terrified but I was laughing. My fear was the fear of the roller-coaster – an instinctive reaction wired into the nerves, not a real terror of possible death. No harm could come to me. I was with Leo. And Leo, I knew, was indestructible.

"So what became of him?" Pablo asked.

"Forgive me," I said. "It's not something I want to discuss."

We walked into the house through the French doors.

"I don't have time to make breakfast," I said, picking up my briefcase from the coffee table. "I have to go into town. I'll bring back some cigarettes tonight. You must be running low."

"You want to know about my brother, don't you?" Pablo said. He flipped a smoke into his mouth. "That's what you're trying to get me to write about."

I nodded, checking through my papers.

"Swapsies, then." He snapped open his lighter. "You tell me about your brother and I'll tell you about mine."

I looked up from my files. "Why would you want to know about that?"

"Why would *you*?"

"I want a book to sell."

Pablo lit his cigarette and blew smoke out over his jutted lower lip. "There are easier books for you to sell than one I haven't even written. I've looked at the manuscripts in your study. There's good marketable stuff there." He shook his head. "No. It's the fraternal thing that interests you."

There was scant sign now of Pablo's adolescent demeanour. He looked his age. The merry blue of his eyes seemed to have deepened. The creases of his smile had become determined. It was if he'd stepped out of the long grass like a tiger; the stripes that had camouflaged him were revealed as intricate and menacing.

I put my papers back into the briefcase. "I'll think about it," I said.

"Please do." He glanced at the carriage clock on the mantle as he tapped ash into his cupped hand. "Well, I've been up for nearly three hours. Time for a drink." He gave a facetious grin, and the tiger melted so smoothly back into the moving shadows of the forest that I wasn't certain I'd really seen it all.

I shrugged on my jacket and checked for my car keys.

"It's a Beaujolais kind of day, I think," Pablo mused, opening the door to the cellar. "Couple of gulps and I'll start knocking out the old deathless."

"Please use a coaster," I murmured, and I headed for the car feeling that the tables had been turned on me. For the first time since I'd met Pablo, I was a little apprehensive about leaving him alone in my home.

*   *   *   *

After confirmation class, I asked the priest what happened to the souls of babies who died.

"They go straight to heaven," Father Lenahan told me, "because they're without sin."

That wasn't the official line at the time; Father Lenahan elided Limbo. But now I think about it, his answer was so prompt and pat that I reckon he must have known about my stillborn twin. If he meant to reassure me about Perdito's fate, he fucked it completely up, because I was asking about myself, not my brother. The priest's answer just confirmed my suspicion that I was the only person in the entire history of Catholicism to emerge from the womb already damned by the commission of prenatal murder. When it came to evil brothers, fratricidal Cain and devious Jacob had nothing on me. What's more, neither bludgeoned Abel nor defrauded Esau insisted on hanging around the place, denouncing their siblings and demanding compensation.

I, on the other hand, was pursued by my victim. My head buzzed with thoughts that were not my own, turning over and over, sleeplessly. I was endlessly tugged by notions of inventive tactile schemes; experiments in sensation.

I was walking home from school on a bright summer's afternoon. A fat brown dog turd lay fresh and moist on the sidewalk under a halo of flies. It seemed almost to pulse.

And the pictures were there in my mind immediately. I could see myself crouching down, scooping the soft turd into my hand, squeezing to watch it slowly emerge in curled ribbons between my fingers, warm and sticky. My stomach turned, and I felt Perdito's thrill as he sucked up my revulsion. He was aroused by it.

It occurred to me to taste the dogshit. Instantaneously the image was alive with such vivid clarity that I had to bite back vomit. Perdito was ecstatic – I could feel him swelling in my head, thrilled and excited, as my knees bent and I knelt on the grass verge, disgusted but electrically charged.

"Pablo! What in God's name are you doing?"

It was my father, getting out of the car and striding across the road.

"Are you completely mad?"

Not me. Not me. Perdito. I owe Perdito. I killed him.

Good little Catholic boy, I was crammed with juicy seeds of guilt like a ripe pomegranate. A few months earlier I'd taken a piss against the back wall of the church, and the fear of Divine retribution had me shivering in my bed for weeks. Eventually I confessed to my dad and he made me apologise to Father Lenahan, whose prescribed penance was fifty rosaries and an afternoon scrubbing the stonework with a stiff brush. Extrapolating from that incident, I didn't have the nerve to admit to murder.

So I did what Perdito wanted. I shoplifted chillies and ate them raw; I poured entire bottles of my mother's lavender oil into the bath; I crushed in my fist every fruit in a punnet of strawberries just because it felt so good – though it might have caused less uproar not to have done it on the sofa.

"You are so naughty these days, Pablo," the Condesa said, hustling me upstairs to my room. "Not just here – at school too. The headmaster phoned again. Third time this month!"

I suffered the consequences of Perdito's adventures resignedly. I reckoned that each small chastisement I endured on his behalf would reduce the terrible punishment I was due when I died. The greater the transgression, the harsher the rebuke and the bigger the chunk knocked off my eventual sentence. The maths seemed to make sense, and any mediaeval Pope would have applauded the double-entry logic of my moral accountancy. On top of which, after each adventure, Perdito would rest, silent and remote – for weeks sometimes – and I could get some peace.

One autumn – I must have been eleven – I built a bonfire on the waste ground at the end of our street, which I spiked with stolen fireworks. I lit it at dusk, and then sat in the dark by the furthest fence and watched while the glow at the heart of the piled branches flickered for a few minutes and then leapt up through the heap as the smaller twigs caught.

The entire construction crackled and sagged into itself. A Roman candle erupted in a whoosh of gold-blue sparks, scattering embers across the ground. Suddenly a rocket shot out of the flames, screaming towards the street, bursting hot-white as it ricocheted off a lamp post. And then all the fireworks ignited at once – silver fountains, banshee hornets, crimson storms, emerald dragons, thunder crackers, sapphire showers – strobing the distant trees, kaleidoscoping on drifts of cordite-perfumed smoke. Hissing rockets skittered across the ground, foundered in the long grass and lay there fizzing for a moment before bursting in plumes of blinding stars and flying dirt. Chesty, explosive thuds echoed against the impassive houses, and screeching whistles thrilled the night air, soaring and dipping like something that whiffles through the tulgy wood.

At the height of the barrage Perdito seemed to wail in my head with wordless joy, and his unalloyed elation washed through my body in a chemical rush. I was already fired up and I felt overwhelmed, overloaded. I was faint and shaking. I closed my eyes and covered my ears with my hands.

Perdito yanked my consciousness backwards, as if I were between him and what was his. He seemed to squeeze past me, and my grip on myself came loose. And then my eyes opened and my ears were unblocked and I was flooded by sensation. The world was all colour and sound – formless, engulfing spectrum; shapeless, smothering noise. Colours pulsed and span in washes of split light that implied no distance or perspective. Noise was pitch and attack and shape and sweep without origin or significance. There was no sense in my senses – nothing had context or meaning.

As I cowered within myself, assaulted by brilliant chaos, I heard a voice – and that, at least, I could understand. Somewhere nearby, almost drowned by the undeciphered din, I heard Perdito yelling.

"Me too! Me too!" he bellowed, between whoops of laughter. *"Yes! Me too! More! More!"*

But he wasn't shouting close inside my ear. He was further away than that. His delirious screams were coming from out there where the explosions and the whooshing and the whistling were.

Perdito was screaming and he was using my voice.

*   *   *   *   **

In my thirties, when I was setting up unannounced public events intended to amuse and provoke, I learned that anyone likely to upset the general populace should prepare either an untouchable excuse or an infallible escape route. What you shouldn't do if you're, say, an eleven-year-old pyrotechnician, is swoon on site and wake up surrounded by the residents' association

"Is two years he act like this – after Florida!" the Condesa yapped at Dad. "Suddenly – bang! – he's a very naughty little boy!"

My bedroom was at the top of the stairs, and my parents had left the kitchen door open as they discussed what was to be done about me.

"He's not naughty – not really. He's adventurous. Creative," Dad said.

"He create bloody world war today! You see everyone stand at the doors? I know what they say! 'What that Lyne boy done now? The parents can't control that Lyne boy!'"

The argument from local opinion was one my mother often cited. You would have thought that after twelve years of marriage she'd've noticed that it never carried much weight with the man who had dropped out of university to become a scuba instructor in the Pacific Islands.

"I don't give a monkey's what the bloody neighbours think," Dad said dismissively. "All I care about is Pablo. He's got a lot to deal with. It's understandable."

"Yes! Yes! You tell a little boy those things! I don't know why you tell him! I say to you, 'No, they're all too young', but you never listen, like always!"

"He asked. So he was ready to be answered."

I could picture Dad sitting at the kitchen table, shoulders hunched, punctuating his words with downward slices of his hand as if he could cut up the argument into Condesa-size bites. He was a very patient man but arguing with my mother pushed him to the absolute limit of his forbearance. Dad approached any problematic issue like a pathologist faced with a body washed up on the beach. He incised, separated and dissected, noting the function and relative position of each significant part, laying individual specimens aside for later analysis. Mum, on the other hand, came on like a flock of seagulls, squawking and flapping, indiscriminately tearing off lumps of loose flesh and pecking at them.

"And he maybe talks to kids at school and they tell at home – then everyone bloody knows our business!"

Now Dad's temper broke. "Oh, for Christ's sake – is that what's worrying you? If Pablo really is upset, that's what we should be concerned about. Not small-minded gossips at fucking Tupperware parties."

There was a brief pause and then the sound of glass shattering. I heard the scrape of chair-legs on the kitchen floor as my father stood up. He said something placatory in Catalan, his voice quieter now. My mother mumbled a reply through suppressed sobs, and they both went through to the living room. As Dad was closing the door, he said, "No hi ha res de que avergonyir-se, Isabel. Ningu en te culpa."

I had to look up 'avergonyir' in the Catalan-English dictionary on the bookshelf above Jazz's bed. It means 'ashamed'. The Condesa, I suddenly understood, wasn't merely upset about Perdito. She was ashamed of him. Ashamed of my twin.

I'd developed a mental picture of him by this time. In my mind's eye he was skinny, like me, and even scruffier. He had shoulder length hair and he wore tatty dungarees. His feet were bare. I see now that I'd modelled him on Huckleberry Finn. He lived in a cave formed of white, wet coils, lit by an oil lamp that stood on a bare wooden table. His bed was a cosy pile of furs and hand-sewn quilts. The room was my brain, of course, and the décor owed a lot to the whale's belly from Pinocchio. Whenever Perdito emerged from his cave, he stepped into a landscape lifted directly from CS Lewis – though I never asked myself whether the green undulating hills and the buttercupped valleys were supposed to be in my head, or in his.

As I stood in Jazz's room with the dictionary in my hand, looking at 'ashamed', I expected him to react – but he was quiet. The firework display must have knocked him out completely. I could see him curled up on the bearskins, mouth open and eyes closed, snoring.

I was furious that my mother was ashamed of him. It wasn't his fault he never got born. It was mine. Dad was always going on about responsibility. Only the previous day, when I'd jumped out of the treehouse and flattened my mother's beloved peony, Dad had run through the accustomed catechism for my benefit.

'You're not a baby anymore, Pablo. No, no – listen. It doesn't matter what you meant to do or didn't mean to do. You have to take responsibility. So – what are you going to do about Mum's plant?"

I had smothered Perdito in the womb. It was my responsibility now to let him get at life. It was up to me to make sure that he wasn't forgotten and ignored. Perdito was not a shameful secret – he was my brother.

I heard the door of the living room open and I scooted back to my bedroom where I sat on the bed, ready to tell the truth. Dad came in and sat next to me.

"So what was that all about then, Pablo?" he asked.

"It was for Perdito," I said quietly.

Dad raised his eyebrows. "Okay. What does that mean exactly?"

"I know you won't believe me," I shrugged.

Dad was much too clever a man, and too reasonable a father, to allow himself to be taken hostage by making any reply at all to that. He just waited.

"Okay," I said. "You know how you told me about Perdito being inside me and everything? When we were babies?"

Dad nodded. "Yes, I do."

"Well – he's still inside me. Like a ghost or something. I mean, not in a scary way. Just like anyone else, except inside me."

I looked up at my father, and he held my gaze, chewing his top lip and thinking.

"How can you tell?" he asked eventually – very seriously and without any hint of surprise or anger. "How can you tell he's inside you?"

"He talks to me. I can hear him."

"And he tells you to do things, like make a bonfire?"

I sighed. "Yes. But he really likes that kind of stuff."

"Okay. Did he like it when you cut your hand?"

That hadn't been my favourite of Perdito's experiments, but I had indeed drawn a carving knife across my palm at his insistence. It hurt like fuck, and I bled all over the kitchen floor.

"Did he like that?" Dad asked again.

I dropped my chin and grimaced. "Yeah. But I didn't. It was stupid."

"Pablo – look at me," Dad said. I raised my head again. "Listen – you are a very imaginative, very clever little boy. And..." His gaze wandered around the room before settling on me again. "And you're certainly bright enough to know that you're in big trouble with this firework thing. Yes?"

I nodded.

"Good," Dad said. "So I need to know if you're making this up about Perdito. Because you're perfectly capable of it, hm?"

"I'm not making it up!" *I insisted, punching my fist into the pillow in frustration.* "See! I knew you wouldn't believe me!"

"No – that's not the point," *Dad went on, more soft-spoken and apparently calmer with every word.* "If what you say is true, it's a very important thing. It's something that we have to deal with, isn't it?"

"That's what I mean!" *I shouted.* "Perdito wanted me to tell you ages ago, but I said you wouldn't want to know about him. Because it upsets everyone. But you and Mum have to know because…"

"Shh. Pipe down, Pablo." *He took both my hands in his.* "All right." *There was a long pause during which he grazed his bottom teeth over his top lip again and again. I could hear the TV from downstairs – Mum was watching* Call My Bluff. *The theme tune always put me in mind of the word* scaevity *which had featured on the show and stuck with me. Now it went round and round in my head like a chant, filling the hiatus in conversation.*

"How long has Perdito been talking to you, Pablo?"

Scaevity, scaevity, scaevity. It means 'unluckiness', by the way.

"Since that day I was sick on the train. Two years or something."

"I see." *Dad nodded. He took a deep breath.* "Now, it was absolutely right to tell me. Absolutely. Good boy. But I think it would be better all round if it was me that told Mum, hm? You see what I mean?"

I nodded. It was a relief, actually. I had thought about telling the Condesa that Perdito was here, and the scene I pictured was not short of melodrama. Dad and I agreed that he would find a good time to introduce the subject with Mum, and that I wouldn't mention it at all until he gave me the nod.

"And one more thing. If Perdito wants you to do anything else that's – well – likely to get you in trouble, or anything dangerous, you come and tell me, all right? And the three of us will talk it over."

"Scaevity," I said, nodding again.

"What?"

"Yes. I'll tell you."

Dad sent me to brush my teeth and then he settled me in bed. I was exhausted and I put up no fight at all although it was barely eight o'clock.

"This'll all get sorted out, Pablo. Don't worry," Dad said as he kissed me goodnight. "Do you want me to leave the light on?"

"No. Why?"

"Just thought you might. Okay. You go to sleep."

"Perdito says good night too," I told Dad as he turned at the door. Perdito had said no such thing, but I wanted to introduce the idea that he might; and I thought Dad would like to know that his lost son was a polite and affectionate kid.

"Well, sleep tight," Dad said, though he looked a little pained. "I love you, Pablo."

Chapter Six
A Record of Accidents

I was not Pablo. I merely occupied Pablo. The hands of Pablo were not my hands and the feet of Pablo were not my feet. I could extend myself into them, like a boy dressed as a monkey for a party, but I couldn't feel with the tips of the fingers. I couldn't instruct the feet where to walk. When Pablo looked in the mirror he saw his own face but I – the twin – did not see mine.

Out there, though, beyond Pablo, was Tomàs. Tomàs was almost Pablo. In the unread library of Pablo's memory I learned that they had been mistaken when they were small.

"Here's one for little Tommy."

Our grandmother offered a lollipop to the nearest toddler.

"That's Pablo," *the Condesa said, seething,*

"Well, if you say so. Of course, if I saw them a bit more often I'd know the difference."

"We were over only last month for the barbecue," *my father said. He didn't want to argue with his mother but neither could he allow his wife to be criticised.* "Come to think of it, you never mixed them up all that afternoon."

"It's easy to tell them apart when they've got no shirts on."

The Condesa stood up and stalked off to the kitchen to make more tea.

By the time my brothers were big enough to pick out their own clothes there was no mistaking which was which. At seven years old, Tom was careful that his trousers were clean and that his top was of a matching shade. He liked his hair combed. He checked the weather before choosing his shoes. Pablo woke up in yesterday's t-shirt and underpants, and he put jeans on only if he had to leave the house. He wore the first two socks that came to hand, regardless of colour or style. He tended to be sick on the day of the appointment at the barber's.

I began to see that Pablo was unusual. Tomàs, the Condesa, Jacinta – they all straightened the world. Things around them fell into lines. Pablo generated entropy – things around him scattered, leaked, cracked, clashed. Nothing in Pablo's world belonged in any particular place. Nothing was what it was for any good reason. When Pablo looked at a staircase, a parsnip, an LP he saw a chance conglomeration of matter that might at any moment rearrange its own atoms into a rhododendron, a spire, a lamb cutlet, a puff of steam.

"Pablo! What is this scratch on the table? Did you do that?"

"I was sharpening a pencil."

"On the table? Are you an idiot?"

"It doesn't matter."

"This ugly scratch on my dining table? It doesn't matter?"

It did matter, though – even to Pablo. Although he hadn't done it deliberately, he preferred the table with the scratch. The smooth surface of the oak was a deliberate and offensive travesty of the random nature of wood. He wanted a table that was a record of accidents and chance events. He saw no reason to sit in an accustomed place at that table when the family gathered for dinner. He sat wherever he pleased. He thought the ingredients of the meal might as well arrive in alphabetical order.

For me, immersed in Pablo's world, the flood of the physical was so overpowering I could barely keep a hold on consciousness. When he did something as simple as read a book, I felt half-drowned in sensation – the print bristling on the page; the citrus page beneath the fingers; the fingers *moving like magic. As he touched a green sweater acrid flavours popped like seed pods. I could taste the texture of the wool. Suede felt like grass smells. Cotton – the sheets on the bed, the blue t-shirt Pablo wore almost constantly – was sugary.*

These were my sensations, not Pablo's. When he looked at a fire engine, he saw an object that reflected red light. To me, red had grain like polished wood, and it was slightly warm. Pablo didn't register these joyous depths of experience. But then he didn't register half of what went on around us.

Jacinta was taking a salad bowl down from the Welsh dresser in the kitchen.

"Be careful," the Condesa said. "Use two hands."

"I won't drop it," Jacinta said, sliding the bowl over the edge of shelf and bringing her palm up underneath it.

But the Condesa wasn't worried only about Jacinta dropping it. She was also suppressing the urge to help, because Jacinta was twelve now and should be trusted in the kitchen. And she was worried that Pablo would think that if his sister could get things from the top shelf, so could he. And she was happy that she had a reason to use the bowl because it reminded her of her own mother. And she was irritated that everything on the dresser seemed to collect dust, however thoroughly she cleaned the house.

All this was so obvious to me that the Condesa might as well have said it aloud. It was evident, but Pablo didn't seem to get any of it. And I understood that it wasn't only Pablo – it's all of you. Flesh misses almost everything, and what it doesn't miss, it forgets.

*   *   *   *

<u>Essay for Alice: School</u>

End of term at St Mary's Primary School. We are nine years old.

"Mr and Mrs Lyne – do come and sit down."

Pablo and I stand to the side, both wearing the expression of uncomfortable expectation peculiar to small children present when teachers meet parents. Mr Betts lays two school reports on the desk before him.

"Well, one at a time, eh? Elder boy first." He rotates one of the reports so that our parents can read it. "Pablo," he says.

"He's not the oldest!" I say.

The Condesa shoots a warning look at me. Mr Betts checks the birthdates on the reports and chuckles. "I shall have to knock a point off your maths score, Tom."

"But he isn't!"

"Tom, please be quiet," Dad says under his breath.

I bite my lip. Our parents scan the column of Pablo's grades as Mr Betts summarises his progress.

"As you see, Pablo has maintained last years' performance, achieving A-grades in most subjects." Dad and the Condesa nod gravely. "He still has a tendency to lose focus, but he brings a unique perspective to everything he does. Overall, a very impressive year, Pablo."

Pablo smiles, smug as a juggler.

"Good boy," Dad says.

Mr Betts spins my report around, and our parents lean forward to see.

"Hugely disappointed in you Tomàs," says the school teacher with a smile. "A mere unadorned B for Art. Apart from that, A-plus throughout. Magnificent effort."

"Well done, Tom," Dad says.

"The Lyne boys are first and second in the year again. You should be very proud of them both." He nods towards the far wall. "Much of their work graces our 'Special Achievements' gallery, of course."

The family follows Mr Betts across the room, and he points out my essay on *Charlotte's Web* – five pages of neatly handwritten literary appreciation that I had planned, drafted, edited, copied out twice and finally decorated with a felt-tip drawing of a pig.

"It's very good, Tom," Dad says, having skimmed the first two sentences. "Isn't it good, Isabel?"

"Very neat. Good writing, Tom. What is this pink thing?"

"And this," says Mr Betts, "is unmistakeably Pablo's contribution."

It's a design for the cover of *Alice in Wonderland* in paint, crayon and collage. I happen to know that Pablo flung it together in about twenty minutes after breakfast on the day it had to be handed in.

"Oh, Pablo," says my father. "Is this really all your own work? It's stunning."

"You are a genius, Pablo! It's beautiful. James – we must get a frame for this amazing picture."

"Needless to say, Pablo's painting was given twenty out of twenty," Mr Betts says.

"Top marks! Well done!" Dad exclaims, ruffling Pablo's hair as the Condesa hugs him.

"And well done to you too, Tom," Dad says, turning to me – but I'm already heading out of the door towards the car.

You'd think, wouldn't you, that being so obviously favoured would be enough for my brother – but no. He was constantly on the lookout for new ways to attract attention, and it was at about this time he came up with the unignorably compelling idea of Perdito's ghost – simultaneously a guaranteed come-on and the ultimate let-off.

One of my cousins was getting married, and the Condesa volunteered to make the wedding cake. It was an elaborate confection consisting of three tiers, each covered in pure-white fondant icing decorated with sugar roses and winding ivy, all hand-made. The Condesa had spent hundreds of hours on it – smoothing the icing until it was as flawless as marble, curling and colouring every edible petal of the roses and every intricate sugar leaf of the ivy, and easing them into place around the cake as if they had grown there, intertwined and spontaneous, perfectly naturalistic, romantically complete with glistening drops of glycerine dew.

Two days before the wedding Mum declared the cake finished and she put it on the dining room table, fully-assembled, intending to deconstruct it for the trip across London the following day. At nine in the morning, I was woken by a scream of such agony and outrage that I was too scared to run down and see what had happened.

"Oh, Mother of God – why do you do this? Why? Are you insane? Are you a crazy child? James – get him away from me. Please. Get him away before I hurt him. Oh, dear God…"

Pablo had come down in the night and pushed his finger into the fondant icing – not once, but scores of times. All three tiers were riddled with dozens of neat and methodical holes, around the sides and across the tops, deep enough to expose the fruitcake beneath. As if that were not enough, the roses had been comprehensively deconstructed, the individual petals scattered across the table, smudged by thumbprints, smeared and licked.

"What possessed you, Pablo?" my father raged, dragging my brother upstairs by the arm. "Why would you do something so wicked?"

"I'm sorry! I'm sorry! I couldn't help it!"

"Couldn't help it? Of course you could help it, you stupid child."

"I'm really sorry!" Pablo sobbed, gulping, as Dad yanked him towards our bedroom.

"It's a bit bloody late for sorry."

And that's when Pablo played the trump card, of course. "I *had* to do it. For Perdito."

Dad stopped dead in his tracks.

"Oh, Pablo, no. No – don't say that."

"He wanted to do it. I had to!"

"He told you to?" Dad seemed close to tears himself now. "Perdito told you to?" He pulled Pablo to his chest, and hugged him, rubbing his back. "Oh, God – you poor boy. You poor boy. What are we going to do?"

Brilliant. He deliberately fucks up all Mum's work, ruins our cousin's wedding – and *still* manages to get my parents to feel sorry for him. You know what they did? They told the family that Dad dropped the cake walking down the steps outside our house, and then they spent hundreds of pounds on a shop-made cake that had to be collected by my father from Plymouth.

My parents protected Pablo, whatever he did. And now I'm expected to protect him too.

Chapter Seven
The Kid with the Haunted Head

*H*uman beings don't like things to happen without good reason. So when some significant event appears to have no identifiable precursor, people call it 'fate' – by which they mean that there's some metal-level order to things; order of such intoxicating purity that it's completely transparent, like vodka.

Natalie Crowther always maintained that she and I were fated to meet. Certainly her outlook was peculiarly suited to a relationship with the Kid with the Haunted Head. Maybe that's really how it works – the entire universe has nothing better to do than ensure that on a summer's day in the early eighties a scruffy boy toting a sackload of guilt should bump into a skinny chick with a Florence Nightingale complex.

I was seventeen. My Art teacher organised a trip to see an exhibition by a local artist presented by the municipal library. As it was my habit to slip away to the library after morning registration anyway, I decided to attend.

I rather liked the exhibits. They were watercolours that seemed at first glance to be no more than twee re-runs of Woolworth kitsch. But as you looked at them you detected something dark and incongruous there. The artist had lifted photographs from medical textbooks – a diseased lung, a sclerotic liver – and merged them with the paint in such a way that they were transformed into chocolate-box images: this skin condition became a Mediterranean sunset; that embolism was a still life with summer fruit. It was at once funny and disturbing – which more or less covered my teenage taste in art, and isn't far off the mark even now.

The artist was a narrow, twiggy woman in her early twenties, her wrists jangling with purple and green bangles, her hair spiky and plum-coloured. She was standing by a painting in which a vertical section through a congested heart had been turned into two kittens peeking out of a battered red hat.

I sidled towards her, holding my paper beaker of complimentary 7-Up.

"Excuse me. I just wanted to say I like your stuff," I told her. I was a gawky kid, and it was a gawky opener. I was nervous enough talking to girls my own age – a mature woman of twenty-three scared the life out of me.

"Thanks," she said. "Listen – do you smoke? I'm dying for one."

I shrugged. "Sorry. I don't. But – well – just wanted to say, you know, it's good painting. So, anyway. Bye."

No, of course that's not what I said at all. The tightly-scripted screenplay of the cosmos wouldn't allow it. In fact I said, "Yeah – we'll have to go outside though."

On our first real date I was roped into helping her move house.

"Can you drive?" she asked, slamming shut the back-doors of the hired van into which we'd loaded her stuff.

"I expect so. I've never tried."

"Funny. I'll drive."

Her new place was on the Isle of Dogs – a Victorian two-up-two-down with a basement she intended to use as a studio. We unloaded all her belongings and heaved them into the appropriate rooms, and then Natalie took me out to a local Indian for dinner – which was all the thank-you I honestly expected.

"It's nearly ten," she said as we left the restaurant. "Why don't you stay over and I'll drive you back tomorrow when I return the van?"

"Oh, okay. I can sleep on the sofa."

Natalie laughed and patted my cheek. "You really are incredibly bloody sweet, aren't you? I like your vibrations"

And then she kissed me open mouthed, and after a moment's confused hesitation I did my best to respond. Over her shoulder I could read the menu in the window of the Mumtaz. The words 'rogan josh' still remind me of that kiss. Natalie tasted of garlic and cardamom. Her hair smelled of gel and tobacco. The bib-buttons of her dungarees dug into my chest.

We went back to the house and I had a wonderful night – but the Condesa, it turned out, didn't.

"Where have you been?" she shrieked when Natalie dropped me off the following afternoon. "We phoned all hospitals and dad drove round the streets! You can be lying dead in the gutter!"

I closed the door behind me.

"Mum, I'm nearly eighteen years old. I stayed at a friend's – so what?"

"I worried to death! We didn't sleep one minute! Not one minute! Can't you use a telephone?"

"She doesn't have a phone. She's just moved in."

"She? Who is 'she'?"

The front-door opened and my dad walked in. He was gaunt and pale.

"So you've decided to honour us with your presence, have you?" he said.

"I stayed at a friend's." I explained again, wearily. "It's not a big deal."

"And you couldn't let us know where you were? Just as a simple courtesy?"

"What am I supposed to do? Request an overnight fucking pass?"

Dad's white face flushed with colour. "I will not have you using that language to me, young man!" he roared. "As long as you live in this house..."

I could tune out any amount of hysteria from my mother, but Dad's anger was impossible to disregard because it was so rare. If I'd upset him I must really have crossed a line. Though I wasn't about to concede that. I simply upped the ante.

"Well, maybe it's time I didn't live in this house then!" I yelled and I bounded up the stairs to my room.

"Don't you turn your back on me! Come down here this instant!"

"He stayed with a woman! A woman, James! All night!"

I could hear Dad coming up so I opened the window, stepped out onto the roof of the porch and dropped down to the front garden, my face flushed and hot as I headed for the street.

"Come back here, Pablo!" my father shouted from the window of my room. "I mean it! I want to talk to you!"

I ignored him and headed for the library where I stayed until dark. When I went back I apologised to them both, but I'd decided that it was time to move out.

I sometimes wonder whether I'd have been so keen on a relationship with Natalie if she hadn't offered such a convenient escape route. I think I would. I was besotted and I was getting a lot of sex. Love may well be blind, but it compensates by indulging the tactile senses. In Natalie's case, apparently, other senses were getting a good work-out too.

"Your aura is just amazing," she told me as we lay in bed. "I've never seen anything like it. It's like a whole rainbow."

"Is it?"

"Really. It's so positive and bright. You have a very positive energy."

In the dew-kissed morning of love's first dawn, this kind of thing is endearing. By love's lunchtime, when the drizzle comes, precisely the same schtick becomes intolerable. Natalie was full of half-baked ideas that she was always ready to share.

"Football is so negative. That's why they push it so hard."

"They?"

"The faceless people who control us. Why do you think the church is so anti-sex? Because they know that a fuck sets you free. Football's attritional, yeah? It traps you in negative karma."

"You think the Pope and BBC Sport are in cahoots?"

She once told me that the Second World War was a put-up job orchestrated by Hitler, Roosevelt and the international banks. Given the outcome, I don't think Adolf can have read all the way through the project plan. But I recognized what was going on here. Natalie's deductive paranoia was just a version of my mother's instinctive trepidation. Nat coped with the fearful uncontrollability of existence by perceiving deliberate malevolence on a global scale. The air was blue with conspiracy and that's what made it through her glasses.

It took eighteen months for my irritation to become unignorable. Natalie was good company a lot of the time and I couldn't fault the sex, about which she taught me a lot. But the enjoyable aspects of the relationship were melodic interludes. For the most part, the constant cello-thrum of Natalie's fearfulness was counterpointed by shrill coloratura passages around the conspiracy theme, and it all made my head hurt.

Anyone else in my position would have got out. People dump people all the time – no big deal. But I couldn't. I had a responsibility. There was

*   *   *   *

That's where the writing came to a halt, mid-sentence.

I returned to the house around nine-thirty having stopped off at the parish church to visit Leo's grave. My instinctive impulse was to reject Pablo's demand to be told about him – but I couldn't quite see why.

It occurred to me that I rarely spoke about my brother to anyone except George. Presented with an opportunity to do so – a question about my family, say, or my time at Cambridge – I steered the conversation elsewhere. It was an unconscious habit and one that I could justify, I suppose, by protesting that the memory was too painful to be rekindled. But Pablo had offered me a trade that was perfectly fair – his painful tale for mine. Standing by Leo's grave in the quiet dusk, I knew only that I didn't want to tell the story – but having no good reason for that disinclination, I couldn't permit myself to refuse.

Driving home I distracted myself by planning dinner. Something formal, with the table properly set. I like the gravitas engendered by ritual, and if I was bound to relate Leo's story I would insist on appropriate dignity. I even considered obliging Pablo to shave and wear a shirt, which, I told myself, would indicate to him how seriously I regarded the occasion. That was a lie, though. My real purpose was to punish him for my discomfort.

Opening the front door, I put my briefcase on the hall table and walked through to the drawing room, expecting to see Pablo sprawled on the sofa with a glass of wine. He wasn't there. In his place was a wiry woman with cropped blonde hair and angular features. A wide red belt held up blue jeans too generous for her small waist, and her cropped t-shirt showed off muscular, hard arms and a tight, flat stomach.

She looked up from the magazine in her lap and nodded at me.

"Stephen Richmond, yeah?"

"Yes," I said, holding out my hand to her as she got to her feet. "I suspect you're Natalie Crowther." I peered over her shoulder through the open doors to the terrace. "Where's Pablo?"

"Good question. I know he's staying here, so you needn't pretend he isn't."

"It's not a secret, is it?" She hadn't taken my offered hand, so I let it drop. "Then again, perhaps it is. Can I offer you a drink?"

As I poured two glasses from a bottle of red wine that was already open on the coffee table, I asked, "Out of curiosity, how did you know where I live?"

"The solicitor gave me your phone number. I just came to the area and asked around. It's not as if you live in an anonymous semi, is it?"

"Indeed. Cheers. Have you been waiting here long?"

She sat down again and I took a seat in the armchair opposite her.

"A couple of hours. So where is he then?" she said.

I shrugged. "All I can say is that he was here when I left this morning. I expect he'll turn up for dinner."

I was less insouciant than I affected. Either it was coincidence that Pablo had gone out for the evening – which would be the first time since he'd come here – or he'd deliberately made himself scarce in order to avoid our unexpected visitor. Whichever it might be, there was a distinct possibility that he wouldn't be back at all. My feeling was that once he'd built up momentum in a given direction Pablo just kept going.

"Okay," Natalie said. "I can wait."

"As you wish."

We sat in silence for a few moments. I was at a loss as to how to initiate a conversation. My guest, on the other hand, seemed to be itching to speak. She fidgeted with the stem of her wine-glass and rubbed her right hand up and down her left bicep. She had something on her mind.

"So you're a literary agent," she said at last. "What do you want with Pablo? He's an artist."

I saw no reason not to tell the truth. "He's writing a book. A memoir, one might call it."

She frowned. "He's not a writer."

"Well – I think he might be."

She snorted and took another sip of her wine, gazing around the drawing room.

"Is that you? Who did it?"

Above the fireplace was an impressionistic painting in oils of Leo and myself as adolescents – fifteen and twelve respectively. Leo was depicted in profile, sitting shirtless beneath an apple tree in the orchard, gazing out towards the lake in the golden early evening. Beyond him I could be seen swinging by both arms from a branch of a second tree, short-trousered legs pedalling the air. I've never had any recollection of posing for the picture, and I've always suspected that my father insisted I be painted in after the event. To be honest, the composition would work much better without me.

"It was commissioned from a friend of the family. He was highly-regarded in his day."

"Was he queer?" Natalie remarked. "Let me tell you – he was. The whole painting screams homo."

She was trying to provoke me and it was working. The back of my neck prickled with annoyance. But I maintained a civil air, which I suspected would irritate her as much as she was irritating me.

"Does it matter?"

She shrugged and began rubbing her bicep again. She carried a tattoo there – a stylized lizard in slate grey and ox-blood red. "Which one's you?"

"The younger of the two," I told her. "What does your tattoo signify?"

She glanced at it. "It's the Native American symbol for intuition and insight, as you ask."

I nodded. "And is there a lot of Cherokee in the Crowther bloodline?"

That got through. She bit her lip and crossed her arms, a pink flush rising in her cheeks.

"Yeah – typical," she said. "Bloodline is what you people are all about, isn't it?"

"Which people?" I leaned across and poured her more wine. Having landed one in her ribs I was starting to enjoy myself. "Literary agents?"

"I know a lot about you," she said. "I've done some research."

"How enterprising."

"You're in *Who's Who*. And so was your father."

That was true – though my father did a lot more to earn his entry than I have. I'm only included in the publication that my mother used to refer to as the Christmas Card List because of my involvement with Sub Judice.

"Barely a column inch. It doesn't really tell you very much."

"It tells enough. You're the establishment personified."

"I was never James Dean, admittedly."

"Actually," she said, sitting forward, "if you're the baby brother, how come you inherited the family seat?"

I may have winced. Her question touched a spot so recently made tender that I wondered whether the poke was intentional. More likely it was simply one of those nail-sharp coincidences on which life occasionally gets snagged – but I'd already primed myself to talk about Leo, and now that anxious readiness welled up in my throat and spilled.

"My brother Leo died young," I said too quickly.

Natalie murmured something I failed to catch. It may have been 'Lucky you", which was designed to needle me, of course. But, yes, I'm sure many would consider that I've been lucky. This house represented the greater part of my father's estate and had Leo lived we would have had to find a way to divide its value. I still regard the place as only half-mine.

"I didn't see a car in the drive," I said. "Did you come by train?"

Natalie nodded. "Then I walked from Aylesbury."

"Quite a hike." I glanced at the clock. "Would you like me to call you a cab to get back? The last train to London goes at ten-fifty."

"I came to see Pablo," she said. "I'll wait all night if I have to."

"Ah. Do you expect me to invite you to stay over?"

"Think I might steal the silver?"

I was overweight and out of condition. Natalie looked like a kick-boxer. I couldn't see that I'd be able to eject her bodily from the house. I might have called the police, I suppose, but even if I obliged her to leave she'd be back soon enough, I was sure.

"I don't think you're dishonest, no."

"I'll sleep here on the sofa so Pablo sees me when he comes in."

I nodded. "As you prefer. I'm going to make a sandwich and take it up to bed. Can I get you anything?"

She shook her head.

"Pablo has no key," I said as I stood up, "so it would probably be best to leave the doors to the garden open. Goodnight."

The kitchen window looks out over the approach to the house and I stood by the sink for a few moments, wondering if Pablo really would reappear. My house-guest was a resourceful and, in his way, responsible man of forty, yet I was worried about him. And I realised that I would miss him should he not return.

I took a plate of cold ham from the fridge and opened the bread bin. Lying on top of a granary loaf I found a few sheets from a legal pad, covered with Pablo's loopy handwriting.

Human beings don't like things to happen without good reason. So when some significant event appears to have no identifiable precursor, people call it fate...

Smiling, I rolled up the sheets and stuffed them into my trouser pocket. I made a sandwich and poured a glass of milk and then, having peeked in to see Natalie flicking through a book on the sofa, I took myself off to bed to read.

* * * *

"It makes total sense. I mean, this sack of blood and bones we think of as a person is just, like – well, exactly that – a sack. The real essence of a person is spiritual. Just visiting the material world, y'know?"

I'd had no trouble accepting Perdito when I was nine years old, and Natalie scooped him up without a qualm at twenty-three.

"You believe me?" I said.

"Of course. That whole thing with the scar on your back, the vibe you have – it all fits. Also it explains why I thought you were Gemini. I was so on the money with the fundamental truth, but I got the belief model completely wrong."

"As long as you don't think I'm nuts."

"You're not nuts. You're amazing." She leaned over me to reach the cigarette pack. She lipped the smoke. *"We should try some sort of enabling thing for Perdito."*

"Some sort of what?"

Ever thorough, Natalie read up on twin-myths and techniques for spiritual channelling. She'd already taken an evening course in hypnotic regression, with a minor in healing pebbles. And what she didn't know about scented candles wasn't worth knowing.

I mock now. I rejoiced then. I realised how lucky I was to have found a girlfriend who didn't scoff or refer me to a psychiatrist. One evening at the house in Docklands, Natalie took me by the hand and led me downstairs to the basement. She had whacked the heat up high in there and draped the walls with tie-dyed sheets lit from behind to diffuse pink-blue light across the ceiling. In the centre of the studio a paddling pool was filled with warm water. Natalie told me to strip and get into the pool while she lit the candles and rolled a joint.

"Is this supposed to be womblike?" I said as I slid my jeans off.

"Interesting you should think that," she said, licking the edge of a Rizla.

I slid into the water and Natalie handed me the glowing joint. As I took a drag, she flicked a switch somewhere and, across the ceiling, a thin red filament flickered then glowed, darkening to the colour of wine. I dragged on the joint.

"Think back to the train," Natalie said, sitting cross-legged by the pool.

I took another suck of the spliff and gazed up at the red stripe.

"Okay."

"Picture the train journey. How do you feel?"

I leaned back in the blood-heat water, closed my eyes for a moment. When I opened them I could see the dancing vein – skipping and wavering across nothing, red as nettle and warm.

"What do you feel?" Natalie said from miles away.

I lifted the joint to my lips again. I could feel the surface tension of the shallow water clinging to my thighs and climbing my scrotum. I was aware of the very curve of the meniscus.

"Whitsun weddings." I said. There was a slur in my voice. "An instant of light reflected."

The library was on the train with me. All the books – hundreds and hundreds I had read when I should have been at school – were in my mind at once. I was happy with the books. I could open them and close them whenever I wished. I could hang them on the beautiful endless red vein.

"Pablo? Hello?"

"Yes?"

"Yes what?" Natalie said.

"What?"

"Pablo?"

I floated in the red and the warm, in the scent of candles. I wasn't paying attention.

And I felt him, roaring towards me like a train from the cut, pulsing like a slick clot along the dancing vein, rising like an unexpected gout of vomit. I felt him push past me as if I were separating him from what was his – the incendiary spectacle of sensation. I slipped beneath the warm water of Natalie's paddling pool, blowing bubbles, holding the lit joint above the surface. Natalie took it from me.

"Pablo? Hello?"

I closed my eyes. Or rather, my eyes closed themselves. I could see the dancing crimson cord but I couldn't keep it in place. It scooted up and slid down. It weaved. It climbed towards me and teased away. I let it. I could smell spilt coffee and the greasy tang of print from a discarded newspaper.

"Pablo! Sit up!" My hair was being pulled. "Sit up!"

I felt myself dragged upright, and my eyes opened. Natalie was there, *shaking water from her hand, reaching for the joint in the ashtray. I saw her as if she were a captured instant between strobing trees.*

"Jesus. You had me worried for a moment there. You okay?" She took a drag and blew out a jet of grey smoke. "You want a hit of this?"

"Fuck, yeah," Perdito said in my head. "Say that." I watched my hand reach. I felt my mouth open. "Take it." I could hear him as clearly as I had that hot day on the London train. "Say it." I was way back, watching. I let go.

"You feeling okay?" Natalie asked.

"Fuck, yeah," Perdito said out loud, taking a long drag on the reefer. "I feel great."

*   *   *   *

I was awoken at three in the morning by small stones rattling against my window. It was Pablo, of course, beckoning me to come down to the garden

"...and bring a bottle," he whispered as I turned to find my dressing gown.

I didn't want to venture to the kitchen, which would take me past the open door of the drawing room, so I collected a bottle of revolting cherry brandy from the box room – a client's gift that I could bring myself neither to drink nor to throw away. At the bottom of the stairs in the dark I retrieved two packs of cigarettes from my briefcase and slipped them into the pocket of my dressing gown. I hesitated, wondering how to get out of the house. The front door tended to creak and Natalie was sleeping in front of the doors to the terrace. I went to the dining room and opened the window as quietly as I could manage.

"Hello," murmured Pablo, popping up from the shrubbery. "Did you bring a drink?"

I handed him the cherry brandy. "Where have you been?" I asked under my breath.

"Shh. Let's get away from the house. Can you get your leg over the sill?"

He helped me clamber out into the bushes and then he loped away across the lawn, gesturing for me to follow. I hadn't put any slippers on and the grass was cool and ticklish under my feet.

"Shall we take a walk around the lake?" Pablo suggested once we were out of earshot of the house. He opened the cherry brandy and swigged from it. "Blimey, that's pretty foul." He swigged again.

"Natalie is an, er, interesting woman," I said, falling in beside him as we followed the path towards the folly. "I'm only faintly surprised to find myself climbing out of a window rather than risk waking her."

"Yeah. Sorry about all these *Mad Bitch at Blandings* shenanigans. I'd just rather not see her at the moment."

"Evidently."

He'd been reading through his pages in the kitchen while making toast, and looked up to see Natalie walking down the drive. He shoved his day's writing into the bread bin ("…as a kind of Natalie primer…") and scooted out of the open French doors. Hiding in the knot garden he watched her stroll around the house and go in.

"Seven hours I've been stuck here, and I smoked my last fag ages ago."

I gave him the cigarettes from my pocket. We settled down in the folly and looked out at the moon floating on the surface of the lake.

"Your piece about Natalie is tantalisingly inconclusive," I said, waving away the offered brandy bottle.

"No kidding," he muttered glancing towards the house.

"So why couldn't you leave her? I mean, those events are twenty years in the past – and here she still is."

Pablo smiled and took a long drag on his cigarette. "Tell me about Leo."

"Ah."

I gazed across the placid lake, remembering other summers in this house. My memories are overwhelmingly those of childhood and adolescence in which Leo features predominantly. Perhaps that's because old age sharpens the recall of youth; or perhaps Leo was the fixing-agent that imprinted images on my mind, and without him to make them vivid the pictures I subsequently captured have faded.

"Actually," I said to Pablo, reaching for the brandy, "I will take a shot of that vile stuff."

So we sat there on the stone bench in the mock Temple of Athena passing the bottle to and fro as I talked about Leo.

*   *   *   *

I arrived in Cambridge in the autumn of 1960, lugging two suitcases and a cello. My brother Leo had gone up three years earlier to read Law. I was unpacking in my rooms when he stuck his head round the door.

"Hello, old chum. Welcome. Shall we shoot out for a pint? I've a restaurant booked for eight o'clock, but I feel the need of a sharpener."

I grinned, tossing a bundle of socks into a drawer. "I want to get everything straight and start on some reading. Nice to see you, by the way."

Leo came over to me and brushed my hands from the suitcase which he then gently closed.

"I am about to embark on a year of crushing slog, and your high-minded conscientiousness is no good to me. I plan to live vicariously through you, so shuck that abominable tie and we'll be about our proper business."

At the Eagle I was introduced to George Sandham. Back then he was a young man with the poise of a cat's tail - his treacle pudding years lay far ahead of him. I also met Abigail, whom my brother had mentioned in several letters over the preceding months. She was a dark-eyed imp who affected a languid theatricality that was intended, I think, to smack of the

Weimar Republic. I found the pose outdated and irritating, but Leo was evidently smitten.

We had a three or four pints apiece – Abigail drank schnapps – and it was dark by the time Leo ushered us to his car.

"There's a wonderful little place out in the sticks run by a French couple," Leo said. "Limoges-sur-Cam sort of arrangement."

The owners greeted Leo – everyone did – as if he were a sorely-missed son returning with news of a discovered diamond mine. We were given a table overlooking the river – the bank and the flowing water illuminated in the autumn dark by lights concealed beneath willows. The food was excellent and the wine unceasing. Leo was peacocking a little, letting his little brother know how well set-up he was, so witty and at ease with his girlfriend, his urbane pal George, his first-name chumminess with the restaurateurs. But I was pleased to note that he was also showing me off to them. "I worked my socks off to get the results I needed for Uni – but Stephen barely broke sweat, the brilliant little bugger. Jet-propelled brain and bloody good-looking too. Obviously I loathe him, and I have since childhood."

I stopped drinking after a couple of glasses of wine – I was tired, and there was a lot to do the following day. When it was time to leave, I told Leo I'd drive.

"Nonsense. Poppycock. For one you don't know the way, and for two you've barely passed your test. I shall be fine. I could do the journey in my sleep – and actually I have, once or twice."

I acquiesced. Leo drove – and on the outskirts of Cambridge he killed a pregnant dental nurse called Marianne Hammond. She died instantly as the car hit her on a clear stretch of road when the traffic signal was in her favour.

Leo killed Marianne Hammond and then he killed himself – but not instantly. It took ten years of determined, alcohol-sodden self-neglect and guilt. At my brother's funeral I wept on George Sandham's shoulder, and he told me I was weeping a decade after the fact. I still weep occasionally, because the fact is still part of the present for me. I can't quieten the impulse to re-run that moment outside the restaurant in the sticks when I might have taken the keys from my brother's hand. I can see myself doing it. "No – come on, Leo. Better safe, eh? Pour yourself into the back and I'll take us all home." He would have given in – he was a very biddable drunk, at least before the accident. Thereafter he was anything but.

"Oh, for Christ's sake, go on then," he says, in my revised version. "George, tell him where to go." And he clambers into the backseat with Abigail whom he subsequently marries the month after he and George graduate. Five years later I help him through a messy divorce and he rooms with me for a few weeks until he finds a new place – and I never have to see him lying unconscious in a police cell covered in vomit and blood while George posts bail in the office outside.

All it would have taken is for me to have lifted the keys from his finger as gently and firmly as he lifted my hands from the suitcase. But I didn't do it, and three lives were not spared.

*   *   *   *

Even hearing myself say his name out loud was a novel shock. It was the first time in decades that my mouth had formed those syllables and that my breath had given them a voice. George and I, of course, had no need to speak about Leo directly – and to whom else would I have spoken? As I described my lost brother, as I related the circumstances of the accident on the outskirts of Cambridge, I realised that I'd made Leo invisible. I'd kept him to myself, thought about him constantly, venerated his memory – but by my private and silent devotion I'd erased him from the world. Who would remember Leo when George and I were gone?

"Well, now I will," Pablo said. He took another swig from the brandy. "Then again, maybe it's you that should be writing a book."

I sniffed and smiled. "I'm trying to encourage you to write one." I nodded towards the house. "Do you think she'll leave if you stay in hiding?"

"I bloody well hope so. Listen, if she hangs around in the morning, can you find a way of getting some food out here to me? I'm starving."

"I will, yes."

The moon emerged from behind a cloud and a fox trotted along the path towards the orchard. Pablo and I sat in silence. He stared across the water at the light in the drawing room; I gazed at a faint black smudge on the Portland-stone floor of the Temple. On a warm night like this when I was ten or eleven, Leo and I had taken some sausages and beer from the pantry and slipped out of the house in the dark. We built a fire in the centre of the Temple to cook the sausages and Leo opened the bottles of ale with his penknife. My father was expected to be away for the night – killing time in Westminster waiting for the Division Bell, I imagine – but he drove home in the early hours and saw our campfire from the house. He called the police, thinking that gypsies had set up shop in the grounds. There was hell to pay. Even Leo couldn't charm us out of the beating that followed.

There's no one left alive but me who remembers that adventure. Given the usual run of things – one in which both brothers had grown up and married, produced children who then had children of their own – it would have evolved into a family story told round the Christmas table and at wedding breakfasts. It would have become a small component of the vehicle that carries us all into the future – shared memory.

But I've never shared Leo. I've never spoken up when I had the opportunity. There was the moment with the car keys outside the restaurant. I should have spoken then but I didn't, and my brother was lost. I've failed to speak ever since, and because of my failure the world will be deprived of Leo once again.

"You know what?" Pablo said, grinding his latest cigarette underfoot. "I reckon a person could inhabit this garden for years without anyone knowing they were here."

I looked at him and he handed me the cherry brandy.

"It's been done," I said, and drained the bottle.

*   *   *   *

I learned the technique – or rather, we learned it – of allowing Perdito to drive. I used cannabis the first few times to loosen my grip on myself, but soon I could simply unfocus and drift backwards, and Perdito would flow into the gap I'd left. I was still there, and still conscious of speaking, of making my limbs move – but the words I spoke, the movements I made were initiated by him, and I allowed them.

"There's a real difference between your personalities" Natalie used to say. "I mean, I can always tell which of you is, like, in the ascendant."

She was right – Perdito and I were dissimilar people. He was the more extrovert and boisterous. He had a quicker temper than mine and little patience. When I was letting him through I still spoke in the first person, but Natalie swore that my voice changed.

"I've had enough of this crap," I permitted him to say, nodding at the television. "Let's go out somewhere."

"Yeah, let's. What do you want to do?" Natalie asked.

"Go and see a band or something. Find some dope. Dance. Anything but stay here."

"Okay. Where did I put my keys?"

Natalie leaned over the arm of the couch to rummage in her bag, and her skirt rode up over the backs of her thighs. I felt Perdito lurch inside me and I allowed through the instruction he sent to my arms. I leaned forward and yanked down Natalie's underwear, then fumbled with the zip of my jeans.

"Perdito!" Natalie exclaimed. "God!"

I made myself transparent – a wireless transmitter of Perdito's impulses – and he shoved Natalie further forward, shifting her thighs apart with my knees.

"Let me see it," he demanded, one hand clamped around the back of her neck. "Show me."

"You bastard. Go on – be rough. Hurt me."

"Uh-huh."

Perdito thrust my cock in brusquely and fucked her over the arm of the sofa. She panted encouragement as he pulled her hair and slapped her arse. He fingered and mauled and squeezed, grunting and talking filth. They came together in a screaming crescendo of profanity and gush – and the moment after orgasm Perdito disengaged from me, detumesced in my head and flopped away, drowsy. Within seconds he was silent and I could feel him darkening and letting go.

"Jesus," Natalie gasped as she slid back into the seat. "It's like having two boyfriends." She looked at me. "Pablo?"

"Yes, it's me."

"I know. Something changes in your face. Did you enjoy it too?"

Not entirely, no. Rough sex just wasn't really my thing. But it didn't matter what I liked – Perdito liked it and it wouldn't have been fair of me to get sniffy about his preferences. Had things gone differently and he had smothered me in the womb, I wouldn't have wanted him telling me what I could and couldn't do when it was my turn with the flesh and blood.

But eighteen months into the relationship with Natalie, I'd had enough. She irritated me – not constantly, but too often. I wanted out. Perdito was appalled.

"What about me? What about what I want? I like her. She's fun. She's great in bed. She understands us. Don't I get a say?"

It was the 'us' that mattered. Perdito knew how lucky we had been. It seemed unlikely we'd find another woman who'd accept us – embrace us, in fact – rather than assume we were lunatic freaks. On top of which, I think Perdito was honestly fond of her, so I had no right to quit. I just clenched, holding my irritation in like a fart, and carried on. Anyone looking from the outside would imagine that Natalie and I have had an intermittent relationship for more than twenty years. We spent time together – a week here, a few days there, the occasional trip abroad. We worked on joint projects. We had blazing rows. It wasn't all bad, but it wasn't much fun most of the time. Now that Perdito's gone, there's no reason to see her any more.

To be honest, I don't care whether I see anyone at all for a few months. I have a date to look forward to in December, but until then I just want to enjoy being alone.

*   *   *   *

I came into the kitchen to find Natalie pouring orange juice.

"Good morning. I hope you slept well," I said.

"Fine. He's not come back though."

"Apparently not."

I filled the kettle.

"How long has he been here?" she asked.

"Three weeks or more. When did you last see him?"

"About a month ago. He's always disappearing. Weeks, sometimes."

I dropped teabags into two mugs. "And do you usually seek him out like this?"

Natalie folded her arms and leaned back against the counter. "I'm not some pathetic, needy girlfriend chasing after a runaway bloke, if that's what you're thinking," she said.

"Of course. Milk and sugar?"

"No sugar."

"I thought not."

"He's been acting very weirdly. He's not well."

I shrugged. "I'm aware of the incident on Wardour Street, though he hasn't talked about it yet. He must have been in some distress."

"God, no – distress?" she scoffed. "That event was brilliant. It's the best thing he's ever done."

I handed her a mug. "It was an event? An art concept?"

"Of course it was. Look at the reaction he got."

"I see," I said, sipping my tea. "So in what sense has he been acting strangely?"

She shrugged. "Personal stuff. None of your business. I just need to see him and talk."

"Perhaps he's back in London. You may have passed each other in transit."

"Yeah, maybe. But I went round to his place yesterday before I came here and he wasn't about."

That was a surprise to me. "His place? He told the police he was homeless."

Natalie laughed – the first time I'd seen her appear anything but aggressively sullen.

"Christ – he has the most amazing apartment on the river at Limehouse. A huge space. It cost him a fortune." She shook her head. "See – you don't know the first fucking thing about him. No one does. No one knows him like I do."

As I flipped bacon rashers in the frying pan, Natalie wrote down her phone number for me, asking me to call when Pablo rematerialised.

"Good luck finding him," I said at the door. "Nice to have met you."

She began to walk away down the drive but turned and came back to the porch.

"Look," she said hesitatingly. "He might not want to contact me, yeah? But if he's, you know, reluctant, can you tell him something from me?"

"Of course."

"Just say that I miss them both. Okay? I miss both of them."

I watched her as far as the gate, and then I walked down there myself to check that she was disappearing along the lane. When I returned to the house, Pablo was eating a bacon sandwich, dripping melted butter on the floor.

"She says she misses both of you," I told him, tearing a paper towel off the roll and bending to mop up the butter.

"She's not going to give up easily," Pablo mumbled with his mouth full. "She's very persistent."

"She means you and Perdito, I take it."

Pablo nodded and wiped his lips on the back of his hand. "Then again – you probably do have to be exceptionally persistent to track down a missing ghost."

*   *   *   *

People love the thrill of coincidence. "Imagine – all the way to Ayer's Rock and who are we sitting next to on the bus? You'll never guess – Matthew's proctologist!" But coincidence is just that category of chance in which it's more than usually easy to divine a spurious pattern. It's the face of the Virgin in the scorch marks on a pita-bread.

*   *   *   *

My function within Sub Judice is chiefly that of coordinator. I organise the time and activities of the writers, lawyers, actors, politicians and so on who are involved in our campaigns. I prefer to stay out of the spotlight, not least because we have at our disposal the talents of so many for whom the spotlight is an accustomed environment. Daphne Cadwallader, for instance, has been involved with us for five or six years. Her father is a novelist whom I represented during the eighties, and despite Daphne's film credits and the fact that she has school-age children of her own, I still think of her as Little Daff. And she, I'm not embarrassed to say, still thinks of me as the family friend who presented her with her first tricycle.

I had an appointment to meet her on location in Sussex.

"Uncle Stephen! Come in, come in. You look so well!"

I stepped up into her trailer and was ushered to a seat.

"We'll need you in about ten minutes, Miss Cadwallader," advised an adolescent flunkey with several earrings. Daphne waved him out of the trailer and offered me a soft drink from the fridge.

"I can't sit down in this thing. God knows how those women managed." She was in Victorian costume – crinoline bustle dress and piled-up hair. The Diet Coke she was sipping looked most incongruous.

"It's so kind of you to find time for me, Daff," I said, opening my briefcase and taking out a folder. "I know how busy you are."

"Oh, sod off, you idiot," she scolded. "It's lovely to see you. How have you been?"

We exchanged news of mutual friends and her family, and then talked about the campaign that Daphne was fronting for us. I took her through recent developments, progress in the courts, the germane legal arguments.

"You're really good at this, Stephen," she said, leaning over my shoulder to look at the papers. "You should have gone into law."

I hesitated. And then I replied, "Well, we already had one lawyer in the family. My elder brother. I couldn't have competed with him."

"Really? I didn't know you had a brother."

"Yes – Leo." Leo. I said it. I caused Leo to exist in another human being's world. "He died too young. In his thirties."

"Oh, I'm sorry."

I imagined Daphne talking to her father, who had known me for twenty-five years. "I saw Stephen Richmond last week. Were you aware he had a brother?" Perhaps there would be other people present – Daphne's mother, one or two writers and theatricals of my acquaintance. "Leo. He was a lawyer apparently. He died many years ago."

There was a knock at the trailer door and the boy with the earrings stuck his head in.

"When you're ready, Miss Cadwallader."

I stood up. "Are you working all weekend?" I asked, just to move the conversation to a close.

"No, we get tomorrow off. Sunday lunch at my parents', and then Rory's previewing his new show."

The children of writers, I've noticed, very rarely go into what George would call 'the useful professions'. Novelists do not tend to raise electricians or nurses. Daphne's brother Rory was a sculptor – for want of a better word to describe one who welds shopping-trolleys to wheelbarrows and displays the results in Shoreditch galleries.

A thought occurred to me. "Could you do me a favour? Ask Rory if he knows a chap called Pablo Lyne."

"Well, I can tell you he does," Daphne said immediately. "So do I – or at least I used to. Contemporary art is a very small world. Why do you want to know about Pablo?"

"He's my house-guest at the moment. He's writing for me."

Daphne frowned. "Sit down a moment, Stephen," she said. "Let me tell you about Pablo Lyne."

Ten years earlier Daphne met Pablo at a party in St John's Wood. He was quite famous in avant-garde circles at the time, it seems, and Daphne was struck by the deference Rory offered him as the three of them chatted on a balcony overlooking Abbey Road.

"I was impressed by him too, although I knew nothing about his work. He was an attractive and intriguing man of about thirty back then, and I was young – what? twenty-three? – and, to use an expression of my mother's, no better than I should be. Isn't that awful? Anyway, I began to act like a complete hussy. It didn't have the desired effect. Pablo just kept chatting away – unblushing, casual – oblivious to what I thought of as my feminine wiles."

"Are you sure you want to tell me this, Little Daff?" I put in. I'm not a prude, but I wasn't comfortable that this kind of revelation fell within the terms of my relationship with a small girl with whom I had once played hopscotch.

"Oh, shut up and listen," she frowned, swatting my shoulder. "Well, I was most put out that Pablo was impervious to my charms. So after half an hour or so of ineffectual trollopery, I just came straight out with it. 'Look – are you going to take me to bed, or what?' I said. And do you know what he replied? 'Yes, okay. That might be nice.' I mean, it's not exactly the thirst that from the soul doth rise, is it?"

Again the earringed boy appeared in the doorway. "Everyone's on set, Miss Cadwallader, ready to roll."

"I'm just coming, Jerry." She turned back to me, tutting. "Rory and I, impoverished artist and actress that we were, shared a tiny flat in Kilburn, to which I eagerly dragged Pablo. It was a one-bedroom place and I had the bedroom. Rory, who we'd left at the party, slept on a fold-out sofa in the living-room. Well, Pablo and I fell into bed, shedding clothes the while and…"

"Wait, wait," I said. "Is this going to become graphic?"

"I'll gloss the details," Daphne promised. "All I'll say is that a change came over Pablo once the main action got underway. Vertical, he was self-effacing, wry, solicitous. But horizontal, and at various other angles, he was aggressive, profane, bullish – not what I was expecting at all."

"Did he hurt you?"

"No, he scared me. It wasn't just that I saw a side of his personality that I hadn't anticipated. It was more like…" She paused and gazed out of the window of the trailer, thinking. She looked back at me. "It was as if he became someone else. The guy I'd talked to at the party was no longer there at all." She shrugged. "I don't mean it figuratively. Honestly, the chap I ended up in bed with was not the one I'd tried to seduce an hour earlier."

I thought of the tiger again, coalescing from the shadows of the forest for a moment and then merging back into the undergrowth.

"Well," Daphne said, breezy again, "I was less than thrilled with the idea of spending the entire night with Pablo, so I suggested that we go out for a drink before the pubs closed, hoping I could shuck him somewhere along the way. By the time we'd got dressed he was back to his original self, so laidback and diffident that I wasn't even sure I'd seen in him what I thought I'd seen. That was rather unnerving as well.

"And this is where it all descends into French farce. We opened the bedroom door and walked out into the living room to be confronted with the spectacle of Rory vigorously rogering a woman with green hair. There were limbs sticking up all over the place. And the woman, believe it or not, was Pablo's girlfriend!"

"Natalie?"

"Yes! Do you know her too?"

"Only slightly."

"Extraordinary. Anyway, Rory pauses in mid-stroke without actually disengaging, and the Natalie woman peers over his shoulder. Pablo, still pulling his jacket on, says, 'We're just going for a quick drink across the road, Nat. If you get a move on we can share a cab home'. And with that he takes my hand and we saunter from the flat. Sure enough, twenty minutes later Natalie appears in the pub, pleasantries are exchanged and off they go."

The door of the trailer opened and a flushed man with a beard clambered in.

"Daphne, please. The clock's ticking."

Daff picked up her parasol from the table. "Sorry, darling. Sorry, sorry. Here I come." She leant down to kiss my cheek. "So you be careful with your house guest, Stephen. He's an odd one. Promise me?"

I promised, patting her hand.

"I wonder if he'd remember me," Daphne mused as we left the trailer.

*   *   *   *

I had a cat once. I was living in Clapham and one day this black-and-white cat wandered in through the backdoor and decided to stay. She didn't ask for much – she seemed capable of finding her own food and she was never that bothered about being stroked – so I was content to let her treat the place as home. I never gave her a name, and I don't suppose she gave me one. We just got used to having each other about. And then one morning I walked out onto the street and she was lying dead in the gutter. She'd been hit by a car. She was totally stiff, utterly unfeline. Nothing is deader than a dead cat. I buried her on the Common.

For weeks afterwards when I was in the flat I'd see movement at the periphery of my vision and I'd think, 'cat'. Or I'd open the front door and, before I could remind myself it was pointless, I'd look for her on the windowsill where she liked to sleep.

In exactly the same way Perdito's absence is taking some getting used to. I keep catching sight of him out of the corner of my mind. For thirty years I had him in my head and I still expect him to pipe up whenever I'm doing something that he'd enjoy – smelling the roses in Stephen's garden; luxuriating under the clean, white sheets of the bed. When I wake up it takes me a few moments to work out what's missing. It's the feeling of being watched

Actually, though, Perdito did disappear once before, just for a while.

I was nineteen and I was in Amsterdam by accident. I'd intended to go to Barcelona – my father had arranged for the Condesa to have her forty-fifth birthday party there. Tom, Jazz and I were to fly out and meet Mum and Dad – but a fault developed on the plane and we made an unscheduled landing at Schipol. We were put up in a hotel near the airport for the night, and decided to go for a drink in the city.

It was early January – dark at five o'clock, the air clear as gin and very cold. The canals were frozen and Amsterdammers were skating on them, past the ice-embedded house boats and beneath the countless bridges.

"They must be suicidal," Tom said as we strolled along the Prinsengracht. "I wouldn't trust that ice to hold."

"Let's try that after dinner," Perdito suggested. Since we'd begun to swap control, I had got used to him chatting to me in the background, and I could feel him there even when he was silent. Sometimes months would go past without my hearing from him. And then I'd feel something noiseless shift inside me like the movement of dust. I'd acknowledge him with a thought, and leave him be.

We chose a bar that was crowded, smoky and loud. Halfway through the second beer I got up to let two girls squeeze past to the table behind ours. They were loose and tall, carelessly lovely in a way that's peculiar to Dutch women. Beauty drapes over them like a hippy scarf; it trails in their wake as they ride their rusty bicycles; it coils about them lazily like reefer smoke.

Because of the proximity of the tables and the volume at which it was necessary to conduct a conversation, the girls heard us discussing how we might spend the evening in the city.

"Excuse me," one of them said eventually, "you are thinking what you do in Amsterdam tonight? You like rock music?"

"Love it," I said immediately. "What have you got in mind?"

"Our friend is in a rock band who play tonight. This is interesting for you?" The girl speaking was high-cheeked and wide-mouthed, her hair trodden-blonde and Medusan.

110

"We have to be up early tomorrow," Tom said. "We absolutely can't miss the flight."

The other girl – darker and shyer – said something in Dutch, and the blonde nodded before turning back to us. "When you want to come with us, you go in the door gratis."

"Well, that should clinch it, Tom, eh?" I said. "It'll cost you nothing."

He tutted dismissively, but I knew that money was a factor with him. Money's always a factor with him.

"We have to check in at eight," he said. "On the dot."

He and I looked to Jazz, not because she had the casting vote but because she was our big sister and even as adults we deferred to her. I'll bet that there are captains of industry, senior civil servants and unassailable spooks in the upper reaches of MI5 who defer to their big sister.

"We can afford a couple of hours," Jazz said.

Before we left the bar with Tineke – the blonde – and Neelie, I needed to buy cigarettes. The cigarette machine was in a low alcove by the stairs, and hanging from the ceiling beams were dozens of strips of sticky tape, each of which had a few coins stuck to it. My head brushed against them as I fed guilders into the slot. When I retrieved the pack of smokes from the tray, I found that a few cents were wrapped around it with tape. The Dutch have a reputation for both fiscal niggardliness and easygoing generosity, and this was a superb example of that apparent contradiction. They would hate to feel the vending machine had cheated them of fifteen cents, so the cigarette companies attach the change to the cigarettes. But having been offered this paltry shrapnel, no one can be bothered to keep it, so they stick it to the ceiling as a demonstration of their cheerful indifference. I like the Dutch.

While we were watching the band at the Melk Weg and I was chatting to Neelie, who was handing round a succession of knee-buckling joints, Perdito nagged me about skating on the canal. I wasn't against the idea, but I resented being cajoled.

"Do you live near here?" I shouted at Neelie over the music.

She smiled. "Three streets away only. Why?"

"Do you have any ice skates? I'd really like to go on the canals."

"Oh, is that all you ask?" she laughed as she accepted a joint from Tineke and dragged on it before passing it to Tom. "Skates are not necessary. We can walk on the ice in our shoes. It is normal."

"Neelie and I are going to walk on the water," I told Jazz and Tom. "Coming?"

Tom had smoked a lot of dope, but it didn't appear to have unbuckled his uptightness by even a notch.

"It's time we were heading back to the hotel," he said. He twisted his arm around so that I could see his watch. "We absolutely must not miss our flight. Tell him, Jazz."

"I really don't feel well," Jazz said, lifting her head from the table. "Don't be late back, all right?"

"If he goes, we'll never bloody see him again," Tom slurred. "I'm not explaining it to Mum."

I assured them both that I'd be there for breakfast at the hotel, then Neelie and I walked out into the clarified, chill darkness of the Amsterdam night. We strolled along the canal until we reached some steps that led down to the ice. Neelie was right – shoes were fine as long as one didn't walk tentatively. The safest way forward was to alternate short sprints and long slides. Whooping and laughing, we skittered along the centre of the canal, looking up at the tall, narrow houses with their bright, uncurtained windows. We yelled at the echoes as we scooted under bridges and we hullooed to passers-by who stopped on the cobbled pavements to applaud us when we held each other's hands and span in reckless circles.

And as I careered along, I listened for Perdito, who was ever eager for this sort of undiluted rush of sensation. I expected to be able to feel his prickled excitement, as I had when I'd parachuted over Salisbury Plain and abseiled in Switzerland. But I couldn't find him. He seemed to have retreated. Speeding towards a bridge, I closed my eyes – which was stupid, but I was pretty stoned – and fumbled around in my head for him like someone looking for a torch in the dark.

"Look out!" Neelie shouted.

Skating blind, I'd veered towards the canal bank where the arch of the bridge was lowest. I opened my eyes in time to see the bricks with which my head collided.

"There's blood," Neelie said, leaning over me. "Come up here in the light."

I couldn't understand why Perdito was so silent. This was exactly his kind of trip.

"We go to my house and I clean you," Neelie suggested. "Maybe we have sex also."

"Okay – why not?" I murmured, wiping blood from my ear. For the first time since I was nine, I couldn't sense Perdito at all. It really felt like he was gone.

"You closed your eyes." Neelie said, helping me stand up. "Are you out of your mind?"

"If I'm not," I told her, "someone else is."

*   *   *   *

I woke up in Neelie's bed at about the time that the plane to Barcelona was taking off. I sighed and reached for the half-finished joint on the bedside table. As I lay there smoking and watching Neelie's breasts rise and fall, I felt around in my head for Perdito. I couldn't find him at all. It was worrying. I could barely remember a time when he hadn't been there, observing, pressing against my mind, rubbing himself on my perceptions like a frotteur.

I closed my eyes and drifted off again, feeling bereft.

A few breathless hours with Neelie later – "Do you want more fucking, or maybe we eat first?" "Can I see both menus?" – she and I went for lunch at a café on the nearest canal. I was totally unhungry, despite the dope. It was as if Perdito had taken my appetite with him. I drank coffee and chatted with Neelie, but I was distracted. The winter sunshine stretched like a cat across the thawing ice; the tall white houses smiled along the seductive curve of the canal, inviting an exploratory stroll. I was about to fall in love with Amsterdam, but I was like a man who had bumped into the knees of his future wife whilst crouching to look for a contact lens. My vision was lopsided and my attention was misdirected.

"I must go to work," Neelie said. "Thank you for the nice night."

"Thank you too. Where's the station from here?"

I dropped into a bar for cigarettes, grinning as I taped the small change to the ceiling. I had a couple of glasses of genever, which gave a tingling boost to the fading maryjane. I wondered whether Jazz and Tom had made the flight – they were both pretty stoned when I left the club. I'd never seen Tom smoke dope before and it surprised me a bit. But then you could pump Tom full of morphine, padlock him in a milk churn and suspend the whole thing over a pit of cobras and he'd still get to check-in early enough to secure a bulkhead window seat with a view up the flight attendant's skirt.

On the way to the airport I stopped at the hotel. I picked up my overnight bag, and also a note from Jazz of which the first line was 'Fucking typical!' That's as far as I read before dropping it in a litter bin.

There was no flight that would get me to Barcelona in time for Mum's birthday dinner, so the money Dad had sent me was spent on a ticket back to London. I realised I'd have to do something about making it up to my parents, though I was sure they'd have a perfectly wonderful time without me.

As for Perdito – it was a whole year before he made himself evident again.

* * * *

I suppose I could have asked Pablo whether he remembered Daphne Cadwallader, just as I could have asked him about the luxury apartment in Limehouse, but there was little to gain from such an interrogation. Even if he recalled her, what was I to do – give him the opportunity to present his version of events, as if I were a schoolmaster investigating misconduct behind the gymnasium?

In any case, Pablo was writing like a fury now and I didn't want to distract him from his task. At whatever time I returned home I would find him scribbling beneath a blue pall of smoke. After sherry, I'd suggest a dinner menu and then there would be a charming interlude of crossfire courtesy in which Pablo would offer to cook and I'd insist that it really wasn't necessary.

Over dinner we'd chat about either the garden, for which he'd developed a custodian passion, or about the craft of writing in general terms, and then Pablo would pick up the bottle – "Don't mind if I finish this off, do you?" – and return to the desk to continue scribbling.

This was the routine at home. Away from Twyborough Cross I was engaged in the project of making Leo visible. It was the kind of monomania one sees in an inebriated dinner party guest who keeps trying to haul conversation back to his favourite topic, ignorant of the resigned sighs and the indulgent swapped glances of the other diners. In client meetings, at lunch with publishers, in telephone conversations and at cocktail parties, I was constantly on the look-out for opportunities to mention Leo. I must have been a terrible bore but I had thirty years to make up. I imagined a world in which I had always been ready to talk about my lost brother. In such a world the references to him would have accumulated gradually, and awareness of his existence would have been part of knowing me. When mutual friends were talking, they might have referred to Leo as an identifying element of my personality.

"He lost his brother, you know. I don't think he's ever quite got over it."

And that would be true. I never quite got over it. Leo – his presence and his absence – was a defining factor in my development and therefore in my achievements, and it had been a betrayal, a dishonesty not to have made that plain to the world. It was as if I were taking credit for a success that was not, in the end, due to me.

This change in attitude was not lost on George. I was hosting a Charity Lunch in support of Sub Judice and George was my guest. Afterwards, when we were alone at the bar, he lit a cigar and looked at me sidelong.

"What's got into you?" he said. "Have you been going to séances or something? Are you all right?"

To some extent George did his best to replace Leo as my big brother, and I was grateful to him for the impulse if not the follow-through. In truth, his regular attempts to guide me, advise me, look out for my interests served to prompt in me speculations as to how Leo would have handled that responsibility. I often imagined what he would look like – he'd be nearly sixty-five. While I inherited our mother's hair – thick and almost white by the time I was forty – Leo had our father's – fine, light brown and poorly attached. Our father was bald at the crown by middle-age, and I expect Leo would have gone the same way. He would have put on weight too, as I have – but all on the stomach and chest. He'd still be thin in the face. He would have been an imposing, solid old man.

I put myself through this torture of forensic projection, I think, because it reminded me that Leo would have grown old and less golden. It discouraged me from reducing him to a beautiful immortal cipher, which was my tendency. But when I imagined conversations with him – and when, from time to time, I had dreams of such limpid immediacy that I awoke from them tearful and angry that I'd woken at all – I was always my current age and he was twenty-two – and there seemed to be no anachronism in that at all.

"I'm fine. I can't imagine what you mean," I told George.

He blew on the lit end of his cigar. "These incessant allusions to Leo all of a sudden. What's brought that on?"

I had a cigar too, still in my top pocket. I took it out and slid off the band, which I handed to George.

"See that? *Romeo y Julietta*. Is that a good cigar?"

"Well, it's not bad. Not absolutely top quality but nothing to be ashamed of. Why?"

"I know nothing about cigars. I always ask for a *Romeo y Julietta* because that's what Leo told me to ask for."

"Did he? I don't think I ever saw him smoke a cigar in his life."

"He said it was necessary to smoke a cigar once in a while merely to remind you why you stick to cigarettes. Didn't he ever say that to you?"

"Never. What are you driving at?"

"Driving. That's another one," I said. I was a little drunk. I was always a little drunk when I was with George. "Do you know why I drive a Bentley?"

"Because you can afford to, I assume."

"I could afford a Rolls. A Daimler. No. I drive a Bentley because it's the car to which Leo aspired. The perfect marriage of pretension and tradition – that was his line."

"Yes – I remember that one."

I rolled my brandy around the glass, watching the meniscus climb. "And these are just the cosmetic fripperies. God knows how many other influences I've taken from Leo that I don't even recognise, let alone acknowledge. He deserves some credit."

"Do you still miss him?"

I nodded, my eyes on the swirling brandy. George tapped the ash from his cigar and pursed his lips.

"Mind if I join in?" he said.

And so, sitting there at the bar of a banqueting room on the Strand, we talked about Leo – really talked about him – for the first time in twenty-five or thirty years. None of what we said was new or surprising. It was dusty and mildewed but immediately familiar, like a scrapbook rediscovered in the attic.

George and I contributed separate happy recollections of my brother – childhood and adolescence for me, college days in George's case. But of course the accident happened on the night that George and I met, so our shared memories of Leo – those that involved all three of us – concerned the decade of his self-destructive decline, and we couldn't reminisce without evoking those years, those painful times.

Memory is not, as the idiom suggests, a lane to be walked down, stopping at a given spot to admire the fondly-remembered view of the fields, averting one's eyes when passing a still-smouldering bombsite. One cannot tour the past selectively because memory isn't a neat parade – it's a kasbah. You may duck into the backstreets intending to buy only a postcard, but in forked alleys and covered passageways, in cut-throughs and unexpected courtyards you'll be waylaid by the importunate peddlers of trinkets, perfumes, gemstones and geegaws that you hadn't expected even to consider, let alone bring home.

"What was the name of the club we used to go to on Frith Street?" George mused.

"God, I don't know. Patti Mills worked there."

"Ah, Patti," George nodded. "I really thought Patti might be the making of him. Well, no – he was fully-made. The saving of him, perhaps."

"He put paid to that," I murmured. I turned a corner in the seething kasbah and was swept by the press of busy memories into narrow, dark alleys that I had not visited for decades.

*   *   *   *

I graduated in the summer of 1963 and I began work that autumn as a sub-editor for a large publishing house in Mayfair. At first I roomed with my father at his *pied-á-terre* in Pimlico but the arrangement was irksome to both of us, so my parents splashed out on a two-bedroom apartment close to the British Museum, and I moved in there. The idea was that I would find a lodger with whom to share the place, but within days of my taking residence Leo had established himself as the second occupant. He simply knocked on the door one evening, drunk and unconcerned – "Lost my wallet somewhere in Soho. I don't fancy walking all the way to bloody Chelsea. Where's the drinks cabinet?" – and he stayed put.

"Better he should be with you at night than gadding about God knows where with God knows whom," my father muttered grimly. We were driving down to Twyborough Cross on a Friday night. "Perhaps you can make him see sense, Stephen. It's time to stop crying over spilt milk."

The milk in question, of course, was Marianne Hammond and her unborn child, the victims of Leo's accident. My father was not an uncompassionate man, but at some selfish, protective level he resented the woman whose death had so affected his elder son. And the effect was obvious. Although Leo was still holding onto his position as a junior barrister, his professional future was balanced on the rim of a glass.

"He needs a woman to put him straight, give him some responsibility," my father continued. "You know I don't want to pry, Stephen, but are there any suitable prospects in that regard?"

Leo was not short of female company, but I'd seen none that would have fallen within my father's definition of 'suitable', by which he meant steady, reliable, determined – my mother, in short. Leo's taste in women appeared, at first sight, eclectic. Padding into the kitchen of a morning, I had encountered dishevelled debutantes, tousled air hostesses, panda-eyed go-go dancers, bleary shop assistants. They formed a representative cross-section of the denizens of London's nightlife, but they had in common a taste for both the fashionable hedonism of the time and the dark rum that was Leo's favoured narcotic. I am certain that in any era and in any city an attractive and fairly wealthy young man could find a way to ruin himself, should he feel so disposed. But London in the Sixties was particularly permissive of Leo's driven self-destruction. My parents assumed that during the week in town their sons would be industrious, discreet young professionals; and that at the weekends we would return home to socialize, attend church; we'd be, in short, the respectable scions of a respected Member of Parliament. I was. Leo was less so.

"There you are! Have you seen Wednesday's *Sketch*?" the old man would rage, flapping the newspaper in Leo's face when he walked into the house. "Page ten! Look!" Leo tossed his motorcycle helmet onto a chair and reached for the paper, turning to the relevant section. Father tapped it with an irate finger. "And who the hell is that woman draped around your neck?"

"Caroline, if memory serves," Leo said, holding the page still and peering at it. "Gosh, I do look rather the worse for wear, don't I? Terribly sorry."

"Have you any idea how embarrassing this kind of thing is for your father, Leo?" my mother put in. "We have journalists telephoning day and night to ask about you. What are we expected to say?"

"I didn't even know that there was a photographer in the place. It's really most tiresome. I do apologise."

He was honestly contrite – at least, he was in the early years. But by the mid-Sixties his visits to Twyborough Cross had become intermittent and his appearances in the gossip columns amounted to a residency. My father, who was simultaneously incensed and distressed by Leo's behaviour, had taken to telling the Press that his son was having a nervous breakdown. Leo thought that hilarious. In fact he thought most things hilarious. He burned with a manic exuberance which, in tandem with his indiscriminate generosity, made him a popular reveller in the clubs and restaurants of the capital. As more than one of his pals told me when I accompanied my brother on an evening out, 'Leo's a riot.'

That's exactly what he was. Just as a rampaging mob gleefully destroys the shops and houses of its own neighbourhood, Leo was devastating himself with a wild grin on his face.

"Dad really shouldn't worry about the papers, you know," he told me once. "They're here and gone. No one will remember me tomorrow."

Indeed.

Patti Mills, though, was an exception to the usual run of Leo's women, and she appeared likely to become a more permanent fixture than any of her predecessors. She was almost Leo's height – taller than me – and statuesque in a way that was completely out of vogue, though I have yet to meet a heterosexual man unimpressed by that sweater-girl silhouette, however unfashionable it might be deemed. I adored Patti. George adored her. My parents, to whom she was introduced one summer weekend, practically adopted her. Within half an hour of her arrival at the house, my father was leading her around the grounds, asking her opinion about the rose garden, promising that he'd get Leo to take her out in the boat on the lake.

"Lovely, lovely girl," my mother smiled. She was sitting with Leo and me on the terrace, taking a gin and tonic before dinner. "Have you met her parents?"

"I've not had that pleasure," Leo said. He was sober and cheerful, and there was no undercurrent of contained mania in his demeanour. "I think they're tradespeople."

"Oh, don't try to provoke me, Leo. I don't care if they're gypsies. She's wonderful."

'Miraculous' was the word my father used when he talked to me on the phone a few months later.

"The change in Leo is a sight to behold," he said. "Do you know, I gave them both lunch at the House yesterday and Leo didn't touch a drop? Four courses and he drank water throughout. It's a huge relief to see him back on the right track. I'd like to pretend that it's due to the influence exerted by your mother and me – but it's Patti. All down to her. Good woman, you see. There's no substitute for the love of a good woman."

I know exactly when the old man said that. It was Thursday, October 20th, 1966. The following morning at nine-fifteen, in a Welsh mining village called Aberfan, the colliery waste-tip slid down the hill, and engulfed the primary school. More than a hundred children died there in the classrooms, buried under tons of black slurry. It was horrific and unforgettable. Forty years later I can summon the photographs and the newsreel images – the villagers digging in the evil muck for the bodies of their sons and daughters, the blanket-covered stretchers carried to the chapel, the mute faces of the little ones who survived.

I was watching the television news at our apartment that evening when Leo came home. He sat in the armchair for perhaps a minute, staring at the TV and drumming his fingers. He looked most uncomfortable. Suddenly he stood up, strode over to the set and turned it off.

"We don't want to see that dismal stuff," he said. "Let's go out on the town."

"Dismal hardly seems the appropriate word, does it?" I said. "And I do want to see it." I hauled myself out of the armchair and turned the television on again.

"Well, I'm not watching it. When Patti gets here, tell her I'm at the club."

He left. I sat there, silenced and made useless by the terrible, monochrome finality of the broadcast pictures. The school and several houses had been buried a little after nine o'clock. Not one child, not one teacher had been found alive since eleven, but they continued to search. In the milling, frantic swarm of digging rescuers there were parents whose children were still missing. To me, a hundred and fifty miles away watching television, it was obvious that they were ripping the nails from their fingers in the filthy rubble only to defer the eventual realisation that there was nothing to dig for. I didn't know whether, if there were some way of doing so, it would be kinder to lead them away from that dreadful place, or to let them scrabble in the ruins of the school until they dropped.

Patti arrived and took a seat next to me. There was nothing we could say to each other. Nothing would do. I have spent a lifetime in the service of words, but I learned then that there are horrors beyond the realm of language. Even now I am uncomfortable writing about Aberfan.

Eventually, Patti stood up and wiped her eyes. "I'd better go and meet Leo. Do you want to come?"

I shook my head. "I'm not in the right frame of mind." Alone again in the apartment, I turned off the television and made a cup of tea. I went to the bedroom and opened my Bible, but I found no comfort there.

A special service was arranged for that Sunday at St Dominic's, just down the road from Twyborough Cross. All over the country people were attending such services – it was all one could think of to do.

"I haven't been able to contact Leo," my father said as we stood outside the church. He looked at his watch. "I hope he and Patti are on their way."

He wandered off to talk to friends and I stood by the lych-gate, staring along the lane. The trees were decked in happy shades of gold and crimson, delighted with themselves in the cloudless sunshine. A squirrel scampered across the graveyard and hopped up onto a headstone, turning and nibbling an acorn in his agile paws. I looked up to see a flock of starlings sweeping the sky above the west tower of St Dominic's, as starlings had each autumn since the days of the Black Death. The sun shone down – on me as I brushed lych-gate moss from my shoulder, on my father as he fretted about Leo's absence, on squirrels and starlings preparing for winter – and I was embarrassed that it was also shining with such merry brilliance on the debris of buildings and the wreckage of lives only a few hours' drive away to the west.

"We'd better go in – come along," my mother said as she and the old man passed me. "Leo and Patti will have to stand at the back. I've never seen such a turn-out."

"Here they come now," I said, nodding towards Patti's red Mini that was bumping down the lane. "I'll bring them in."

I walked over to the car as Patti and Leo got out. Leo acknowledged me with a twitch of the eyebrows and no smile. Patti looked rather solemn too.

"We'd better get inside pretty swiftly," I said. "It's going to be standing-room only."

"There's time to finish my fag," Leo muttered. "The faithful are still filing in." He leaned on the church wall, head tilted back to blow smoke into the air.

Patti took my arm and led me towards the gate. "He's been very acting very strangely," she whispered. "He hasn't stopped drinking since Friday night."

I glanced at Leo. "He seems quite *compos mentis*."

"I know. But he got through most of a bottle of vodka on the way down here, and he's had barely three hours' sleep." She shook her head. "And he's so withdrawn. I've never seen him like this. Usually when he drinks he's the life and soul, isn't he?"

Leo flicked his cigarette-end across the lane into the nettles and pushed himself up off the wall. "Come on, then," he said, strolling towards us. "Let's see how the old fuck in the dog-collar explains this one away."

The church was indeed packed, but the three of us managed to squeeze onto the end of the final pew. I was wedged against the wife of the local butcher who, as the organ twiddled and the congregation settled down, interrogated me in a whisper about what I was up to, where I was living and whether there was any prospect of a nice wedding here at St Dominic's.

"Your mum's waving," she said, pointing towards the front pews.

"All right?" my mother mouthed.

I nodded.

She pointed at Leo and frowned. I looked to my left, around Patti who was bent low, apparently whispering to Leo whose forehead was resting on the back of the pew in front. I doubted that he was praying.

I shrugged theatrically for the benefit of my mother, and tried to convey that I'd keep an eye on my big brother. Mother shook her head and turned back to face the pulpit as the organ was abruptly silenced in mid-phrase and the Reverend Rawlings led us in a rendition of 'O God, Our Help in Ages Past'. He was a solid pastor in every sense, Joe Rawlings, sturdy as a buttress and just as integral to the parish church. My father considered him not only a friend but also a counterpart – the two of them were clerical and political pillars that held up the community.

"Over the last two or three days," Rawlings said when the hymn had been sung, "I've had more visitors to my house than at any time since I first came here. And, one way or another, everyone I've spoken to had the same question on their minds. 'How could God allow what happened in Aberfan?' I've been struggling with that too."

To my left I heard the hiss of a match. Leo was lighting another cigarette.

"In these modern times," Rawlings continued, "when we can send a man into space, when we can turn on the television and see pictures sent from the other side of the world, there are some ideas that seem old-fashioned – mediaeval, in fact. All this shiny science blinds us to some ancient truths." He leaned forward in the pulpit. "We've forgotten the nature of evil. We've lost sight of the Devil."

There were nods and murmurs from the congregation – but I heard Leo snort, and I nudged Patti who glanced at me worriedly.

"But Satan is still there, going about his destructive, malicious work, visiting misery and horror on ordinary folk. He's still engaged in the eternal battle with God. He was there in Aberfan, at a quarter past nine in the morning on Thursday. If the school had been buried just half an hour earlier, there would have been no one inside. We would be thanking the Lord now for that good fortune. But on this terrible occasion, evil won the fight."

"It's not bloody arm-wrestling," Leo said, loud enough to be heard in every corner of the hushed church. I looked at him. He was slouching with his head back and his eyes closed, the cigarette drooping in his hand. People turned to see who had spoken – pews creaked and clothes rustled. Leo opened his eyes and met the gaze of the congregation.

"Morning, all," he said.

"Actually, Leo, that's a very good analogy," the Reverend Rawlings said calmly. "The constant tension, the shifts in balance between good and evil. It's going on around us all the time. And it affects us all."

"Fabulous," Leo snorted, taking a drag on his cigarette. "We're all side-bets in a cosmic pub-game."

"Be quiet, Leo!" My father had risen from his seat and was walking back along the aisle. "Come outside. That's enough."

Leo got up too, steadying himself with one hand on the pew in front.

"No – it's *not* enough!" he shouted, suddenly animated. "All this cant just lets us off. It's an excuse for someone's ineptitude and carelessness." He pointed at Joe Rawlings "Are you telling me that a God who can part seas can't stop a slag-heap sliding downhill?"

My father grabbed Leo by the arm, but Leo swung with the other hand and the swipe knocked Dad backwards onto the stone floor.

"Leo, please," Patti said, standing up next to him. He shoved her down too.

"*People* kill children," he yelled. "Indifferent, irresponsible people. And if God's so disinterested that he allows it, then fuck God!" He leaned his head back and he stared up into the vault of the church. "Fuck you!" he roared.

The echo rumbled and rolled around the barrel roof, fading into the grey stone of the ancient walls. My father struggled to his feet, cradling a bruised elbow. Everyone else in St Dominic's was immobile with shock. Leo exhaled and shook his head, dropping his arms to his sides – he appeared exhausted.

"Car keys," he muttered, holding his hand out to Patti without looking at her. She fished the keys from her handbag and gave them to him. "Thank you." He ran his eyes over the congregation. "He doesn't refer to you as sheep for nothing," he said – and he walked out of the church.

My father forbade me to allow my brother further access to the apartment, and he had the locks changed. "If he has to put a roof over his head, he'll knuckle down to his responsibilities." But Leo didn't show up – not for months. My father also stopped Leo's allowance, on the premise that the less money he had the less he could drink. "We've made it too easy for him, that's the trouble."

But it wasn't alcohol that was destroying Leo, any more than it's the bridge that kills a leaping suicide. It's the determination to jump

*   *   *   *

I've often wondered where Perdito went when he disappeared on the canals. I'd always imagined that without me he had no substance – no weight or form. It didn't make sense that he had got out or got away. He would be a candle-flame with no wick, a bubble without a skin. I convinced myself that he must simply have sunk deeper into me than ever before, and was sleeping.

I can certainly remember the day he woke up. It was a Saturday, and I'd had lunch with Tom – the first time we'd met since the bar in Amsterdam – and later I'd dropped in on Natalie – who I also hadn't seen for months, come to think of it.

The football results were being read out on the TV, and I was incorporating them into the act. One thrust for each goal scored.

"Fulham 3..."

"Ah! Ah! Ah!" Natalie squealed.

"...Portsmouth nil."

"Shame."

Suddenly Perdito was there, shouting gleeful encouragement. "Fuck her! Fucking fuck her!" *Talking dirty was a particular quirk of his. He liked words in general – not on the page, but in the mouth. When we were abroad he picked up foreign languages with astonishing speed.*

I was startled to hear him, but also relieved. I grinned.

"What?" Natalie said, looking up at me.

"Nothing."

"Hull City two…" the TV announcer intoned.

"Ah! Ah!"

The phone rang.

"Leave it!" Natalie and Perdito said together. But it kept on ringing, right the way through to the Scottish Second Division. I couldn't ignore it any longer.

"For Christ's sake," I muttered, rolling over to pick it up. "I'll bet there's a four-all draw coming up."

"Pablo, it's Jacinta. There's been an accident."

I gestured to Nat to turn the TV down.

"What's the trouble?" I said. I hoped it was merely appallingly inconvenient – a kitchen fire at my parents' house, say. But Jazz wouldn't have let the phone ring so long for that. An injury then. It couldn't be Mum, because Dad would have called. So it was Dad. Dad had had an accident. Perhaps he was okay. Badly hurt but okay. No. When everyone's okay, that's the first thing people make clear. "Listen – everything's fine, but there's been an accident." So – everything was not okay.

All this dominoed through my head in the eternal half-second before Jazz spoke again. And when she did, I knew what she was going to say.

"Dad's had an accident." She paused. And then she began to sob, choked and breathless. "Pablo – Dad's dead! He's dead. Oh, Jesus Christ – I don't know what to do…"

"What happened?" I asked. "Jazz – listen to me. What happened?"

"Come home, Pablo. Mum's going crazy. I don't know what to do."

"Okay – I'll be there soon as I can. Tell me what happened."

"I can't believe it. It's just… I can't believe it. I can't believe he's dead."

"All right. Don't worry. I'll be there soon."

I hung up the phone and sat naked on the edge of the bed, hands cupping my nose and mouth. I closed my eyes.

"Fuck," I whispered.

"What's happened?" Natalie asked, putting her hand on my shoulder.

"My dad's dead."

"Oh, Christ, Pablo. How?"

In my ear I could hear Perdito – not speaking but panting. A wordless rhythmic gasping like the approach of orgasm or the containment of pain.

I turned to Natalie. "Can you give me a tenner? I've got to get home."

"Of course."

I stood up to pull on my underwear and jeans.

"Mum must be in a right state," I said. "Jazz sounds awful. I expect she's getting in touch with Tom. Perhaps I should call him before I leave. He might be driving down so…"

I stopped jabbering in mid-sentence and slumped back onto the bed. I burst into tears.

"My dad, my dad," I wept as Natalie put her arms around me. "Nat – my dad's dead."

I was unable to swallow, convulsed by sobs, breathless. But as hard as I cried, I could still hear Perdito in my head, mainlining on the anguish pumping in my chest.

"Oh my God," he howled. "More! More!"

* * * *

People say that although it fades with time, the ache of bereavement is constantly present. Not true – at least, not for me. The sorrow fluctuated like a shortwave signal from hour to hour and from place to place. In the days following my father's death, I sometimes felt crushed by grief – immobilised and constricted, as if rocks were being piled on my chest. At other times I found myself thinking of Dad with wistful affection – and I was sad but not overwhelmed. There were even moments – usually when I was reading, or late at night, drunk – when I forgot about the whole thing entirely. These periods of remission were brief. Soon it all came crashing back in and I felt guilty about having escaped the pain for a while. Perdito made sure of that.

"*Do you remember when Dad used to put on those little puppet shows behind the sofa?*"

As kids, Tom and I had a small collection of glove puppets – Pinocchio, Mickey Mouse, a red-nosed policeman – and Dad would crouch behind the sofa and improvise sketches with them that were rug-rumplingly funny to two spellbound six-year-olds. Reminded of those afternoons, I felt my heart cave in. Loss percolated in my chest and caught in my throat. Sniffling, blinking, I pressed the heels of my hands into my eyeballs and whimpered.

Perdito had done this to me a few times recently. Whenever I found a crevice of myself in which to be calm and forgetful, he fired off a memory that illuminated my misery like a distress flare. All I wanted was a break from the eye-pricking sorrow, but he kept turning my face to the painful light.

"*I don't want to think about the puppet shows. Just leave it be.*"

"*They were so funny though. We fell about laughing.*"

We did. That is, I did and Tom did. Perdito hadn't been there. He hadn't been aware in those early years. The memory was one that he'd found in my head and was now holding over the fire as if it were a long-lost teddy-bear.

"Stop it! Just leave it alone."

He was getting off on it. He was sucking up my misery, gorging himself. I could feel him becoming bloated and drunk with it.

"And Jabberwocky. *You remember how he used to recite* Jabberwocky *at bedtime?"*

Instantly the covers were against my cheek, the wardrobe was striped streetlamp orange, and I could hear Tom shifting and fidgeting in the top bunk. Dad sat on a ladder-back chair by the door where both of us could see him in the twilight.

"Twas brillig, and the slithy toves…"

The reassuring rituals of childhood. By the time we were three or four, we were joining in, murmuring along with Dad as we teetered on the cusp of sleep. One, two! One, two! And through and through… *I was eight before I discovered that my father hadn't composed* Jabberwocky *himself. I remember it fondly now, but in the days after his death the memory was a wire brush on a blistered burn.*

"Shut the fuck up, Perdito!" I shouted aloud – and he bulged in my head, gleeful and drum-tight, squeezing me into the crannies of my brain, suffocating me. With the wine bottle clasped to my chest, I stumbled to the bathroom where my housemate kept her Valium. I palmed three or four and scooped them into my mouth, washing them down with a long glug of Merlot.

"Come to my arms, my beamish boy!" Perdito whooped. *"Remember? Remember?"*

Still swigging from the bottle, I staggered to my room and flopped across the bed, curling up with my face wrapped in my arms. Perdito babbled and sang, intoxicated by unhappiness, and I had to listen to him until the drugs kicked in and I melted gradually into white-blind unconsciousness like a hot chestnut dropped on fresh snow.

Chapter Eight
Posthumous Encouragement

<u>Essay for Alice: My Dad's Influence</u>

The Condesa had never admitted to me that Pablo sponged off her, but he'd never held down a job for longer than a fortnight, so if Mum wasn't supporting him, I couldn't see how he stayed afloat.

I think that my father could see this propensity for indolence in Pablo, which is why he set his will up in such an inventive way. Unfortunately the terms applied to all three of us – Jacinta and me, as well as my twin – which was profoundly unfair as I have always been hardworking and not in the least profligate. The same goes for Jacinta, but as her fiancé owns a chain of steak restaurants that stretches right around the Pacific Rim, the issue of access to our inheritance is purely academic to her.

A week after my father's funeral, we three children assembled at the house in Hook to meet the family solicitor. My mother, who is at her most Iberian in times of emotional stress, was dressed in layers of black. Suddenly I could see why such clothes are called widow's weeds – they hung from her arms and shoulders in loops and tails, as if she had just risen from a stagnant lake like an Arthurian witch. I went into the front room where my sister was watching television. She zapped it off as I sat on the sofa next to her.

"How's she been?" I asked.

Jacinta shrugged. "Not great. She keeps making huge meals that neither of us eat, and then spends hours cleaning up after herself." Indeed, the house was antiseptically spotless – another indication of the depth of the Condesa's grief. Half an hour before we'd had to leave for Dad's funeral, she'd still been on her knees in the kitchen, using a toothbrush to scrub imaginary grime from the slotted crossheads of the screws that held the hinges of the cabinet doors.

Jacinta reached for her handbag. "I'm going out for a cigarette. Do you want one?"

I still smoked back then. We sat on the low wall of the patio. The sky was a flat, luminescent grey that threatened late snow. The lawn was edged with exhausted purple crocuses, splayed flat and past their best. My sister nodded towards the small wooden shed.

"Did you know that that thing isn't nailed down? It's just sitting on those two-by-fours."

"No," I said. "Why would you mention it?"

She gave a mirthless smile. "I caught her trying to move it so that she could sweep out underneath."

"Christ."

We smoked in silence. From a house close by I could hear someone playing scales inexpertly on a trumpet. I ground out the cigarette and cupped the butt in my hand to take indoors and put in the bin.

"Want another one?" Jacinta asked.

"No, thanks. Have you been to work or did you take the week off?"

"I told them I wouldn't be in, but Mum insisted I went." She lit her cigarette from the stub of the last one. "It's funny, you know. Even at work I think of everything in terms of Dad. If I'm making pastry, I remember him taking me to the patisserie in St-Jules-le-Croix. Very early in the morning, just him and me. Or if I'm serving jambalaya, I can hear him singing that pop song when he was driving us all to the swimming pool."

"I wish I could remember things like that. I just don't seem to have that kind of recall."

"God, really? I remember everything." She stood up and walked to a corner of the patio in which were set mementos of trips we had taken as a family when we were kids. Crouching, she pointed at a clutch of pebbles embedded in the concrete. "Lipsi – I was ten. You threw a huge strop because you had to share a hired bike with Pablo." She touched her fingertips on a deep green cluster of malachite. "Goa. I bought it in a street market with my holiday money because I thought it was exotic. Dad laughed and said it probably came from England. This knobbly flint – do you remember that?" I shook my head. "Pablo found it in the garden of a cottage we rented in Kent when you two were about twelve."

I frowned "Are you sure?" I had absolutely no recollection of a cottage in Kent.

She came back to sit on the wall. "So haven't you been thinking about Dad at all?"

Of course I'd been thinking about him. The man was only forty-three, which is no age to die. Actuarially speaking, he had a good thirty years ahead of him.

"I've been thinking about him a lot." I rolled the cigarette stub between finger and thumb and looked at Jacinta. "I've been trying to come to terms with the realisation that I'll never speak to him again."

"Oh. As opposed to those long chats you so frequently used to have with him far into the night," my sister remarked, stubbing out her cigarette on the brickwork.

I would have argued the unfairness of this snide comment – I was away at University, for God's sake. Unlike her, I wasn't still living at home, rent-free – but the front doorbell chimed and we could hear my mother and Pablo exchanging hellos in the hall. After a few moments Pablo emerged onto the patio. He was wearing an ankle-length Army greatcoat and Cuban heels. And eye-liner, for God's sake.

"Did I leave my keys here?" he asked Jacinta, without so much as a how-do-you-do. "I'm sure I had them at the crematorium. I had to break a window to get into the flat. Complete pain in the arse."

Typical Pablo. Not a word about Dad. Just me, me, me.

Mum tapped on the kitchen window. The family solicitor had arrived. The three of us trooped back indoors to the living-room and sat in a row on the sofa. Mr Hilary Underhill – a pink, jolly little man with child's hands – was perched on an armchair with his briefcase on his lap. As he fished out a blue file, Mum came in with a pot of tea and three hundredweight of homemade cheese scones.

"You have sugar with your tea, Mr Underhill? Or maybe you like some coffee? Stupid of me – I make some coffee. You all right for tea? Is no problem to make coffee. Two minutes only. You are sure? And you take a scone. Take two."

When this overture of displacement hospitality was concluded, Mum looked around for somewhere to sit. The only empty seat was Dad's – his big armchair in front of the fire. Cup and saucer in hand, the Condesa was momentarily at a loss. I got up.

"You sit next to Jacinta, Mum. I'll get the piano stool."

"Go ahead, Mr Underhill," Jacinta said. "We're ready."

The solicitor's jam-doughnut face did not easily lend itself to a sombre expression. Delivering his required preamble of condolence, he looked as if his professional gravity might at any moment disintegrate into a fit of giggles. He mentioned his personal relationship with our father – "whom I met as a client, but who, over twenty years, became a friend" – and he said how proud Dad had been of his offspring. Apparently Mr Underhill felt he knew us as well as he knew his own children – though I hope his own children saw him more often than once a year at pre-Christmas drinks. Throughout this peroration, Mum sniffled quietly and Jacinta and I paid respectful attention. Pablo, lounging back with his left ankle resting on his right thigh, picked absent-mindedly at a flap of loose rubber on his Converse.

For the most part the will was standard stuff – the house and everything in it went to Mum, along with all the money and investment stocks. This was as I'd expected. I thought there would probably be a bequest of a few thousand to each of the three of us – perhaps enough to put a deposit on a flat. So my attention was wandering when Mr Underhill started to talk about the travel company of which Dad had been a director.

"Idyll Holidays took out insurance against the death of any of the principals, so that the remaining directors could purchase the deceased partner's shares," the solicitor told us. "The monies accruing from the sale of shares will be split between Mrs Lyne – fifty percent – and the three children, each being entitled to a third of the remaining fifty percent."

Jacinta glanced at me. She and I were obviously thinking the same thing – to wit, a bit more than expected, then. But I wasn't going to be so crass as to ask, and neither was she.

"Mrs Lyne is aware of the numbers involved, of course," Mr Underhill said, with a nod towards Mum who gave a Latin pout that was simultaneously confirmatory and dismissive. "And at the present time," Mr Underhill continued, addressing the three of us, "the figures are of little interest to you, I'm sure. When all of you feel ready to talk about this in more detail, please contact me and we'll sort out the mathematics."

Pablo looked up from fiddling with his shoe. "That's an argument waiting to happen," he said. "No one'll want to be the first to suggest that a decent period's passed and it's time to get our hands on the loot."

"For God's sake," I muttered.

Pablo turned on me. "What? That's true, isn't it? I mean – why set ourselves up for a mourning contest?"

"The choice of words could be better, but the point's well-made." Jacinta said, nodding. "I think we should be told now, Tom."

"Yes – now when we are all together," Mum said. She got to her feet. "I make more tea. You tell them, Mr Underhill, please."

I don't think it reflects badly on me – in fact, I'd like to think quite the opposite – if I admit that I was very interested to know how much money we were talking about here. Dad had been conscientiously thorough; he would expect no less of me.

"Very well," Mr Underhill said, riffling his notes as Mum picked up the tray and went out to the kitchen. "Now, Idyll is not a publicly-quoted company, so an objective formula must be applied to determine a valuation."

I bit my lip. There's no point trying to hurry a solicitor. Mr Underhill explicated, qualified and caveated for another ten minutes. I could hear Mum clinking about in the kitchen, running water in the sink, opening and closing the oven. I could smell fresh *polvones* – a biscuit that she usually made only at Christmas. Smelling that warm, sugary aroma, I felt a rush of Proustian excitement – the childish anticipation of treats and gifts. It was as if Dad were holding a big wrapped parcel up in the air, and little Tomàs, still in his pyjamas, was jumping up and down with his arms stretched towards it, halfway between laughter and tears – "Give it to me! Pleeease, Dad, pleeeaase!" It was the oddest sensation – there I was at the reading of my father's will, and suddenly I felt nostalgically happy. I smiled – and Pablo caught my eye. He gave a quizzical frown

"What?" he mouthed.

I shook my head. "It's nothing."

I snapped my full attention back to the solicitor, whose discourse was circling like an airliner stacked over Heathrow. If the size of the inheritance was proportional to the tortuousness of Mr Underhill's run-in, I reckoned we must be up to thirty or forty grand each by now – or, to put it rather more pointedly, a house.

"So, having explained all that," Mr Underhill said, taking a sheet of paper from his blue folder, "the question is: what does it all mean in pounds, shillings and pence?"
He looked around at the three of us, evidently wanting a cue. I was beginning to suspect that Mr Underhill was a bit of a ham.

"And what's the answer?" Jacinta said at last.

"What it means, in round figures," he said, "is that the surviving directors expect to pay for your father's shares a sum in the region of…" He glanced down at his sheet of paper. "…um…in the region of…sixteen million pounds." He looked up. "Give or take a few pence."

There was a brief silence and then Jacinta said, *sotte voce*, "Fucking hell."

"Sixteen million," I said, awestruck. "So that's…"

"Eight for Mum and two million apiece for us," said Pablo hauling himself from the sofa. "I'll go and help with the tea."

Mr Underhill smiled. He looked much more comfortable smiling. "Admirably swift mental calculation," he said as Pablo closed the door behind him, "but a little awry unless there's a sibling I don't know about. Two point six million would be closer to the mark."

At that moment, six hundred grand either way didn't seem to make much difference.

"I had no idea Dad was worth that much," Jacinta said. She was quite breathless.

I thought of my second-year exams which were two months away. The hell with them – there was no need to graduate now. There was no need to do anything, in fact. I *could* do anything I wanted, but I wasn't *obliged* to do anything at all.

"Do we get it all at once?" I asked. "Or as an income?"

"That's a very good question," Mr Underhill said. "And it has a very interesting answer. Let's wait until Pablo and your mother come back."

I didn't like the sound of that. I immediately extinguished the mental bonfire on which my textbooks were beginning to smoulder.

*   *   *   *

As a professional in the field, I have to say that Dad really did his homework when he was devising the mechanisms of the Trust that administers his legacy. He made a very good job of what is the most difficult part of writing a will – that is, imagining all possible scenarios and catering for every one of them in a way that avoids anomalies. It's an exercise in creative imagination – in speculative fiction, actually – and it's the part of my job that I enjoy most. Well, inasmuch as I enjoy the job at all. If it weren't for Dad's posthumous encouragement of the work ethic, I wouldn't have had to make a career of it in the first place.

"He worked hard all his life," the Condesa said, her bottom lip a little unsteady. "When we come to England after you boys are born, we have no money. We live four months with Nan and Grandad. Jacinta sleeps in with us and you two go in beds I make in drawers from the sideboard. You don't remember this but we always remember it, your Dad and me. Always we remember it."

There was more in this vein, of which the upshot was that Dad felt that everything he'd achieved – getting a grounding in the travel business, setting up Idyll, growing the company – had been driven by the need to provide for his family. Apparently he considered himself at heart a lazy man, but the necessity to earn money had inspired him to make something of himself and to overcome his natural inclination to bum around on Pacific beaches having a ball. That's admirable, I suppose, but I was hurt by the implication that if it weren't for us kids he'd have had a more enjoyable life.

"If by some unfortunate circumstance I should die before what I'd like to think is my time," Dad said in a letter to the three of us that Mr Underhill handed out, "you would all become very wealthy in an instant. That would be a tragedy. It would irrevocably damage your potential to create fulfilling lives for yourselves. Not because money makes one miserable, but because the need for money pushes one to do all sorts of things that bring happiness.

"And yet, it would be absurd to deny my children what I've worked so hard to provide for them. I can see how you might resent me if I left it all to the National Trust, and I don't want to be resented, even if I'm not there to know about it."

So Dad's solution was what Mr Underhill called a salary-match scheme. Every year on the tenth of June – which was Dad's birthday – I have to present proof of my previous twelve months' earnings to the trustees. A month later they send me a cheque for precisely the same amount.

"In this way," Dad's letter said, "I'll be helping you to exactly the extent that you help yourselves. Your inheritance will make life a lot easier, but it won't stunt your self-reliance. One day, I hope, you'll thank me for it."

There was a lot of other stuff too – quite touching stuff actually that made me rather misty when I first read it – but the immediate practical upshot was that I couldn't avoid my exams.

"I'm really not sure what I think about this," Jacinta said, though tears were running down her face and dripping onto her copy of the letter.

"I think it's brilliant," Pablo said. His cheeks were as streaked as Jacinta's, but he was smiling too. "Instead of having barely two pennies to rub together, I'll have barely four pennies to rub together."

Sitting there in my mother's living-room, gazing at the letter from my dead father, I was already thinking about the implications of the arrangement. I could work only six months of every twelve. Or I could earn flat out for five years and then take five years off. Or I could just live hugely beyond my apparent salaried means – which is, in fact, what I've done for the last two decades.

But there was another little twist.

"Mr Underhill," my mother said "Please now tell about the other thing James want to do."

"Ah, yes." Mr Underhill cleared his throat. "This arrangement is intended primarily to stimulate, umm, industriousness now, when you're young people just starting out. But your father hoped that you'd get to a point where there was no longer any need for this drip-feed arrangement."

"Ah," I said. "That's good. So at what age do we get the whole lot?"

"Not age – amount," Mr Underhill said. "Your father felt that if you ever earned a hundred thousand pounds gross in any one year, that would indicate you were no longer reliant on your inheritance. And at that point, you can have all of it." He chuckled like a cartoon bear. "It's a bit of a paradox, when you think about it."

Pablo laughed out loud. "*How* bloody much?" he said – which was one of the rare occasions on which my twin expressed my thoughts exactly. This was the early eighties, remember. The average wage was seven-k per year. My university grant was six hundred quid. I could no more imagine earning a hundred thousand pounds than I could foresee the Internet or mobile phones. None of us could.

"Let me write that down," Jacinta smirked, reaching for her bag. "Just in case I ever get to ninety-nine grand and then forget to earn the other one."

Even I laughed then, and Pablo positively howled.

"You all stop," Mum said, frowning. "Your father knew what he's doing. It's not funny."

But all three of us were chortling merrily now. I think it was relief of tension as much as anything. Certainly it was the first time I'd laughed since Jacinta had called me with news of Dad's death.

"It's not funny! Daddy think very much about all this!" Mum insisted, flapping an annoyed hand at Jacinta, who was closest to her. "Stop laughing! Stop!" Suddenly her face crumpled and she put her hand to her mouth. "He love you," she managed through sudden sobs. "He just want you to be happy."

At that, of course, I felt utterly ashamed of myself and stopped laughing immediately. Though I have to point out, even at twenty years' remove, that Pablo started it.

Chapter Nine
Days Burning in our Wake

That night Pablo gave me some pages and – to my ill-concealed astonishment – he cooked a meal for us while I read them.

"What do you think?" he asked. He placed a Spanish omelette in front of me at the table and poured two glasses of wine.

"I'm amazed," I said, "that you're capable of throwing together something so evidently palatable and so professionally presented."

"Ha-ha," he said flatly, taking his seat. "Obviously I was talking about the writing."

"So was I."

Pablo's latest section needed work. He hadn't mastered his inclination to wander off at tangents, for instance, and he still indulged his idiosyncratic taste for ten-page paragraphs. But he was at last sticking to a roughly chronological structure, and I congratulated him on his self-discipline.

"I didn't realize I was doing that, to be honest. It's just how my thoughts went."

"Of course they did. We perceive life as a progression of related events because that's what it is."

He shook his head, smiling. "Look – a big bear," he said. "And a little bear right next to it. And a scorpion! And a pair of scales! The stars are laid out in pictures!"

I reached for a poppyseed roll. "Just keep doing what you're doing, that's all. And while we're on the subject, you also need to consider such fundamentals as character development, plot strands, dramatic tension, resolution. You have the beginnings of a good story here – a good and original premise – but it'll have to progress in a compelling way."

I glanced up from buttering my bread and Pablo was gazing back at me with a weary, almost disappointed expression. He put down his cutlery and picked up his cigarettes. He nodded at the manuscript lying on the table beside my plate.

"It isn't fiction, Stephen," he said, fishing a cigarette from the pack. "If you think I'm inventing it all, we're going to have a problem."

The tiger was there again in Pablo's eyes as he looked at me over the flame of his lighter. His implicit question was difficult to sidestep – *do you believe me?* Although my first instinct was to protest that, no, of course I knew that all he had written was true, I realised that I had in fact read it as fiction. An equivocal response – 'Well, I certainly believe that you're telling the truth as you see it' – would diminish me in Pablo's estimation. But I couldn't honestly maintain I was convinced that he had been haunted by the ghost of his stillborn brother.

"This is what I'm talking about when I mention plot and character," I said. "Your story hasn't demanded my belief yet. It's still teasing me with circumstance. As a reader, I'm not obliged to take a position until the narrative forces me to."

Pablo blew smoke out over his jutted lower lip. For a moment I was afraid he'd say I was fudging – which I was – but he sniffed and said, "In ordinary English, you're waiting to see what happens next."

"Precisely," I said, not a little relieved. "That's what makes people read any story, true or fictitious."

"Okay." Ash dropped from his cigarette onto the tablecloth. "So what happened next with Leo?"

"Ah. My turn, hm?"

"That was the deal."

And so, over a couple of bottles of wine, I told the story that had been pressed to the forefront of my memory that afternoon. Patti, Aberfan, the service at St Dominic's. Pablo smoked and drank and listened, silent throughout and patient when I faltered, which was too often.

"So what became of Patti?" he asked, as we moved outside to the warm dark of the terrace.

I settled into one of the wrought-iron chairs and looked out across the perfect lawn. Pablo topped up my glass.

I took a deep breath. "That Sunday, Leo simply disappeared. None of us knew where he'd gone. Almost every day I'd call my parents or George would contact Patti at the club, all of us hoping that one of the others had found him. Eventually – a month or so after Leo had walked out of St Dominic's – Patti telephoned to say that he was alive but that he didn't want to see anyone. I learned later that he'd taken rooms in Eastbourne, and Patti visited him there." I picked up my glass. "Why Eastbourne I really can't imagine. Though when people flee, they often seem to go to the sea."

"There's no family connection with the place?" Pablo asked. "No childhood holidays or day-trips to the beach?"

"Not that I know of," I said, sipping wine.

"Which is why he went there, then."

That comment sounded to me like the resonance of a chord struck in Pablo's own memory. Not long before I would have taken it as an opportunity to steer conversation away from the subject of my brother. But not now.

"The months passed and Patti supplied regular bulletins: Leo was depressed; Leo was drinking too much; Leo wasn't speaking at all. And then, in the April of '67, Patti asked George and me to meet her for lunch in the West End.

"Whenever I'd seen her in the preceding months she'd been drawn and anxious, brooding over Leo's state of mind. But when she arrived at the restaurant in Shepherd Market she seemed happier. She'd put back some of the weight she'd lost and there was a calm resoluteness about her. She told us, very straightforwardly, that she was going home to Worcester and that she had no plans to return. 'I can't help Leo. If I stayed, eventually the situation would damage us.' I remember very distinctly her choice of words. 'It would damage us.' George and I pleaded with her to keep in touch, but she wouldn't promise that. And so we parted on Curzon Street amidst embraces and tears, and I never saw her again."

Pablo said nothing for a few moments. I glanced at him, wondering whether he'd nodded off in the dark. But he got to his feet, saying, "I'll make some coffee. Glass of port to go with it?"

"Yes, thank you."

I looked out at the moon floating in the lake. Perhaps if things had gone differently this would be Patti's home now. Had she and Leo married, I would have found a way to extract myself when the house came down to my brother and me. There might have been children who'd have grown up with these grounds as their dominion, making campfires in the folly, racing along the allées, swinging from the branches of trees by the water's edge. Sometimes I feel that I have no right to this place at all.

As he returned with a tray and laid it on the table, Pablo said, "Leo wasn't raging at God because of Aberfan, was he?"

"Well, he was. It was a terrible, faith-shaking thing. But I know what you mean."

Pablo poured a small glass of port for me and a large tumblerful for himself. "And you – the one who thinks that benign order is evident in the design of a sunflower and the majesty of the Alps – how did you explain what happened?"

"I clung to Joe Rawlings' proposition that the battle was won that day by malevolent forces in the universe."

"And on the night of Leo's accident? Was that down to the forces of evil too?"

I said nothing. Pablo was nudging me towards a conclusion that I knew I couldn't support.

He kept pushing though. "If it happened because the Devil wrestled God's wrist to the table, then Leo needn't have felt any responsibility for that woman's death, need he? Actually – no one has to take responsibility for anything at all. As Leo said, we're just side-bets."

I shook my head. "No – we're instruments." I stopped and thought again. "That's too passive. We're recruits. We choose our side."

"And Leo chose the evil side?"

"No, that's not what I'm saying. He made a small, bad decision that led to large, terrible consequences. He decided to drive when he shouldn't have."

"Ah, okay. So God turns up for the big gigs, but the minor stuff – just one or two deaths – that's down to the frailty of human beings." Pablo grinned in the dark – not unkindly, but certainly enjoying my discomfiture. "It sounds a very complicated system to me," he said. "Isn't it more likely that the universe is just thrown together any which way – like your books?"

Then I smiled too. "Perhaps one sees chaos only when one doesn't share the concerns of the organising mind," I said. "I hate to disappoint you, but my books are very carefully arranged. You just can't see it because the rules by which they're ordered aren't of interest to you."

"Really?" Pablo said, puzzled. "Excuse me a moment."

Getting to his feet, he drained his glass of port, refilled it and headed into the house. When I went to bed ten minutes later, he was still prowling around the shelves, head tipped sideways, muttering.

It was a rare event to have surprised Pablo, and I was pleased. I toasted myself drunkenly in mouthwash. Then I went to bed and I dreamt of a dog behind a wire fence, running to and fro, barking pointlessly at passers-by.

*   *   *   *

I can think of nothing so arbitrary as a given person's assessment of what constitutes acceptable tidiness. The very word 'acceptable' makes my hackles rise.

The range of tidiness is a line drawn from New York to San Francisco. One end, where the line begins at Ellis Island, represents rigid order; ultra-tidiness, in which leaves fall from trees into neat racks and the smoke particles from my cigarette follow each other to the ceiling in a regimented line like the links of an anchor-chain; every human head is shaved for fear that a hair or two might rebel against the orientation imposed by the comb; all books are the same height and two hundred pages long so that they fit neatly into standardised bookshelves; there are daily executions of those who fail to wash up their cereal bowls.

The line of tidiness terminates in San Francisco Bay, on the jetty at Alcatraz. This is not the opposite of tidiness, but its philosophical complement. Atidiness. Active disarray. Buildings shed bricks all over the street like a dog in spring; parking bays generate at random across the pavements; fallen leaves never decompose but blow around in vast clouds darkening the sun; used cutlery fuses to the edges of kitchen surfaces, dripping eternal Bolognese sauce onto the handles of the cupboards beneath.

And on this scale, between these two conceptual extremes, the range of the human practice of tidiness is represented by a section one foot long on the sidewalk outside a general store in Hays, Kansas. My mother's a notch – a tidy notch, very precisely marked – about seven-eighths of an inch from the eastern end of the twelve inches. And I'm a biro-mark an inch-and-a-half from the western end. The gap between us is so tiny that statistically it doesn't register. To worry about it would be a waste of energy; and to attempt to drag another human being along the line towards your own favoured spot would be neurotic.

So, although I'm pissed off that I can't see the order in Stephen's books, I'm more irritated that there's order at all. It alters my view of Stephen, somehow. His life is a symphony of careful organization – the neat files in the study, the knives in their rack by the cooker, the immaculate and formal garden. The chaos of his bookshelves was an intriguing indicator of good sense. I never quite trust people who are organised. I knew a woman once whose closet was arranged so that the clothes were aligned to the visible spectrum. Looking along the rail, you'd see the white frocks, then the creams, followed by the reds and the orange ones and the yellows gaining battle in vain until you got to the black numbers at the far end. She was the sort of person who, if asked to take a Dalmatian for a walk, would dress in black and white. It all smacked of an unsettling obsessiveness, not to mention a complete misunderstanding of how colours work.

That kind of preoccupation with control usually springs from either fear or guilt. Certainly it does in my mother, and in Natalie too. I think it might in Stephen, and I understand why.

*   *   *   *

"How does one go about setting up a scholarship fund to help an undergraduate?" I asked George.

He laughed. "Good God – are we so old that we feel it's time to leave memorials to ourselves?"

"Not in my name. In Leo's."

"Ah, I see." He shrugged. "I imagine one simply tosses the Bursar a bundle of fivers and asks him to slip it into the trouser pocket of the deserving poor."

We had just emerged from a Sub Judice case meeting, during which I had not been concentrating at all. I had been doodling on my notepad like a distracted schoolboy. *The Leo Richmond Law Scholarship*, I'd written. *Criteria for award? Balliol necessarily?*

"What do you think of the idea?" I asked.

We were standing on the corner of High Holborn and Chancery Lane, and George was looking around for a taxi.

"I don't see that it could hurt," he said distractedly.

"I take such encouragement from your boundless enthusiasm."

George turned. "Oh, come on, Stephen. What do you want me to say? If this scheme makes you feel better, that's fine. I just can't see what good it'll do, that's all."

"It'll keep his name alive," I said.

He rolled his eyes. "And what does that mean? Do you envisage some future High Court judge saying he owes his entire career to the sainted Leo Richmond?" He peered up the street towards Holborn Circus. "My God – it would be cheaper and more effective to have a rose named after him."

"No, that's not the point," I said, flushed. "A grant to study law would permit someone – several people – to do the work that Leo might have done."

"But that he didn't actually *do*, Stephen! You seem to want a succession of hapless undergrads to take on the responsibility of making up for Leo's failure. Christ, man." He raised his hand and stepped off the kerb. "Taxi!"

"I can't imagine why you're being so bloody about it," I muttered.

The taxi pulled up and George bent to speak through the window.

"Fulham Palace Road, please," he said, opening the passenger door. He turned to me again. "Stephen, you've just come out of a four-hour meeting concerning a possible miscarriage of justice, and I know you were working on the case all day yesterday. On Monday you hosted a fund-raising dinner that took three months to organise. You must give at least thirty hours a week to Sub Judice." He climbed into the cab and pulled the window down. "You don't need to pay anyone to live your brother's life. You've always done a fine job of it yourself."

The cab pulled away and it seemed to drag the world with it. I was left alone on the pavement, stunned and suddenly distant from everything, as if I had collapsed into myself. People walked towards me, around me, brushed against me but I didn't register them. I remembered the dog behind the wire fence, barking.

"Are you okay, sir?"

It was a young man with an American accent, his girlfriend standing a little further back, both wearing expressions of honest concern.

"Yes. I'm fine. Miles away. Thank you."

I set off along High Holborn, walking, as the poet has it, in a shower of all my days. I took a side street at random and I passed the spot in Red Lion Square where I once found Leo unconscious against a wall in the snow. Turning into Great Russell Street I recalled an occasion when George and I carried my brother home as he extemporized a drunken aria in the style of Verdi. One night he was beaten up and robbed in Montague Place, though he remembered nothing about it. A month later he was arrested during a police raid on a brothel in Sidmouth Street, the cost of which to my father was several redeemed favours and unplumbable embarrassment. Memories seeped through the cracks of the Bloomsbury pavement like a water-table rising, and I saw Leo sprawled in every doorway, heard his laughter issuing from every open window. I waded on, thigh-deep in recollection, until I reached Tiller Street, and I stopped outside the mansion block in which my parents had bought an apartment for me. I was so immersed in the flashflood of memory that I almost felt I might catch sight of Leo at the first-floor window, staring broodingly out to the street.

Despite the old man's edict, I always took my brother in. When he returned from Eastbourne, only a few days after Patti left, he was unemployed and short of money. Within a fortnight he found a low-paid job as a legal advisor for an organization that represented young people accused of drug offences. For a while he was diligent and relatively sober, though so withdrawn that we barely spoke. He would work at the dining table all evening as I read manuscripts in the armchair. I'd cook and he would sometimes eat. We might catch last orders at the pub on the corner and make sporadic conversation about his latest case or my current line-edit. It was a dull, featureless existence and I was grateful for it. It seemed to indicate an improvement in Leo's condition, though not, as I told my father, in his mood.

"It's a step in the right direction – let's be content with that," the old man declared. Neither he nor I were yet familiar with the exhausting cycle of disappointment, despair and brittle hope that is the lot of those who love an alcoholic.

I often wondered whether it was significant that Leo's next descent into destructive self-loathing began within three or four weeks of the first anniversary of Aberfan. By the November of '67 he was back into his familiar routine, though his new haunts were less expensive and rather shadier than he'd been used to when my father was paying him an allowance. I shan't record the details of Leo's activities – there's a dogged repetitiveness to the process of slow suicide that's edifying neither to relate nor to read. But it was during these periods of determined madness that Leo unwittingly mapped out Bloomsbury for me in pools of blood and vomit. He charted Soho too. And Kensington and Whitechapel and the Square Mile.

And it was on those evenings when he was absent that I developed the habit of trying to complete Leo's paperwork. I'd do what I could – and what I did became more competent with practice – so that, at the very least, I could pack him blearily off to work in the morning with something to show at the office. These days, I suppose, experts would say that I was enabling Leo's dependency. At the time, I was just trying to help.

So it continued for three years. The months of sullen respite. The inevitable return to the bottle. It seems naive now, but I really didn't expect Leo to die. I knew that he was taking the curves too quickly and that he was contemptuous of invisible dips in the road, but it never crossed my mind that he might come off the motorcycle. He was Leo. He was indestructible.

Friday, October 2nd, 1970. Another date I can summon exactly. The publishing house for which I worked threw a party at the Curzon to celebrate the publication of a biography of Buster Keaton. It was the first book I'd personally commissioned and edited, and I was immensely proud of it.

"Formal tonight, is it? Or just the workaday suit?"

Leo was making tea and toast for breakfast, unshaven but not particularly hungover. He'd been laying off the drink for a week or two – which is to say he'd been getting through no more than a couple of bottles of wine each night, usually at home in the apartment.

"Not even that formal," I told him, knotting my tie. "Swirly shirts and yellow cravats, I expect. I'll nip back to change this afternoon." I glanced at the clock. "Shouldn't you be thinking about getting dressed?"

"I'm not going in today. I have plenty to do here." He opened the fridge for milk, looking at me sidelong as he straightened up with the bottle in his hand. "Don't worry. They're not expecting me."

I hesitated to speak. My impulse was to warn Leo against spending all day in the pub – but when he was in a relatively abstemious phase I didn't want to give the impression that I mistrusted him. At the slightest hint of a nag he'd start drinking merely to demonstrate that he was not to be browbeaten.

He handed me a cup of tea and sat down at the table. "Are you taking anyone?" he asked.

"George is coming – I wangled him a ticket. But he's not going *with* me, exactly."

"I should hope not. People would talk." He looked up at the plate rack. "Did I leave a packet of cigarettes on the top shelf there?"

I tossed them to him and he leaned back to light one from the gas-ring.

"Thanks. You know George is queer, don't you?"

I paused in the act of combing my hair. "Do be sensible. What about Genevieve?"

"Oh, he makes the effort, certainly. But his heart's not in it. Nor any other part of him."

"I shall tell him of your theory," I chuckled "He'll laugh his socks off."

"Oh, I wouldn't mention it to him. I only brought it up in passing. But no need to embarrass me by relaying it to George, eh?"

"I was joking, Leo."

Leo nodded and picked up his tea. "They all say that."

"So what do you have planned for tonight?" I asked, taking my jacket from the back of a kitchen chair.

"I'm going to a birthday party."

"Oh – anywhere nice?"

"Local. Quiet affair. Very low-key."

"Well," I said in a murmur, as if I were saying nothing at all. "You know. Moderation."

"In all things. See you later. I'll iron a swirly shirt for you."

It was my habit to walk to Mayfair if the weather was fine, which it was. October 2nd 1970 was a beautiful autumn day in London.

*   *   *   *

I returned to the apartment at five, intending to change my clothes. As I climbed the stairs to our front door, I could hear Leo singing 'Happy Birthday' at the top of his voice.

"Busy day?" I asked, walking into the front room. In the centre of the coffee table sat a birthday cake that looked as though it had come from our local patisserie. It bore three candles, and three shot-glasses were arranged around it, each filled with dark rum. A bottle of milk stood to the side. Leo was holding a fourth shot-glass and filling it as I walked in.

"Whose turn?" he said, looking from the empty sofa to the equally empty armchair. "Graham?" He looked at me. "Ah, join the party, Stephen. I'm afraid the guests are imaginary. They don't say much, but then again they drink very little."

"I have to get changed," I said, irritatedly. "I thought you were working today."

"What? When there's a party? Very popular day for birthdays, the second of October." He knocked back the rum in a single swallow. "Graham. Groucho. Mohandas. Jonathan." He poured another. "All my phantom guests have a birthday today."

I bit my lip and turned to go to my room.

"Sorry! Too informal?" Leo called. "That's Messrs Greene, Marx…"

I slammed the bedroom door, furious at my brother. I didn't go out much, didn't often attend functions. Tonight's do was important to me and I was looking forward to it. If Leo expected me to cancel in order to nursemaid him in his irresponsible drunkenness, he had another think coming.

Except, of course, that Leo expected nothing of the kind. He'd never asked me to take care of him. Not once had he relied on me to get him out of any scrape. He borrowed the occasional few pounds and he was always grateful to discover that thanks to my diligent shepherding he'd woken up in his own bed – but he never took for granted that I'd come to his rescue. I had assumed that responsibility unasked.

Not tonight. I was going out and he'd have to fend for himself.

I changed my clothes and went back into the living-room.

"I'm off. Look, stay at home this evening, all right? I don't want to get any phone calls in the small hours from O'Malley's or Paddington police station."

"Why would I go out?" He reached forward and pulled all the glasses of rum into a group at the edge of the coffee table. "I have all the company I need right here."

"Evidently," I said. "Another evening living it up with Captain Morgan."

Leo grinned. "Ahoy," he said, and gulped a shot.

As I walked down the stairs to the street, I could hear him singing 'Happy Birthday' again. Whenever I hear that nursery rhyme tune these days, I see the polished banister in the stairwell of our mansion block and the pile of letters on the table in the entrance hall. I hate it.

*　　　*　　　*　　　*

I often think about the unique flash of light reflected from the pane of a greenhouse that I saw out of a train window when I was nine – the flash that no one in the universe would ever see but me.

Any greenhouse in the sunshine summons that memory: the heat of the carriage, the red cable, Stig of the Dump, *the smell of warm travel-dust. Actually, any glass that throws the sunshine around alludes, less evocatively but unignorably, to trains and delightful solitude. A skyscraper in the city's shimmer might do it, or a wine glass on a garden table in August. And if that August wine glass were diamond-cut lead crystal, it would have its own specific mnemonic power. It would trigger a rush of Christmas Eves.*

There was a cabinet in the dining room at home – walnut, I think. The grain of the wood flowed in concentric circles like sepia ink dripped onto a saucer of milk. Inside was the Condesa's neurotically comprehensive collection of wine glasses. She felt that a Burgundy should be served in a different glass to a Bordeaux, and that neither of those would suit any other red wine, for which an all-purpose vinho tinto *glass was required. There were similar requirements for differing types of white, rosé, champagne, sherry and dessert wines.*

The cut-crystal glasses were invariably used for dinner on Christmas Eve. I was fascinated by the candlelight refracted through them as we all sat at the table and my mother ferried in dish after dish of hybrid Anglo-Catalan food that would give us indigestion.

Experience forms associations, and associations inform experience. They accrete on each other like coral – and for each of us the accretion is unique and arbitrary. No one in the world but me tastes turkey paella and pa amb tomaquet when he sees candlelight though diamond-cut lead crystal – not even Tomàs.

"What does that remind you of?" I asked him once. We were at a restaurant in Paris, I think.

He picked up the glass and looked at it. "Isadora Duncan," he said.

Isadora Duncan. I don't know why, and it's possible that he didn't either. But my twin's experience of a wine glass is utterly different to mine – and this is just one object among millions, all of which might be encountered in an infinity of combinations.

Uncontrolled explosions are going off around us constantly as we move through the world. We each live in a firework display of personal meaning, deafened by thumping retorts of memory and blinded by the starburst rockets of our own incendiary past. We're enveloped completely by the smoke of days burning in our wake and we have no concept of the spectrum-flickered landscape that any other human being inhabits.

It's amazing that we manage to communicate with each other at all.

*   *   *   *

George and I came back to Tiller Street at about one o'clock, having had a wonderful evening. Leo was lying with his legs on the sofa and his head on the floor. The birthday cake was smeared around his mouth. His cigarette had burned out between his fingers and scorched a black line on the carpet. His eyes were closed. He'd died of asphyxiation, having inhaled vomit while unconscious.

George telephoned the emergency services while I lifted my brother's body back onto the sofa and put a pillow under his head. I tidied up. I think I even washed and dried the glasses and plates. I did the things that I always did when Leo passed out. It wasn't until they covered his face to take him to the ambulance that I really understood that he was dead.

And then I stood in the dark on the pavement as the ambulance drove away, and George stood next to me.

"No siren," he said.

"No."

"You had better phone your parents."

I nodded.

"Where are the candles?" I wondered.

"The what?"

"There were candles."

It turned out that Leo had eaten them. The post-mortem found them in his oesophagus, and there were burns in his mouth. He'd eaten them while they were alight.

The following Monday Leo's boss called to ask my brother whether the case notes were ready. I was packing to go down to Twyborough Cross for the funeral the following day, but I found the required notes and completed Leo's tasks. I dropped the paperwork into his office on the way to the train station.

And, as George says, I have been doing Leo's work ever since. Thirty-five years after my brother's death, standing on the pavement outside the apartment, I was holding a briefcase stuffed with legal documents intended to rectify an unresolved injustice. I have been tireless in my efforts to prove that the verdict of guilty was a terrible, ill-considered error and that the victim of that miscarriage should be set free.

Gazing up at the first-floor window on Tiller Street, I didn't need to see a white, haggard face there to understand that I am no less haunted than Pablo.

   *   *   *   *

The day after Dad died we were all at home consoling Mum, and Tom took me into the garden for a cigarette. We stood by the shed smoking for a few minutes, and I was wondering why he'd brought me out there. It wasn't just so we could commune in silence, I was sure.

Eventually, still staring across the lawn, he got up the nerve to speak.

"I'm not looking forward to the funeral, I can tell you," he said.

"Be bloody odd if you were, wouldn't it?"

"Look – do you think it's absolutely necessary to attend? I mean, what real difference does it make?"

"You can't not go," I told him. I was honestly shocked at the thought. "What about Mum?"

He turned to look at me. "Mum's out of her mind. Nothing could make her feel worse than she does. She probably wouldn't even notice."

"It's you that's out of your mind. Christ – it's Dad's funeral."

"No," he said. "If we both said we weren't going, it'd be a sort of solid gesture. I mean, she expects you to be unconventional and I'd be backing you up, so everyone would just accept it."

"Are you listening to me? It's our father's bloody funeral, Tom."

He shuffled. "Well, you didn't go to Mum's birthday."

"That's hardly the same thing," I said, flicking my cigarette butt into the flowerbeds. "Forget it. I'm going. You're going. Be a fucking grown-up."

He did go. And then he gave me a hard time about how I was dressed. I didn't have a suit – in fact, I had very few clothes at all. I just wore my ordinary stuff.

"What the bloody hell have you come as?" Tom hissed when we met outside the crematorium. He was done up in a sober suit, black tie – the complete mourning costume.

"I've come as me. As opposed to a minor character from *Bleak House*," I told him. "Where did you get that outfit?"

"I had the decency to buy the appropriate clothes. This isn't a night out at the Roxy, you know."

My brother, let's not forget, was only there because he couldn't find a way to cry off, but the 'appropriate' clothes apparently gave him the right to berate me. The snide implication was that my clothes suggested I was less grief-stricken than him. But all the black-tie stuff is just emblematic – it **represents** *the pain of bereavement, but it's not* **evidence** *of it*

I was still furious with him when we all gathered at the house for the reading of the will, and his demeanour on that occasion did nothing to improve my mood. He was itchy with impatience, slavering to find out how much money he was in for. As soon as the solicitor arrived Tom started bustling about, ushering Jazz and me to the living room, hurrying the Condesa up as she made tea and put cakes on a plate. His eagerness was revolting.

The solicitor – a florid little chap like a plum in a suit – rambled on at length, riffling papers and talking legal gibberish. The proceedings seemed completely irrelevant to the emotional circumstances and I found it hard to concentrate. Tom didn't. At one point, when the plum's discourse was meandering towards Dad's bequests, I glanced at my brother and he was smiling – a huge great grin, like a kid listening to the headmaster's speech before the presentation of the Scholar's Cup. I caught his eye and he immediately adopted a grave expression, but he was embarrassed, I could tell. So he should be.

It turns out that Dad was worth a fortune, eight million pounds of which was to be divided between us kids. I immediately calculated it as two million apiece – which, of course, included Perdito. Not a very realistic assumption, I admit, but the one that I instinctively made. Perdito, who'd been silent since the night of the vodka and Valium, picked up both on my maths and on the obvious impossibility of applying it.

"No! You're right! I should get a share too!"

I ignored him. I stood up and went to the kitchen where Mum was making more tea.

"How're you doing?" I asked, leaning on the counter.

She didn't look at me. There were biscuits to arrange on a plate, cups to be rinsed, milk jugs to be replenished.

"Someone left open the box," she said. "The Bourbons are soft now."

"It doesn't matter," I said. *I walked up behind her and put my arms around her.* "Don't worry about the biscuits."

Her breath caught. She turned and pressed her face against my chest, shoulders trembling. I said nothing – I just let her cry.

"Always it was your father," she sobbed. "You babies – you were a lovely prize. Something extra. But your father was always all I want."

Looking through the kitchen window I could see the shed that Dad had built. The Condesa had been nagging for months about the bikes rusting in the side-return and the wheelbarrow being unsightly parked at the edge of the patio, so one day when she was out, Dad put the shed up as a surprise for her. When she got home he took her out to the garden, proud of his efforts. For a man who never really mastered scissors the successful erection of a shed was a remarkable and unprecedented achievement.

"It's close outside the kitchen window, that ugly thing!" my mother said. "I don't want to look at that all day!"

Dad bit his lip. "Well, it's there now. I'm not going to move it."

"Why not at the end of the garden where trees hide it?"

"Look, you said you wanted a shed. You've got a bloody shed."

"And the colour! So orange!"

"It's new wood! That's the colour new wood is! It'll fade."

This went on for about an hour. Actually, it went on for years. Whenever Dad mentioned how nice the garden was looking, the Condesa would say, "Yes, except your bloody ugly shed."

I used to worry that my parents didn't really like each other – they argued like this constantly. I didn't know then that the terms of a relationship are a secret hex incomprehensible to any outsider.

"Now – enough silly crying," Mum said, turning from me and reaching for a tissue to blow her nose. "Take the biscuits, Pablo. I quickly do my face."

I leaned against the counter again.

"I don't want the money, mum," I said.

She had taken a compact from her handbag and was wiping smudged mascara from her eyes as she peered into the mirror. "Don't be stupid. It's your money. Dad worked hard for you."

"To give us a good life. Not to give us money."

Mum fished a lipstick from the bag and talked as she put it on. "Money is good life. Same thing." She blotted her lipstick on another tissue. "Anyway, it's not so easy. Dad knows you don't care about money. It's not a problem with you. But perhaps for Tomàs and Jacinta it's more a problem."

"What does that mean?" I asked. "Tom's brilliant with money. And who knows about me? I've never had any."

Mum smiled and patted my cheek. "You're so like Daddy. Is why you argued all the time." She handed me the plate of biscuits. "Go. I bring the tea."

As I reached the kitchen door, she said, "Pablo – you understand what I say about you boys and Jacinta? I don't mean you are not important."

I understood. Dad had been the wheel in which the roulette ball of her life had spun. We kids were a payout – a welcome bonus, but not the game itself. That was okay. Actually, I thought it rather romantic.

"It's okay," I said.

"I'm very lucky to have you all. Very lucky."

"All?" Perdito murmured in my head. "Lucky?"

He was really beginning to piss me off.

*   *   *   *

If I could be bothered, I could claim a small annual income from Dad's estate, but frankly I've never been able to face the paperwork.

There's also a mechanism by which I might trigger a siren-wailing, strobe-flashing jackpot that'll cascade over me in glittering doubloons. Tom has spent most of his adult life trying to line up the three cherries that make the bells go off. On one occasion he even persuaded me to go into a scheme with him. Or rather, him with me, as it was my artwork that was going to pull the handle. In the end it came to nothing, much to Tom's comical fury. He actually threw a punch at me – it was like being assaulted with a violet.

He wasn't the only one who was cross with me about money. After the reading of the will, Perdito envisaged us embarking on an orgy of carnal excitement – drugs, travel, speed, sex – the usual self-indulgent fantasies of a young Croesus. But he also proposed more creatively outrageous experiments in sensation. He wanted, for instance, to be shut naked in a brilliantly-lit confined space with dozens of bats.

"What would that feel like – all of them flapping and crawling over us, panicking and blind? All it needs is money."

"It's academic. I'm not going after the money."

"That's just selfish."

We argued about Natalie too. He wanted to see her more often than I did, and he nagged at me constantly.

"Call her. We could go round tonight. Just one night, Pablo. Just let me drive for one night with Natalie."

If he couldn't sway me to that, he urged me to swap seats for whatever else I might be doing.

"I hardly get to be in control ever. It's my body too. It's my blood. We should be sharing fifty-fifty. You act as if you're doing me a favour letting me swap."

Eventually he'd wear me down and I'd agree to loosen my grip, step back and become his transmitter. I'd watch from behind my eyes, often embarrassed and sometimes appalled. Over the years his behaviour became worse and worse.

My sister Jazz emigrated to New Zealand in the mid-nineties. Her friends organised a farewell dinner at a restaurant on the King's Road to which Tom and I were invited. Perdito wanted to be directly involved, and his argument was one that I couldn't deny.

"She's my sister too, isn't she? I mean, you're the one who's always going on about my being included in the family."

So we agreed that he could take over halfway through the evening. From cocktails to entrees, I chatted to a rather chubby girl on my left and, on my right, a bald guy in his mid-twenties. Throughout, Perdito was pressed nose-flat to the window of my perceptions, like a street-urchin outside a fish-and-chip shop.

"So what do you do?" asked the chubby girl, Heather.

"Various temping jobs – in offices and so on. I dabble in painting and sculpture, but I'm not single-minded enough about it, if I'm honest."

"Do you sell much stuff?"

"Yeah, once in a while."

I could feel Perdito sucking up the juices of our surroundings – the smell of garlic on the croutons, the glint of light from Heather's earrings, the pitch and attack of spoken phrases that peaked above the babble of general conversation. I rolled warm wax from the candle between my fingers and he thrilled at the translucent pliability of it and at the way the whorls and loops of my prints were preserved like engraving on the blob as it hardened. He was tugging at me, impatient and excited.

"My turn! My turn!"

As soon as I'd finished my steak, I went to a cubicle in the Gents where I relaxed, released, loosened, as Natalie had taught me. Perdito leapt forward into the cockpit of my mind, and everything around me immediately sharpened – the odour of disinfectant, the bass thump of music from beyond the door, the taste of mustard on my tongue.

I know of course that there's an element of schlock-horror farce in all this. And, to be honest, it would have been a damn sight easier if, when Perdito took over, I'd collapsed groaning behind a sofa and emerged with mad eyebrows and pointed teeth. Easier for me, and a lot easier for those around me. We'd long before realised that it would pointless – counter-productive, in fact – for Perdito to present as himself, as it were. People would be forgivably confused if I suddenly started referring to myself as 'Perdito'. So whatever he did, he did as Pablo

I left the toilets and went back to the table, watching like an anxious backseat father as Perdito revved my senses and adjusted the rake of my mind. I sat down between Heather and the bald guy again, and I reached for the wine – or, to be more accurate, I didn't prevent Perdito reaching for it. I poured a generous measure into my glass and then leant across to top up Heather's.

"No – I'm fine," she said, putting her hand over it.

Perdito wasn't having that. I pushed Heather's hand away. "Rubbish," I said. "It's a party."

"Oh, well – okay," she giggled, picking up the brimming glass. "Cheers."

I felt Perdito's prickly delight, and I groaned inside. He'd clocked Heather as pliable and wax-soft, and he intended to leave the impression of my fingerprints on her.

"Nice earrings," I said as I lit a cigarette. "I like the way they catch the light."

The bald guy to my right tapped me on the shoulder. "Would you mind not smoking?" he asked.

"Would you mind fucking off?" I replied evenly.

I could have refused to say it – but I had no right to censor Perdito. He wasn't a child.

Jazz leaned across the table. "Pablo – just go to the bar to smoke, eh?"

"Why? It's a smoking table, isn't it? Why can't he go to the bar to breathe?"

"It's okay," the bald guy muttered, getting to his feet. "I need the loo anyway."

"I'm sorry, Graham," Jazz said. "My brother's an arsehole." She scowled at me and returned to her conversation.

Heather reached for my cigarettes. "Well, if you can, I can. Mind if I nick one?"

"Do."

"I promised my boyfriend I'd give up, but what he doesn't know can't hurt him, can it?"

Wincing, I replied, "Does that apply to anything else you're not supposed to do because of your boyfriend?"

The subsequent conversation was a minuet of smirking innuendo. I disengaged and let Perdito cruise. At the other end of the table, Tom got up to go to the Gents and his seat was taken by the returning Graham who shot me a disgruntled look. I grinned and blew smoke towards him which he flapped away irritatedly. When Tom returned, he sat down beside me for want of anywhere else to sit

"Having a good time?" he asked, glancing at my hand on Heather's thigh. "Where's Natalie tonight?"

I felt Perdito glow warm. He always did when Tom was around.

"She's got her period," Perdito had me say. "Stomach cramps, the lot." Which was true, but not information I'd have volunteered myself.

"How delightful," Tom muttered.

"Oh, God – that can be awful," Heather put in. "It's a recognised syndrome, you know. Really debilitating."

Perdito was on to the idea like a shot.

"So what does it feel like?" I asked. "What's it like when blood comes out of you? Can you feel it trickling inside?"

"Er...well. I've never had to describe it. Um..."

"Hey, Jazz," I said. "What's a period feel like? "

Jazz glanced at me with weary disgust. "Shut up, Pablo."

"No – come on," I insisted, raising my voice to be heard above the hubbub of conversation around the table, "Half the people around this table bleed every month, and the other half have no idea what it feels like. Why's it such a big deal to ask?"

All chatter had ceased, not only within our party but also at neighbouring tables.

"Tom," Jazz said, glowering "can you take him outside?"

Tom nodded and grasped my arm at the elbow. I tugged it away. I was almost yelling now. "Look – there are seven women at this table. The *chances are that – what? – two of them are bleeding from their cunts. It's a perfectly natural function and I'm just asking how it feels."*

Tom and two waiters bundled me out of the restaurant and shoved me down the steps to the street. I turned to go back in, but Tom barred my way and pushed me against the railings.

"Why do you always have to be the centre of attention?" he demanded, his hands pressing my shoulders against the wrought-iron. "It's Jacinta's night, you idiot."

Perdito could feel me shuffling forward inside, ready to take back the wheel. He shoved me away.

"Not yet," he said.

"It's Perdito," I said to Tom. And that surprised me. Even with Natalie, Perdito had never used his name when he was driving. Never. "It's me." I stared Tom in the eyes. "Really. It's Perdito."

Tom immediately let go of my shoulders and staggered backwards. He looked terrified.

"Don't start that shit, Pablo," he said shakily.

"It's me," I heard myself say. "You know me. It's Perdito."

"You're insane. Just shut up."

"You know me, Tom."

"What the fuck are you on, you freak?"

He bounded up the steps to the restaurant and pointed me out to the guy on the door.

"Don't let him in under any circumstances," he said. He ducked back inside, and the doorman positioned himself squarely in the threshold, staring at me threateningly.

"What was all that about?" I asked Perdito.

He said nothing, keeping a tight hold on the wheel. I reached into my pocket for cigarettes but I'd left them on the table, so I just waited to see what my twin would do next. He was fizzy with excitement. I could hear the hum of the streetlamp twenty feet away. I could taste the scent of chilli from a kebab in the gutter. I could feel each individual eyelash moving in the breeze that blew along the road from Sloane Square.

"Pablo?"

Heather was coming down the steps, shrugging on her coat.

"It's still my turn," Perdito muttered as I turned to meet her.

He was brutal that night. I don't think Heather enjoyed it much, and I certainly didn't. But it was none of my business. I had no right to stop Perdito being himself.

*   *   *   *

On the way home from Bloomsbury I visited Leo's grave. He's alongside my mother and my father, to their right. There's a plot to the left reserved for me.

Leo's funeral was brief and bleak. It was the first I'd attended. I've been to so many since that I'm almost blasé, but that October day in 1970 was the most awful of my life. I couldn't imagine how I would ever again be happy. When my parents died – the old man, suddenly, in 1981 and my mother mercilessly slowly three years later – I was aware that the immediacy of the grief would fade. Their lives had been lived – lived well – and the time had come. Not so with Leo. He was thirty-three when he died. Twenty-three when he'd started dying.

My parents erected a simple headstone that bore Leo's name, his dates and the single word 'Beloved'. I'm not against understatement, but I always considered it a shabby memorial; an indication of embarrassment. A few years ago I replaced it with one a little larger – though no larger than those that mark my parents' respective spots – on which are engraved four lines from Tennyson.

*And thou hast vanish'd from thine own
To that which looks like rest,
True brother, only to be known
By those who love thee best.*

Perhaps my choice was sentimental. Selfish even, because it commemorates Leo as my sibling, rather than as his parents' son. Maybe it was conceited of me to have claimed him like that. Doubts assail me these days – about everything.

"I don't believe I've told you about Pablo," I said as I picked the seedlings of weeds from Leo's grave. "You'd like him – he's your sort of chap." I should mention – in case I appear odd – that I don't consider I'm speaking to Leo when I talk aloud at the graveside. It's just a way of thinking things through that I find useful occasionally. "At least, he likes to drink and smoke. And he makes me laugh. So the two of you would probably get along." I stood back, rolling the weeds between my hands. "He loves an argument, just as you did. He provokes me to conclusions that I'd prefer to avoid."

Dusk had settled over the trees and I could hear barking from somewhere behind me in the village.

"I always tell myself I did all I could, Leo. But perhaps I'd have done more had I not thought you were right to feel so guilty."

My mind ran back and forth along the line of moral logic like a dog at a wire fence – a fence that had always been there, although I'd never before wandered this far from the house. When Pablo dragged a stick up and down the mesh, I'd rushed out barking and I'd come up against the boundary of my province. "I've made bad decisions too. I should not have let you drive. I should not have let you be forgotten. I shouldn't have tried to atone by replacing you." It was dark now and I couldn't make out the lettering on his headstone. "I'm sorry. I'll find another way."

As I drove home to Twyborough Cross, another snippet of Tennyson came to mind.

Vague words! but ah, how hard to frame

*In matter-moulded forms of speech,
Or ev'n for intellect to reach
Thro' memory that which I became.*

*   *   *   *

"Stephen, I'm so sorry for what I said as I got into the taxi. I've been feeling a bit under the weather and that always makes me bitchy. Give me a call and let me apologise properly."

I turned off the answering machine and walked through to the drawing room. I was melancholic and I wanted to sit alone on the terrace and count the stars. I poured a whisky and took it out to my accustomed seat overlooking the lawn.

The garden lights were on, lending subtle illumination to carefully chosen aspects of the view from the terrace. The folly was lit from within, giving substance to the columns and reflecting them in the lake. Hidden spotlights in the shrubbery led the eye towards the water where the moon hung and rippled. Beneath the oaks that represented myself and Leo there was a soft glow – and my gaze rested there. It was not as it ought to be. The light was splayed across the ground, when it should have been thrown upwards, diffused through the branches.

"Stephen! Over here!"

Pablo was waving from the knot-garden, silhouetted against the oaks. I tutted. It had taken me ages to position those lights correctly. I'd had the entire system modernised in the nineties, precisely replacing the one my father had put in thirty years before. One could only set them up at night, of course, and as the effect was to be seen from the terrace I'd had to tramp to and fro around the edge of the lake several times, adjusting the angle of the lamps, coming back to the house, returning to the trees – over and over again.

I walked down the steps and made my way along the gravel path that follows the edge of the lawn to the knot garden.

"I've got a surprise for you," Pablo said, grinning in the dark. "This way."

Already disgruntled, I followed him between the low box-hedges and through the arch to the Old Pasture – an area of sloping ground where the grass remained uncut and a trodden path led down to the orchard. The lamps that should have been directed up into the branches of the oaks were slanted across the Pasture now, and I could see why. Pablo had needed the light to work by. He had planted trees – quite mature specimens, twenty and thirty feet high – dotted across the open space.

"What do you think?" he asked. "There are a couple of beech, some silver birch, a native hazel or two." He wandered between them, touching each trunk. "They were delivered this afternoon and I wanted to get them in before you came home."

"There must be two or three thousand pounds' worth here," I said, trembling with fury. "And all on my account, I assume?"

Pablo looked pained. "No, of course not. Wouldn't be much of a present if you had to pay for it yourself, would it?"

"Don't you think it would have been polite to consult me before making a decision like this about my garden? If I'd wanted a patch of woodland here, I'd have done something about it myself."

"But think of what it'll be like in ten – even five – years," Pablo said. "Instead of this boring patch of grass, you'll have…"

"I *like* this boring patch of grass. It's been here for two hundred years. I simply cannot believe the presumption." I shook my head. "Take them all out. I want them gone by tomorrow."

I turned and stalked back to the house, alight with self-righteous anger. It had been a mistake to let Pablo loose in the garden. However well meaning, he lacked the discipline and the sense of history necessary to care for Twyborough's grounds.

I sat in my seat on the terrace again and sipped whisky, glowering. The percussive thwack of a spade in earth drifted to me from beyond the knot garden. I drained my drink and went into the drawing room for another. Pablo appeared outside the French doors as I turned from the sideboard.

"I've taken the hazels out," he said flatly, kneeling to untie one shoelace. "I'll do the rest in the morning." He pulled the sneaker off and tossed it aside on the terrace.

"Pablo," I said, a little calmer now, "I'm sure you meant well, but a garden like this isn't something you can improvise."

He swapped from one knee to the other and started to untie the second shoelace. "Edition date within publishing house," he said without looking up. "Disregarding imprint."

I glanced at the books lining the walls. "Yes."

"The concern of the organising mind is to maintain the order of the past." He lobbed the left shoe after the right and stood up. "I'm off to bed. There's a lasagne in the oven – should be ready in about twenty minutes."

It was only half past ten. Pablo had never gone to bed before midnight in all the time he'd been my guest.

"Oh, don't sulk, Pablo," I said. "Let's not part for the night as bad friends. Stay and have a drink at least."

He walked past me to the door, where he turned. I knew him well enough by now that I braced myself for an incisive parting shot. He hesitated, as if he were having second thoughts, and then he said, "It might need a little black pepper. See you in the morning."

As I ate lasagne alone in the kitchen, I wondered what his first thought had been.

*   *   *   *

I rarely dream, but when I do the dreams are convincing and potent.

The night of Pablo's trees, I dreamt of Vivienne Belitho-Fitzwarren, of whom, despite her memorable name, I have not thought for a decade or more. In my early forties she and I were close, and I often brought her to Twyborough Cross. My father had died a year or so earlier and my mother was increasingly frail. In the end the relationship with Vivienne withered because I simply couldn't give it the attention it deserved, what with my mother's illness and the increasingly time-consuming work of Sub Judice. When it all finally fizzled out I was disappointed, but too busy really to grieve.

In the dream, I was sitting on the terrace and I could see Vivienne walking around the west side of the lake towards the folly. When she reached it, she put both hands against one of the columns and pushed. The column tottered. I stood up and began to run across the lawn, but my feet sank into the grass until I was wading through mud. I was concerned that I was ruining the perfect lawn, but I was also desperate to stop Vivienne destroying the folly. As I struggled towards her, she heaved at the column and it toppled. The entire building collapsed, roof caving in and walls buckling. I was there beside her, outraged, and I pulled her away by one arm. I bent and tried to lift the column upright; she was standing in the middle of the lake screaming, "You can't do this! What about me?"

I was woken by a commotion in the garden. I rolled out of bed and went to the window. Pablo was backing across the lawn holding a spade, and Natalie was advancing on him.

"What about me?" she yelled. "You can't just pretend I don't exist!"

I couldn't hear what Pablo replied. He was talking at a conversational pitch and by this time he was almost at the edge of the lake.

"And what does Perdito say?" Natalie shouted. "I know he doesn't want this. You can't just decide something like that on your own."

Pablo took two steps back, shrugging and shaking his head, but always with his eyes on Natalie, warily.

"That's a lie! It's impossible!" she yelled, and she rushed at him. He raised the spade in both hands as a barrier, but Natalie ignored it, grabbing him by the throat. "Where's Perdito? Perdito!" She shook him, and he seemed not to resist, though he could very easily have swung the spade upwards and dislodged her arms. "Let me speak to him, you bastard!"

I remembered how tightly muscular Natalie had appeared when I'd seen her close up. And Pablo, though not actually weedy, was no bodybuilder. In the event of an all-out brawl, one's money would be on the girl.

"Stop that!" I shouted.

Natalie looked over her shoulder, and Pablo ducked from her grasp, dropping the spade. He grabbed her about the waist and swung around on his heels, releasing her as he came to face the lake. Before she even hit the water, he was running back to the house. He looked towards me as he bounded up the steps of the terrace.

"Thank you for having me!" he shouted – and he disappeared through the French doors.

Natalie stood up in the water, her blonde-white hair flat to her head and dripping, her clothes hanging in sodden folds.

"Come back, you fucking bastard!"

She waded from the lake and squelched across the lawn. I had to withdraw from the window into the bedroom so that I could chuckle unseen. I pulled on my dressing gown and straightened my face, then went downstairs. My car keys were gone from their hook by the door, and the Bentley was no longer in the drive. Natalie was drenched on the terrace, and I took her a towel.

*   *   *   *

That evening the telephone rang.

"Hi. Has she gone?"

"Hello, Pablo. Yes. I tumbledried her clothes and let her have a shower. She was not happy."

"I can imagine. The car's at the Bentley dealership on Berkeley Square being serviced. It'll be ready by the weekend."

"Thank you. Where are you – Limehouse?"

He laughed. "How do you know about Limehouse, you sneaky old sod? Ah – Natalie told you."

"You're still welcome here. I'm sorry I snapped at you last night."

"It's okay. The tree nursery people'll come tomorrow to get the saplings. I'm going away."

"Where?"

"Away. Thanks for everything."

He hung up.

I warmed up the leftover lasagne from the previous evening and opened a bottle of wine. I ate on the terrace, watching black clouds gather over the oaks. The terracotta pot at the top of the balustrade was full of cigarette ends. The twilight was still and humid. I turned on the garden lights.

Having finished the wine, I went inside to pour myself a brandy. The telephone rang again and I hurried around the sofa to pick it up.

"Hello?"

It was one of my authors, fretting about the lack of response from prospective publishers. I soothed him and promised to chase a few people in the morning. I flicked through the channels on the television but nothing held my interest, so I went back out to the terrace. Lighting fractured the sky as I sat down, and thunder snarled beyond the orchard. Fat raindrops slapped against the flagstones – one here, two there – and then the downpour came.

There was a hollow pop from the shrubbery and all the garden lights went out. I slouched there in the warm wet dark, watching the little splashes of rain in my brandy, lonely for the first time in years.

Chapter Ten
A Mere Bag of Blood

There was no constancy in Pablo. For weeks he would do nothing but read books, contemplate his art projects, daub. I would sit behind his eyes, smothered and unexcited, removed and padded. I was barely conscious, as if I were dozing on the sofa in a dim room on a summer's afternoon.

But suddenly, without warning, burning white light would atomise the curtains; the TV and the hi-fi would spontaneously burst into pounding life; the roof dissolved and hot, multicoloured rain poured in from the incandescent blue sky. I was instantly an electrified fulcrum of sensation, drunk on light, dazzled by orchestras. I hungered to taste and touch, to inhale and soar. I scrabbled for control of our hands and mind, begging him to let me connect with the world.

And as he stepped aside, I was awash with chemical reality, eager and powerless. I rampaged for ecstatic, stupefied days at a time – until, in an unpredictable moment, the tumult receded and the colours paled; the realm of the material shrank away from me and became monochrome – and I fell back into Pablo, nauseous, bloated and ready to sleep.

When I was active, I hated to be so in the thrall of sensation – so jacked up on hue and skin, on perfume and vibrato and the sour texture of velvet. I felt like a child spun on the lawn by an uncle holding his wrists, screaming and delighted and afraid, recognising the house whipping past, the smeared kaleidoscope of the summer border, the angled yellows and blues of the swing and the summerhouse – but not in control, not able to touch the ground. I didn't like that sensation. I didn't like that it was only *sensation. And I was not at all fond of who I was. I was an embarrassment to myself.*

During the long, dim days of repose, I dreaded the next bout of totality. I wanted a measured and sane experience of the world out there. I longed to negotiate with Pablo – but it was only when I was animated that I could put my case, and then I didn't want to. Roaring like a bejewelled dragon, spitting sparks, I hadn't the patience to think.

I sensed that Tom's world was not like Pablo's. I sensed that if I were trapped in Tom, then I would be able to consider. I would recognise myself. I knew that the face I saw in Pablo's mirror was not my face. Even then, even before I knew what I know now, I felt that Tom had my face.

*   *   *   *

I never leave my telephone answering machine on when I go out of the house. It's like having a slot in the door through which people can push little packets of unwanted hassle, like fresh dogshit. Tradesmen in particular take full advantage. "Thing is, mate," says the plumber who failed to show up, "I left a message on your machine asking you to confirm. But you never called back so I thought – y'know – you must've changed your mind." No matter that you've had four prior conversations, mailed a letter of agreement and paid a deposit. The fat turd of responsibility has been deposited on the doormat in your absence, pal, and now it's up to you to scoop it onto a magazine and flick it back.

I always have the machine on when I'm at home though, in order to screen calls. There are very few people I wish to speak to.

Beep. "Tom, you old bastard. It's Angus." Angus Jakes, my boss. I looked up from my desk. "We've picked up a lead on a client in Malaga. Bit outside our usual catchment area but it could be mucho lucrativo, and I'd like you to handle it. The meeting's set up for Friday. Give me a buzz and I'll fill you in."

Having been distracted, I opened the spreadsheet in which I keep track of my salary and commission. There were two months left of my financial year – which would end, of course, when I presented proof of my earnings to the trustees in June. I projected a year-end figure of fifty-plus, my best performance yet. But it depressed me, as it did every spring, that I'd be back on the treadmill next year, plugging hopelessly away at earning the upfront hundred thou that would free me from the daily grind for good.

Ever since I left University I'd been looking for a way to make that much in one hit. It wouldn't be easy under any circumstances, but the terms of my father's will were very specific about acceptable means of achieving the target figure. Gambling was out, for instance – so there was no point in amassing fifty thousand and putting it on red at a casino. For me, the risk-to-reward ratio would be a lot better than evens, and my father had obviously anticipated that calculation.

Share-dealing was out as well. During the stock market boom I broached the subject with both my mother and the Trustees, and the idea was vetoed. I complained that this was somewhat unfair – hypocritical even – as the money I was due had been raised in the first place from the sale of shares.

"No, no," my mother insisted, sweeping the floor around me as I sat in her kitchen. "When Dad and his friends start the company they have no money – none. We sell car, Dad's scuba things, jewellery – all to pay for office in Chiswick. Your dad work very hard. Twenty years – and then Idyll is worth money. Work, work, work. Not sit and watch TV screen like stupid yup."

"Yuppie," I corrected.

"And with the shirts with stripes! Like pyjamas! No class, these yups."

"What if I start a company and eventually sell the shares?"

"Feet up!" She swept under the table as I lifted my legs out straight. "Yes, yes. You start company like Dad. Make a new thing from nothing. That's hard work. You have a good idea for some company?"

Actually, no, I didn't at the time. I just wanted to establish the principle.

I've invested in a few business ventures on the side – a wine bar, a company customising VW Beetles. Once I even went into a scheme with Pablo. This would have been the mid-nineties. I got a call from Jacinta.

"Pablo and Natalie have managed to get a joint exhibition at a gallery in Charlotte Street. Mum and I are going to the opening. Do you want to come?"

"I'd rather nail my scrotum to a passing train."

Jacinta tutted. "I'll rephrase the question. Would you like to explain to Mum why you're not going to be at your brother's first West End exhibition?"

We agreed to meet outside the gallery at seven-thirty, and I was punctual, which was utterly pointless given that my mother was involved. By eight o'clock I was tired of standing in the drizzle so I went inside to wander amongst stubbly, unironed men and wristy, chain-smoking women with fidgety eyes. As I walked around clutching a glass of pineapple juice and a plate of nibbles, I realised that the terrible thing about contemporary art is how utterly artless it is. It seems to be no more than a series of visual puns and one-trick jokes.

"Like it?" asked a voice beside me. It was Natalie. Her cropped hair was dyed flame-orange and she was wearing a white mini-dress over white tights. She looked like a freshly-lit cigarette. Like Pablo, she purported to be an artist – for which calling she had exactly the necessary qualifications of vacuous secondhand pretension – Emperor's clothes, and all from Oxfam. Her contribution to the exhibition was a collection of careful copies of famous landscapes into which she had incorporated twentieth-century environmental developments. So there was a Sixties housing estate on the far side of the stream in which Constable's haywain was stranded; and an oil refinery could be seen dominating the landscape beyond La Gioconda's balcony. The notion raises a smile, I suppose, but having smiled, one has got from it everything one is going to get.

She nodded at the piece by which we were standing – her parody of Millais' *Blind Girl*, behind whom fenced fields were reaped by a bright yellow combine harvester, while huge aluminium barns gleamed beneath the rainbow's arc.

"It certainly makes you think," I said, which was as ambivalent a platitude as I could manage on the spur of the moment.

"This one's my favourite," Natalie said. "Because – you know – it says that how we're irrevocably changing our landscape is really important even if we're unaware of it." She sipped her wine. "With the girl being blind and everything, y'know?"

"I'm speechless."

"That's exactly the reaction I'm after. Like – mute outrage."

"And I'm certainly outraged," I said.

"Have you been in the other room yet – Pablo's work?"

"I'm on my way there."

She put her hand on my arm confidingly. "He's a total genius, your brother. I mean, in a way I suppose he's sort of been my pupil – but I've learned so much from him about seeing the world and having that whole open-minded attitude towards creativity and, well, just life, really. Come and look."

My brother's genius had been channelled into the creation of the most repulsive collection of objects I have ever seen in my life. There were thirty or forty paintings on parchment in daubed brown-red – rough studies of a foetus at various stages of development.

"It's not paint," Natalie told me. "It's blood. Pablo's blood. Isn't that incredible?"

"Jesus Christ," I murmured queasily.

"But the really mind-blowing piece is over here."

It was a refrigerated glass cabinet filled with some sort of clear liquid in which floated a balloon sculpture of an unborn child. The balloons were filled with – I was afraid to ask, but Natalie told me anyway – more blood. Pablo's blood again. There must have been two or three pints of it, dark crimson and viscous.

"The baby's hair is Pablo's too. And its little fingernails are bits of his skin."

I felt quite faint. The cocktail sausages I had just eaten were rebelling against being confined to my stomach.

"Excuse me – I need to sit down," I said.

I took a seat at the side of the room and lowered my head, sipping from my glass of juice. I couldn't help wondering how Pablo had collected the blood. At home, with a needle in his arm? Over how many days do you siphon off three pints of blood? Did he keep it in the fridge in milk bottles? The whole idea was quite disgusting.

"Are you all right?" Natalie asked. I could see her from the knees down as she stood in front of me. She was wearing black patent shoes with a strap across the instep, like a schoolgirl's. "Can I get you something?" She put her hand on my shoulder and I shrugged it away. The last thing you need when you feel sick is to have someone fussing over you – particularly someone you don't like.

"I'm fine," I said, not looking up. "Just give me a minute or two."

"Okay. I'll go and see if Pablo's arrived yet." Her feet turned and walked out of my view.

I chanced a quick glance at the refrigerated cabinet. From this side I could see a sign that gave the name of the piece – *Blood Brother.* There must have been some mechanism to create a slight current in the clear fluid that surrounded the sculpture, because it was turning – head over heels and round and round in slow motion. I dropped my head away for a few seconds, and then forced myself to look back again – because I was damned if anything created by Pablo was going to be permitted to overwhelm me. The model was not, in fact, made of balloons exactly, but some kind of moulded latex, very thin like a condom. An umbilical cord trailed from its belly and the fine brown hair on its translucent skull floated wispily, waving. As the foetus pitched and rolled, the blood shifted and flowed within the plastic membrane, making it bulge here and cave there. It was as if the infant had to struggle to hold its shape, to remain in a recognisably human form – it seemed constantly on the verge of reverting to a mere bag of blood.

A couple came in to the room – he was bespectacled and evidently much too cerebral to bother about combs, and she looked like an eel – and they circled Pablo's floating foetus.

"Jason's already bought it for his Brussels exhibit," the man said. "It'll be a bugger to transport, of course."

"It's perfect for Brussels," the woman replied. She nodded towards the rust-coloured daubs around the walls. "I'd seriously consider buying one of these. Rather more in my price bracket, I suspect."

"You could probably pick one up for eight or nine hundred," the man told her, still gazing at the turning infant in its glass case. "I know Jason wrote a check for twenty-five thousand for this piece – and that may well turn out to be a snip."

I had begun to feel better but suddenly I came over faint again. As the couple wandered out into the other room, I made a quick count of the framed pictures on the walls and did a sum that included the rubber baby – and I concluded that I was surrounded by at least fifty grand's worth of Pablo's bodily fluids.

"Hello. Nice of you to come, if only for Mum's sake."

I looked up and there was Pablo, unshaven and tired, but wearing a rather stylish and well-cut suit in charcoal grey. No tie of course. And green Converse high-tops. But, for Pablo, this was the equivalent of a formal get-up for tea at the Palace.

"Don't worry," he said. "I'm not going to ask you what you think of the work. I don't want you to have to lie, and I don't suppose I'd like to hear the truth."

"Actually," I told him, getting to my feet, "I'm rather impressed."

"Are you? I thought you'd be appalled."

"That too. The subject matter is unarguably appalling." I considered expanding on this appraisal – not least in terms of Mum, whose reaction to Pablo's art I couldn't begin to imagine – but I didn't want to get into an altercation. "What I'm impressed by is the money this stuff apparently commands. Is it true you've accepted twenty-five-k for that creation?"

Pablo took a cigarette from his pack and performed his wearisome little trick of flipping it into his mouth from waist height. He grinned as he snapped open his lighter. "Yeah. I suppose I ought to say that I'm not interested in the money, but frankly, I'm pretty fucking impressed myself." He inhaled. "Though it's not all profit. It cost a fortune to make the thing."

He'd borrowed from Natalie, he said. Once he'd paid her back and cleared his accumulated debts, he'd be a couple of thousand ahead.

"Is it worth that much because it's the only one?" I asked. "Or could you sell more of them at that price?"

"There are eight or ten collectors who'd probably be interested if there were more available. But I can't afford to make an edition even that limited." He grinned again. "And that's assuming I could spare the blood."

Eight clients. Two hundred grand gross. More importantly, actual invoices sent to buyers and demonstrably paid. It was late May. As long as Pablo could turn out the run in thirteen months, we'd both hit our father's arbitrary and ludicrous target, and we'd be set for life.

"So it'd be – what? – something around thirty pints for a limited edition of eight." That meant that Pablo would have to give blood at the rate of a pint a fortnight, which sounded like quite a lot to me. "Though of course it doesn't have to be *your* blood specifically, does it?"

"Of course it does. That's the whole point of the thing."

"I'll take your word for it that there's any point at all," I muttered, still thinking.

Pablo frowned, eyes narrowed as he took a long drag of his cigarette – and I reminded myself that, difficult though I found it to believe, he did actually take this macabre doodling seriously.

"Sorry – strike that remark," I said. "How much do they cost to make?"

Pablo shrugged and prevaricated, but I pushed him to tot it up. What with the custom-made refrigerator cabinets, the insulating fluid that had to be of a very precise density, the moulded latex for the model itself and Pablo's living expenses – five thousand pounds apiece.

"So forty thousand for eight – yes?"

"About that," Pablo agreed. "Including needles."

I was soon to submit my annual claim to the trustees, so I knew I had thirty-eight thou imminent. My proposition to Pablo was very straightforward. I would put up my whole cheque to finance the production of eight more blood-filled babies, on the condition that he could get written commitments ahead of time from the interested parties, and that he could knock out all eight pieces before the end of May the following year. We'd split the two hundred grand straight down the middle, and by July we'd be sitting on two million each.

I was expecting to have to sell this idea hard but Pablo, to my surprise, saw the sense of it immediately.

"I don't suppose there'll ever be a better opportunity to make that kind of money so fast," he said.

"Exactly. And can I just head off any subsequent complaints about you doing all the work by pointing out that forty-k is a considerable investment on my part, and without it there would be no work to do."

"Yes, massa."

"Incidentally, I don't think we need tell Mum about this venture, okay?"

"No?"

"No. It doesn't need to be mentioned."

"If that's the way you want it," Pablo shrugged. "But I can't see why not."

At which moment there came a shrill, screeching wail like a skewer pushed into one's ear. Pablo and I turned to see the Condesa standing in the doorway, her eyes fixed on the revolving foetus. Her hands were clenched to her face, which was stretched tight with horrified shock.

She turned to look at my brother. "Why do you *do* this, Pablito?" she demanded shakily in Catalan. Her voice was tremulous and high. "Mother of Jesus, let him sleep."

As tears spilled, she turned and pushed past Jacinta who was standing a little behind her, and scurried away through the outer gallery.

For a moment Jacinta stared at Pablo with furious intensity, and he gazed back, expressionless. "You really don't give a fuck, do you?" Jacinta spat, pale with rage. And she strode out, following our weeping mother.

Pablo and I stood silent in the white room. Beyond the door I could hear the chink and chatter of the guests. From behind me came the low hum of the refrigerated cabinet in which the blood baby floated and tumbled.

Pablo lipped another cigarette, and snapped open his lighter.

"Then again, you may have a point," he said.

*　　　　*　　　　*　　　　*

I know what it is not to be alive. I remember.

Imagine that you're driving along the motorway at night in a downpour, immersed in the slushy white-noise of tyres on the tarmac, the thrum of rain on the car's roof, blurring the windshield, the relentless pulse of wipers, splashed crimson and amber sliding across the monotone wet dark for mile upon mile, for hour after hour, forever – no hissing second different to any other in the shapeless drone of noise and black and red.

Suddenly you drive beneath a six-lane overpass – and for a held breath of a moment, there's light – other cars have shape, drivers have faces, the radio's music is audible, everything is defined and carries meaning, not swamped by wash and hum but contoured, solid, coloured, significant. You cruise for a long bright instant. You are alive.

Hold the breath.

Exhale and the bridge is gone. At once the formless thrum and the slushy white-noise envelop you, splash and blackness, monotone burr. The overpass drops away behind, and you must drive in the dark rain forever.

I remember. And I'm not yet ready to emerge again into that endless dark rain.

*   *   *   *

Pablo managed to elicit five letters of intent to purchase the blood babies, which was enough to convince me that the market was there. Flushed with confidence, I wrote the cheque. My mistake, in retrospect, was twofold. Firstly, I should never have given him all the money upfront. Secondly, I should have kept in closer contact so that I could manage the project. Oh, sorry – threefold. I should have had Natalie killed.

Two months after I'd bankrolled Pablo, I got a call asking me to meet him at a café on Covent Garden Piazza. Concerned that some problem had arisen, I was more than usually punctual. Amazingly, so was Pablo. He was sitting outside the café with a bottle of beer in front of him and his forearms resting unnaturally across the table like the forelimbs of a Trafalgar Square lion.

"Hello," I said. "Can I get you anything from the bar?"

"Another beer please. With a straw."

I brought them out to the table in time to see Pablo picking up his previous beer between his wrists and levering it towards his mouth.

"What have you done to yourself?" I asked as I sat down. "It's not going to stop you working, is it?"

"I bloody did it working," he said. "I can barely move my fingers. Could you get a fag out of my top pocket and lodge it in my useless claw?"

"So how did you get yourself in this state?" I said, taking the pack from the pocket of his shirt and extracting a cigarette.

"Signing seven thousand autographs with both hands simultaneously. Light it for me, will you?"

I fired up his ancient silver lighter and cupped the flame as he put the cigarette awkwardly to his lips. "Seven thousand autographs?"

"Thanks. Yeah – I've been thinking a lot recently about the relationship between money and art."

"Me too," I said. "I rarely think of anything else."

"So I imagine. It seems to me that there's no inherent or intrinsic value in any manufactured artefact – from a thrown pot to *Guernica*. Value is a function of the perception of an object, not of its existence."

"I have no idea what you're talking about," I said. "But if I did, I'd say that I don't give a monkey's as long as the blood babies are perceived to be worth thirty grand a pop."

"Well, that's my point," Pablo nodded. "Why aren't they worth a million quid each? Or twenty pence? I was talking to Natalie about this, and she said that the only thing that has a universally-agreed value is money itself."

I grimaced. "How I envy the fascinating dialogue the two of you must conduct over your bread and cheese."

"Look inside my cigarette packet again."

Something was rolled up in there. I pulled it out and flattened it on the table. It was a five-pound note.

"What's that worth?" Pablo asked me.

"Do I have to do this? Some of us have real lives to get on with, you know."

But he wasn't to be diverted. "A fiver is worth a fiver," he said. "By definition. The system would completely disintegrate if we didn't all believe that that was so." He lifted his curled hand and managed to take the cigarette from the corner of his mouth. "Now turn it over," he told me, nodding at the banknote. He sipped beer through his straw.

On the other side of the five-pound note was Pablo's signature, scrawled in pink magic-marker.

"So now what's it worth?" Pablo said, lodging the cigarette back into the corner of his mouth. "I've signed it. I say it's art. Is it worth more than a fiver now? What would it mean if I charged fifty quid for that five-pound note?"

I blinked. "Fifty? Really?"

Up to this point I had been suppressing weary irritation – but suddenly Pablo had touched on an exciting idea. Barking mad, of course – but then everything to do with contemporary art is insane. In an instant I could see the potential. "Do you think we could do that? Charge people for money? Would that work in the art world?"

My mind was whirring. This was a much better notion than the blood babies. Less effort, swifter production, potentially staggering margins. But like all inspired schemes, it needed an entrepreneurial mind behind it. For a start, Pablo was thinking too small. If you could ask fifty for a five, there was no reason you shouldn't sign fifties and charge a thousand for them. "What's the biggest denomination note they make?" I wondered aloud.

Pablo shook his head. "No, no. You see what you're doing? Despite knowing that there's an absolute value to this piece of paper, you've instantly developed a perception that negotiates that value. Natalie pointed out that if we were to sell these things, we'd be perpetuating precisely what we're trying to undermine."

"These things? You've made more of them?"

There was an excited yell from the far side of the Piazza. Then another. I turned to look. There was Natalie, standing behind one of those machines that blows streamers and glitter into the air at football stadiums. And from the upturned mouth of the machine there spurted a blue fountain of paper. Each piece whooshed twenty feet into the air before fluttering groundward, or being caught on the breeze and looping away across the Piazza.

"I've made precisely six-thousand nine-hundred and ninety-nine more of them," Pablo said. "Do you have any idea how long it takes to sign that many fivers?"

The shoppers and tourists on the Piazza had realised what this cloud of litter was made of. People were chasing the tumbling banknotes across the cobbles, bending as they ran, colliding with each other. More were emerging from the stores to investigate the commotion, and they started grabbing at the five pound notes drifting in the air and skittering past their feet. Waiters and patrons outside bars and cafés abandoned their tables and rushed into the throng. Traffic wardens stuffed fistfuls into their shoulder bags. There was shouting and screaming. Fights were breaking out.

It was chaos. Seven thousand five pound notes – thirty-five k – swirling and tumbling in the summer breeze. And all of it straight out of my bank account.

"I have people up there filming this," Pablo shouted above the din, waving his crippled hand at a balcony behind us. "It'll be the centrepiece of an installation."

"Will the installation be worth two hundred grand?" I screamed at him. "Because if it's not, this ridiculous fucking display is costing me two million quid, you stupid bastard."

"Ah, now," Pablo smiled. "You were always a man who knew the true value of money."

I believe I told Alice a little while ago that I couldn't remember the last time I was truly angry. Well, it's just come back to me. Before I left the

Piazza, I fractured Pablo's jaw with a punch that had every penny of my squandered investment behind it.

I decided then that if I was going to make the kind of money necessary to release me from the yoke of daily work, it would have to be through my own efforts. I couldn't invest in anyone else or rely on anyone else – least of all my brother, who had not even the dimmest conception of how difficult it is to create wealth.

I was on my own. And I really can't imagine why I didn't see that sooner.

*   *   *   *

In a moment of inattention, I answered a phone call from my boss, the appalling Angus Jakes – a pot-bellied smirker with high blood pressure and a higher forehead. He was still pressing me to go to Malaga. Apparently some gold-encrusted, sclerotic ex-pat wished to make his peace with the taxman, and he had asked his legal advisers to organise the drafting of a will.

"There's the possibility of an ongoing relationship with this firm of solicitors, Tommy-boy. They've got clients all over the shop – Portugal, Spain, the Med coast – and they're looking for a partnership. Do a good job on this and we could find ourselves opening an office in St Tropez, mate." He paused, presumably to mop up drool with a handy memo. "According to the back of my fag-packet, we're in with a chance of doubling turnover if we can get at all these loaded wrinklies."

"You know I don't fly, Angus. Can't you send someone else?"

"It's only two hours' flight time, you girlie. Take a pill and have a couple of Scotches in Departures, you'll never even know you were on a plane. Business class, natch."

"No. I'm sorry. I'd resign first."

This may seem a petulant thing to have said, but it was a calculated stymie. I generated more revenue than his other four sales-people put together, so Angus was desperate to keep me on the strength. Indeed, he seemed to think that the best way to secure my loyalty was to adopt an attitude of unsolicited intimacy towards me.

"Listen, Tom, old mate. It needn't come to that. Stay down there an extra week on me. Fill your boots."

This concession so readily made told me that the man could be pushed further. I had studied the most recent accounts of the company. By Angus's own figures, this trip was potentially worth something not unakin to four million pounds in the first year alone. With that much at stake, I wanted more out of it than a tan.

"A week of sex, sun and sangria – can't say fairer than that, Tommy-boy, can I?"

"Well, you could, yes. As I understand it, for my *sine qua non* contribution to doubling turnover, you're prepared to give me five days sucking up salmonella with burned-pink plumbers and their squalling families."

Angus gave a you-got-me chuckle. "What'll convince you?"

"Let me think about it," I said. An idea was turning over in my mind and I needed time to tune it. "I'll come in and see you at one on Wednesday. If we can thrash something out, I'll drive to Spain straight from the office."

Sitting in my study I considered the feasibility of making enough out of this to rack my earnings up to a hundred grand. It would all depend on manipulation of the psychology of Angus Jakes.

Angus was turned on by money – but it wasn't avarice. To Angus, the getting of money was proof of his creative, strategic mind. He would rather make a hundred pounds on some arcane, convoluted deal that would baffle a forensic accountant than rake in ten times as much on a straightforward and conventional sale. I needed to put together a proposition that would enhance Angus's view of himself as a can-do, make-it-happen outside-the-box prime-mover – which, I swear, is how I once heard him describe himself. By teatime I had sketched out something that I was pretty sure he'd go for.

At about seven I popped down to see Jeremy in the ground floor flat to ask him to pick up my mail from the foyer while I was away. The door was opened by a woman in her mid-thirties. Before she said a word I had her pegged as American (unnaturally even teeth, blonde hair that shone with the light of a thousand products), educated in Florida (her sweatshirt read *Gators*), moderately wealthy (her expensive trainers were carelessly battered) and actively single (as I lifted my left hand to push my hair back, her glance checked for a wedding ring).

"Can I speak to Jeremy, if it's convenient?"

"I doubt it is," she said. "He's in Italy skiing." The accent was East Coast but she pronounced the *t* of 'doubt' as a glottal stop, like a Londoner, so she had evidently lived in the UK for some time. Her name was Barbara. She was house-sitting for the week and – sure – she'd take in my mail. Why not?

"You're most terribly kind," I said. "Perhaps I could buy you a drink as a thank-you?"

She dipped her head sideways and looked at me through narrowed eyes, though smiling. This was a learned gesture – it's what lazy actresses do when they're trying to express amused thoughtfulness. Before it became a cinematic cliché no one ever did it in real life, but now it's part of a shared vocabulary of body language that's about as convincing as Esperanto.

"Yeah – let's do that," she said. "Is right now okay? My schedule's clear. Give me five minutes to change."

I went back upstairs to fetch my jacket, mentally awarding her a definite mark-against for the celluloid choreography – but two or three ticks in favour for the lack of coy messing about when faced with a simple proposition. And another for the eyes. Very blue eyes, the colour of Himalayan poppies.

It turned out that she was the IT director for a budget airline – not the most exciting job, she said, but dirt-cheap flights and discounted hotels all over the world. She was recently back from a few days in Athens. Just amazing town. The culture, the architecture. She wondered if I'd ever been there.

I nodded. "I believe so."

"You believe so? Aren't you sure?"

"I vaguely recall being taken there as a child. My father was in the travel business. We went to all sorts of places."

She was sipping a Bloody Mary straight from the glass. Like all Americans, she seemed to know by instinct when there was a red residue on her paper-white incisors, and she discreetly patted her teeth with a napkin from the bar. I sipped my pineapple juice.

"You were a lucky kid. I never even left Pennsylvania until I went to college."

"University of Florida, I bet. You were wearing a Gators sweatshirt earlier."

"I'm impressed. Do you know the nicknames of pretty much every US college?"

Actually, I did. I'd associated with enough American women to have built up a comprehensive body of information. Americans love to talk about their college years, and it helps if one can show some measure of familiarity with the subject.

"So of all the countries you've visited," she asked, "which is your favourite?"

"To be honest, I think abroad is over-rated," I told her. "I've don't subscribe to the idea that travel broadens the mind. People are much the same everywhere – only the weather and the standards of hygiene change."

"You're kidding, right? What about seeing amazing buildings and landscapes, experiencing different cultures?"

"I've never encountered a building that was worth getting diarrhoea for. And culture is just a sociologist's word for habit. Why am I supposed to be interested in other people's habits?"

Barbara gave me a sideways look with one eyebrow raised – another Hollywood pantomime – but I was serious. You won't discover anything about the world from mastering chopsticks in Peking that you couldn't learn from taking lunch every day in your local greasy-spoon. If the proper study of mankind is man, there's a lifetime's material within a hundred yards of your doorstep.

But I didn't want to get into an argument with Barbara. I changed the subject.

"So where do you live when you're not house-sitting?"

"I just bought a place in Greenwich. It's being totally re-wired, so Jeremy's trip was timely."

A definite plus, that. Her usual habitat was miles away on the other side of South London, so after this week there'd be very little chance of us bumping into each other on the street.

I offered to take her to dinner.

*   *   *   *

I tiptoed out of Jeremy's flat at five in the morning, carrying my shoes and shirt, though I was tempted to stay. From bar to brasserie to bedstead, Barbara had been highly entertaining company, and her attitude towards world travel – that of indiscriminate adventurousness – was one that she seemed to apply to any activity in which she took part. But I would leave to her the decision as to whether we would take things to a second encounter. It was only polite.

That morning I had another appointment with Alice. I was fifteen minutes late, and I can't abide unpunctuality.

"My apologies. I couldn't find a parking meter within half a mile," I said, unscrewing the cap from my mineral water.

Alice looked surprised. "You live in Kennington, don't you? And you drive across the West End when it's only twenty minutes on the Underground?"

"Nothing on God's earth would get me on the Tube," I told her. "I was last on a tube train during the IRA bombing campaign in the eighties. I reported an unattended sports bag to the driver, who peered at it for a few seconds, then kicked it. As it didn't splatter him all over the carriage, I suppose he concluded that it wasn't a bomb. Would you entrust your life to a cretin like that?"

"So you're not keen on aeroplanes and you avoid the Underground. What about boats?"

"Dull. There are few things duller than the sea. It takes you forever to get anywhere and there's nothing to occupy you on the way." I took a swig of my mineral water. "I used to take the ferry to see a girl on the Isle of Wight. The return on investment was less than satisfactory."

"Did you care for her?"

"Not enough, apparently."

"Which would you say was the most important of your relationships? The one you most cared about?"

"Louise," I said – too quickly. "Well, at least, that was the longest."

"Tell me about Louise."

I glanced at the clock. "I really don't think we have time."

"It's a long story, is it?"

"It would take a long time to tell, and a nanosecond to understand. But it has nothing to do with my fear of flying. I hope you're not of the school that thinks that everything's about sex."

"I'm just trying to get some idea of how you see the world and why."

But she obviously thought she was onto something. I imagined she'd already sketched out some textbook theory about my phobia and she was trying to get me to supply colours to fill it in.

"Listen – I'll talk about anything," I told her. "I have no problem with that, all right? I just want to avoid reducing a two-year relationship to a ten-minute anecdote – especially when it's completely irrelevant to what I'm here for." I swigged my water again. "I just want to avoid wasting time, that's all."

She jotted something on the pad that she held on her knee, and I groaned.

"Oh, no. What now? What did I say that was worth writing down?"

"Do you know how often you use the word 'avoid'?" she said, still scribbling.

"What?"

Alice looked up from her notes. "Let me ask you something. Say I wanted to make a will. Rather than engage someone like you, couldn't I save time and money by just handwriting a letter and leaving it with my personal effects?"

"Good God, no," I said. "That would be very risky. There's a carefully thought-out format that structures the thing so that an experienced professional can ensure a…"

Alice interrupted. "It's the same with my job. I'm not just sitting here listening to you chat. That would be very risky. There's a carefully thought-out format that structures…"

I returned the interruption, hands held up. "Yes. Okay. Point taken."

"Thank you." She closed her notebook and slipped the pen through the ring-binding. "I'm a guide here, Tom. It's your journey and in your country, but I know this sort of terrain. If I'm to be any help, I need your trust. Can you give me that?"

Obviously I was supposed to say yes, so I did. I couldn't see that it made any difference either way. If her methods were any good we'd get to where I wanted to go with or without my trust. She was supplying a service after all, and if she failed to deliver I was not about to allow her the *post eventum* get-out that it was somehow my fault for not 'committing'. One wouldn't put up with that from a decorator or a dentist. "I'm sorry, Mr Lyne, but you were not committed to the amalgam, which is why you now have an abscess on your gum."

But – as Alice insisted – I reminisced about Louise. Actually, I haven't thought about her for years, and once I started I found myself going off at tangents – my University career, other people I knew there, the various jobs I had between terms. I tried to relate the facts about my disastrous relationship with Louise, but it was all somewhat disjointed. The sequence of events seemed jumbled in my memory.

"Now, we're out of time again," Alice said as the clock on the wall ticked to the hour. "Same time next week?"

"Actually, I have to go away on business. So the week after?" I screwed the top on to my mineral water bottle and got to my feet.

"That's fine. Where are you off to?"

"Malaga. By car."

"Ah. Well, hopefully it won't be too long before you could go by plane, if you so chose."

I shrugged my jacket on. "Can't wait," I said.

*　　　*　　　*　　　*

I needed to pack a suitcase for my trip. I keep one in the bedroom closet, pretty much ready to go – wash-bag stocked, reference books strapped in, one large and one small towel, because I hate those meagre, thin efforts that you get in even quite good hotels. But I always leave packing shirts until the day before I travel, otherwise they get creased. I can't stand a creased shirt. I had a woman come in to do my ironing for a while, but I fired her. She just couldn't get the collars right and, anyway, I didn't like her being here while I was out. She kept moving things. If I leave a magazine on the chair in the hall it's because on the chair in the hall is where I want it. I don't expect to come home and find it's been put on the coffee table in the living room.

I was loading the tumble dryer when the phone rang and the machine kicked in.

Beep. "Tom – I forgot to ask you to write down everything you told me about Louise. If you could e-mail me a day or two prior to our next meeting, that would be helpful. See you in a fortnight."

"Oh, for Christ's sake," I muttered. I walked into the living-room, picked up the phone and hit call-back. Alice seemed to be either unaware or unconcerned that I had other things to do – a vitally-important business trip, for a start. She had no right to order me about like a lackey.

"Alice – it's Tom Lyne."

"Hello, Tom. I'm just going into a session. Is it quick?"

"Look – I've already told you about Louise. And I really am going to have a hell of a busy couple of weeks. Is this homework thing absolutely necessary?"

"Yes, I think so."

"No – surely not." I kept my voice even and civilised. I didn't want to make it such an issue that she found it impossible to back down. "I mean, I just want to avoid duplicate effort and inefficient use of both my time and yours."

"Sorry, I lost the signal. You want to avoid what?"

"I want to avoid – hello? – I want to avoid duplicate effort. I mean…"

"Tom, sorry. I'm not catching half of what you're saying. And I really do have to go. Can you hear me?"

"Yes, perfectly. Honestly there's very little to tell that I didn't cover during our session. I know I wasn't that articulate, but…"

"No, sorry – you keep dropping out. Look – I really would like you to write about Louise for me. It will be worthwhile. By the way – when did you last fly?"

"What?"

"The last time you flew. Write about that too. Have a good trip. Bye."

I slammed the phone down, seething. I have never understood why women seem to think they can take this airily cavalier attitude to one's time. They all do it. "I'll be ready to be picked up at eight. You can get that stuff into the attic while I'm out. We're going to Martha's for dinner on Thursday so you'll have to move your gym night." It's indicative of absolutely monstrous egotism. And it's infuriating because it leaves one no reasonable options. One can't simply acquiesce to such offhand dictatorship – not even for a quiet life – because it will just get worse. Then one's resentment will build and eventually, when it all becomes intolerable and one decides to get out, they act as if it's a huge surprise. "Why didn't you tell me you were unhappy? I thought we were getting on so well." Too late, sweetie – all the tenderness I felt has been crushed beneath the Panzer tracks of your invasive bossiness. Your toiletries are in a plastic bag on the porch, next to your spice-rack.

But you don't have to be in a relationship with a woman for her to imagine that she has the right to impose. Apparently, just being a man marks you as part of an infinite and free natural resource, like the rainforests, to be claimed, cut down and exploited in precisely the way that Mother Nature – that merciless old witch – intended. It makes me tremble with fury.

I was still trembling when there was a knock on the door. It was Barbara. I fucked her on the carpet and we went for a late lunch, then back to bed at my place for the afternoon. She had a business dinner that evening, thank God, otherwise I would have had to have come up with a story to get her out of the flat. I really wanted some time on my own.

*   *   *   *

I couldn't see when I was going to get any chance in Malaga to do my homework. Even if I had a free evening or two, I didn't want to be stuck in a hotel room tapping away at the laptop. It would be such a waste – writing about moribund periods of my past when I could be out somewhere living my present. That was the problem with the entire bloody exercise, actually.

As soon as Barbara left I showered, and then sat down at the computer to write my essay – straight into e-mail, no editing and no proofing. I just wanted to get it out of the way, and if Alice didn't like it, tough.

*   *   *   *

Dear Alice,

You asked about the last time I flew. There's not much to tell. A friend encouraged me to meet her in Prague, where she was working. She was a most compelling dinner companion and I enjoyed spending time with her, which led me to the self-deceit that I'd be able to handle the plane. I'm really not prepared to go into the shaming details – the hours of anticipatory sweats the night before, the jumpy eternity in the departure lounge, the innumerable paper bags into which I attempted to throw up quietly so as not to draw attention to myself during the flight. No one unafflicted could ever understand the encompassing terror of being trapped in that cramped seat. The feeling of utter infant vulnerability, the dreadful powerlessness. If I had been offered a parachute even when we were over the sea, I'd have strapped it on and jumped.

I didn't fly back. I bought a used car in Prague and drove home.

So what does that tell us? Nothing. Can we dissect my experience, pinning out the physiological and emotional trauma like the innards of a lab rat? Well, if you like – but to what end? It merely humiliates me. It gives the impression that I'm some sort of neurotic hysteric. Oh, hang on. I suppose I ought to look up the precise technical meaning of those terms. God forbid I should step on any professional toes.

However, there it is. Now let's move on to Louise – another episode of cringing humiliation, though rather more prolonged and, if I may just make this absolutely clear, one that is not in the least germane.

In my entire life I have only had one moment of rebellion, and my mother has never let me forget it.

"You see that boy on the television, Tomàs?" The boy in question would be forty years old and invariably smug. "In the programme where they talk about the newspapers? So smart, that one with the nice suit. Very clever! And he was at Cambridge! Yes – I read in a magazine! If you listen to Dad and you went to Cambridge, you will be on television programme now."

At seventeen, I refused point-blank to take the entrance exam for Cambridge. Though they'd never discussed it with me, my parents and my teachers had long assumed that the dreaming spires would be the next stop on my academic journey. You'd think they'd have understood that their lack of consultation and their complacent supposition were practically guaranteed to move any self-respecting adolescent to bloody-mindedness. My petulant obstinacy was an attempt to take control of my life and they are entirely responsible for it.

I went to a well-thought-of red-brick in the Home Counties, where I read Philosophy and Politics - but Cambridge was to feature anyway. During the Christmas break of my fresher year I was invited to a week-long party by an old school friend, Malcolm Norris. The first night I ended up sleeping on the living-room floor of his shared house, surrounded by empty gin bottles and comatose undergraduates. I was soft-focus drunk but completely awake. I watched snowflakes settle on the window pane and listened to Malcolm in the next room having sex with Louise Parsons. The following day over a breakfast of gin and orange, she and I chatted while Malcolm was out hunting and gathering cornflakes. By the time he returned, I was irretrievably smitten.

Louise was minuscule – barely five feet tall. Her hair reminded me of autumn – not just the shade of evening russet, but the way it seemed to be constantly in motion like forest leaves lifted on a swirling gust. Her eyes were dragonfly-green, bright with the reflected pure white light of the snow outside the kitchen window. And she made me laugh.

Over the next few days I fell into the habit of drinking and smoking in whichever room contained Louise, attempting to end up next to her so that some casual chat could be initiated. At the end of each night – which was usually more like the morning – I would try to time my descent into inebriated unconsciousness so that I flaked out in her vicinity so that I could stymie the possibility of anyone else smoothing in there under one of the increasingly-stained sleeping-bags that were scattered about the place. There were plenty of candidates. The one that concerned me most was Robin, a soft-spoken, cologned aesthete with mountain-blue myopic eyes and a high blink-rate that made him appear simultaneously vulnerable and aloof. I didn't like Robin at all.

And soon it was the morning of the twenty-third – the day I was supposed to leave for home. All over the house groaning young people were staggering from bedrooms, scratching their hair, sniffing their t-shirts, looking for a passably clean glass from which to glug copious water. Outside in the garden the snow was shin-deep, and the kitchen was crystal-lit by the still, hushed brilliance of reflected winter sunshine.

I made a cup of coffee and sloped down the hall, wearing a duvet over my clothes like a cloak. I pushed open the door of the living-room with my shoulder.

Louise was curled up under a beige blanket, her hair across her face. I prodded her shoulder gently.

"Coffee?"

I can't remember how we progressed from crouching together and talking to making love. But it was unlike any sex I'd ever had – playful, unselfconscious, giggly. There was no tension or anxiety, which were always the predominant feelings in my previous experiences. It was extraordinary sex, and yet merely what we happened to have chosen as the vehicle for a relaxed and perfect afternoon. It was like, for instance, enjoying the smell and the texture of tomatoes, the bubbling slide of butter in a pan, the gradual infusion of paprika's scent into rice – as opposed to cooking risotto merely because one was hungry.

Christ, I haven't really thought about this in twenty years. It's two o'clock in the morning now and suddenly I have a craving for gin. How Pavlovian. I keep a cupboard full of alcohol for guests – I think I'll get myself a London Dry and orange. Anyway, I've spent too much time on this already. I shall keep typing until the glass is empty and call it a night. I have an important meeting with my boss tomorrow, and probably a very long drive after that.

Louise and I fell into a routine. Each Friday I'd trek to Cambridge, spend the weekend, then head back early on Monday morning. But Louise was looking ahead to her Finals, and by the autumn she was suggesting that meeting every other weekend might be a more convenient arrangement. I acquiesced to this without a bleat. In fact, disappointed as I was, I think I acted as if I would have proposed exactly that, had she not got in first.

Then, one Wednesday before a scheduled Cambridge weekend, I received a call from her.

"There's a college function on Saturday. It'll be all academic shoptalk – not your thing at all. I was thinking we could meet in Euston for lunch on Sunday?"

I was stunned that she felt able to postpone me so casually, but I replied in tones of equally casual reasonableness. "No, it's okay. I'd like to come to the party. I'm sure I'll hold my own amongst the boffins."

"No – really. I'm going to be totally preoccupied with schmoozing for my post-grad. To be blunt, I don't want to feel responsible for you. You see my point, don't you?"

"Tell you what – I'll come up on Sunday and stay over, then we can have at least one night together, eh? Please?"

"All right," she agreed grudgingly. "Sunday. But I doubt I'll be at my best and brightest."

I got up at five on Sunday morning. At twenty past nine, I emerged from Cambridge station and took a cab I could ill afford to Louise's digs. One of her house-mates let me in, grumbling about the godforsakeness of the hour. I bounded up the stairs to Louise's room and opened the door. Louise was sleeping with her face to the wall, squashed between the cream wallpaper and Robin, who opened his eyes and looked at me – blankly for a moment and then with instantly-alert alarm.

"Good morning, Robin," I said. "What are you doing in bed with the woman I intend to marry?"

"Nothing!" he said panickily, sitting up. To my surprise, he was afraid of me. "Nothing. Just sleeping."

"Don't treat me like an idiot, Robin," I said wearily. "I'll go and make some coffee."

I have to analyse this. I have to understand why I didn't scream or hit someone or break down in tears. I'll think about it while I'm topping up my gin and making a sandwich.

I've got it. I didn't go berserk because that would have disempowered me. Ooh, good psychotherapy word! To put it in more pragmatic terms, I was determined not to appear disarmed by the turn of events. Any reaction but the one I managed would have left me nowhere to go other than out. But calm good manners put Robin – drinking pal Robin, blue-eyed Robin, star Cambridge undergrad pure mathematician Robin – in the position of having to be as civilised as I was. I made the bastard coffee and he had to sit there in the kitchen with me and drink it. And that, of course, was very uncomfortable for him because all he wanted to do was flee before Louise appeared, which he suspected would be more uncomfortable yet.

And appear she did, in a long red t-shirt and just-fucked hair. She slid onto a chair at the breakfast table and spooned sugar into the coffee I'd made for her.

"What bloody time do you call this?" she asked, scowling.

"Sunday morning," I said.

"I ought to be going," Robin ventured, draining his cup.

"No, no. I'm making toast," I said, again the fulsome host. He sighed and stayed put. I looked at Louise. "Good event last night?"

"Very," she said, hands clasped around her mug.

"Super."

I stood up. Robin flinched, shuffling his chair back towards the door.

"Raspberry jam or marmalade?" I asked, opening the cupboard.

"Either," he said. "Er…cigarette?"

"Yes – thank you. Oh, look, there's a jar of honey here, if you'd prefer it."

I strung breakfast out for a good half-hour. In my memory of it I made omelettes and pancakes and conjured maple syrup from the air with a wave of my cool clean hand. But, actually, the meal probably consisted just of toast slathered with discomfiture straight from the tub. And throughout the entire thing, as I bantered and Robin squirmed and Louise grimaced sullenly, all I could think of was her thighs beneath the long red t-shirt and his come slick on them like butter.

She apologised later – but only in the way that she might have apologised for spilling milk on my newspaper or rearranging my cutlery drawer unasked. The implication was that, tiresome though it was of me to be upset, it was a downside of the relationship that she'd have to tolerate. So – hey – sorry, okay? And I settled for that. *I settled for that.* Why? Because I thought that my jealousy and grief were my problem, not hers. It was my failing that I was so petty and narrow-minded, so conventional and territorial.

Just one more gin, while I finish this off. It's half-past three. If I get to bed by five I can sleep until about eleven, which'll be enough.

The summer following her finals Louise needed to be in Cambridge during the holidays, working all hours at the lab. I went up there to stay, and got a job pointing at architecture for the benefit of brightly-coloured groups of awestruck Yanks.

In the evenings I usually had Louise's place to myself – she didn't often come in before ten. Having got home soon after six, I'd make a cup of tea and turn the television on. I'd watch ten minutes or so of the news without taking a word of it in, and then perhaps I'd go to the bedroom and try to read a chapter of whatever I had on the go. I drifted from room to room like dust. Without Louise, I had no particular reason to settle anywhere. It didn't matter, because when she wasn't there I wasn't really there either. I was just a place-holder for myself. I would stand by the sink in the bathroom with the window open, staring along the road to the corner of the street. And when I caught sight of her I would run along the corridor to the front room and turn up the TV, then doubleback to the kitchen. As she came through the door. I'd be dropping a tea-bag into the cup.

"Oh, hi. Do you want a cup of tea? I'm just making one. God – what a day. I lost a tourist at Corpus Christi. Only got in about thirty seconds ago myself."

Nothing but her presence animated me and gave me purpose. Gave me anything like life, in fact.

My one respite from this pitiable golem existence was provided by Pablo. At that time he was living in some kind of artists' commune just outside Cambridge, and my mother, who hadn't heard from him for months, had insisted that I check up on his welfare. He was in one of his more reasonable phases and – not in the least coincidentally – he wasn't seeing the ghastly Natalie either. We went for a drink one early evening and it became a weekly habit. Sometimes we'd go on to a cheap pizza place, though I'd be anxious about the speed of service because I'd want to get back to the house minutes after Louise arrived home. (Not, of course, minutes before. It was important that she knew I'd been out having an independent good time.) Once in a while though, Louise would join us for something to eat when she finished at the lab. She and Pablo got on well, and as he was just about the only man of our acquaintance that she hadn't slept with, I wasn't distracted during dinner by a jerky flickbook of reconstructed filth soundtracked with the feedback screech of retrospective jealousy.

"How's it going with Louise?" Pablo asked, one December night in the pizza place. It was a cue to confide – but not one I could respond to because I didn't think that my relationship with Louise was anything other than fine. That I was so destitute and bereft without Louise was ungainsayable proof of our fathomless passion.

"Everything's superb. Never been happier," I told him.

"Sex alright, is it?" Pablo asked, flipping a cigarette. "On a scale of one to ten?"

"God, you're coarse."

Although I would never have told him so, sex with Louise was too infrequent to register on any scale at all. I would lie awake at night next to her, trembling with desperation, afraid to venture my hand across the unnegotiable inches between us. Or I would press myself to her back, moving against her, clasping my arms around her as she clenched rigid, and I would rub and chafe and whimper, wordlessly begging her to want me, to love me, huffing and gulping until I ejaculated joylessly and fell back, weeping in silence and ashamed.

Christ. One more gin, I think.

"It's none of your business, frankly," I told Pablo. "What's happened to Natalie? No longer in the picture?"

"It's a moving picture," he said. "It'll sort itself out. Or it won't. Or something."

"I don't think it will if you're so what-the-hell about it," I told him. "These things require work. Actual effort."

"That must be why you look so grey and exhausted. Another bottle of wine before we order?"

"Have you called Mum, as I told you to?" I asked as we ate.

"Not yet – there's no phone at the farm. I'll call her from Scotland this weekend."

It had been a month since I'd urged Pablo to call our mother, and one would imagine that he'd been somewhere near a phone in that time. I quite properly reprimanded him, at which he merely shrugged. "Anyway," I said, "What takes you to Scotland?"

"A friend's invited me to hang out up there for a while. I could do with a break."

"I can see how you might be exhausted from all the sitting around and thinking, or whatever it is you do all day."

"It takes it out of you, yeah," Pablo agreed.

I speared the last forkful of my pizza. "Listen – it's only nine-thirty. Come back to the flat and call Mum now. I'll pick up a bottle of wine on the way."

This suggestion didn't spring entirely from altruism. If I could persuade Pablo to speak to the Condesa she would stop phoning me to ask about him.

"Make it two bottles of wine and a sofa for the night, and you're on," Pablo said.

As we approached the house, I could see the light in the living-room, so Louise was back. I wished I'd thought to bring her a pizza. The front door was ajar, which was typical of Louise. Fridges, windows, tupperware – she was incapable of closing anything properly.

"Hey, it's me," I shouted as we stepped into the hall. "Pablo's with me, so don't wander out of the shower."

She didn't wander out of the shower. She wandered out of the bedroom, carrying the duvet and followed by Robin. He was clutching an applebox under one arm and dragging Louise's suitcase behind him. Once again I had arrived earlier than expected. And once again, Robin looked apprehensive and Louise was annoyed.

"Fuck," she sighed, looking at me.

I think it took me a moment to understand, but I got there eventually. "Oh, Christ, no," I murmured. Then I shouted. "No, Louise! Don't go – please! I'll do anything!" I was crying now. I stumbled forward and tried to drag the duvet out her arms. "Please don't go. It'll be all right. I'll make it all right."

She snatched the duvet back from me. "I can't stand it any more. I'm sorry. I'm miserably unhappy and so are you."

"I'm not! I'm not!" I sobbed. "I'm perfectly happy!"

"You'll be better off – you'll see," she said. "I'm really sorry." She pushed past me, and Robin scurried after her. I slid down the wall to the floor with my face in my hands. For the next – I don't know – fifteen minutes perhaps, I kept my eyes shut and my head down and I snivelled as Louise and Robin strode to and fro past me, ferrying her belongings out of the flat.

And the door slammed. And I wailed again, rocking back and forth, not dying but dead. I was no one. I didn't exist anymore – she was gone. I didn't open my eyes for fear of seeing nothing. Blank white. No floor or walls. No carpet or paint. A featureless universe that provided no context for me at all.

"Come into the living-room."

It was Pablo, somewhere out there in the nothing.

Eyes shut, I shook my head. There was no reason to go to the living-room. Or the kitchen. Or the bedroom. There was no reason to move, because everywhere was nowhere now.

I felt Pablo's hands on my biceps and he pulled me to my feet.

"Look at me," he said.

I opened my eyes and he was staring gravely back at me, blurred by my tears.

"What am I going to do, Pablo? What am I going to do?"

"Come into the living-room."

I collapsed on the sofa and howled. I howled all night and Pablo sat there and watched me, smoking cigarettes and running his fingers through his hair.

Jesus, I've had enough of this. Why do I have to think about all this again? It's half past five and I have things to do today. I'm going to bed.

Just to finish it off – Pablo talked me into going to Scotland with him, where I was miserable but at least out of Cambridge. I was miserable for years, actually. You get over it. Five years, more or less. You get over it.

My typing's becoming less and less accurate. I'm going to hit 'Send' and go to bed. I seem to have drunk almost an entire bottle of gin. I've got better things to do than rake up all this crap. I'm going to bed.

I've just read back everything I've written. God, I was such an idiotic, weak, pathetic excuse. My alarm has gone off. It's seven in the morning and I haven't had any sleep. If I go to bed now I can get three hours or so.

Why do you want to know all this anyway? Well, I just hope you enjoy reading it more than I've enjoyed writing it, that's all. Stupid waste of time.

Your client,

Tomàs Lyne.

*   *   *   *

Then one night there was Tom, screeching, curled up on the sofa in the house in Cambridge.

"Jesus – what am I going to do? I'm lost. I'm so fucking lost."

Pablo said nothing. He watched. From time to time, across the small hours, he made mugs of tea that Tom drank between retching tears. I watched too, pressed against the panes of Pablo's eyes.

"Oh, Jesus, fucking Jesus. What am I going to do?"

Pablo smoked, piling the dog-ends in a souvenir ashtray from Lyme Regis.

"Not Robin, that bastard," Tom sobbed. "I can't believe she'd go with him. Christ."

Pablo lit another cigarette. "Did you suspect?" It was the first time he'd spoken for three hours.

Tom mashed his eyeballs into the heels of his hands; he ground them in. "No. No. No. Didn't suspect." He dropped his hands and looked straight at Pablo. Straight at me. "I fucking knew. I fucking knew, Pablo. And I ignored it."

Looking into our eyes, he seemed to open before me, inviting me in, wanting to be made full. He was vulnerable and disarranged. He was ready for me at last.

I leapt forward against the glass of Pablo and ricocheted off. I hammered with my fists on the blank, ignorant door of him. He couldn't hear me. I was alive, priapic, slavering with the purity of Tom's misery, inhaling it through Pablo's every orifice. The stench of Tom wafted in, but I couldn't get out. I couldn't leap across the few feet to my other twin. I had supposed that I'd be able to smash through the pane of Pablo's perceptions in a cascade of glittering slow-motion smithereens. I thought that if Tom were open and loose, I could erupt from one brother and dive into the other. Not so. I needed Pablo to be as loose as Tom.

So I waited, hot and restless as he gaped wide, suppurating, a void pulsing to be filled. His miserable emptiness keened through the night, though no one but me, it seemed, understood it.

Dawn broke on the morning after, and Pablo rose from the armchair where he had sat all night while Tom wept and snivelled. He picked up the orange bucket into which Tom had puked from time to time, and he took it to the bathroom to rinse.

In the kitchen he made two cups of tea and a plate of toast.

"Here," he said, coming back to the sitting room. "Sit up. Drink some tea."

"Thanks," Tom said, gulping.

Pablo sat down. "Do you want to come to Scotland with me?"

"No. Thanks, but no."

"Why not? What are you going to do here?"

Tom sniffed. "I don't know."

"I do. You'll just sit on the sofa and feel like shit." Pablo reached for a piece of toast. "You'll feel no better in Scotland, but at least you'll get fed."

"I don't know." Tom picked up the butter knife and held it in his hand, studying it. He tapped it on his knee. He put it back on the plate. "Look – I'm sorry about all this. But thanks for staying."

Pablo lit a cigarette. "When you feel better, you won't thank me. You'll despise me for having seen you so flayed and fucked-up." He blew out smoke. "You won't be able to forgive me for it."

Tom shook his head and sipped his tea. It looked like 'no', but it meant 'yes'.

I waited.

Chapter Eleven
Dumb Luck and Cigarettes

A month or so after Pablo departed, George came to Twyborough Cross for the weekend. Over chicken curry on Friday night he said, "Is everything all right? You seem rather subdued. "

"Do I? I suppose I have been a little bereft since my house-guest flew the coop."

When Pablo left I assumed that I would never hear from him again. He didn't strike me as the type who'd arrange the occasional brunch or send newsy Christmas cards.

"Surely it's good to have the house to yourself again though?"

"Well, one would think so. You'd imagine I'd be delighted not to have to endure a fug of cigarette smoke and sandwich crusts between the sofa cushions. But, actually, I do miss having Pablo about."

"You old softy," George said.

I swallowed and patted my chest. "I wish cardamom didn't give me heartburn."

"It's our age," George said. "I've had indigestion for a month. You get used to it." He spooned lime pickle onto the side of his plate. "So did he finish writing a book for you?"

"No. Which is a pity, because I was becoming more and more convinced that there was something there. I don't expect it'll ever be completed now. Pass the rice, would you?"

The following morning an envelope dropped through my door bearing Pablo's handwriting and a Dutch stamp. Inside I found a hefty sheaf of paper and a covering letter.

Hi, Stephen,

Some pages for you. I'll keep them coming from time to time. If you want to let me know what you think, you can call me. I've got myself a new mobile phone – see the top of the page.

I'm in Amsterdam. Every fifteen minutes or so a glass-topped sightseeing boat chugs past on the canal outside, and the tourists spot me in the window at my desk. They often wave, and I wave back. I wonder if the guides have got used to me being on show, and have incorporated me into their spiel. "On the right you can see a typical mediaeval house. Note the stepped gable, the hook at the top for winching furniture into the windows, and, on the second floor, the Englishman with the low-tars and two bottles of Pinot."

I fell in love with this apartment the first evening I saw it. A girl I knew lived here, and six years ago she decided to sell, asking the equivalent of two hundred thousand pounds. I'd never before wanted anything that cost serious money and I was penniless. But I offered her the asking price and told her I'd pay cash at the end of the month. Then I went out and obtained the necessary.

No one in England knows about my home here and I'd like to keep it that way, which is why I haven't given an address. Has Natalie been bothering you since I left? Please tear the phone number off and eat it. You'd be astonished what that woman can dig up, given an inkling that there's anything to be discovered.

Talk to you soon.

Pablo

I called the number immediately, lodging the telephone under my chin as I filled the kettle.

"Hello, Stephen," Pablo said blearily. "Have you read my stuff?"

I could hear George moving about upstairs, so I took two tea-mugs from the cupboard.

"Er, no. Just the covering letter."

"Oh. Okay. What are you calling for then?"

I had no idea. All of a sudden I felt a little foolish.

"I just wanted to let you know it had arrived safely."

"That's a relief," Pablo said, deadpan.

There was a short pause. "Are you at your desk in the window overlooking the canal?" I said.

"I just woke up. It's only nine o'clock, you know."

"Ah. Sorry."

Again a pause. George wandered into the kitchen and I nodded towards the toaster as I opened the bread bin. He took the loaf out and began to slice it.

"So – if you don't mind my asking – how did you get the money for the Amsterdam apartment? And Limehouse, come to that?"

Pablo yawned. "I'll write a bit about it. How's things with you?"

"Oh, much the same."

"Did the people come for the trees?"

I hesitated. "Yes – thank you."

I could hear Pablo lighting a cigarette. "Well, call me when you've read the stuff so far."

"I will," I said, making the tea. "I'm looking forward to it."

"And I'm enjoying writing it. Thanks for persuading me to. I owe you."

"The work is all down to you, my friend. Like a signpost, I just set you off in that particular direction."

"Was that your waif?" George asked when I hung up.

"It was." I indicated the envelope on the table. "He's still writing, I'm pleased to say."

"And he feels indebted to you?"

"Authors often overestimate the momentum gained from tiny pushes. You see it in their acknowledgements. Long lists of everyone who ever patted or stroked them as they made their way to the podium."

"I think you deprecate yourself." George sugared his tea. "Just as you take no credit for all your altruistic effort on behalf of Sub Judice."

I lifted the toast from the toaster and buttered it, slotting each slice into the rack. "I've been thinking about what you said – about how I was living Leo's life. If you're right, my motives for putting so much of myself into Sub Judice were selfish, weren't they? Not in the least altruistic."

George took a piece of toast and bit it. "I look at it this way," he said, mumbling through crumbs. "The work is all down to you, my friend. Like a signpost, Leo just set you off in that particular direction."

I laughed. "Sometimes I forget that you make a living from arguing."

*   *   *   *

Dumb luck and cigarettes. When we're looking for a title for this stuff, Stephen, that might do.

Not far from here, a stroll along the Prince's Canal, there's a gallery called de Parelboom *– the Pearl Tree – in which one of my installations is a permanent fixture.*

It didn't require any real effort to make – I just had to talk some suppliers into giving me the machines. There's a photo-booth to take your picture, a bucket full of loose change and a supply of glue. But the important element of the work is one of those Penny Falls machines that you see in arcades. You drop the coins into slots at the top and they push each other over a series of sliding steps until a handful of coppers cascades into the hopper beneath.

As soon as someone has stuck their face to a coin and dropped it in, they become intensely interested in its inconsequential and random progress through the game. They'll hang around for hours watching other people put their pennies in and they become very excited as their coin edges towards the drop. "Hey, the blonde guy's pushing me! You! Look – you're shoving me out of the way!" When the piece first went on show at de Parelboom *the crowd around it was four-deep and the queue to make penny-portraits trailed right out to the street.*

On the evening of the opening, the gallery owner tugged me around, introducing me to a succession of faces with whom I tried to make small talk. I'm not good at it. Eventually I snaffled a bottle of wine, bought cigarettes from the vending machine and sneaked up the backstairs to the roof terrace. I perched on the wall and looked out over the gables of Amsterdam.

The door from the stairway opened and a svelte, grey-haired man in his fifties emerged. He lipped a cigarette and nodded at me.

"U ook ontnapt voor een paar minuten, hé?"

"I'm sorry," I said. "My Dutch isn't good. If you repeat that very, very slowly, I might get it."

"You've escaped for a few minutes also, eh?" he said, immediately dropping into perfect and barely-accented English.

"Yeah. I can't do the chat."

He lit his cigarette and leaned back against the wall. "My wife insists I come with her. I don't understand most of this art myself."

"Don't you like it?"

He shrugged. "It's not Picasso, is it? Did you see that one with the game from the amusement arcade? Interesting crazy idea – but as art, it's a joke."

"Perhaps it's meant to be."

"Yes, maybe. In that case, I'd like it."

I grinned and he looked directly at me, then rolled his eyes. "Ach – typical. You're the artist, I suppose."

I admitted I was.

He laughed. "I'm Piet Visser. Nice to meet you." As we shook hands he said, in the casually direct way the Dutch have, "So you make good money as a joke-artist? How much do you ask for the arcade game, for example?"

I had just come from a lunch date with the woman who owned the apartment in which I now live. I'd promised her that by the end of the month I'd pony up half a million guilders – so that's the figure I gave.

"Does that include the pennies?" Piet asked. "Or are they extra?"

"You Dutch drive a hard bargain," I told him. "What do you do for a living?"

"I'm a Director of Marketing," he said. He held up his cigarette. "These."

"Difficult job, I imagine."

"Exact. I'm the most low cockroach in a profession crawling with vermin."

As we stood on the roof watching dusk settle on the canal, Piet talked about the problems of marketing cigarettes. "What the industry needs," he said, "is an image improvement. Even the people who buy our product hate us. And to the others we're worse than heroin dealers."

I took the fresh pack of smokes from my pocket and unwound the tape that held the small change.

"That's our brand," Piet said, nodding at the carton

"Listen," I said, sticking the tape to an air-conditioning vent, "could you get me into a meeting of the Board of your company?"

He raised his eyebrows. "Why?"

"Because I have interesting crazy ideas."

*   *   *   *

"Thanks for letting me come in at such short notice," I said to the members of the Board of van Brug Tabak. "I'll be very quick."

I'd bought a suit and I'd shaved. It was vital that I inspire confidence in the nine men sitting around the long oak table in front of me, and I'm not so contrary as to deliberately undermine my chances.

I held up a brown envelope. "This is what I'm here to offer. The contents of this envelope will save your company money – not a huge amount, but some. That's not the important bit though. It'll also give you some high moral ground to stand on. It'll make the government reluctant to raise the tax on cigarettes. And – as if all that weren't enough – it'll help find a cure for cancer."

I tossed the envelope onto the table.

"Would you like it?" I said.

There was a short silence and then all the guys along the sides of the table turned to look at the big man at the top – a squat, bristly chap without much by way of a nose. He looked like a friendly though hirsute toad.

"If you present your proposal," he said, "we'll assess it and pay you what we think it's worth."

I shook my head. "No, sorry. It's a very simple idea. Once you've got it, I wouldn't be able to take it back. I'm asking you to gamble. You give me a banker's draft and I'll give you the envelope."

The toad shifted in his seat. "And how much do you want for it?"

"I'm English," I said. "So my idea of an impressive amount of money racks up in sterling. I'd like a million pounds. Say, three million guilders."

There was a spontaneous group gulp from the junior members of the Board, and the toad said, "Out of the question."

"Okay," I said. I picked up the envelope. "If you'll excuse me, I must dash. I have a similar meeting with the Board of Rood Galjoen Tobacco at two o'clock."

That wasn't true, but it didn't need to be.

"Wait," said the toad. "We need to discuss this. Can we have an hour?"

I nodded. "Certainly. Is there somewhere in this building I can smoke?"

I was shown to the cafeteria, where I ordered coffee and a pastry. Having no book to read, I watched the lady behind the counter making sandwiches. She spread the butter with the back of a spoon, which looked to me much easier and more efficient than using a knife. An hour and a half passed. I couldn't imagine what they were discussing all this time. It wasn't as if debate was going to give them any more to go on. The decision was very simple – either, "Yes, let's chance it" or "No, let's have him beaten up in the car park." I decided that I'd give them another thirty minutes.

"Mr Lyne?"

"Hi."

"Would you come back to the meeting, please?"

"I'm sorry for the delay," said the toad as I sat down. "We were waiting for a courier from the bank." He nodded at the man sitting to my left who showed me the draft for three million guilders, though he kept it out of my reach.

"Let me ask you, Mr Lyne," the toad continued, "how do we know that there is anything in that envelope at all?"

"You don't," I said.

"And how do you know that we won't just take the envelope and refuse to give you the draft?"

"I don't."

He smiled. "Piet tells me you're an artist. Are you sure you've chosen the right profession?" He nodded at the guy with the banker's draft who handed it to me, not without obvious reluctance.

"Thank you." I put the draft in the right-hand pocket of my new suit and took the envelope from the left one. "There you go," I said, sliding it onto the table. "Would you like me to stay while you open it?"

"At these prices, Mr Lyne, I think it would be nice to have it from the horse's mouth. Is that the correct expression?"

"Okay. Mind if I smoke?"

"I insist."

I produced a pack of cigarettes that I'd bought from a vending machine at a bar the previous evening.

"Look at the change you attach to these packs," I said. "It must be terribly labour-intensive sorting out the few cents to the right sum and sticking them on. It probably costs as much as the change itself. And no one cares. It's an amusing irritation."

I stripped off the tape and peeled the small change into my hand.

"So – you announce that you're not going to be putting these few coppers on the vending machine packs anymore. Instead you're going to donate the money directly to cancer research. You make a big publicity deal of it."

I tossed the coins onto the table, and they rolled towards the Managing Director.

"The next time the government's thinking of raising the tax on cigarettes you remind everyone that your donation to medical science is only the difference between the retail price of the cigarettes and the next convenient half-guilder that the vending machines will take. So, if the government puts the price up, they'll be depriving the researchers of funds."

Taking out a cigarette, I tossed it neatly into my mouth and snapped open my lighter.

"In short – you reduce the cost of sale; you get to come over philanthropic; and you put the government in a difficult position in the eyes of the public."

I lit my cigarette and took a very deep drag, which caught me wrong and I coughed, spluttering and thumping my chest with my fist.

"It's a good idea," said the toad while I hacked. "It might even be worth the price." He instructed one of his colleagues to slide the envelope down the table to him. "Tell me," he said, "what do you plan to do with all that money?"

I wiped my eyes and wheezed.

"I thought I might buy some lungs," I said.

*   *   *   *

Having money changed a few administrative invisibilities in my life – for instance, I owned the floors on which I dropped my clothes at night – but it didn't have any other effect. There wasn't anything I really wanted to spend money on once I'd bought the apartments in Amsterdam and Limehouse.

That summer Jazz returned from the Antipodes for a month in order to show off her new man, Scott. At that time he owned a steak restaurant back in New Zealand. Jazz invited Tom and me to meet him at a bar in South London, and I liked him immediately. I like anyone who swears on a first date.

"No more fucking about in Christchurch – we need to open up in Oz," he said. "Target the major cities. The timing's fucking perfect."

"I can run the business in NZ while Scott sets up branches in Australia," Jazz put in. "All we need is money. A couple of hundred thou would be a start."

"I'm going to look for investors as soon as we get the fuck home," Scott said.

Tom sat back in his chair, shaking his head. "I don't want to tell you your business, of course," he said, "but I've dabbled in the catering trade. It's really high-risk. I can't see anyone putting up that kind of money without some collateral."

My brother's pompous antipathy was all I needed. The following day I went to Scott and Jazz's hotel.

"I've got two hundred grand going spare," I told them. "I don't need it."

They were a little surprised – incredulous, even – but Jazz is her father's daughter. Within two days she'd organised legal documents and shoved them under my nose.

"Get a lawyer to check it all out," she advised.

"I don't suppose you're going to cheat me," I said as I signed. I imagined all those greenbacks that had languished, dispirited, in my account now flourishing in Scott's, flexing their biceps and running on the spot, eager to do something useful. "But I don't want anyone to know about this, okay?"

"Why not?"

"I have my reputation as a feckless layabout to consider."

The truthful answer was that Tom, if he knew I had access to real funds, would start pestering me to invest and speculate and generally feed the slot machine that would pay out our inheritance. That wasn't why I'd given Scott and Jazz the money – I just thought that it was more valuable to them than to me. Still, when I signed Jazz's paper I bought a large stake in the company and, as dumb luck would have it, Scott turned out to be some kind of entrepreneurial genie. Every year he sends me a fat cheque, each more grossly swollen than its predecessor. Jazz tells me that these dividends are only a fraction of the company's worth. Apparently I'm a very rich feckless layabout.

Perdito was delighted that we had access to cash at last. The Limehouse apartment had been his choice – too close to Natalie's house for my liking and too immodestly modern for my taste. And he insisted that it be decorated in gut-churning merry-go-round colours and furnished in as many textures as the sample swatches could offer. The effect wasn't exactly understated. It gave me a headache.

But at that time – a couple of years either side of the turn of the century – everything gave me a headache. The part of my life that followed making lots of money is blurred in my memory. My body ricocheted to and fro between London and Amsterdam, and also between Perdito and myself, and my mind lagged behind somehow.

"You haven't done any work at all since we made the Cash Fountain," Natalie said. "What's wrong with you? You were on the verge of real success there."

Behind her, out of the window, were the boats in the Limehouse Basin. If I focussed my eyes just so, I could make her head a huge ball spiked on top of one of the masts. Or I could force a shift in perspective so that her face became a little bubble floating an inch in front of me. I was tired. Perdito had been in the driving seat for most of the preceding two days and he'd *dragged me around the clubs of the West End, dancing, drinking, sprinting along Oxford Street at dawn. I was approaching forty, for God's sake, and I couldn't take that kind of pace anymore. Didn't want to.*

"I haven't got the urge to be creative," I said. That wasn't true. Art would have been a relaxation – but I lacked the energy to fight Perdito for space and silence. He was a constant, insistent buzz that prevented me from thinking straight. I could no more ignore him than you can ignore a hornet in a hot car. I was distracted every minute. There were scorch-marks on the counters in the kitchen and on the windowsills where I'd put down and forgotten burning cigarettes. I rarely ate. I couldn't be bothered to. And anyway, when Perdito was in control, he ate like a waste-disposal. I just smoked cigarettes to keep myself awake and drank wine to help me sleep. Open books lay flat all over the bedroom floor – having started one, I couldn't concentrate. In bed, eyes watering, I'd read the same page again and again, but not a word stuck.

I was a passenger in my own body. I was covered in bruises I didn't deserve. I was taking drugs I didn't enjoy. I was waking up in beds that I hadn't chosen. The more frequently I allowed Perdito to drive, the less I controlled our speed and direction. And his pursuit of sensation seemed an attempt to stifle a growing jadedness. He wasn't getting the buzz he'd once enjoyed, and his solution was to go faster, skid further, taking every corner with his foot down. He was discovering that there were limits to what the vehicle could do, and it frustrated him.

One morning, after riding shotgun while Perdito went on a spectacular all-night cocaine bender, I found myself standing at the entrance to Clapham Common underground station in rush-hour drizzle, exhausted and weak. I bought a ticket and joined the damp and silent commuters carried down to the crowded platform, and I jostled for position amongst the umbrellas and parkas. I was standing close to the edge of the platform, ready to sidle to the spot nearest the opening doors of the packed train. There was only one guy between me and the platform's edge, so my odds were good.

My back hurt. My chest hurt. And my feet, that had walked coke-fuelled miles around London all night, were blistered and sore. As the warm whoosh of wind from the tunnel heralded the next northbound train, I shifted my weight from one raw foot to the other. At that moment the guy in front of me bent to pick up his briefcase and my knee caught him – just hard enough – on the arse. He teetered forward over the edge of the platform arms grabbing backwards as the train roared out of the tunnel. I reached, grasped his elbow and yanked him to me, turning him – and the train rattled past, swiping through the block of air in which he'd been hanging a half-second before.

We clasped each other, both panting with shock and relief. There was no anger or apology – just the eye-to-eye realisation that one of us was very nearly dead. As the carriage doors slid open we let go, still wordless but exchanging nods. He turned and pushed onto the train. I stood back, clammy with sweat.

I could have killed him. Had the train hit that guy, he would have exploded in front of me. Dumb luck – just as my father's death was dumb luck. Or, if my feet hadn't hurt, I wouldn't have moved at that instant and he'd have gone to work as he always did, having come no closer to death than breathing takes you. One penny pushes against another – no history to it, no intention behind it – and something happens, or it doesn't. It's just how the penny falls.

I boarded the next train, shaky and dry-mouthed.

"It would have been an accident," Perdito said. "Everyone would have said so."

I was surprised to hear him. After a night like he'd just orchestrated he tended to be quiet for days.

"The guy would have been just as dead, accident or not," I said. My body was pulsing with adrenalin; crimson-spattered images of other outcomes were flash-carding before my mind's eye.

"But what would that be like? I mean, killing someone?" It was my jangling alarm that had roused Perdito, I realised – the snapshots in my head and the chemicals in my veins. "Just accidentally, obviously."

He fell silent, but I could feel him slurping up the sticky overspill of my shock.

I got off the train at Stockwell to change for the Victoria line. As I was walking down the escalator, Perdito tugged at my foot and I stumbled into a woman carrying a portfolio case. I apologised and hurried on.

"What did you do that for?" I asked him. He'd never before taken control, however briefly, without my permission. He'd managed it then only because I hadn't been expecting it.

"It was just a muscle spasm or something, from the coke," he said. "Weird, huh?"

But it wasn't. I'd felt his touch. He was testing his strength, and I knew why. Perdito had seen a way to turbocharge his experience of the world.

*   *   *   *

Three days after the night of the chicken curry, my phone rang as I was getting ready for bed.

"Mr Richmond? Margaret Slattery here."

George's PA. "Good evening, Margaret. How are you?"

"I'm afraid George has had a heart attack. He's at St Thomas's."

I got there at eight the following morning.

"How are you feeling?"

His face was the colour of porridge, and his eyes were barely open. A heart monitor beside the bed bleeped constantly, which ought to have been reassuring, but it sounded to me like a repeated threat.

George managed a smile. "I still say it's indigestion," he whispered.

I sat with him for a quarter of an hour or so, making trivial conversation. Margaret arrived with flowers and best wishes from colleagues. I promised to come in again that evening, and I withdrew to the corridor where I waited for Margaret to emerge.

"I feel so awful," she said as we walked to the car park. "It's my niece's wedding tomorrow. I have to drive up to York, but I feel I should be here."

"There's nothing you can do at the moment," I said.

She showed me the keys in her hand. "But he asked me to fetch a file from his house and…"

"I'll get it," I said. "Just tell me what he wants."

"Would you? I hate to be a bother."

"It's no trouble."

"He asked me to destroy it at first. But then he changed his mind and told me to bring it in to him."

"I'll make sure it gets to him safely. Go to the wedding and try to enjoy yourself."

George had lived in the same small mews house in Kensington since the late sixties, and a lifetime's bric-a-brac had accumulated there. The walls of the tiny study were covered top-to-bottom with files and ring-binders. I was looking for a lever-arch file to the right of the desk. On the spine I'd see 'P & J' in orange felt-tip pen – which, I noticed, was an uncharacteristically cryptic designation for George to have given. Most of the labels were precise and self-explanatory: *Utility Bills 90's*; *House Insurance Docs*; *Michael & Helen (Correspondence)*.

It took only a minute to find the file in question. I pulled it out and tucked it under my arm. I had no intention at all of reading its contents. But as I turned to leave the study, my elbow knocked against the desklamp and in an attempt to stop it from toppling, I dropped the file which fell open on the floor at my feet. As I bent to pick it up I couldn't help noticing a word in the first paragraph of the document facing me. *Patti*.

It was a letter dated March 2002. Stooped over, I read it.

Dear George,

I've been going through Patti's papers which is a job I've been putting off for weeks. I found a bundle of your letters to her and I think the best thing is to send them back to you. Please find enclosed.

I didn't thank you properly at the funeral for coming. Obviously I wasn't quite myself. It was strange meeting you face to face after all this time. I know Patti would have been pleased you were there. I told the kids you were an old friend of hers from London which was true of course.

The kids and their respective 'other-halves' have been a great help and comfort to me these last couple of months. Jonathan stayed until the end of January but he had to get back to his job. I'm hoping to go out there in the autumn.

I don't suppose we'll meet again but I'd like to thank you for all you did for Patti, not only before I met her but since. We were both grateful for your discretion all those years.

Yours truly,

Ed R.

I picked the file up and sat back in George's swivel chair, staring at the letter. There was a lot to understand. Patti was dead. She'd married and had children. And George had kept in touch with her – secretly. I undid the clip that held the documents in place and I flicked through. Astonished though I was, I did have the good manners to feel guilty about looking at George's private papers, but my over-riding feeling was one of betrayal. George had kept this from me. From *me*. Had he walked in at that moment, my sense of outrage would have been my defence against accusations of snooping.

George's letters to Patti were interspersed in precise chronological order with hers to him. The earliest was dated *7th December 1967*, from an address in Worcester.

Dearest George,

I should have followed up my phone call rather sooner, but things have been hectic, as you can imagine.

I'd forgotten how steadfastly Victorian people are out here in the sticks. Ladbroke Grove this most certainly is not! I've found a place now, thank God. Just a tiny house but very nicely presented and, most importantly, sharing with another girl my age, as opposed to some dry old witch who assumes I'm a fallen woman. I couldn't have managed these last months without your generosity and please be assured I shall repay you one day. It might not be this week though!

I have invited my mother for lunch on Christmas, but she hasn't replied. I'm not too worried. Eventually she'll get over the shock of having raised a hussy and once she sees Jonathan she'll forgive me everything.

You'd adore him. He's a delightful chubby little thing, always smiling, no trouble at all. Masses of dark hair and the most intelligent eyes. Leo's eyes, actually. Sometimes when he looks at me...

It still hurts, of course. No one understands better than you. I may never get over it but I'd rather be miserable without Leo than with him.

You're in an impossible position, George, but I have to ask you not to forward any more correspondence from Leo. The note when Jonathan was born was heartbreaking. But even that – beautiful and sincere though it was – reminded me of how sick Leo is. He'll never change. Perhaps if I were on my own... God, I don't want to talk about it. Don't send me news of him, even if I beg. I do have moments of weakness and the last thing I need is to have them indulged.

There's no phone here in the new place, but please write. Tell me what exciting things are going on in London – parties, clubs, who's being naughty with who! It'll brighten up my day.

All my love,

Patti.

I wiped my eyes with the back of my hand and turned the pages. A letter every few weeks. Patti meeting someone; George not meeting anyone;

Jonathan crawling; Jonathan walking; Jonathan talking. I was faint and breathless, but no longer furtive. I read on. There was a letter from George dated October 4th, 1970.

Dear Patti,

I'm afraid I have news from which I can't protect you. I wish I could.

Leo died in the early hours of this past Friday, 2nd October. He'd been drinking heavily all day at the flat. Stephen and I found him.

The details are sordid and upsetting, but it seems to have been unintentional. An inevitable accident, one might say. I think you should know that he appears to have been celebrating Jonathan's birthday. There was a cake, and Stephen tells me that Leo had talked about throwing a party (though the significance of that was lost on poor Stephen, of course).

I really don't know what else I can say. He's to be buried at the church near Twyborough Cross and the funeral will have taken place by the time you get this. His suffering is over now, for which perhaps we should be grateful. For those of us that loved him, a new suffering begins.

I feel that I've lost Leo for a third time. The first was when I came to understand that I would never be close to him in the way I so wanted. Then, when he changed wretchedly after the accident, I lost him again. And now he's gone completely and I'm distraught.

I can talk to no one but you about what Leo meant to me. I expect you feel the same. Please call me. I'm unutterably sad and alone. Only you can comprehend how ghastly it all is.

Ever your friend,

George.

I closed the file and stood up, shaking. I left the house and hurried to the main street. I had to talk to George. However ill, he was obliged to explain. I had a nephew. Leo had known about his son. George had known too. Was I not to be trusted with all this? What reason could there possibly be for excluding me? Those closest to me had conspired in silence.

But a nephew!

Furious and excited, despondent and confused, I clutched the file to my chest and looked up and down the street for a taxi. I waved at one cruising on the far side of the road and it turned, waiting for a gap in the traffic.

"Come on, come on," I muttered – and I felt a white hammer-shot of pain to the side of my head, and my legs buckled.

That's the last I remember until a voice said my name in the darkness.

"Mr Richmond? Do you know where you are?"

I couldn't reply. I seemed to have no control over my tongue. In any case, I had no answer to give, because I hadn't the slightest idea where I was.

I was blind.

*   *   *   *

For the first time since I'd been aware of Perdito, I was frightened by him.

"I know what you're thinking, Perdito. If you kill someone, I'll be held responsible."

"Not if it's an accident."

Perdito saw the law like a ferret sees the wire around a chicken coop – just an obstacle to be negotiated. To be the blameless bystander in a fatal misadventure would get him inside the run. He could sink his fangs into fluffy newborn chicks without taking the rap for opening the gate.

"No – I'll be responsible because I'll know, whatever anyone else says."

"That's stupid. You're the one who believes everything is dumb luck."

For a long time I'd been ground between the twin rocks of conflicting culpabilities – the long-term guilt of having been lucky enough to smother Perdito; and the close and present blame I bore for all that Perdito did when he was in the driving seat – the fights he started, the women he abused, the hotel rooms he wrecked, the chaos in his wake. I wasn't sure he'd really attempt to kill anyone. And there was nothing I could do about it anyway, other than refuse him access to the world. But that wouldn't have been just. You can't lock someone away in anticipation of what they might do one day.

On the first morning of 2003 – that is, the day after my fortieth birthday – I came round in a police cell and I had no recollection of how I'd arrived there. That had never happened before. I had always known what Perdito had got up to, as if I watched from the rail. But this time, like a werewolf returning to human form naked at the zoo, I was blank about the events of the previous night.

"Perdito?"

No response. I sat up and gave myself the once-over. My head was throbbing. My belt was missing and I had no shoes on. My knuckles were bruised and it hurt to flex my fingers. I wondered who I'd hit, and how hard. Very hard, by the state of my hands. But, apart from the bang on my forehead, there was not a mark on me.

The door of the cell opened and in came a thin, stooped sergeant of about my age.

"How's your head?" he asked.

That, to my relief, didn't sound like the kind of question a policeman would ask a murderer.

"It's pretty empty. Embarrassing question but – where am I?"

"Hook police station. No idea why you're here, huh?" He handed me my sneakers. "Come and have a cuppa."

In the canteen I was given tea and a bacon sandwich.

"Don't remember me, do you?" the copper said. "Darren Ellison. I used to do your history homework in exchange for dirty magazines."

I peered at him. "No," I said. "Don't remember you at all. Sorry."

"Charming. So what were you on last night? Speed? Spirits? Both?"

I shrugged. "No idea. Have you got a fag I could ponce?"

He went to another table and came back with a box of matches and two cigarettes.

"The last thing I remember," I said, lighting one, "is walking across the concourse at Waterloo station."

I'd been awake for three days. At Christmas I'd promised Perdito he could take the wheel during the New Year break and our birthday. By the time we boarded a train on New Year's Eve, I was phasing in and out, losing it.

"What did I do? Am I going to be charged?"

"Not this time," Ellison said.

He told me that at midnight the police had received a call about a disturbance in Beeches Avenue. It was me, pounding with my fists on the door of my mother's house.

"Don't ignore me! Let me in! It's me – Perdito! Let me in."

Ellison dunked a biscuit. "I suppose 'Perdito' is a pet name, is it?"

"Sort of."

The house was dark, but apparently I didn't believe there was no one home. I climbed onto the porch and tried to prise open the window of my old bedroom using a splintered branch from the shrubbery. At that point a squad car arrived. Ellison recognised me immediately.

"Pablo? Pablo Lyne?" he said, standing on the lawn. "What are you playing at?"

I looked down at him and he could see I was crying. "I just want to see my mother. It's my birthday. I've never in my whole life spoken to her on my birthday."

"There's no one there, Pablo. Why don't you come down and we'll wait for her?"

"I've never spoken to her at all. Can you imagine that? Never even spoken to my own mother."

"Pablo…"

"I'm not fucking Pablo!" I screamed. "He stole my blood. Everything."

"Okay. I just want you to come down. Take your time."

"I exist," I sobbed, sitting disconsolately on the windowsill. "Look at me." I held my hands up, palms exposed. "I'm not Pablo. I'm not Tom." I lifted my feet and waved them in the air. "I move my feet. I make my feet move. On my own. See?"

I lost my balance. I slid feet-first off the porch and dropped to the path, sprawling face down. I was motionless as Darren Ellison and his colleague came to help me up.

"I feel everything," I said, and I slammed fist into the crazy paving. "Felt that."

They hauled me upright and I allowed myself to be led to the squad car, in which I immediately threw up.

"It wasn't pleasant," Ellison said.

I lit the other cigarette. "Sorry."

"I've had worse shouts on New Year's Eve. So what you doing these days? Got a job?"

"Nope."

"On drugs?"

"Intermittently."

He shook his head. "You look like shit. How did you get into this state?"

I shrugged again. Now I'd ascertained that I hadn't killed anyone, all I wanted was to go back to sleep.

"It's a real waste," Ellison said. "You were far and away the brightest kid in our year – just lazy. You could have done the homework ten times better than me." He took a card from his pocket and pushed it across the table. "Go and see these people. They're good – not just busybodies. They'll help you sort yourself out."

"Thank you. Can I get my wallet and stuff now?"

"Yeah. Come on."

I was given my belongings and Darren showed me to the door of the station.

"You get yourself straight, Pablo – all right?"

"I will. Thanks."

"By the way – whatever happened to your brother? See much of him?"

I nodded. "We're inseparable."

*   *   *   *

For want of anywhere else to go, I walked towards Beeches Avenue. I thought I'd drop in on the Condesa so she could wish me a belated Happy Birthday.

Ellison was right – I was in a state. And I couldn't see any chance of things improving. It wasn't as if I could evict Perdito. I had no mechanism for doing so and no right even to consider it. But I was truly scared by my lack of any memory of the previous night's escapade. Christ knew what my brother might do without me to chaperone him. It looked as if I would spend the rest of my life wincing and apologising. Or serving twenty-five to thirty without leave to appeal.

When I reached the house, I was dismayed to see Tom's flashy car parked in the drive. I wasn't up to sparring with him over elevenses. I was about to skedaddle but Mum came out to put the milk bottles in the porch and she spotted me lurking behind the lilac.

"Pablito! What a lovely surprise!"

Tom was sitting at the kitchen table and he raised his eyebrows when I walked in.

"Both my boys together!" the Condesa said, putting the kettle on. "We just this minute get home ourselves, Pablo. Tom took me to the Ritz for New Year party last night – such a wonderful place. And the bedrooms! So beautiful!"

"And where did you see the year in?" Tom asked me. He looked me up and down. "In a dungeon?"

"Yes."

"I have a Christmas cake here," the Condesa said, oblivious of the exchange between Tom and me. "I find some birthday candles."

"Nice of you to take mum out for the night," I said as the Condesa bustled away to the other room. "Are you driving back to London later?"

"No. I've somewhere to go on to."

"Lucky you." I took out a pack of cigarettes I'd bought on the way from the police station and I turned it over in my hands. The next question was going to cause ructions but I couldn't see any way round it. "Could you lend me a tenner? I seem to have left myself without a bean."

"Perhaps you shouldn't have spent money on cigarettes."

"Yeah – I wasn't thinking. I'm not feeling too clever at the moment." I twisted the cellophane off the smokes. "I'd rather not have to ask mum."

Tom produced his wallet and opened it. "We'll just add it to the forty grand you owe me, shall we?" he said wearily.

"Thanks," I said, reaching for the ten-pound note.

And as I touched it, I saw me. For a flash, I seemed to be looking at myself from my brother's perspective. And I felt a thrill as I looked at him, exactly like the thrill I feel from Perdito when he takes the wheel. Then I was back again, looking at Tom – and he was wearing an expression of stunned surprise. It had happened to him too – I knew it had.

"Tom?" I said.

He remained stone-still for a moment and then he stood up brusquely, pushing the chair backwards and stuffing his wallet into his back pocket.

"I've got to go," he said. He looked pale suddenly, and jumpy.

The Condesa came back in. "No, no – please stay for cake, Tom. Look – I found candles."

"Really, I have to go, mum." He bent to kiss her cheek. "I hope you enjoyed yourself last night."

She followed him to the door. "Happy birthday, darling. Thank you for taking me – I had a lovely time."

I took a cigarette from the pack and held it between my fingers, rolling it to and fro. Perdito was awake, I could tell, but he was feigning sleep. He made me wary, like an intermittent headache that might not be hurting right now but you know it's going to stab you behind the eyes at any second.

"This is very nice, you coming," the Condesa said as she made tea. "I don't see you enough these days. Are you working? And where are you living?"

"I've got a place in the East End."

"So you write down the address, okay?"

"I move about a lot. You can always get me through Natalie."

"Oh – that is still going on? I never know with you two."

I was pushing Mum away, I realised, which was the last thing I wanted to do just then. But it had been like that all my life.

One day and forty years previously the Condesa was in labour, alone and unable to speak English, in a military hospital in Samoa. Tom had been born in the Solomon Islands before the US Airforce lifted Mum and the newborn out of the path of a typhoon, and Dad had been left behind with my sister. The pre-natal care in the Solomons had been pretty rudimentary and Mum didn't even know that she was having another baby. Two other babies, actually.

So the circumstances of our birth were pretty traumatic for her. First she was told that there was a foetus embedded in me. Then she had to consent to an operation to remove it, which was risky. They had no way of knowing whether my internal organs were as they should be, and they wouldn't find out until they sliced me open. There was a real chance of me dying.

It was over a week before my dad could get to Samoa, so after all her grief and confusion the Condesa had to bury the lost child, and mourn alone while caring for the surviving boys. You can see why she'd rather forget the whole thing. She's avoided ever talking to me about it and I haven't pushed the subject since my late teens.

But I wanted to talk to her now. The symbiosis that had sustained Perdito and me was falling apart. Recently he'd felt like a parasite. I was ashamed of that thought; I was angry with my twin; I was scared; I was exhausted and sick and I wanted my mum. But I had no language to say that.

"Yes, talk to her." Perdito's voice was a whisper in my head. "Ask her about me."

The Condesa was putting a few candles on a small Christmas cake. "Now – you blow them out. Is a bit of fun, hm?" She struck a match and held it to each wick. "I love candles."

I blew.

"Make a wish!" she said, clapping.

I blew out the candles, and then leaned back in my chair and put the unlit cigarette into the corner of my mouth. I wished my dad was there. I could talk to him.

"I'm going to have a fag in the garden," I said, getting up. "Back in a minute."

As I opened the back door, Perdito leapt forward in my head and grabbed the wheel. I was taken by surprise, too slow to stop myself turning and saying, "Did you see Perdito? Before he was buried?"

The Condesa froze for a moment in the act of reaching for the sugar on the shelf. And then, as if the pause button had been released, she took the bowl down and put it on the table, and then hurried out into the hall and went upstairs without a word.

I wrested control back from Perdito and walked into the garden.

"Don't ever do that again," I said. I sat on the low wall of the patio and lit my cigarette.

"Let me talk to her! Perdito screamed. "You've got no right to keep me from my own mother!"

He was struggling to take charge again. I could feel him jerking at my legs, and they twitched and shook.

"Stop it."

After the complete shut-out he'd pulled off the previous night, I wasn't at all sure I could keep him at bay, and I didn't want him pursuing Mum all over the house, interrogating her. I walked down the side-return to the street and headed back towards the station. Still he yelled, digging me in the ribs, rifling through my mind like a burglar looking for the key to the safe.

"Fucking stop it," I muttered. "Leave me alone. Just fuck off, Perdito."

I shook my head as if it that might dislodge him. I must have presented a worrying sight – unshaven, bruised, three-day old clothes, shambling along the avenue muttering obscenities, twitching and wincing with a cigarette hanging from my lip.

"Let me! My turn! My turn!"

"Fuck off!" I yelled, grabbing two handfuls of my hair.

"No!"

My legs buckled and I sat down heavily on the front wall of the house I was passing. I felt a needle-jab behind my sternum and I tensed, my whole body shuddering, arms rigid against the brick.

"Perdito…"

"My turn!!

I was jolted by spasms, the cigarette crumbling in my tight fist, my head whipping side to side. Another thin spike of pain jabbed within my chest and I doubled up. Across the road a man walking his dog stopped to look at me. Trembling, drooling, rocking to and fro, I looked up and my eyes met his. He turned and walked on as if he hadn't noticed me.

"Jesus!" I groaned as another spike was rammed into my throat. Gulping for air, I toppled over the wall onto the front lawn of the house, convulsing, my arms wrapped around my ribs as I tried to hold myself together. I could feel foam on my lips and my head was swelling, tight, about to burst. I writhed on the grass as if I were on fire. The pain ebbed.

"Go on – kill me," I panted. "Then what happens to you, you stupid fuck?"

"I don't need you!" Perdito howled. "I don't fucking need you!"

On my back, I tried to breathe slowly, straightening my legs.

"Good," I said breathlessly. I looked up at the grey sky, featureless and matt, just as it had been on the day of my father's funeral.

"I don't need you!"

"Jesus!"

Again the spring-loaded barb skewered my heart, and I rolled onto my side bringing my knees up to my chest. I lay there waiting for the next stab, taking gentle, unprovocative breaths. Perdito was silent. Perhaps it had occurred to him that it's a short-sighted parasite that kills the host. Maybe he didn't know what would happen if I died. I certainly didn't.

After a few minutes I closed my eyes, daring to relax. I unclenched my fists. I was shivering with cold and I could feel tickles of wetness on my cheek. It had started to snow.

"Are you all right?"

I opened my eyes and saw a pair of fur-trimmed knee-high boots and a shopping basket. I rolled gingerly onto my back and the booted woman crouched to look at me.

"What happened? A seizure?"

I laughed – or, at least, I managed a smile with a groan attached. "More an attempted coup," I said.

*   *   *   *

Stephen, I'm very pissed off.

Having spent all night writing, I left the flat and walked along the canal to a café near the Westerkerk for breakfast. Strolling back to my place, I saw someone standing on the steps, waiting for me. It was Tom. I turned and hurried away before he could see me, and now I'm holed up in a hotel. I risked going to the apartment after dark for clothes and my manuscript, but I can't stay there. If he's come all this way to find me, he's not going to give up after one attempt.

Stephen, no one but you knows I'm in Amsterdam. You must have told him.

Actually, fuck this. I'm going to phone.

*   *   *   *

It had been a month since Pablo's last envelope had arrived. When the phone rang, Mary answered it and brought it to me.

"Stephen, it's Pablo. Why did you tell my brother where I was?"

"I didn't."

"Well, he's laying siege to my apartment and no one but you knew I was here."

"I don't even know your address, Pablo."

"Oh." He thought for a moment. "Yeah, that's true. How did he get it then?"

"I have no idea."

"Weird. Anyway – how are you? Who was that woman who answered the phone?"

"That was Mary, my nurse and housekeeper."

"What? What's up with you?"

I sighed. "I had a stroke. I've lost my sight and I'm slightly paralysed in my left arm."

"Blimey. Completely blind?"

"Completely. They say that it might return, but there's no way of knowing for sure."

"That's a bit of a sod."

"It is, yes."

He exhaled, and I could picture him tipping his head back and blowing smoke out,

"Listen, I can't stay in Amsterdam," he said. "Either I pick a city at random and disappear, or you'll have to hide me for a while. Obviously I wouldn't expect such beautifully presented meals as before, but at the very least I could cut up your food for you."

"It's a generous offer, Pablo, but I can manage."

"Bollocks. I'll be there tomorrow."

He hung up.

"Shall I take the phone, Mr Richmond?" said Mary. She was soft-spoken and there was a trace of the West Country in her accent.

"Yes, thank you."

"I've laid out your lunch on the terrace," she said. "Ham and crudités."

"I'd prefer to have it here, if you don't mind."

"I do mind. You have to learn to get around. Your stick is to your right."

I cannot begin to explain my sense of panic when I discovered I couldn't see. Not to be able to read, to look at the garden, to recognise my friends.

The constant and horrifying darkness. In the evenings, after Mary went home, I would sit alone in the drawing room, concentrating on nothing but the effort it took to quell the terror churning in my gut. I would go to bed and pray for sleep, because in dreams I saw. In the morning when I awoke, it would be a few moments before I remembered I was blind. I would weep, crushed by the black prospect of another day of sightlessness to be borne before I could sleep again.

I was utterly alone. I didn't even have George to speak to. He had passed away the day I'd visited him – another heart attack. I have to say that I envied George. I would rather have died than have ended up as I was – dependent and useless, deprived of the sense with which I made sense of the world. I couldn't find many reasons to continue in that state. Just one, in fact.

As he'd promised, Pablo arrived the following day. I heard Mary let him in.

"He's out on the terrace," she said.

Pablo's plimsolls squeaked across the parquet floor of the drawing room and I could smell cigarette smoke.

"Nice shades," Pablo said. "Very Ray Charles."

"Hello, Pablo," I said, turning my head towards his voice. "It's so good of you to come."

Chair legs scraped on Portland stone.

"It's nice to be back. Does Mary serve drinks, or should I go and get something myself?"

That evening Pablo cooked chicken and chips.

"I thought stuff you could eat with your hands would be best," he said. "Mary told me not to help you cope, but spaghetti bolognese would have been bordering on the cruel and unusual."

"It's so humiliating," I said. "I'm reduced to eating like a toddler."

"Would you like a Tommy-Tippee cup for your Semillon?"

Pablo's fatuous helpfulness was a refreshing change from both the efficient solicitude of medical people and the tentative, cheery sympathy of friends. Despite everything, he made me smile.

"I've put a ramekin of ketchup to the right of your plate," he said. "So tell me what happened."

I recounted the events of the day I lost my sight – poor George, the file of correspondence, the lightning bolt of the stroke.

"I imagine George intended to destroy the letters. I am – well, I was supposed to be – his executor, so I'd have seen the file when I went through his things. That's why he asked Margaret to fetch it for him."

"Do you still have it?"

"No. It went missing somewhere along the line. Just left in the street where I dropped it, I expect."

"And how do you feel about having a nephew?"

I reached carefully for my wineglass and took a sip, then guided it slowly back to the table. "Amongst all this ghastliness, the prospect of Jonathan is the only thing that has kept me going. I shall find him, of course."

"Are you sure that's wise? He may not even know that Patti's husband isn't his dad."

"I have no choice. There are matters of which he must be told. For instance, he's entitled to inherit this house."

I'd thought a lot about how I'd find my nephew. It would require research – I didn't know where Patti's family lived or her husband's surname, which, I assumed, would be the one Jonathan had taken. But when I tracked him down, I'd be able to tell him about his father. I'd worried so long that Leo might be forgotten, but by God's grace there was one in whom my brother would be sustained. Leo's blood was in Jonathan's veins and I'd be able to offer memories to complement that blood.

"So you're going to appear to this bloke like a genie and bestow upon him a past he might not suspect, an estate worth millions and perhaps the news that his dad's been lying to him for forty years."

"It might be a shock, yes, but…"

"What if he tells you to get lost?"

"Why would he? It's only natural that he'd want to know about his father. "

I heard the chink of a wine bottle against glass and the glug of Pablo pouring out one of his liberal measures.

"Thing is," he said, "Jonathan might not need Leo like you do."

I smacked my hand angrily on my thigh. "I have become heartily sick of people telling me what's wrong with my attitude to Leo. Either I'm too protective of his memory, or I'm living in the thrall of his unfulfilled potential, or I'm pushing him in people's faces. Why is it so difficult to understand? My God, is it so unusual to regard a lost brother with respect and fondness?"

Pablo laughed, spluttering wine. "Jesus," he said, "you're asking *me*?" He stood up. "I'll go and get coffee, and then I'll read you what I've written recently."

So, as I drank coffee and ate sugary biscuits brought from Holland, Pablo read aloud to me, his voice counterpointed by the evening chorus of birds in the garden.

"What became of this woman, then?" I asked when he finished.

"Shall I tell you? Or do you want to wait until I write it?"

I pondered. "No – I'll wait. I look forward to the next instalment."

"Makes two of us," Pablo said.

*   *   *   *

Her name was Sally and it was her lawn I was lying on. She took me into the house, which was a mirror-image of my mother's. I sat on the sofa and Sally brought me a glass of water.

"Have you had an attack like that before?" she asked.

"Not that I remember."

"You should get yourself checked out. That's advice from a professional."

"You work in medicine?"

"Urban planning. But I'm very professional."

She was mid-thirties, I guessed. Small and slim as a narcissus-stem – with a face that was every bit as heartening as the first daffodil.

"Do you want me to call someone?" she said.

"No. I've just been visiting my mum, but I don't want to worry her."

"Your mum?"

"At number 43."

"Ah – you're one of Mrs Lyne's boys! I thought I recognised you from somewhere. I've met your brother."

"I'm sorry about that."

"He was charming."

"Is that a euphemism for slimy?"

She laughed. "As seaweed."

Behind all this banal to-and-fro, something very odd was happening to me. I was falling in love. I knew the signs – sunny feeling of bewildered happiness, inability to tear the eyes away from the object of affection, ambivalent anticipation of being overwhelmed by soggy yearning when the time comes to part. All that was welling up, but rolling over and over in the fizzy spring there was a pearl-white sphere of something more material. I could see it bobbing in the bubbles and I knew that when the effervescence subsided I'd be left holding it in my hands above the still pool, perfect and whole. That, I suppose, is love at first sight.

But there was a problem.

I nodded towards a photograph of a gap-toothed boy in a maroon jumper and striped tie.

"Is that your kid?"

"Yes – Josh. He goes to Atlee, just down the road. Started in September."

"That's where I went. Well – from time to time."

"He's at his dad's for the holidays."

It was all I could do not to leap into the air whooping.

"Ah. You're divorced."

"Separated."

"I see." I put the empty glass down on the coffee table. "Is there any chance I could take you out for a meal one night?"

*   *   *   *

"This is lovely," Sally said as the waiter went to fetch the wine list. "I've never eaten Lebanese food before."

"Me neither," I said. "I picked it from a restaurant guide with my eyes shut."

I have to say that I wouldn't have thought I was the love-at-first sight type. Actually, there was very little to suggest I was the love-under-any-circumstances type. And yet, when I was around Sally I was as dazed and happy as a purple koala. I wanted to identify what it was about her that compelled me. I wanted to crystallise it and mainline it. I wanted to pull down the blinds and freebase her, to fill myself with her, to trip out on the essence of her. I had to know why I was so immediately hooked.

The waiter returned with the winelist and I indicated that he should give it to Sally.

"You choose", I told her. "I've always avoided learning anything about wine because I like practically all of it and I don't want to complicate matters."

I remember nothing about what we ate or drank, not that night nor on any of the dates we arranged over the following fortnight. I assume I picked at something, and I know I put away some alcohol, but all I can remember is the two of us talking. About our childhoods, our love affairs, our aspirations, our favourite books. This is the standard new love stuff, isn't it? Memories, dreams and, evenually, flirtation. It was the last element Sally and I omitted. Me, I avoided the carnal because I didn't want to appear predatory – she'd met Tom, remember. I was waiting for a cue from her, but it never came.

On our final date I walked her home and she stopped at the corner a hundred yards from the house. She turned to me and kissed me on the cheek, like a sister.

"Pablo," she said. "I know what you're thinking."

"Oh, good. Because I have no idea what I'm thinking."

"Fourth night. This is where we either sleep together or never get round to calling again."

"Well, not necessarily."

"Yes, it is. I know I'm not as experienced as you but I understand the rules."

"I never give much thought to rules."

She stepped back and looked at me, crossing her arms.

"All right. Then what if I told you that there's no chance of you sleeping with me on the next date, or the one after that, or the one after that? Not in the foreseeable future, actually."

"Ever?" I said. "Oh, Christ. Is this one of those things where you tell me I'm a really sweet man? I hate that. That means you find me entertaining but about as sexually alluring as Ronald MacDonald."

Sally shook her head. "No, that's not what it means. To be honest, I'm desperate for you. But not yet."

I took out a cigarette and lit it. "Yet?"

"Can I have a drag of that?"

I handed her the cigarette. She'd never smoked around me before and it occurred to me that the gesture was some kind of symbol of intimacy. It would have helped the symbolism if she'd've appeared to enjoy it.

"God – how did I ever get through twenty of those a day?" she said, wincing as she gave it back. "Look – I'm still married. When I took those vows I meant them. Unlike you, I give a lot of thought to rules."

"But you're separated. Mike's off with Bella or whatever her name is."

"Donna. That's his decision – to break the vows. But I won't. We're still married."

I looked up and down Beeches Avenue which was glowing orange in the streetlights. Thirty years ago I'd stood on this corner at midnight having hopped down from the porch of my parents' house with no real objective but to be illicitly awake and out. It was a thrilling adventure for a ten-year-old boy. I had no idea where I intended to go, but I was elated to be going there.

"What do you want me to do?" I said. I took a drag from my cigarette and threw it into the gutter. "I'm helplessly in love with you. I don't know what I have to do next."

"The divorce will come through in November," she said. "I can't keep seeing you all that time, because I don't have the willpower not to sleep with you. And if I do that, I'll feel..." She wrinkled her nose, thinking. "...wrong. Dishonest."

"So you want to stop seeing me?"

She nodded. "Until December."

"December? That's a year!"

"Ten months."

"Jesus." I turned and paced, turned again. "You think there's still a chance for you and Mike, don't you?"

She shook her head and laughed. "If I thought that, I wouldn't even go to dinner with you."

"But you do think there's something important between us?"

She nodded. "Definitely. Really."

"Then I don't see the problem," I said. "I don't understand it."

"I'm not asking you to understand it," Sally said. "I'm asking you to accept it."

"Fucking hell." I leaned my back against a lamp post and slid down to sit with my elbows on my raised knees. I looked up at her. "How do I know you won't meet someone else? Someone who blows away all that dishonesty stuff?"

She crouched so that she was at my eye level. "How do I know you won't? That's much more likely."

I bluffed. "Yeah – I might. It's always a possibility."

"Do you think so?"

I felt outmanoeuvred and defensive. Despite my instinct that insouciance was not the attitude to adopt, I said, "Well, you never know."

She could have done anything then. Reached for my hands and squeezed them. Kissed me meaningfully. Got up and walked away in tears. But any of those would have left the issue hanging and I wouldn't have known quite what I was being asked to accept. But Sally's response to my self-protective casualness was perfectly unambiguous. She grabbed me hard by the balls, looked me in the eye and said very calmly, "You sleep with anyone else and I'll kill you."

I was astonished – but I was also convinced. I knew that if I rejected her terms, she'd walk away; and if I accepted them, she'd stick to them and she'd expect as much of me. In the precise meaning of the phrase, Sally was sure of herself. Like the daffodil in Stephen's garden, she was exactly what she was intended to be. That's a neat trick. That, I realised, was what compelled me – she knew who she was.

"Well – that sounds like love all right," I said. "Is it too soon to tell you what I want for Christmas?"

         *   *   *   *

Consider losing the ability to conduct internal monologue, so that you always had to think aloud.

"Take a seat, please. Would you like a coffee?"

"Yes, thank you. I'm very nervous. I really need this job but I don't want you to know that. I hate your tie. I wish I'd had breakfast because my stomach's rumbling. Cream no sugar. I couldn't face that commute every day. I'm keeping my jacket on because my armpits are soaked. Don't ask me about my résumé – I made most of it up. You look the type who'd be screwing his secretary."

That's what it was like. I couldn't have a thought without Perdito knowing about it. When he was quiescent – which he was for weeks after the New Year – he seemed unaware of what I was thinking – but it was all there to be caught up on when he came to. In my mind's eye I saw a cluttered library, with books open on the tables, magazines strewn across the floor, scribbled notes stuck to the edges of shelves and the windowpanes. And Perdito, having dozed in a leather armchair, would wake up and stretch, glance around. He'd get up and walk towards the door, carelessly kicking over piles of paper. An open book would catch his eye – a book I'd left there while he slept. He'd realise it was one he hadn't seen before, and he'd pick it up and leaf through it, skimming.

He'd frown. "Sally? Four dates? Who's Sally?"

I hadn't mentioned him to her. My feelings for her were nothing to do with Perdito, and her feelings were for me, not for us. I didn't want him to be part of what I anticipated, and what I anticipated was the rest of my life.

Which led to a conclusion that I didn't dare think about when he was awake.

"My turn."

It was Thursday – a week after my last dinner with Sally. Perdito was alert now, and itchy.

"Not today," I said.

"I want to see Natalie. It's been ages."

"No."

"Why?"

I couldn't allow myself to frame the answer to that. I shut down the thought as soon as it was sparked. I tried to lie to myself.

"I have to work. I'm painting again."

There was a silence. Perdito knew something was amiss.

"What's going on?" he said.

"I'm just preoccupied with the painting, that's all."

I could feel him casting around in my head for whatever was out of place – pacing the library, turning over sheets of paper, checking the covers of books, scanning the shelves for a new, unbroken spine. I needed to distract him.

"Actually," I said, "To hell with the work. I deserve a break. Let's go out and get drunk."

"My turn to drive."

"No – I will. We'll have a good time. Trust me."

Springheeled Jack's is a bar in Whitechapel, always crammed with people and the smell of sweat, the music so loud it's nauseating, the action on the pool tables rapid and dangerous, the strippers on the tiny stage garishly-lit and sleazy. I drank fast; I offered high stakes for eight-ball; I allowed myself to be jostled and threatened. I fed Perdito an overload of sensation, and I kept my mind off Sally.

"Here's an idea," I yelled above the din to a tattooed thug who was racking up the balls. "I'll get a bottle of vodka from the bar, and every time one of us sinks a ball, the other has to take a swig."

He turned out to be a very good player, and over seven frames I knocked back most of the bottle.

"One more," I said, slapping a fifty-pound note on the table. "Can you cover that?"

"You can hardly fucking stand up."

"Easy money for you then, isn't it?"

The shriek and squeal of guitars zipped around my head like comets. As I bent to make the first shot, the blue baize crackled with static beneath my hand and the triangle of balls shattered like a detonated rainbow. With each breath I could taste hot smoke, warm piss and icy vodka. Perdito was ablaze with sensation and I kept piling it on – light, sound, odour, flavour, texture – in the hope of building a fire so high it would burn him out, leaving me to make plans while he slept in the ashes.

It was a dangerous strategy. What didn't stun Perdito tended to make him livelier, and he tugged at my consciousness, over-excited and eager. I was already driving drunk and it didn't help to have him reach over and pull the wheel this way and that. I was barely keeping myself on the road.

I potted three or four balls before I missed one and stood back to let the yeti approach the table. He soon cleared all but the black which he left over the pocket.

"Want to lose another fifty after this, mate?" he asked, chalking his cue.

"Arrogant fuck," Perdito said.

"You've got to put that one down first," I said. I meant it as chummy banter, but what happened next made it look like attempted intimidation.

As the yeti leaned across the table to sink the eight-ball, Perdito made his move – yanking me back and lunging for the wheel. My limbs spasmed – and one hand caught the end of the yeti's cue. He scuffed the shot completely. As he straightened up and turned, he seemed less than thrilled. The butt of his cue hit me on the left temple and I fell backwards through the door of the Gents.

*   *   *   *

Pablo and I soon settled into a routine again. At nine or thereabouts he would yell up the stairs that breakfast was ready. He refused to help me negotiate my way to the kitchen, saying that Mary had forbidden it. While we ate, he'd read to me from the newspaper and then we'd go upstairs and he'd pick clothes from the wardrobe for me.

Mary would arrive at ten, and Pablo went to work in the garden until lunchtime. During the afternoons he'd write, and I'd listen to the radio or force myself to tour the house, tap-tapping with my stick. I also made phone calls. I was maddened at first by my inability to master the keypad but then I realized that as long as I could dial Directory Enquiries, they would put me through to whatever number I wished. Eventually I tracked down a Registrar in the Midlands who cross-referenced Patti's maiden name and came up with a death certificate, of which I ordered a full copy.

That afternoon I had an appointment at the hospital. Pablo drove me there and guided me around.

"What's the latest?" he said on the way home.

"There's nothing wrong with my eyes, so the culprit is the visual cortex. But I've undergone scans of brain activity and everything seems to be working. They think my blindness might be hysterical." I shook my head. "It's really most insulting. They're implying that, somehow, I'm doing this on purpose."

"It's an unconscious reluctance to see the food I cook."

That evening, as we sat on the terrace before dinner, I said, "What time is it, Pablo?"

I heard him turn to look at the clock in the drawing room – he didn't wear a watch.

"A little after seven."

"So it's not dark yet. The sun must be behind the folly."

"Yeah."

I hesitated. "Help me see it."

"You can see it – it's in your head."

"Please, Pablo."

"I don't think I can do it justice." He took a breath, and after a few moments he began to speak. "Okay. The lake is saffron and the copper beeches are glowing purple. The marguerites along the stone-walk are ghost-white against the dark foliage of the dahlias, and above them the clematis shifts in the breeze, flowers winking – they look like the lights of a town seen from the sea." He sipped his wine. "A pair of magpies are playing hopscotch between the shadows of trees stretched across the grass, and on the arch to the knot-garden, the rambling roses are smouldering ember-orange as the evening closes in." I heard him strike a match. "Blimey. That wasn't bad, off the cuff."

I could smell nightstock and nicotiana in the beds below the terrace, and I could feel the last warmth of the sun on my tear-streaked face. I sat in silence – as if by concentrating very hard I might be able to hear the colours of my garden. I raised my head, listening for the resonances of the twilight, but the sound that reached me was the laughter of two small boys tumbling over each other on the endless lawn, knowing that it was nearly bedtime and hoping that the adults' call from the house would never come.

Chapter Twelve
Unalloyed

I opened my eyes.

Look at those words.

I opened my eyes.

Who opened?

I.

Opened what?

Eyes.

Whose?

Mine.

I opened my eyes.

"You asked for that, mate." A bald man was holding a damp cloth to my temple. "You all right?"

I wanted to know where I was, so I lifted my head and I moved it. I used my eyes to look around. My ears listened.

I was laid out on an upholstered banquette in Springheeled Jack's. My eyes saw a stripper stepping offstage clutching her clothes, the man who had hit me drinking at the bar, horsehair tufting from a split in the fabric of the seat. I lowered my head and it throbbed – but I was alone in it. I had no sense of Pablo about me.

No Pablo. That had happened only once before – at New Year's – and I barely remembered it. Pablo had passed out under the combined weight of drugs, vodka and exhaustion, and I had roared on. I was barely even aware that my host was unconscious on the backseat.

But now – in Springheeled Jack's – I was compos mentis and I seemed to be in sole possession of our senses. I sat up.

"You'll be right as rain in a tick," said the bald man. He reached a glass from the table and offered it to me. "Knock that back."

I sniffed it. Brandy.

The bald man nodded towards Pablo's pool opponent at the bar. "Danny stood you it. Close as you'll get to an apology. Salt of the earth Dan is, to be fair."

I tasted the brandy, anticipating the usual pizzicato-studded timpanic rumble – but all I got was sensation in the mouth, aroma in the nostrils, heat in the belly. There were no musical stabs, no chaotic overloads. The experience of brandy was both enjoyable and – the word suddenly meant something – sensible.

"I'll be fine," I said – and I said it without anyone's tacit consent. The bald man went back to the bar.

I stood up. I was facing a pinball table that bleeped and pinged, strobed and flickered in an attempt to attract my attention. I watched the sequence – three crimson blinks on the back panel, the roar of a Harley, the bumpers flash in unison, a siren wails and neon chases itself around the specials lanes. I watched it over and over, but it didn't drown me. I understood it. It made sense.

I flexed my fingers. I sucked in the cigarette smoke and the smell of beer – and what I tasted was no more than cigarette smoke and beer. It was as if the world was coming to me uninterpreted. My connection was direct, was unalloyed, was – mine. Pablo was not there.

Which raised the question of where he was. I felt around for him, like someone feeling for their spectacles in a loaded rucksack, and I found him. The shape of him, but not the sound of him. He was out cold. I was on my own.

I was on my own.

I left the bar and I went to the only place where Perdito on his own would be considered remarkable.

*   *   *   *

Natalie opened the door of her house in the Isle of Dogs.

"Hello," she said. "This is a surprise. I thought you were abroad this week."

"It's me," I said. "It's Perdito."

"Ah. I should have seen it in your face. Come in."

"No. It's me. It's just me." I took her hand and put it against my cheek. It was warm. The scent of marmalade that I was used to from her was absent. Absent and, all of a sudden, comical. I couldn't imagine why it had ever seemed to make sense. "Look. It's me. It's Perdito."

She looked at me closely.

"I don't get it," she said. She drew her hand back. "Come inside."

The living room was as it always had been – the Indian table with its crude rivets, the Kandinsky posters, Natalie's collage portrait of Pablo made from crumpled sweet wrappers; all of them merely objects, not booby-traps of sensation primed to explode in my face. It was as if Pablo crosswired everything, plugging his senses into the wrong receivers for mine. The colour brown was corrugated; the word epaulette was yeasty; mustard tasted like a violin-note. It had always been that way. Now, for the first time, I was experiencing flesh purely.

"What happened to your forehead?" Natalie asked as she brought me a glass of wine.

"Pablo got in a fight."

"Pablo did? That's unlike him."

"You mean it's more like me." I touched the bump with my fingertips. "Listen – something weird has happened. Pablo's – I don't know – asleep. Not here. And everything makes more sense without him. He wants to get rid of me, Nat. He doesn't want me to see you. He doesn't want me at all."

"What do you mean? How can he get rid of you?"

"I don't know. But if he can do it to me, I can do it to him first. He wants rid of both of us."

She frowned. "He wants to dump me?"

"Yes, yes – but I don't." I leaned forward and took her hands. "I want to be with you."

"I don't understand. I want to talk to him." She snatched her hands free. "Let him take over. Make him explain."

"No, no – he's out cold. Everything's clear now." I stood up. "Don't you want to be with me? Really me?"

"Let me speak to him, Perdito. He can't just dump me."

"What do you care about him? This is me."

She grabbed my shoulders and shook me. "Both of you – it has to be both of you. Pablo!"

I pushed her back on to the sofa and I made for the door. I didn't want Pablo revived – not now I was alone. I leapt down the front-steps to the street, and Natalie pursued me, screaming at me to come back. I ran. I wanted to run and I ran. I made the decision to duck into an alley, and I ducked. No one permitted me. No one tried to rein me in. I twisted and turned where I wanted to twist and turn, and I lost Natalie in the cuts behind the old houses. The hell with her.

I headed along the river to Canary Wharf. In the shadow of the tower I took several hundred pounds out of an ATM, and then I hailed a cab.

"Leicester Square, please," I said.

*   *   *   *

Having mailed my long letter to Alice, I went to bed drunk and unhappy, and I had a vivid dream – or more like a total recall – of the trip to Scotland with Pablo after Louise left.

We went by plane – back then I could still fly, though it wasn't a pleasant flight. I spent the entire journey with my face turned to the window so that no one could see I was crying. I stared at the bed of cloud below us and Louise was lying there on her back, her legs wide as Robin fucked her. She gasped and laughed and got on all fours. She clambered over him, guiding him in. She kissed him and fellated him, stroked him and wanked him – and I watched, lashed in my seat, fingers digging into the armrests. She was happy and relieved to be having an unselfconsciously horny good time. She wasn't thinking about me at all.

The friend with whom Pablo had been invited to 'hang out' was not, as I'd expected, some Caledonian hippy with a windswept croft on the shores of Loch Ness, but a minor member of the nobility – a narrow, tall woman in an ankle-length black coat drifting towards us like a wraith as we emerged from the Arrivals gate.

"Hello, Pablo," said Moira McLachlan. "Lovely to see you again." She kissed him on both cheeks in the continental manner. "Flight all right, was it?"

"Very smooth," Pablo said. He put his arm around her shoulders and turned towards me. "This is my brother Tom."

"Nice to meet you," I murmured, holding out my hand. I wondered whether Pablo was sleeping with this woman. She had that clear, fresh-breeze kind of face on which age doesn't accumulate, but I'd have guessed her at forty or so. Twice our age. Surely he couldn't.

"Nice to meet you too, Tom. My God, you look awful – are you unwell?"

"I've been crying for twenty-four hours straight," I said. I was much too miserable, and much too interested in my misery, to bother lying about it.

"Oh, dear," Moira said, obviously nonplussed. "Well – the car's just outside. Is that all your luggage?"

I can't think what reply I expected her to offer, but I was incensed that she'd so incuriously glossed my terse explanation of washed-out complexion and red-rimmed eyes. With Pablo in good-humoured attendance, Moira led the way to a chauffeured vintage Rolls and I trudged behind, working up an epic sulk that I intended to impose on both of them for the duration of my stay. We piled into the back of the car and as Moira and Pablo toasted each other in malt Scotch, I glowered silently out of the window.

I'd never been to Scotland before and I've never been since. I hate the place. There are those, apparently, who see an enduring, untamed magnificence in the desolate glens and the implacable mountains, the malevolent coastline and the sinister lochs. But I watched the drizzle-smeared landscape roll past as we drove, and the place might have been created for the sole purpose of reflecting my mood. Dank, bleak, devoid of fauna or feature; from horizon to horizon a wilderness onto which chill darkness descended like a thick headache. I've never been anywhere so sodden with loneliness.

Moira's home was a nineteenth-century pile stacked on a crag rising from cliffs that rebuffed the insistent waves of the North Sea. Though it was called Dunvigan Castle it was actually no more than a large square house spiked with ornamental turrets. Very comfortable though – huge stone fireplace in the main room, numerous well-upholstered bedrooms, snug kitchen with an ancient oak table.

"I asked for something to be left for us," Moira said, opening the oven. "Sit yourselves down. You must be famished. Could you light the candles, Pablo?"

She brought out a casserole dish and lifted the lid. Steam rose from a beef stew in which dumplings sat like toads. Pablo uncorked a bottle of wine he'd taken from his rucksack and Moira turned off the lights.

"A bit of atmosphere, I think," she said as she took her seat.

I hadn't eaten since Pablo and I had shared a pizza the previous evening in Cambridge – and I'd thrown that up an hour after Louise had walked out with Robin – so I probably presented a rather unappealing spectacle as I wolfed three bowls of the stew. Pablo, whose appetite varied from month to month between the voracious and the disinterested, paddled his meal around the plate and chain-smoked. And chain-drank. Moira and I were still on our first glass when he opened a second bottle of wine.

The plates were cleared and Moira produced stilton, biscuits and a bottle of whisky. I wasn't exactly cheered up but I was certainly more in control of myself. And then Moira said to Pablo, "So, you were going to tell me more about Perdito."

I suppressed a groan. I'd seen quite a bit of Pablo over recent weeks and I was relieved that I'd detected no sign of my brother's ephemeral alter-ego. Now the subject had come up, I didn't want to instigate a private argument in front of a stranger. Then again, I didn't want Pablo making a fool of himself – and of me by extension – with any candlelit tales of post-mortem fraternal possession.

"Perdito's a sort of personification of Pablo's creative muse," I said to Moira, hoping she'd pick up on my 'humour-him-it's-easier' tone. "You know what these artistic types are like."

"What the fuck do you know about it?" Pablo said, immediately needled. "He's my twin, not yours."

"Well, if he's yours, he's got to be mine too hasn't he?" I replied soothingly, giving Moira a smiling shrug. "I mean, by definition."

"Not necessarily, no. You have no idea what you're talking about."

I nodded, maintaining the calm smile. "As you wish."

Pablo sloshed himself out another brimming glass of scotch. "Don't patronise me, you supercilious creep. Jesus – no wonder Louise got fed up with you."

Stew and dumplings lurched in my stomach. For a few minutes there, distracted by Pablo's idiocies, I'd forgotten. But now I felt the heat rise in my cheeks and I had a vision of Louise climbing the stairs of Robin's house, following him to the bedroom, asking him to unzip her dress. It was about that time of night. I could feel all self-control slipping away from me.

I pushed my chair backwards and stood up. "Thank you for dinner, Moira," I said a little shakily. "I think I'll retire now, if you don't mind."

"Are you all right, Tom?" she asked.

"Very tired. Excuse me."

As I closed the door behind me I heard Moira say to Pablo, "That wasn't very nice of you."

I cried myself to sleep in a four-poster bed that was much too big for one person.

*   *   *   *

My relationship with Louise is parenthesised in my mind by deep drifts of snow.

When I woke up in the four-poster, the room was bright with the same pure reflected light that had surrounded us the first time we made love amongst the gin bottles in Cambridge. Snow was piled on the windowsill and I could see the odd flake drifting lazily against the crayon-blue sky. I pulled the covers over my head and wept again – as I did every morning for a year. It shames me now to think how bonelessly bereft I was.

"Shall we take a walk along the cliffs after breakfast?" Moira suggested. "It's beautiful out there."

A vertiginous stairway led from the house down to the clifftop – an ancient wooden arrangement of which one side was bolted unconvincingly to the face of the rock. The handrail on the other side wobbled on its struts, and I was careful not to rely on it to take my weight. My hand slid tightly along the rope that looped along the rockface and I kept my eyes on my feet, watching each cautious, snow-covered step of the descent to the path below.

"It's perfectly safe," Moira called from a few steps below me. "In the old days they lugged huge barrels of contraband booze up and down here, and the instances of the stairs giving way are comparatively few."

She waited for me to pussyfoot my way to the bottom. Pablo was standing with his back to us on a snowy little promontory gazing out to sea, the brisk wind flapping his denim jacket and rippling his hair. I think he was attempting to look far-off and intriguing. Moira gestured towards the path that tracked the cliffs around the bay.

"We'll just go as far as Priest's Point," she said. "There's a wonderful view from there."

"I'll catch you up," Pablo said over his shoulder. "I want to stay here and look at the sea for a minute or two."

Further off and more intriguing by the second. Maybe he didn't get what he expected last night.

The path followed a gentle curve six reassuring feet from the cliff's edge, the line of which was ragged as a ripped envelope, its mounds and hollows deceptively smoothed out by the snow. At one point, where the ground had fallen away in a pie-slice that almost reached the path, I peered down at the woozy drop – a hundred feet or more – to where suicidal waves white with fury flung themselves against the widow-black rocks. I stepped back quickly and my foot slipped a little on the snow. I was in no danger, but it was enough to invoke hot-flushed visions of plummeting over the edge. As we walked on I kept tight to the far side of the path.

"How are you feeling today?" Moira asked.

"Okay. Sorry if I appeared petulant last night. Personal stuff."

"We all get some of that."

"Apparently. Did Pablo tell you about Perdito?"

"Yes, he did. Perdito is a real person to Pablo, you know – not a metaphor."

I stumbled as I put my foot into a hole filled with snow. "So, you think he's literally haunted? Possessed?"

Moira pursed her lips. "Well, I'm trying to imagine what it must be like to know that you were born with another human being inside you. What must that do to your view of the world? You might, for instance, feel guilty that you'd somehow prevented a person from living. And one way to assuage the guilt might be to give that person a form of vicarious existence."

"No, no," I said, shaking my head. "You're thinking about it too much. The whole thing's an attention-seeking strategy. And a particularly callous one."

"Then why would Pablo want to seek attention like that? There must be a reason for it."

I knew the answer, but I couldn't express it without appearing arrogant. The truth is that Pablo's need for attention was a reaction to having me as a brother. I was the one who made the effort, the one who achieved. As a child I never caused any trouble, unlike Pablo who was always in hot water of some kind. When we were there in Scotland I was between terms at University and Pablo, by contrast, was taking time out from idling penniless in a commune. In the decades to come, I'd hold down a proper job, which he seemed incapable of doing, and I'd earn good money and all that goes with it – a flat in London, an expensive car, an active social life. I could see how Pablo would be jealous of me.

So the invention of Perdito had two benefits for my brother. Firstly, it was impossible for me to compete with the mystic and creative abilities in Pablo that Perdito implied. Wouldn't want to, of course, but that's not the point. Secondly, Perdito was a brother that Pablo could lord it over. Even in Pablo's own twisted explanation of what Perdito was, the imaginary little spook could communicate only through Pablo, experience the world only through Pablo, could exist at all, in fact, only because Pablo permitted it. Perdito, in short, represented the control that Pablo would like to be able to exercise over Tomàs. If it weren't so irritating, it would be pathetic.

My reply to Moira was simply, "Insecurity, I imagine. He has a whole firework display of attention-getting techniques. Perdito is just the most incendiary of them."

At which point we were interrupted by ecstatic whooping, and Pablo hurtled past us, skittering along the cliff's edge, bounding from one snow-covered mound to another in his tractionless summer sneakers. His jacket billowed behind him as he leapt and skipped and stumbled, losing his balance and going down on one hand before launching himself again, kicking up chunks of frozen snow that span out over the void and dropped in a tumble to the churning sea.

"Oh my God," Moira said. She shouted after him as he ran full pelt from us, laughing ecstatically. "Pablo! Be careful! Get away from the edge! Pablo!"

And I thought, "This is it. This is how Pablo dies." It would be my fault, of course. My mother's argument would be that I should have prevented it. 'You let him fall from this cliff? You just watch him and let him fall? Why you didn't hold him?'

"What? So both of us could go over the edge?" I could imagine myself saying. Well, I could imagine myself *not* saying. But if Pablo was about to plunge to his death, at the very least I'd have to be able to claim to have made an effort.

I was about to run after him when suddenly – just for an instant – I could see the rocks and the spray of the waves as if they'd been projected in front of me. I stopped in my tracks. Instantly the cliff path was back and my eyes were on Pablo astride a white outcrop, arms spread like a crucifixion, looking down at the raging breakers. Again, from nowhere, the drop to the sea flashed up before my eyes. I saw thrown spray and sucked-back water as the next wave gathered. I could feel the ground under my feet and I could hear Moira beside me, murmuring concern about Pablo – but all I could see was the snow-covered cliff's edge and the jumbled sharp boulders below. I was seeing what Pablo could see. But it wasn't Pablo seeing it. I was getting Pablo's view as he teetered at the cliff edge, but it felt like me. *Not* me. *Like* me.

The vision of the rocks disappeared and I was looking along the cliff path again. Pablo was gone. A gull looped and squawked over the place he'd been standing.

"Are you all right?" Moira asked, tipping her head to one side and staring into my eyes.

"Where is he?"

"He went around the curve there. God, man, you're completely grey."

Over her shoulder I saw Pablo stroll back into view, grinning, his hands in his pockets.

"I want to go home," I muttered. "I just want to go home."

*   *   *   *

Still Tom didn't remember. None of you do. None of you remember where you come from. None of you has any idea how unlikely life is. If you knew you could not risk it so casually.

Every day Pablo stood within kissing distance of death, as sleek boxes of rushing metal bore down on him and swerved at the last moment, avoiding him by inches. The cars stampeded around the curve from the Fulham Palace Road like bison, gaining speed and heading directly towards Pablo and fifty other pedestrians standing at the top of King Street. Two or three dozen cars, as many drivers, aimed head-on at the defenceless commuters by the lights. And not one of those pedestrians moved. Not one shrieked or turned tail or even closed their eyes and held their breath. They were not afraid, because they believed that every one of those twenty or thirty drivers – those strangers, with their unknown infirmities of mind and body, with their madnesses and angers and unresolved despairs – every one of those human beings whose cars were accelerating towards the pavement would turn the wheel and follow the curve of the road. So the pedestrians just stood there unconcerned and relaxed when it would take only a slight misjudgement or a momentary malice to kill them.

More deeply, more implicitly than you believe in God or Hell or Truth, you believe that no approaching driver will see that it's quicker to cut across the pavement; you trust that the guy behind you on the platform won't push you into the path of the oncoming train. No one roars around the curve straddling the line and everyone assumes no one else will. You risk your life each minute, assured that every dumb sack of bones around you has agreed to that bargain; you're convinced that every other soul sees the world the way that you do.

That's the least true thing I've ever heard.

But in the dazzling few seconds of form and sense beneath the overpass, flesh forgets the endless miles of white-noise and black rain through which we travel for all but a strobed blink of our existence. Memories of emptiness are overwhelmed by the immediacy of everythingness. Given a boundless palate of sensation to play with, imagination fails, incapable of conceiving infinite blurry nothing.

I hear static hiss all the time. From the corner of my eye I see the smeared darkness never further away than a missed heartbeat, a synaptic short-circuit, a ruptured artery. Only warm flesh holds us in the light. Bone and blood anchor us to this vivid hiatus between eternities of relentless rain.

I'm not ready to go back. I am determined to cling to flesh – any flesh – and I have as much right to that as anyone with whom I shared the womb.

Chapter Thirteen
Flame without a Candle

I woke up to bright morning sun reflected from the water in the Limehouse Basin. I was lying on the edge of my bed, and by the far wall I could see a pinball machine that hadn't been there last time I was paying attention. My sinuses were dry and raw – the after-effects of cocaine – and my suede tongue was explained by the litter of brandy bottles and beer cans on the floor.

I rolled over and came up against a body. It was a dark-haired girl asleep with her mouth open, dribbling.

"Oh, Christ – no," I murmured.

A redhead walked in from the kitchen, wearing my bathrobe and carrying a tray of tea.

"Morning," she said. "I couldn't find any sugar." She kicked a few empty cans aside and put the tray on the floor before shucking the robe and getting back into bed. She prodded the dark girl's shoulder. "Siobhan – wake up. Tea."

"Excuse me," I said. "I'll be back in a second."

I went to the bathroom and locked the door. I turned on the shower and let it run as I inspected myself in the mirror. I looked dreadful – flaky, washed-out, haggard. Nasty bruise on my temple, too.

"Thing is, Sally," I said to my reflection, "it wasn't actually me that slept with them. No – really. See, my body was being used at the time by my twin. I don't even remember what he did with it. So – you know – I'm still keeping my promise."

It didn't sound very convincing. And, for the first time, I cared. It mattered to me what Sally thought, and I couldn't see any way in which she'd think it reasonable to spend her life with a man who disappeared for days at a time to go on drug and alcohol benders with loose women. Fair enough, really.

My jeans were lying on the bathroom floor and I picked them up in the hope that there might be a packet of cigarettes in the pocket. I pulled out a cellophane twist of coke, an Underground ticket from Piccadilly station and a book of matches from a casino in Mayfair.

I went back to the bedroom. Siobhan and the redhead were sitting up in bed watching television.

"What day is it?" I asked them.

"Tuesday. Your tea's getting cold."

Five days. Good God.

I found some cigarettes in my jacket and I was heading back to the bathroom when the TV newscaster said, "And lastly, the story of one lucky Londoner who fell under a tube train and survived. It was just an ordinary night out for sales manager Gareth Beatty..."

Piccadilly station, seven thirty. The platform was crowded. As the train came in Gareth was nudged by someone behind him and he fell onto the track – into the safety pit, fortunately. The train went over the top of him. Lucky guy.

In the bathroom I checked the time of issue on the Underground ticket. Seven twenty-three. Not only had Perdito made a philanderer of me, he'd damn nearly made me a murderer too. He had to go.

As did the women. Having washed and dressed, I shooed them out of the apartment like pigeons. Then I made a cup of tea and sat cross-legged on the bed with an ashtray in front of me, thinking.

I had never really resolved the problem of what Perdito actually was. I thought of him as kind of a Zen paradox – a flame without a candle. He *flickered in me and he stayed alight, I assumed, only because my tallow sustained him. If I were to rid myself of him – and I had no idea whether I could – would the flame still burn? Perhaps I was contemplating murder, just as he was.*

Speaking of which, I had to consider the fortunately unfortunate Gareth Beatty, cowering under a speeding tube train. I couldn't keep Perdito on a leash for every day of the next thirty years. Eventually he'd use my hands to kill someone. Better that Perdito should be extinguished than some hapless commuter with a family and a real lived life.

All morally watertight, certainly. But of no practical use as I hadn't the first idea of how I could rid myself of my conjoined twin.

"I dunno, I really don't," I muttered tapping out a cigarette.

As I flicked open my lighter the phone rang, which was a bit of a shock because it had never done that before. I had never given anyone the number - not until last week.

I dived off the bed and scrambled across the floor to pick up.

"Sally?" I said.

"Hi. How did you know it was me?"

"Telepathy. That must prove something. How are you?"

"Missing you more than I expected. That must prove something too."

"I can be there in an hour and a half."

"No. Tempting, but no. I'd feel..."

"Yeah, I know. It's okay. But phone calls are allowed, are they?"

"As long as they don't get steamy."

"You have no problem at all with deferring gratification, do you?"

"None. Do you?"

I was very careful not to hesitate or waver. "I'll cope."

We chatted for half an hour. She asked what I planned to do during the week and, for want of anything better to say, I told her that I was going to a preview at a gallery in Soho that evening. The invitation was lying by the phone.

"It's a retrospective of work from the nineties. One of my things is being shown."

"I'll go and see it next time I'm in town."

"No point in my suggesting we meet up, is there?"

"Please don't make this difficult, sweetheart."

"All right. But it's not easy either way."

When we hung up – after lots of adolescent you-first-no-you stuff which I rather enjoyed – I lay flat on the floor and calculated the number of weeks till December. It was many. But it gave me plenty of time to get shot of Perdito.

"Gareth Beatty's a convenient moral justification," I told myself aloud. I sat up and reached for the cigarettes. "It's Sally really. You're prepared to kill for her."

    *   *   *   *

A couple of hours later I took a tube into the West End. A lot of people I knew were there at the preview – though not Natalie, thank God – and I was quite enjoying myself. My work was represented in the exhibition by what I suppose was the best piece I ever made. It was a foetus formed of moulded rubber and my own blood, floating in a refrigerated tank. When it was first shown it created a lot of complimentary interest as well as eliciting, to my gleeful satisfaction, spluttering outrage from those newspaper critics who think that the visual arts have been on a downhill slide since the day Stubbs daubed his last fetlock.

I hadn't actually seen the thing since it was first shown, so when the crowd began to thin out – all the Soave having been drunk – I slipped away to the small room in which the piece stood alone, humming like a macabre vending machine. And I was taken aback.

My memory of it was all about the manufacture – the meetings with the people who produced the latex, the experiments with the composition of the fluid in which the baby was suspended, the painful trouble I had finding a vein from which to siphon off the blood. I'd forgotten that the finished article was so realistic. Not that it was an accurate anatomical representation of a foetus – but it certainly looked like something alive.

As I stood there and watched it drifting in its synthesised amniotic fluid, I remembered why I'd made it. I'd wanted to give Perdito a separate existence. I wanted to represent him to the world and make him real. Everybody who saw the piece would carry in their head forever that image of my twin as an individual, and so, in a way, he would have a life of his own.

Ten years later the concept seemed pretentious and futile. Perdito was still with me, and that circumstance remained completely unchanged by my having contrived a trite symbol of his imagined autonomy. If I wanted to free us both, I was going to have to do something a damn sight more practical than play with dolls.

"You want to kill me again, don't you?" Perdito said.

I was so startled I actually jumped in the air.

"Well – don't you?" he insisted.

"I just want to be on my own," I said. Or rather, I thought.

"This is our body. Just as much mine as yours."

"No, it's not," I said. "It's not." I'd never before allowed that idea to cross my mind, and I knew it wouldn't go down well. "It's my body. I've just let you share it. But now..."

"But you killed mine! It was your fault."

"It was dumb luck. I'm sorry."

I could feel him becoming agitated. Pain started to spout behind my ribs.

"So what do you expect me to do? Where am I supposed to go?"

"I don't know. But I know you can go. You went once before. In Amsterdam."

"No!"

A spike shot up through my heart and I staggered, fell forward and clung to the refrigerated cabinet, knees sagging.

"Jesus," I gasped.

"You go! You leave! You die!"

"Oh, God." It felt as if claws were tearing my heart to tatters.

"Get out! I don't need you!"

And I realised that might be true. If my flame were extinguished, it might be that Perdito could burn on in my body alone. Despite the barbed agony behind my ribs I tried to work out whether it made sense. A candle needs a flame. One flame. A flame needs…

But I couldn't think straight. Perdito was running riot in my head, like a vandal in a library, sweeping books off the shelves, rifling the index files. As fast as I attempted to construct thoughts he kicked them down. Everything was jumbled and haphazard. Ripped sheets of memory were swooshed up from the floor, turning over and over, fluttering across the stop-frame of my perceptions. It seemed to me that the gallery was in Amsterdam and that my father was talking to me on the roof which our feet sunk into like icing. I was clinging to a sky-rocket that skittered along Beeches Avenue, ricocheting off lamp posts, exploding in a sunburst of blood like a heart ripped apart.

"Get out! Get out!" Perdito screamed. But he wasn't inside now. He was the blood baby, floating up to my face, mouth wide open and wailing. I felt another stab, sharp and metallic. I lost my balance and I fell, tumbling over a cliff towards the jagged black rocks and the crimson spray. I clung to the cabinet as the baby screeched at me, and we hit the bottom in a crash of splintering glass, reflecting the sun for me alone, strobing on the red dress of the little girl at the top of the slide. The waters broke and I was drenched, rolling onto my side, knees pulled up, hugging Perdito so that we went down together.

Another steel rod of pain impaled me and I whimpered, curling up tighter. I could feel the snow of unconsciousness flurrying about me, and I bit down hard on the flesh of my forearm. I gasped and bit again, but now my mouth was full of rubber, and Perdito was howling. His blood-baby face was pressed to my cheek, and his tiny hands were scrabbling at my chest. Again I bit, and I pulled, ripping at the latex skin of his face like a savage. The skin tore. I gripped the flap in my teeth, clasping him tight to me, and I jerked my head left and right, opening the wound.

Blood spurted out – cold and sticky – and I squeezed his tiny body, making red viscous fountains that spattered back down on me. I managed to stand up, still embracing him. I staggered to the wall and pressed him to it with my chest. More blood erupted from the gash in his face, hitting me full in the eyes, running down my cheeks.

"Pablo – please." He was back in my head now, and the pain was ebbing. He sounded weak. "Please. No."

"You tried to kill me, you bastard." I lurched back from the wall, the deflating rubber bag in both hands. I twisted it like a wet towel and blood squirted out over my baseball boots. "Go, Perdito. Now."

"I can't – not now. Please."

I twisted tighter, splattering my shirt.

"Go! Just go!"

I held the bag upside down at arm's length and it haemorrhaged onto the floor. I listened, and all I could hear was my own shaky breathing and the *drip, drip, drip as the last of the borrowed blood dribbled out of the dead baby and congealed in a pool around my feet. I dropped the latex body into the puddle and one empty arm flopped flat, the fingers curled and tiny.*

I wiped my face on my sleeve and licked blood from my lips. Four or five people were standing in the doorway, staring at me, horrified. I walked towards them, blank-faced, the broken glass of the cabinet crunching beneath my feet – and they parted to let me through. I went out onto Old Compton Street, still listening.

I hadn't heard him leave, but neither could I hear him there.

*   *   *   *

I didn't know what to do. I wasn't so much calm as mechanical. I was walking, but walking was instinct. A gust of wind blew a plastic carrier bag up in front of me and my arm shot out and snatched it from the air – an involuntary motor response. I laughed. I'd got rid of the one who wanted to control my body, and now my body was doing things on its own. I stuffed the bag in my pocket.

I turned onto Wardour Street and my eyes reacted to the stimulus of neon. My ears registered bells and electronic beeping. My brain interpreted this input as an amusement arcade and instructed my feet to take me there. I got change – lots and lots of change because my hands offered the woman the first piece of ultimately worthless paper that came out of my wallet – and I went to play my game.

I slotted the pennies in and watched them bounce down through the maze of pins to the shelves, jostle each other, edge towards the brink. I sought design in the confusion of shuffling coins, and I saw patterns that looked pretty for a few moments – but they were fabricated by my order-loving human brain. Really the pennies were just pushing each other around at random, without plot or purpose, and every penny had the same face. That was okay. It's only dumb luck which face you get, just as it's only dumb luck which face shoves which other face over the precipice of the Penny Falls.

My hands put in another coin, and another, and another; and my eyes watched them bump and slide and teeter. Eventually a cascade of small change poured out into the hopper – chink-chink-chink.

I felt as if I'd won.

Chapter Fourteen
Dragging Hector

When I woke up on the Wednesday morning after mailing my homework to Alice, I was bemused and disorientated. I was also somewhat wet and sticky – which must have been the first time that had happened in twenty-five years, and it only added to the odd sensation that I was fifteen again. All morning I felt as if I had pulled on an adult-Tom body that zipped up at the back like a gorilla suit. I was very good at walking in it and moving the big hands to pay for a newspaper or hold a coffee-cup, and no one in Starbuck's seemed to suspect that I was just a kid in a costume. Back at home I put my feet up on the desk and they seemed a very long way away. I felt as if I – the conscious me – didn't extend to the end of my legs. It was a happy coincidence, rather than the result of any instructions I might issue, that my feet tended to walk to where I wanted to go.

I loaded my suitcase and laptop into the car, checked my pocket for my passport and drove to town to talk to Angus Jakes about the Malaga trip. As most of my work was done in the evenings at the homes of my clients, I rarely attended the offices of Jakes and Allen – which I considered one of the perks of the job. I had nothing to say to anyone in the organisation, although unfortunately Angus Jakes had plenty to say to me. He once saw me walking along Charlotte Street with two women I'd met that morning in Leicester Square, and from this slight circumstance he'd extrapolated the notion that I was some sort of incontinent Lothario. It was his sole topic of conversation, apart from work.

I was hoping for a brief meeting at the office, but Angus insisted on taking me to a fish restaurant in Fitzrovia.

"Superb quarter, Tommy-boy," he said, waving a sales report at me over the bread rolls. "Eighty-two per cent closure on leads in your territory. Bloody marvellous, my son."

Angus was five years younger than I. 'Son' was not just patronising – it was inappropriate. I poured a glass of mineral water and bit my lip. At a table behind Angus, the oleaginous maitre-d was pulling out a chair for a slender woman of about thirty. She had plumb-straight chestnut hair to her waist and an arrestingly short skirt. She was accompanied by a dapper greying man who had his back to me. Personal Assistant and her executive, by my guess.

"I've got a little bet on with Davey that you'll top ninety next quarter. Reckon you could manage that, Tommy-boy?" Angus asked chummily.

The PA was sitting at a slight angle to me, and her thighs were like something out of *Song of Solomon*.

"No prospect is closer to my heart," I said.

"You'll bloody walk it, son."

The waiter arrived with a bottle of wine and poured a little for Angus to taste. He downed it in one lip-smacking toss.

"Lovely. Slosh it out."

I put my hand over my wine glass. "Not for me," I said.

"Doctor's orders, is it?" Angus guffawed. "Touch of the old knob-rot?"

While her boss was occupied with the wine list, the PA glanced at me – for just a moment longer than could be explained by mere looking around. The trick in such situations is to repress the instinct to avert one's gaze. If one can maintain eye contact for only half a second, a mutual conspiracy is immediately engendered. At that point even a microscopic movement of the corner of the mouth is enough to convey a smile. Both the PA and I gave the merest twitch of the lips before returning to conversation with our respective companions.

"I never drink. It's not obligatory, as far as I know," I told Angus.

He held up his hands "I'm not saying a word. Listen, if I was still single, I'd be chin-deep in muff from dusk till dawn – trust me."

Wincing, I looked at the menu. "I think I'll go for the whitebait."

"Fucking oysters is what you need, son!" Jakes roared. "Whitebait, my arse. *Jail*bait more like! Eh?"

He was attracting glances from other diners, and I wished that somehow I could freeze him in mid-chortle like a video and then go to each nearby table in turn to make it clear that I was as appalled and offended as they. I particularly wanted my discomfort to be evident to the PA, who was at that moment uncrossing and recrossing her legs in a most persuasive way.

Here's the galling thing about Angus Jakes, though. His loudmouthed oafishness was a complete affectation. He'd attended an obscenely expensive school. He had a first-class degree in Classics from Oxford, and his father was a High Court judge. When he was very drunk – which was often – his accent rode up like a debutante's hemline and his rounded vowels showed. I couldn't imagine what chemistry of insecurity and rebellion led him to adopt his plebeian demeanour, and I really didn't care. My concern was that I was inescapably stuck opposite him for the next hour and it made my scalp itch.

"So – let's not fuck about," Angus said when we'd ordered. "What do you need as an incentive for the Malaga trip?"

"I haven't really given it much thought, to be honest," I said. I shook out my napkin and put it in my lap. "There's plenty of time to talk about that." I topped up his wine. "Are you still driving the Audi?"

I knew full well that he'd recently acquired a new Jaguar. He was very proud of it, as became apparent over the next ten minutes during which he extemporised a slavering paean to its legion virtues. I forked whitebait and tried to look enthralled. When he paused for breath between the chrome alloy gear-shift and the heated walnut steering wheel, I asked, "So how much would one of those knock out at?"

A brief aside here: when you're trying to win someone over to an idea, it helps to speak in the vernacular with which they feel comfortable. Otherwise – as I hope is evident – I would never have employed so inelegant an idiom.

Angus grinned and picked up his wine glass. "Well, let's say you'd have enough change out of fifty-k to get a BigMac on the way home from the showroom." He took a mouthful of wine, his eyes on me. He swallowed and put down the glass. "Why? Do you fancy one?"

My eyes widened. "Who wouldn't?" I exclaimed. It was all I could do not to gild it with a breathless '*Gosh*!' Then I paused and looked downcast. "But – well – fifty thousand. I don't think I could ask for that much." I was keeping my voice down in case the PA was eavesdropping. I wouldn't want her to think I was as ingenuous as the circumstance required me to pretend.

"Well, nobody actually pays the list price for a motor like that, Tom," Angus said. "There are ways and means. For instance, the company could buy it on the never-never and lease it to you for a nominal amount – or actually to your mum or your cat, so it wasn't taxable. After three years, we'd flog it to recoup a chunk of the outlay and start again."

I shook my head admiringly. "Brilliant."

That exchange established two things, as I'd intended. Firstly, Angus had indicated that he was prepared to offer me the equivalent of fifty thousand pounds. Secondly, we had made it explicit that the value to me and the cost to Angus were separate issues. Having fixed that principle, I could now coax Angus along to the next hurdle, which I planned to reach about halfway through the entrée.

"How are things progressing with the employees' share scheme?" I asked, as my lemon sole arrived.

This was one of Angus' favourite topics. Shares would be awarded to employees in order (I quote from the e-mail) 'to integrate the rewards for individual performance with the ultimate growth of the company.' I'm sure riotous parties broke out all over the office when that one zapped into the inbox.

"We're just finalising the allocations. I expect you're wondering how much you're up for, eh?" Angus said, dipping a hunk of bread into his peppercorn sauce. It is somehow typical of Angus that he would book the best fish restaurant in the West End and then order steak. "Want me to put a figure on it?"

I did actually – though the shares themselves were of absolutely no use to me. Even if I were to find someone who'd buy them, the money accrued wouldn't count towards my required total.

"I don't want to put you on the spot," I told Angus. There was a black husk of peppercorn between his front teeth that was most distracting. What with that and the PA, who was licking each fingertip in turn, it was difficult to concentrate on the matter in hand.

"You'll find out next week anyway." Angus ran his tongue around his mouth and felt the peppercorn. He took a business card out of his pocket and flicked the corner of it along the gap between his teeth. "As our senior consultant you'll be getting shares to about the value of two Jaguars." He grinned. The peppercorn was still there. "Not bad, eh?"

A hundred grand in shares. I very nearly let my frustration get the better of me. "Just give me the bloody money!" I wanted to shout. Not that the shares were really worth that much. Their value was a reflection of Angus's own estimate of what his company might sell for, in the unlikely event of a bid for it.

"That's most welcome," I said. "Thank you."

"And who knows what they'll fetch when we float?" Angus pointed out. "Twice or three times the current value, eh?"

The PA was fellating a king prawn.

"Imagine that," I murmured.

Oh, Christ. 'Imagine that'. It was a feeble, flaccid response that would get me nowhere. I could feel the conversation slipping out of my control. I excused myself and went to the loo, where I sat in the cubicle and tried to refocus.

I really had been close to blowing it when he told me about the shares. It was the PA's fault. I was conducting probably the most important conversation of my life – a painstaking psychological seduction, really – and she was muddying my clarity of thought by coming on all lips and thighs. God knows, I enjoy female company as much as any well-balanced heterosexual man – but you have to get them out of your head when you're trying to achieve anything that requires uninterrupted application. And there's only one way to get a woman out of your head.

I closed my eyes and worked rhythmically on evicting the PA. Five minutes later, feeling much more relaxed and in control, I washed my hands, splashed cold water on my face and returned to the table.

"It must be painful for the directors to give away shares in their own company," I suggested to Angus as I sat down.

He was tapping the back of his spoon on the caramelised sugar of his dessert. "Well, not really," he said. "The shares we're giving away aren't mine or Dave's, exactly. They're allocated for employee incentives and sale to investors. I've already got my own sizeable wedge. This *crème brulée* is fucking quality." He leaned forward and beckoned me towards him. "Don't make it too blatant, but take a look at the bird behind me with the legs. Wouldn't mind having those wrapped round your neck, eh?"

I glanced at the PA. On closer inspection she wasn't quite as stunning as I'd previously thought. And she held her fork like a peasant.

I topped up Angus's wine yet again. It was time to reveal my agenda and let him come up with a stratagem of breathtaking lateral invention.

"I'm grateful for the shares, Angus, but the thing is – I need fifty grand in cash, and I need it fast."

He raised his eyebrows and reached for his wine, but didn't speak.

"So I was wondering," I continued, "if you knew of any investors who might be interested in my shares. I mean, obviously I'd prefer to hang onto them until we float, but, well, I have an immediate priority I have to cover."

Angus put down his glass. "Do you know what I'm not going to do, Tom? I'm not going to ask you why you need that sort of money in a hurry." He sat back, giving me time to marvel at his magnanimous sensitivity. "Let's just establish that boundary, yeah?"

I adopted the gratefully sheepish demeanour of one who has been let off the hook through the compassionate generosity of a more enlightened soul.

"Angus, I really appreciate that. So – do you know anyone who might want to buy? I mean, I'm willing to sell cheap. I need to move quickly and I realise that weakens my position."

"What would you be willing to sell for, if I could find you an investor?" he asked.

I shrugged. "All I need is fifty thousand. I'd sell the hundred-k's worth of shares at half-price." Given that I concoct wealth-management plans for a living, it was tongue-bitingly difficult for me to appear so naïve a negotiator. I was nervous that I might be overdoing the virgin-in-Vegas pose, but Angus was now in prestidigitator mode and his vanity blinded him to anything but his own prowess as a conjuror of fiscal spells.

"Well, the obvious buyer is me, isn't it?" he said. "Clearly I'd want to increase my stake in my own company. But there's a small problemo there."

There was indeed. He was faced with the delicious possibility of acquiring at half-price shares worth a hundred thousand pounds but, as I knew, he couldn't do that without consulting his fellow director who would undoubtedly want a cut of the action.

"Oh, right," I nodded. "You don't have that kind of money to hand. I understand."

"No, no," Angus said, eager to disabuse me of this muddleheaded notion. He explained that I shouldn't worry about his ability to come up with such a sum – he could get it in a phone call. But – was I paying attention here? – it would be necessary to put in place some pragmatic arrangements.

"So, on paper, you'd sell to my sister. See? You walk away with the money you need, and I keep the company in the family. Sorted."

Glory be – there it was. The offer of fifty thousand actual negotiable pounds. I breathed deeply. We were one jump away from the final stretch now, and I just needed to get him over it without a stumble. I could see the fifty thou piled up in the winner's enclosure. It was stacked on a safe that held a further two million, and the key was lying on top.

"But the thing is, Angus, I need the money to appear on my payslip as part of my annual earnings."

For a moment Angus was irritated. He'd come up with a watertight mechanism that benefited us both, and here I was punching holes in the cladding. "What the fuck for? You'll be done over on the tax, for a start." He sighed and rubbed his eyes, thinking. "All right, all right. Hang on a minute while I figure this out."

I simpered apologetically. "I'm really sorry to make this so complicated. Look – maybe we should just leave it for now and look at it when I get back from Malaga."

"Shut up a minute," Angus muttered. "I'm working."

"Sorry," I said again. Then, as an afterthought, "As a matter of fact, we ought to talk about the whole Malaga thing now anyway. I need to be on the road soon, if I'm going."

"Yeah, yeah. In a tick," Angus said distractedly. "See, what we need is an excuse to pull the funds out of the salary budget."

It was all I could do not to drag him across the table by his dreadful rugby-club tie and scream, "Malaga! Malaga, you idiot! That's your excuse!" But I just sat there, my fingernails digging into my palms as he stared blankly across the restaurant sucking his teeth.

"Wait, wait," he said at last, grinning. He looked across the table at me. "Jesus, I'm a genius. You ready for this?"

"What?" I asked, adopting an expression of moronic expectation.

"Fucking Malaga," he said. "Listen."

Angus would persuade Dave that it was worth offering me a fifty-k incentive to bring in both the client in Spain and the partnership with the firm of solicitors. I'd sign over my shares to Angus's sister, and the bonus would be paid in my May salary cheque. Upshot: I'd get my money, he'd get his shares and – he could hardly contain his chortling glee – the company would foot the bill for the entire deal.

"That's awe-inspiring, Angus," I breathed. "Absolutely amazing."

He grinned modestly. "Hey – it's just what I do." He beckoned a waiter. "Let's have a look at the cigars, mate. I deserve one." He turned back to me. "But one thing needs to be clear – the whole shebang depends on you doing the business in Spain. Without that, I've got no excuse to pay you the bonus."

"Don't worry about that," I told him. "It's just a question of making them think it was their idea. And that's what *I* do."

"Yeah, I know," Angus grinned. "I must come along on one of your appointments one day. I'd love to see you in action."

His mobile phone chirruped the vamping intro to *New York, New York* and he picked it up to look at the screen.

"It's the office. Hang on – I'd better take this." He took a slug of wine and put the phone to his ear. "Hey, Linda – what's up?" He looked at me. "Yeah – he's with me now. Yeah. Are they? What the fuck for? Alright – give us five minutes." He put the phone back on the table. "There's a copper at the office who wants to talk to you, Tommy-boy. We'd better take a raincheck on the cigars, eh?"

I tutted as I folded my napkin and put it on the table. "What a shame," I said. "We were having such fun."

*   *   *   *

However blameless a life one may have led, an unexpected visit from the police prompts panicky self-appraisal. As we walked back to the office, I undertook just such a review, which was not made easier by Angus's burblings of speculative concern.

"Maybe you got some bird up the duff, Tommy – you wouldn't be the first. Then again, the police've got better things to do. Oh, hang on. Under-age, could it be? Listen, who can fucking tell these days, eh? I mean, the kid next door to us at home – fourteen she is, but if you saw her in a club you'd put your mortgage on eighteen or nineteen." As we reached the door of the building, he grabbed my arm and turned me to face him. "Look, Tom – if it turns out you need to have been somewhere else when you could've been, like, somewhere *else* – you were with me, yeah? Playing pool at my place. I'll have a word with Jules and she'll back us up on it. All right?"

"I'm sure that won't be necessary, but thank you."

"No sweat, Tom. What are friends for?" He paused and leaned forward to whisper close to my lapel. "Unless it's – you know – rape, or something. I mean, *I'd* be there for you like a shot – but Jules might go a bit charlie on us for – well, serious stuff, eh?"

"I haven't raped anyone, believe me," I assured him. "Nor have I pulled off any major bullion raids or cut up arbitrary vagrants and distributed their body parts across the West End in plastic bags." I detached his paw from my wrist. "Excuse me – I'd better go in."

But he did have a point. As I walked up the stairs to the first floor, I was concerned about rape allegations – not because I had forced myself on anyone, but because it is such an easy charge for a disgruntled correspondent to bring. Looking back over the previous months, I identified two or three women who were perfectly capable of concocting some lurid episode in which they would be cast as the violated innocent. And, God knows, women need very little excuse to plant such a device. A missed phone call, an unforeseen let-down. Detach the wrong wire and they go off in your face.

"In the meeting room at the end," Linda said as I walked into reception. She was wearing a nothing-would-surprise-me expression that was almost smug. Case in point, actually – it had been two years since she and I had a brief fling and still she nursed spiky resentment out of all proportion to the episode that prompted it.

I hurried down the corridor to the meeting room and opened the door. By the window stood a brunette woman of about my age. Her black suede jacket looked about my age too – shiny at the elbows and dog-eared at the collar.

"Mr Tomàs Lyne, is it?" she said, holding out her hand to me. "I'm Detective Inspector Ruth Pontin. Please sit down."

"What's happened?" I asked as we took seats on opposite sides of the table. Her smile reassured me that nothing dreadful had transpired but the only alternative question would have been a guilt-assuming "What have I done?"

"Well," she said, folding her hands on the table top, "the very fact that you're here to ask me suggests that not much has happened at all. How are you feeling?"

I frowned. "Fine, thank you. Why?"

"Not dead at all?

I crossed my arms and sat back in the chair. "Is this cryptic joviality part of some new public relations initiative?"

She smiled. "I'm sorry. It's just my way of expressing relief." She sat forward and studied me. "You look very like your brother, Mr Lyne," she said. "Not quite identical, perhaps – but uncannily similar."

And then I got it.

"Oh, for Christ's sake!" I said, tipping my head back and covering my eyes with my hands. "This is something to do with Pablo, isn't it? Of course it is – stupid of me. It's always bloody Pablo." I looked across at the policewoman. "What has he done now?"

"Actually," she said, "he's confessed to your murder."

"What?"

"He claims to have killed his twin brother." She was more serious now. "He's a very unhappy and disturbed man, if you ask me."

I tutted. "Why do people always feel sorry for him? He needs a damn good slap."

DI Pontin told me about my brother's arrest on Wardour Street the previous evening. At the police station Pablo had been medically examined, showered and given clean clothes. They took a sample of his DNA. It was four o'clock in the morning when DI Ruth Pontin sat down to interview him. She didn't feel there was any hurry to grill their self-confessed murderer, because she had received a laboratory report saying that the blood in which Pablo had been soaked was his own. There was going to be no body to find, no gory high-profile case. Just a huge disappointment for the Press corps who were gathered outside the station.

"What happened this evening, Mr Lyne?" the detective asked my brother.

Pablo was obviously very tired, but seemed completely aware. He rubbed his eyes.

"We had to let each other go," he said. "Good luck to him."

"Your brother?"

Pablo nodded. "Yes. I killed him and I had to let him go. Dumb luck. It could have been me."

"And where is he now, Mr Lyne?"

"Not Mr Lyne. Everyone is Mr Lyne. My father was Mr Lyne. Tomàs is. You would be Mr Lyne if you were me. You could have been me. But I got to be Pablo. Dumb luck again."

"Thomas?" Pontin asked. "Is Thomas your brother?"

Again Pablo nodded. "And I'm Pablo. That's how the penny falls."

"Okay. Tell me about the blood, Pablo."

"It's noble Catalan blood with a South London chaser."

"Whose blood?"

Pablo shrugged. "I got everything – it's very unfair, very arbitrary. I got the body. But the blood is his. His share. "

"I think it's yours, Pablo," Pontin said quietly. "The DNA matches yours. It's your blood."

Pablo smiled for the first time, and leaned forward across the table. "We're twins. Identical DNA. My blood is his blood. His blood is mine."

Up to that point DI Pontin had been taking the case at a pace that allowed her to exercise real concern for Pablo on the basis that he was harmless though disturbed. But the news that Pablo was a twin invalidated that approach forthwith. Pontin was up and out of the room in seconds, yelling at her subordinates to start a search for Thomas Lyne whom she very much hoped she would find upright.

"Lyne is not that common a name," she said, as we walked along the corridor towards the elevator. "We googled it and came up with a Spanish version of Thomas at this company's website. It seemed to tie in with the name Pablo – and as soon as I saw you, of course, I knew you were his brother."

"I'm afraid so," I said. "Are you going to charge him with anything? Wasting police time? Wasting *everybody*'s bloody time?"

"I don't think we will, no. I must say, you don't seem very concerned about his well-being. Will you at least come down to the station to collect him?"

"That's not necessary," I told her. "Believe me, one gets used to the chaos Pablo causes. He always comes out of it unscathed. This instance is particularly bizarre, but otherwise unremarkable."

She pursed her lips. "Well, I'm sure you know him best."

She could hardly have said anything better designed to make my skin goosebump with irritation. I hate that patronising tone that women adopt. The implication is that although you are quite obviously a fool, they are wise enough and gracious enough to allow you to persist in your folly – but they'll be using this against you later.

My phone rang as we reached the foyer and simply to make the policewoman stand there and wait for me to finish before she could take her leave, I answered it. It was my mother yet again – in full flow, as if the call had been connected when she was in the middle of a paragraph.

"…I see it and I think, it's wrong what they say – they don't understand my Pablito. Where is he, Tomàs? He is on news like a criminal or someone! Poor Pablito – what have they done to him?"

I turned away from DI Pontin and walked a few paces back down the corridor.

"You'll be pleased to hear I'm not dead," I told her. "But thanks for asking."

"Oh, I know you are okay – you're a good boy. But where is Pablito? Go find him!"

I get so frustrated when she talks like this. My immediate impulse was to pursue the absurd generalisation that no one who was a good boy could possibly be the victim of fratricide. And then there was the utter lack of any concern about me specifically, good boy or otherwise. On top of which, I resented the assumption that I had nothing better to do than track Pablo down and make sure he was all right. I have spent my entire life being told to track Pablo down and make sure he was all right. Never once has he been expected to exercise any duty of care towards *me*.

But there's no point arguing.

"Mum, he's at a police station here in town. They're about to let him go home," I said, raising my eyebrows at the DI Pontin, who nodded. "I have no doubt he'll call you immediately," I added, though irony is completely wasted on the Condesa.

"Listen, Tomàs – you come and bring me to your place. We have nice dinner and talk – me with my boys. I make something delicious."

I turned away from DI Pontin again, flushing with anger now. "Mother – I can't. I'm going away on business – to Malaga." Somehow I hoped that the mention of a Spanish destination might sway the conversation in my favour. It was a forlorn move.

"You take time off work. Are you a shop boy? No – you're senior consultant! I talk to your boss. This is family. I make him understand."

"You most certainly will *not* talk to my boss," I hissed into the phone.

"I see Pablo on the television. He looks so ill, so tired. And you will just go off happy-happy to Spain? It's your brother, Tomàs!"

"Christ," I muttered. I did a quick mental rearrangement of my schedule. If I caught the last Chunnel train from Folkestone, drove all night across France and Spain – twenty-odd hours with my foot down – I could be in Malaga early Friday morning, just about. "Listen – all right. We'll both come down to you, okay? But I can't stay late."

"Only dinner and nice chat – that's all. Good boy, Tomàs. I was talking to Mrs Aitken today and she ask about you. He's a good boy, I said to her. He…"

"We'll see you about seven. I have to go. Bye."

I turned off my phone and slipped it into my pocket, then walked back to DI Pontin. I'd forgiven her for being condescending. They all do it – I think it's chromosomatic.

"You know – on second thoughts, perhaps I should come along and make sure Pablo's all right. Where are you parked? I'll follow you."

"Thank you," Pontin said. "I'd feel happier if he left with you." She pressed the button for the lift, smiling. She had nice teeth. Small and very straight. Were it not for the fact that my evening was spoken for, I'd have asked her out to dinner. "So why does your brother want to own up to killing you?"

"Not me," I sighed. "Not me."

"You have another brother?"

"Not exactly." I took a deep breath. "Believe it or not, Pablo and I were born in different countries and in different years…"

*   *   *   *

I returned to consciousness in a dream of wholeness, as if I had grown alone. I could see myself – wisps of hair floating in the fluid, fingers clenched, my tiny body tethered by a cord, turning over and over slowly; waiting.

I came into focus.

I looked out from behind Pablo's eyes and there I was as I should have been – individual and made of my own blood; tumbling without falling; immersed in heartbeat hum and saline glow; the blood in me viscous and sticky, in motion.

"You want to kill me," I said.

"You have to leave."

"No!"

I pushed forward, past Pablo. I thrust myself into his limbs. I swelled in his head. He pushed back and we toppled. Everything turned about, jumbled. I felt his arms around me, squeezing me, and the crimson vein was tangled between us, wrapped around us. We were rolling together – all three of us – in the soft, hot red. We were kicking and quickening. In the dark confusion I was torn from one and hugged by another, my blood wrung from me, my organs constricted, my head crushed out of shape. The looped red vein tightened around my throat.

He was killing me again, just like the first time. He was pulling me down, closing me in, smothering me. The soft red dimmed and darkened; the thump of hearts began to fade. I remembered this, as I remembered everything. Just like before, Pablo's embrace was lethal. I had to get out – and risk the world – or stay and die.

I released from him. I pushed myself, breathless, into the light. The cord that held me unravelled and I gripped tight, terrified by the white-noise splash and the rolling wet dark that stretched endlessly beyond the periphery of the light. I didn't dare let go of the filament that connected me to Pablo's flesh. Without that anchor I might be sucked away into the slushy nothing.

Floating, I drew my focus close. I listened not to the static hiss of forever, but to the world of sense and form in which I was suspended. I did what all of you do – I blocked out infinity by immersing myself in the immediate.

In the art gallery, watching Pablo, there was a woman. She knew she had a disease, but she had told no one. There was a man who had been happy until he saw the blood on the walls, which reminded him of Afghanistan. There was another man. He hated Pablo and was pleased to see him in pain.

I picked up these impressions like flavours in the air – like the individual scents of a pack to which I had always belonged. At a distance from my brother, though tethered to him still, I could taste other flesh, other perceptions contained in that flesh, other comprehensions of those perceptions.

Pablo stumbled towards the door and pushed through the knot of onlookers. I was pulled after him like a balloon flapping from the window of a taxi. As we passed people, I could hear their secret whispers, see their unintended colours, smell them. I understood each of them immediately, though only for a moment.

On the crowded street the susurration was constant. This man was preparing to sidle into a sex-shop. This one was drunk and he missed his son. Associations and memories burst like skyrockets in the minds of each passer-by who glanced at blood-soaked Pablo. The thin philosophies and garish fancies of flesh billowed and tumbled around me like plastic bags in the wind – and the wind itself gusted from the dark highway on which the rain fell endlessly. As I drifted from Pablo, I could hear, behind the murmurs of flesh, the slushy white noise of eternal downpour.

At the amusement arcade – amidst the insanity of light and sound that seemed far away from me and unimportant – I listened to the whispers of the woman in the change booth. She was frightened of cancer but more frightened of finding out whether she had it. Even as she lit another cigarette, she thought of tumours in her lungs. Every person she encountered was dying, and she assessed each as either destined to die before her or likely to see her out. If there were more of the former than the latter, she wouldn't get cancer that day. For her, the universe existed merely to tussle over the issue of her mortality.

I had thought that Tom's view of the world was conventional, and that Pablo was odd. But as I listened to whispers from all around me I realised that none of you has any idea of how others experience reality, although you're all certain that everyone lives in the same world as yourself. Each of you is the creator of a unique universe with a population of one. Each of you is his own God.

The police came. Pablo dragged me to the police station. I felt that if I wished, I might let go – but I had no idea what would happen to me then. Without Pablo, perhaps I would simply float away like a soap bubble. And if I tried to go back to him, he would kill me. I had little choice other than to be tugged around.

Pablo was interviewed by a policewoman whose whisper told me that she was certain the universe existed for no other reason than to keep her from boredom. I half-listened as she questioned Pablo, but I was preoccupied with keeping a grip on him. If I lost concentration, I might be sucked out onto the night-time highway to travel forever in the slushy white-noise of the endless rain.

*   *   *   *

My brother was waiting in an interview room with a portly legal representative. He looked ghastly; washed-out and scrawny; dark-ringed eyes and dry, flaking lips. Why anyone says he resembles me, I can't imagine. He was wearing some kind of blue police overall and his hair was hanging over his face.

"What in Christ's name do you think you're playing at?" I asked him. "Are you happy now you've got everyone running around after you?"

He peered at me from under his ratty fringe, a sullen fourth-form scowl on his face. He glanced at Ruth Pontin.

"You didn't need to bring Tom into this. He's not my keeper."

"See?" I said to her. "He doesn't want me here any more than I want to be here." I turned back to Pablo. "You scared the life out of Mum – she's worried sick about you."

"Perhaps we should leave them to chat," the fat lawyer suggested to DI Pontin, getting to his feet. She nodded, saying that she'd be just outside if we wanted her.

"I'll call Mum," Pablo said when we were alone. "I'll explain."

"Explain what? That you want to drag up the whole Perdito thing yet again – that you want to make her think about all that awful stuff? It's so fucking selfish, Pablo."

"It's all right. I've let go of him. I'll explain."

This was a recurring obsession with Pablo. I used to think it was some kind of mental illness, but actually it was just infantile self-dramatisation. Most of us have a secret friend when we're children, and we grow out of it. But not Pablo. His secret friend had always been the triplet that never was. Pablo ascribed to him an individual personality and a separate existence. He acted as Pablo's life-coach – though on the evidence of Pablo's life one would have to conclude that Perdito couldn't coach anything more demanding than a racing snail.

None of this would have mattered, I suppose, if Perdito were completely the product of Pablo's imagination – but he wasn't. He was a dead baby – a mourned lost child with a grave in the grounds of a military hospital in Samoa and a memorial in a Surrey garden. To my mother he was the child she failed. In her Catholic view of the universe, all good things were a blessing and all bad things were a punishment. Two of her babies were healthy and whole, but the third was stillborn – stunted and mixed up with a living one. What had God meant to convey by that? That she was good but could be better? That she should contemplate the fragility of existence? That the Almighty was merciful but not a pushover? I think she fought this battle with herself every New Year's day at Pelham Grange, and I'm sure she mourned the child whom she believed she would kiss one day, but not yet.

But when Pablo used his invented Perdito as an alter-ego, it was as if he was dragging the corpse like Hector around the avenues of Berkshire. I wasn't in the least sentimental about our unfortunate unborn sibling but I was protective of the Condesa. She was completely infuriating and a real drain on my time, but she was also my mother, and I was the eldest son. I had a sense of duty – which is more than can be said either for Pablo, who had all the filial feeling of a sunflower seed, or Jacinta whose support of my mother was expressed by e-mailing me ski-resort photographs that I had to print out and send on. Someone had to keep an eye on Mum, and it was me.

"Listen," I said to Pablo. "The Condesa wants us to go down there for dinner tonight, and I've promised to take you. But I don't want any mention of this Perdito nonsense, all right? We'll just tell her you were doing one of your art performance things and the police misunderstood it. Are you paying attention?"

Pablo was staring unfocussed at the desktop, head slightly inclined. His eyes flicked from side to side, and then he looked at me.

"I wasn't sure he'd gone. But…" He reached for his smokes. "Yeah. It's like hearing a door closing softly. I just heard that." He closed his eyes and leaned back as if he were listening to music on headphones. "No, he's not there," he said, looking at me again. He nodded as he lit his cigarette. "He really has gone."

I slapped my hand down on the table. "That's exactly the sort of crap I don't want you saying, Pablo! Jesus – don't you care whether you upset her at all?"

He smiled like a simpleton – which is an affectation, by the way. He acts as if he's a gifted fool, when in fact he's a bright and perfectly able person, though preternaturally lazy. You'd be amazed how many people – especially women – fall for this brilliant-but-helpless pose.

"I'll call her and explain," he said.

"Christ," I said, turning to open the door. "Give me strength."

*   *   *   *

"Are you happy now? Now you have everyone running around after you? God, you're a selfish bastard, Pablo."

Tom was there. He was agitated and flustered. Incompatible concerns were pulling him apart. He was gleaming with sprung joints and gaping seams.

Relieved, I slid into him and nestled in his soft hot red. I wormed in deep, safe in the cage of his bones, cosseted in the cushions of his flesh. I burrowed, gulping tears of relief, barely able to hear the endless rain that was now faint wash of hiss behind the thump of a real heart and the throb of blood in hot veins.

Pablo lit a cigarette, listening.

"He really has gone," he said.

But I hadn't gone – I had arrived. I had leapt through the void to where I was safe, where I belonged, and I would never let go again. I would live in Tom.

I just needed to make him understand.

*   *   *   *

The lawyer wasn't around, but DI Pontin was in the corridor talking to another officer. I told her I'd take Pablo as long as there was absolutely no official sense in which I was being held responsible for him. I was given a plastic bag containing his bloody clothes – which I dumped in the car park – and I drove Pablo to my flat. I made him change into some of the less expensive items from my own wardrobe before setting off to Hook, calling the Condesa from the car to tell her we were on our way. She asked me to stop for wine somewhere, and perhaps some chocolate 'with the whole nuts, not broken in pieces'.

It was the start of the rush hour, and I wanted to clear town before the bridges clogged up completely. As we headed west I made a call to change my cross-channel reservation. The last train left Folkestone at a quarter to midnight, which would mean getting out of Hook by nine-fifteen and hoping for the best on the motorway.

"Listen," I told Pablo. "I've got to be away from Mum's sharpish, so I don't want you turning this evening into a Tennessee Williams drama, all right? Just be calm and sane and apologetic. No arguments, no mad retrospectives. Please."

"I've never felt less dramatic in my life," he said, leaning his head against the passenger-side window.

We made surprisingly good time. Pablo was dozing even before we got to Fulham Broadway and he was snoring and dribbling by the time I pulled off the motorway into the Fleet services for petrol and to pick up wine and chocolate as instructed. Against my better judgement I bought Pablo two packets of cigarettes, though I wasn't going to let him smoke them in the car. Still, as we were ahead of our schedule and the Condesa would undoubtedly be behind hers, I thought we might stop at a pub and have a drink and a civil conversation. I didn't want us to turn up at the house still out of sorts with each other.

No danger of that, as it turned out. When I got back to the car park, Pablo was gone and so was my Alfa.

*   *   *   *

I should not have left the keys in the car. And I should not have left my phone in the car. But what I really should have avoided leaving in the fucking car was Pablo.

I went back into the services building to find a public telephone from which I could call a cab to take me to Folkestone. I also intended to call Mum and tell her that her poor Pablito had made off with thirty-grand's worth of Alfa Romeo and I was going to report him to the police.

I had some loose change but no folding money at all, having spent the last of it on cigarettes for the car-thief. I sought out an ATM, wondering what exorbitant cab fare I'd be charged for the hundred mile trip to the coast. The Chunnel ticket was paid for and only needed to be collected but I'd need to buy clothes of course, and hire a car on the other side. I checked my jacket pocket for my passport, thanking God I hadn't put it in my briefcase.

I slid my card into the machine and entered my PIN. There was a discouraging whirr and then some arrhythmic grinding, like a robot with a dry cough.

"Oh, no," I murmured. "Come on."

The screen flickered.

There is a fault with this machine. Please remove your card.

I waited with my hand out, but the card did not reappear. I smacked the slot with the side of my fist. Nothing.

"Swallowed it, has it?" An old gentleman was peering around my shoulder like an inquisitive puffin.

"You haven't got a penknife I could borrow, have you?" I said, running a fingernail to and fro along the slot.

"Oh, Lord, you don't want to go sticking a penknife in there," the puffin said. "That'd be criminal damage." He glanced up to the ceiling. "I expect they've got cameras."

"Marvellous." I muttered, straightening up. "Look – could you give me a lift somewhere? To Hook? Or back to London?"

He shook his head. "I'm sorry. What with the wife and the grandchildren and all the luggage, we've no spare room. Otherwise I would, really." He shrugged. "Anyway – best of luck."

I glanced at my watch and then checked the change in my pocket. I had enough for two calls – assuming I could find a phone that was working. I looked around and spotted a public telephone by the amusement arcade.

"Hello?"

"Mum, it's Tomàs."

"Tomàs! You find Pablo? I make nice lamb with herb. And good bread from the delicatessen. Pablo is okay?"

"Mum – listen. I'm stuck at Fleet services. I've got no money and Pablo has run off with my car. I need…"

"Run off? You found him and now you lose him? Where did he go?"

"I don't care! Look, I need you to send me a cab and some money."

"He's all right in his mind? Not – you know – in one of these strange moods?"

"Listen!" I tried to stay calm. It wouldn't get me anywhere to become agitated. "Yes – he's fine. Actually, he said he'd drop around to you this evening. He said he'd rather see you on his own."

"Ah, you see!" the Condesa crowed. "When is there a problem, he wants to speak to his mama. Yes – I give him a good meal and we have nice chat."

"Exactly what he needs – a nice chat. In the meantime, I have a problem too. I let him have my car but I stupidly forgot that I had no money with me. So…"

"You are in Fleet service?"

"Yes. So…"

"Okay, you have cup of coffee now. When Pablo is here, I tell him to come pick you up."

"No! For Christ's sake, listen! I need…"

"You are a good boy to let him have your car, Tomàs. Oh! The cooker bell is ring. Go have some nice coffee. Bye!"

And she hung up on me. It's a testament, I think, to my unfailing self-control that I didn't scream with frustration and smash the handset to smithereens against the wall.

Again I checked my watch. A little after seven o'clock. Time wasn't a problem as long as I could get to Folkestone before midnight. I had enough change for one more phone call. I could order a cab and worry about being penniless once I reached the port – it would be an uncomfortable dialogue with the driver, but I couldn't see what choice he would have but to take my details on trust. Or I could call Angus and have him send a car and some cash. As I pondered these options, I glanced out of the window and saw the geriatric puffin leaving in a spacious family saloon devoid of spouses, descendants or any form of luggage. Bastard. Human beings really are the most duplicitous, unhelpful and mean-spirited species. I could honestly do without them completely were it not for the need to have the streets cleaned and the sewage treated.

I decided that the call to Angus was too risky. I might well get his voicemail, which would mean I'd have no option but to wait. I'd have no control at all over the situation.

On the wall above the phone there was a number for A1 Cars.

"My car's broken down and I don't have time to wait for assistance, so I need a cab to Folkestone."

"Blimey, that's a bit of a run. Cash job or card?"

I was in a position to be obliging. "Whichever you prefer."

"Two hundred quid cash then."

"You're joking."

"Well, the driver's got to come all the way back. Not much chance of picking up a fare in bloody Folkestone, is there?"

Duplicitous, mean-spirited and avaricious. Irredeemable. I decided that should I survive nuclear Armageddon, I'd side with the cockroaches.

"Fine. How soon?"

Half an hour, he assured me. I gave my name and a brief description of myself and said I would be standing outside Burger King.

"Gotcha. Go and have a coffee – the driver'll come and find you."

I wandered aimlessly around the service station, seething. There are times – and it has nothing to do with any prevailing mood of misanthropy – when everyone looks to me like a Mervyn Peake caricature. Each human face I see is magnified and open-pored and soupy. I'm crowded by flaccid, slimy lips between which strands of spiderweb spittle stretch and snap; rubber skin – spam pink, maggot white, toadstool brown – sweating like camembert or dry-cracked as cheddar rind; piggy noses, rotting strawberry noses, papercut and bullethole and weeping-sore noses; and eyes like something that blooms on the soggy satin lining of a month-buried casket. Gargoyles and monstrosities confront me everywhere I turn, hideous and blithely insensible to the ghastly spectacle they present. I swear, there were one or two specimens at Fleet services – sucking up dish-froth coffee and gumming the custard out of etiolated pastries – whose inexcusable repulsiveness was almost more than I could stomach.

I stationed myself outside Burger King and looked at my watch yet again. I'd developed a series of tics – stare at passing grotesque, wince, check watch. It was more than half an hour since I'd ordered the taxi. Twenty minutes later there was still no sign of it.

I went back to the telephone and made a reverse-charge call to the cab company. To my relieved astonishment, it was accepted.

"Cab to Folkestone? Ring any bells? Name of Lyne?"

"What you doing reversing the charges? You're supposed to be holding two hundred quid."

"No one in this hellhole will give me change of a fifty-pound note. Now where's my cab?"

"Buy a cup of coffee then. This isn't the bloody Samaritans."

If one more person suggested that I buy a cup of coffee, I'd torch Starbuck's. "Look – I'm sorry. I'll give the driver extra for the call. Just get me a cab, I beg you."

"It'll be with you in fifteen minutes. White Mondeo. Wait by the main entrance."

"No – we said I'd wait inside by Burger King."

"Did we? Suit yourself. By Burger King."

"You will tell him that, won't you? Hello?"

You see, this is what I mean about the drooling incompetence of every damnable cretin on the face of the earth. The taxi-dispatcher's inept stupidity concerning the agreed meeting-point would have caused me to have missed the taxi completely, were it not for the compensating inept stupidity of his not having dispatched the bloody thing at all.

As I paced up and down outside Burger King, I planned my revenge on the owner of the cab company. Once I'd inherited, I would establish a free taxi-service in the area. I'd subsidise it completely, undercutting A1 Cars and depriving them of business. Then, when they were on their last legs, I'd contact the proprietor and tell him I'd close down my operation if he would personally pick me up from Aberdeen and drive me home to London. I would not, of course, be in Aberdeen. When he called me from

Scotland, I'd say, "No, no. Not *Aberdeen*. Abingdon. In Oxfordshire. Chop-chop, my man."

This scenario so engrossed me that forty-five minutes simply flew by. I was about to make another call to the moron at A1 Cars when a voice at my shoulder said, "Name of Lyne for Folkestone?"

It was the cab driver, at last – a slight woman of about thirty in a baggy t-shirt and faded jeans. My first observation was that she'd made a mistake wearing her hair up, which accentuated the rather corvine structure of her face. My second and more practical thought concerned the admission I'd be obliged to make at journey's end that I had not a penny on me. I knew it wasn't going to go over too well, but I felt sure a hundred-mile drive would give me ample time to demonstrate my honourable and trustworthy nature.

"Yes, that's me. Thank God you're here – I was beginning to give up hope. Fifteen minutes, I was told, and that was nearly an hour ago." I smiled. "Not that I blame you. I'm sure you came as soon as you could."

"An hour ago?" the woman said, shaking her head. "God, I'm sorry. I only got the job just now when I called in."

See? Absolutely hopeless. After Abingdon, Aberystwyth.

"Well, it's very good of you to take it on. I know it's a bit of a trek." Again, I smiled, and glanced at my watch. It was nine o'clock. That left very little leeway for roadworks, pile-ups or traffic jams. I'd have to tell her to put her foot down. "Shall we be on our way?" I said, holding a hand out towards the car park. "After you."

As she walked ahead of me – very trim figure, I noted; tiny waist – I asked, "What's your name, incidentally?"

"Melanie."

"Tom," I told her. "Nice to meet you, Melanie."

Everything was suddenly going very well. It might even turn out to be a pleasant drive.

"I'll need to get some petrol." she said as we reached the car. "Oh, that reminds me. The boss said I had to ask for the fare upfront. There are some really crooked people about."

"Sadly true," I said, nodding. "Let me ask you this – would you say that I had an honest face?"

*   *   *   *

At a quarter to midnight I managed to find a lorry driver who was willing to give me a lift from Fleet services back into London. I had to walk from Putney Bridge to Kennington and, having no keys, I woke Barbara up to let me in to the building. She was less than cheerful about it – not because it was three o'clock in the morning, but because she had company, the shameless slut. She handed me my spare apartment-keys from Jeremy's cork-board with impatient bad grace.

I let myself into the flat, poured a glass of milk and slumped in front of the computer. I looked at journey-planners, car hire sites, train timetables. I calculated the fines I'd accrue if I drove right across Europe at a remorseless hundred-and-twenty. It couldn't be done. By the time I'd picked up a spare laptop from the office, hired a car, got out of London, it would be early Thursday afternoon, at best. There was no hope of making Malaga by ten on Friday morning – not by car and not even by train.

Two and a half million pounds. When I was young I couldn't imagine that sort of sum – but once one understands what money is, what it can do, two and a half million pounds ceases to be abstract. Angus was fond of the cliché that time is money. At the workaday level, that was true. If I spent the day writing up legacy plans for clients, or poring over the Chancellor's latest scheme for robbing graves, I earned nothing but what would feed me while I did it again tomorrrow. I'd converted my time into money, proving Angus right – and I was a small but measurable span closer to death.

But there's a critical mass of money – and two and half million was massive enough for me – that would set in motion a reversal of the Einsteinian alchemy. The problem is no longer, "How much money can I turn this year into?" but "How many years can I turn this money into?" I knew that I could turn my inheritance into at least thirty years – and they wouldn't be cheese-paring years, either – which would mean that nobody could ever again tell me what to do, where to go, how to run down the remaining revolutions of the clock. What I was after, you see, was not a new Alfa and the ingratiating approval of my bank manager. I didn't actually want the money at all. I simply wanted time enough to live my life. I wanted to be in control of the expenditure of that time.

But as I turned off the computer and shucked my clothes ready for bed, I couldn't see any way of getting what I wanted that did not involve doing what I cannot bring myself to do. It's not cowardice. It's not just some disinclination that I've turned into a neurotic block. It's a crippling disability, and I can't overcome it by force of will, any more than a quadriplegic, though offered kingdoms, could make himself walk across the room by thinking positive thoughts.

Even for two and a half million pounds, even for thirty years of freedom, I could not subject myself to the suffocating, paralysing terror that would engulf me were I to step aboard a plane.

*   *   *   *

As early as I dared – about three minutes past seven, actually – I called Alice's mobile.

"Hello, Tom," she said, sounding very awake and breezy. "Are you in Spain yet?"

"As you ask, I'm in Kennington. That's what I'm calling about. I have to be in Malaga this time tomorrow and I need your help."

"And how can I help?"

This was going to be tricky.

"I was hoping," I said, "that you could spend some time with me today and – well – speed up the process. I have no recourse but to get on a plane tonight and I need some sort of therapeutic crash course."

She laughed. "Interesting choice of words. But I'm afraid that it's not that simple or that quick. There's no cognitive equivalent of penicillin, Tom."

"Oh, come on," I urged. "You know where we're going with treatment. You know what you're going to tell me. All I want to do is skip to the denouement."

"Really – that's not how it works. I'm sorry."

I knew she'd say that. She was obliged to. An admission that what I was suggesting was achievable would undermine the very basis of her livelihood. I had to find some angle that offered an upside for her.

"Look – how long were we expecting me to be coming to you? Six months?" I did a quick mental sum. "What if I were to pay you for the equivalent of a year's weekly visits? Just for seeing me all day today?"

As soon as I'd said it I realised it was a mistake – completely the wrong strategy.

"It's not a financial issue, Tom" Alice replied, rather tightly. She was of that prim post-hippy persuasion that regards any allusion to the value of money as a kind of cosmic vulgarity. Not, I might add, that that stopped her charging thirty quid an hour. However – I had made an uncharacteristic error of pitch and hit a jarring bum-note, which I put down to lack of sleep.

"No, no," I soothed, "I'm not trying to buy a solution. I just don't want you to be out of pocket, that's all. I want money not to be an issue."

"Not only is it not an issue, it's not relevant," she said. "Look, Tom, I can see that you're in a pickle here but there's really nothing I can do"

Everyone, as they teach you in trite selling seminars, has a hot-button. You just have to find it. Alice, for instance, had chosen a profession in which she could fulfil her desire to understand people's problems and help solve them. She'd let me know that she appreciated I was 'in a pickle' because that displayed her empathic nature. All that was stopping her taking the next step – which was to come to my rescue – was her professional *modus operandi*. It was intrinsic to her worldview, and to her way of valuing herself in fact, that problems such as mine were so deep-rooted that their resolution required lengthy and complex treatment. Any suggestion that we could get it all sorted out in an afternoon was anathema to her.

I paced to and fro in my living room, my tired brain rummaging through files of tactics like someone looking for a lost insurance document.

"Alice – you've told me dozens of times that I need to be ready to deal with whatever it is that's causing my problem. You've said I'm avoiding it. Yes?"

"Well, you do currently take the view that the world has an issue rather than you, yes."

I walked through to the study and took my back-up credit card out of the desk drawer.

"Fair enough. And the point of the counselling is to get me to a position in which I truly want to change my behaviour or my perception or whatever, isn't it?"

"Which is a long way off yet, if you want my opinion, Tom."

Clenching the phone between ear and shoulder, I sat down in front of the computer and brought up the webpage of flights to Malaga. There was an early evening departure from Gatwick that would suit me perfectly. But merely looking at the details – schedule, flight number, check-in time – made my palms damp with apprehension.

"Well," I said, "extraordinary circumstances have accelerated me to that point. I'm ready to change. I really want to move to a resolution, Alice."

I could hear her thinking this over. I could also hear her making tea. A spoon was chinking in a mug. Earl Grey, I'd bet. Or possibly blackcurrant and camomile. Something sanctimoniously unpalatable.

"Actually, this is not unknown," she said. "A crucially significant event can sometimes trigger a cognitive shift that permits new realisations of…"

"Yes! That's what's happened!"

"But I've never heard of anyone using that as a basis for accelerated closure through intensive therapy. Quite an idea."

I'd got her interested. The professional gobbledegook indicated that she'd found a possible justification for seeing me. Now she was trying to sell it to herself. As she mused aloud about the possible dynamics of decision-point crises and focussed counselling, I'm sure she had visions of her face all over the cover of *Brain Boilers' Quarterly*. The clincher would be to get her to believe it was she who was pushing the thing forward.

"Hang on a minute," I said, suddenly nervous. "Do you mean no one's ever done this before? I mean – are we sure it'd be safe?"

"Oh, God, yes. Don't worry. My approach will be to utilise proven techniques in a way that…"

I stopped listening when she said 'will' rather than 'would'. She was sold.

She hadn't been intending to work that day, as it happened. Someone else was using the consulting room in Camden, so we agreed that Alice would come to my place.

"I'll see you around nine, Tom – is that okay?"

"Perfect. And thank you. I'm looking forward to it, in a strange kind of way."

"It's all very exciting. See you soon, Tom."

That's another thing about people like Alice. They insist on constantly using your name. She must have said 'Tom' a dozen times during that conversation. It's also, incidentally, a well-known trick in selling. A potential client pays more attention to you and finds it more difficult to dismiss you if you keep addressing him by name. So I knew what she was doing. She was selling me a solution just like I sold solutions to my clients. I recognised all the techniques. And that's why I was sure that she could come in and supply whatever it was she usually puts off delivering for six months or more. It was just a question of cutting the spiel.

I typed in my credit card details and booked the flight.

*   *   *   *

My study overlooked the garden. There was a knotty wisteria growing up the wall from Jeremy's patio and when the window was open the scent of it infused my room, which I found relaxing. That morning I sorely needed to relax.

As I was making coffee and toast, the phone rang and the machine kicked in.

"Tomàs? Where is Pablo? He didn't come here last night. Go find him and…"

No. I was never going to find Pablo again. Nothing the Condesa could say – nothing anyone could say – would ever persuade me to waste another single minute of my life finding bloody Pablo. Walking past the machine, I switched it off in mid-fret and took my breakfast to the study. I leaned back in my swivel chair and put my feet up on the sill of the open window, enjoying the early sunshine. I might have dozed off. A little before nine o'clock the entry-phone buzzed.

"What a lovely flat," Alice said as I took her coat. "Very smart."

"Thank you. Would you like some tea? I've only got the ordinary stuff, I'm afraid."

"Just a glass of water would be fine."

She followed me into the kitchen, complimented me on the colour scheme and said how clean and tidy everything was, considering I was a man on my own. I get that a lot from women. Apparently the ability to wipe up a coffee stain is so remarkable in the human male as to be almost unnerving.

"Fizzy all right?" I asked, opening the fridge and taking two glasses from the cupboard.

"Yes, fine." She ran her eye over the shelves. "I like these mugs."

"I'll give you the catalogue," I said, closing the cupboard door. I put the bottle and glasses on a tray with some coasters. "Shall we get started then?"

"So," Alice said when we'd settled in the living room, "what significant event prompted your phone call?"

"The company I work for is in trouble. There's a contract on offer in Spain, and if we secure it we'll avoid redundancies and all the attendant trauma." I clasped my hands in my lap and dropped my head. "Friends and colleagues are relying on me." A pause, and then I lifted my gaze again and looked directly at Alice. "I don't want to go into the office on Monday and say, 'Sorry, guys, you're all out of work because I couldn't get on the plane.'"

Alice raised her eyebrows, which was a bit of a disappointment. I was hoping for a single silent tear.

"Without wishing to appear rude, Tom," she said, "I really wouldn't have expected your motivation to be rooted in altruism. Well, well. Perhaps we'll both move forward in our separate life-journeys today."

"As long as mine ends in Malaga, I'll be happy."

She opened her bag and took out a sheaf of paper, which she laid on the coffee table between us. She started to turn over the pages, scanning.

"This is the e-mail you sent me the night before last."

"My God, was it only the night before last?"

"Mm-hm. I have to say I found it fascinating."

"Glad to have captivated you," I said, "but do we really have time to go any further into my past relationships? I mean, we've only got a few hours and I'd really prefer to concentrate on the aeroplane problem."

Alice looked up from the print-out and fixed her eyes on me. She said nothing. I stared back for a few seconds and then slumped in my seat.

"All right, all right," I said, holding up my hands. "I trust you. We'll do it your way."

"Thank you," Alice said, returning her attention to the sheets of paper. She tapped a finger on them. "You know what strikes me about this? It's easy to see why Louise split up with you – you're very explicit about how demanding you were to be around. But it's more difficult to see why she got into the relationship in the first place."

"Oh, thanks," I said.

"From what's on the page, I mean. What do you think attracted her to you when she had so many suitors to choose from?"

"I was absolutely fantastic in bed," I said immediately.

Alice blinked at me silently, and then she jotted something on her notepad.

"Okay," I said. "I suppose it's unlikely to have been that alone." I topped up my water, spilling a little on the coffee-table. "Why me then?" I stood up and went to the kitchen for a paper towel. "I certainly wasn't the bookies' favourite at the off." I came back in and wiped up the spill, dabbing the coaster and drying the bottom of the glass. "I must have been doing something right, I suppose." I went to the kitchen again to put the soggy paper in the bin and then returned to my seat. "Let me think."

I frowned, looking at the bubbles rising in my water. I noticed that there was a little chip on the base of Alice's glass. That's what you get for putting them in the dishwasher. I reached to pick it up. "Oh, God – look at that. It's chipped. I'll get you another one."

"Tom – sit down!" Alice said sharply.

"It's okay. I'll just…"

"Sit down!" She took a deep breath. "Listen. What you're exhibiting here is displacement activity, which is an avoidance technique. Usually I'd wait it out, but you have expressly asked me to accelerate the programme, so I need to be more proactive than usual."

I bit my lip. 'Proactive' is therapist-speak for 'bossy', of course. I felt told off and my instinct was to ask her who the hell she thought she was to clip me round the ear like that. But I needed to keep her focussed on the task in hand, so I nodded and looked contrite.

"I agree. Sorry."

"Thank you." She shifted in her seat and folded her hands in her lap. "Now – I'd like you to think back to the start of your relationship with Louise. I know that's difficult for you, but I want you to try."

I closed my eyes. I have trouble even summoning Louise's face, to be honest. When I picture her I actually see a photograph taken at Camden Market. She's standing on the bridge above the lock, her back to the camera, looking over her shoulder and smiling. I don't remember taking the shot. It might not even have been me that took it. And yet that's the Louise I carry with me – not the actual animated real girl but a photograph of her in a moment and in a place at which I might not even have been present.

Casting my mind back to the early days of the affair, I remembered something that I'd missed, I think, when I e-mailed Alice. Louise and I alternated visits. One weekend I'd go to Cambridge and the next she'd come to me. She'd show up Friday night and we frequented my pubs and we went to my restaurants. We slept in my bed.

"I missed you this week," she said one morning as we lay there after sex. "Did you miss me?"

"Well, to be honest," I said, grinning, "I was so preoccupied with fighting off wanton and lubricious philosophy undergraduates that I barely gave you a thought."

Louise propped herself up onto one elbow and looked down at me. "I bet that's true. I bet you're inundated with offers."

"I don't suppose I get any more than you do."

She dropped back on to the pillow and reached for her cigarettes. "The thing is," she said, lighting one, "that people like you. You could get someone new to love you tomorrow. I couldn't. I could get fucked no problem – but that's all."

"Oh, come on…"

"No, no – it's true." She passed me the cigarette. "I don't mind. You love me even though you have this huge choice of women. It makes me feel special. But I need you a lot more than you need me."

"Well, you are special," I said. "You're very special."

At the start, mine was the stronger hand. By the time Louise walked out, it was a stump. As long as she was tugging me around like a hambone on a string I didn't notice that I was incapable of independent movement – but after she cut the cord I could only lie where I was left, immobile and picked clean of flesh. I remember going into the kitchen a week or so after she dumped me. I opened the larder and stood for I don't know how long, staring at the food. I had no idea what I liked to eat. I knew what Tom-and-Louise ate – they ate beans on toast and paella and pasta sauce made with frankfurters. I knew that. But Tom? I couldn't imagine what Tom ate. I pressed my forehead against the shelf and sighed, ashamed of being so stripped of personality that I couldn't even tell whether I liked baked beans.

Having touched on the Louise disaster, Alice and I started talking about the Scotland trip and the weird waking dream I had on the clifftops.

"The first time we met," Alice said, "you told me that you'd never had any odd experiences attributable to a psychic connection with your twin."

"Did I say that?"

Maybe I did. The process of talking to Alice about my past was bringing to the surface memories that had been long submerged, as if tectonic shifts on the ocean floor had toppled a sunken liner and the gas-swollen corpses trapped inside were now floating up through a rip in the hull, rising past the coral reef, drifting there blind and gruesome in the sunlight. And Alice was proposing a day's snorkelling.

"Anyway," I said, "it wasn't anything psychic. I was just out of my mind with grief and exhaustion. It was some kind of synaptic short-circuit."

She nodded. "You're very resistant to the suggestion that you might be unusually close to Pablo."

"I'm resistant to the suggestion that I ought to be."

"And you dismiss the idea that he might really be disturbed. I mean, clinically unwell. But from what you say about his perception of Perdito, that seems a reasonable hypothesis."

I sighed, and went to fill the kettle.

"Mental illness tends to run in families, doesn't it?" I called as I turned on the tap. "It's a hereditary thing."

"Often, but not always."

"Well, there you are then. There's no history of lunatics on either side of the family. Morons, possibly, but not nutcases. Would you like a biscuit?"

"Don't open a packet especially."

"It's okay." I brought through the Tupperware in which I keep biscuits. "I'll get a plate, hang on."

There was an open pack of Lincoln biscuits in the Tupperware, alongside an open pack of Digestives. When I got back with the tea and two plates, I discovered that Alice had tipped them all out into the plastic box and the wrappers were screwed up in a ball on the coffee-table.

"Hm. You've unwrapped all the biscuits," I observed, putting down the tea.

"Oh, sorry. Does it matter?"

"Well, not really. I just don't want them to get stale."

"Don't worry. That's what Tupperware's for."

"And now they're all mixed up. They'll get broken and there'll be crumbs everywhere. There're crumbs on the table already."

I brushed them into my cupped hand. I picked up the wrappers and took them into the kitchen to put them in the bin. It was infuriatingly presumptuous of Alice to make casual unilateral decisions about how I store my biscuits. Yes, it's a small thing but the principle is huge. How would she like it if I went into her house and started rearranging the cushions on her sofa or folded her tea-towels differently? I couldn't believe the gall of the woman.

The black bag in the bin was nearly full so I pulled it out and tied it up.

"Forget it. It doesn't matter," I said, returning to the living-room. I opened the front door and dumped the rubbish bag on the landing to take down later. "Where were we?"

"We were trying to pinpoint precisely when you became so uncomfortable with flying that you couldn't board a plane. Can you remember the next time you flew after the Scotland trip?"

"I suppose I could look it up in my journals," I said taking my seat again. "I keep them all in an antique chest under my bed."

"Do you?" she asked.

"Of course I don't," I snorted. "Do I strike you as the kind of man who has nothing more useful to do than jot down that kind of irrelevant minutiae every night of his life?" I shook my head. "I'd've thought you might have known me better than that by now."

"I can only work with what you tell me, Tom," she said tightly.

"And I can only tell you what I remember. And I don't remember what I did every day of every week twenty years ago. It'd be a pretty pathetic person who did, I imagine."

Alice crossed her arms and sat back in her seat looking at me. She was cross – which was rather unprofessional of her. It was hardly my fault that her therapeutic techniques were difficult to apply to someone who wasn't narcissistically obsessed with his own past. I was doing my best to cooperate but it was up to her to find a way to help me. That's what she claimed to be able to do and that's what I was paying for.

She just sat there glaring at me and I – a man who has been glared at by Gorgonian tax inspectors and Sphinxine excise officers – just gazed back, waiting her out. Picking up my tea-mug, I sat back comfortably in the chair and crossed my legs. There was no point in continuing until she'd calmed down.

Eventually she chuckled and slapped her thighs with her open palms.

"Oh, dear me. You're a piece of work, Tom, aren't you?" she declared. She reached for a biscuit and bit it. "You know – the bargain we strike as counsellor and client is that you tell me about your life, but I don't tell you about mine. That's how it works. However – I don't think it would be a betrayal of professional ethics to tell you that I have a husband."

"I'm flattered to be made privy to that domestic snippet."

She took another bite of the biscuit. "Well, I mention him for a reason. He doesn't like you."

"What?"

"Obviously he doesn't know your name – but he said to me the other evening, 'You saw the fear-of-flying chap today, didn't you? You always come home grumpy when he's been in.' And he was right. Our sessions invariably leave me angry, and then I'm irritable all day. That's never happened with anyone else. It goes against all my training."

"Well, yes," I said. "It does sound rather unprofessional."

Alice threw her hands in the air. "There you go again! Bang – right on the spot that's guaranteed to get my goat. I've been asking myself why that happens."

"Perhaps I'm just more difficult to treat than your other patients and that frustrates you," I suggested.

"No," Alice said. "I found the answer in the end." She leaned forward. "It's not me that's angry. It's you."

This, I felt, was a pretty typical psychobabble get-out. Alice was losing control of her emotions and it was noticeable even to her spouse. But – Good Lord – it couldn't possibly be *her* fault. It must be someone else's. Oh, look – Tom Lyne! He'll do.

"I'm perfectly calm and rational," I said. "I rarely get angry."

"So you've mentioned and I think it's true. You rarely get angry, but that doesn't mean you don't feel anger. You've developed the strategy of making other people angry on your behalf. It's a twofold win for you. You get to see the anger expressed, and you also get to congratulate yourself on your superior self-control – because Tom Lyne, as we all know, doesn't get angry." She paused and took another biscuit, scattering crumbs across the coffee-table. "It's a very sophisticated technique. Very clever."

"It's very unlikely. How do I do this then? Telepathy?"

She smiled. "Do you think I really care how you store your biscuits?"

"Huh?"

"I did it to annoy you, simply to test the theory. You stayed quite calm, but within two minutes you were needling me. You needed me to be angry because you were."

"Nonsense."

"You should have seen how relaxed you became as soon as you realised you'd got to me," Alice said. "Drinking your tea, grinning. You were smug as anything."

I sighed. "Is any of this relevant to the problem in hand?"

"We'll see. Shall we move on?"

She told me to close my eyes and imagine myself back home after the Scotland trip. I recalled the flight to Heathrow and going straight from the airport to the West End to buy gifts for my parents. It was miserable, that Christmas season after Louise left. We met up two or three times in London to sort out the practicalities of separation – dividing up the refunded deposit on the Cambridge flat and similar mundane but painfully symbolic disentanglings. I tried to conduct myself with stiff dignity during these encounters but I quickly slid from matey solicitousness – "How's it going with Robin? Are you happy?" – to desperate pleading – "Don't you love me at all any more? Can't you ever see a time we'll be back together?" Louise was understandably revolted by such unappealing appeals.

So when I turned up at home for Christmas I was in a less than festive mood, which my father considered impolite and self-indulgent.

"You'd better bloody cheer up before your mother's birthday," he told me. "I've got enough on my plate worrying about what stunt Pablo's going to pull this year."

And as I thought back to that conversation with my father, I remembered. God – I remembered. Continental plates jolted against each other on the ocean floor and in the depths of the wreck a distended, squid-flesh cadaver was dislodged from under an upturned bunk. It tumbled slowly upwards, bumping against the metal walls, printless fingers brushing jumbled furniture as it rose out of the gaping hull. Foul bubbles of gas escaped from its frayed mouth as it drifted up into the light.

Sitting there in my living room, I felt panic erupt in my chest and sudden sweat bloomed cold on my back. My scrotum tightened and I couldn't breath.

"The Barcelona trip," I said. "Oh, Jesus."

Dad had arranged for us all to gather in Barcelona for the first weekend in January. We'd meet up with Mum's family, have a celebratory dinner and generally indulge the Condesa's nostalgia. My parents had flown out there directly after the New Year break, and Jacinta, Pablo and I were to join them on the Friday night. But the plane developed some kind of fault and we were forced to land in Amsterdam for a stopover.

"A fault? Were you afraid?" Alice asked.

"No. Well, yes. But that wasn't the flight that matters."

The three of us decided to make the best of a bad job and go out on the town in Amsterdam. We went to a bar on one of the canals, where Pablo ingratiated himself with a couple of local women who offered to take us on to a rock concert.

"How far is it to this club?" I said as the two Dutch girls stood up to lead us out. "We absolutely have to be back at the hotel by midnight."

I bumped clumsily into the table as I got to my feet. I was drinking quite heavily at the time. Directly after Louise left I'd survived on orange juice and cigarettes, but since Christmas I'd taken to spiking the juice with vodka and chasing it with bottled beer. It was the only way I could get to sleep at night. When we got to the club – a rather nasty dive decorated entirely in black paint and blue neon – Pablo's new Dutch fan-club handed out fat, neatly-rolled joints. I'd smoked marijuana before, of course – if you were taking a Philosophy degree in the eighties, cannabis was practically a core element of the syllabus – but the Amsterdam stuff was to undergraduate dope as the Andes are to the South Downs. Not having eaten, and soft-focussed by several vodkas, I was peculiarly susceptible to the hallucinatory capabilities of the drug.

We were sitting at a gloomy table in a corner. Jacinta was slumped with her head in her arms and Pablo was chatting to one of the girls he'd adopted. The other seemed to be talking to me, but I formed the stoned idea that she was actually addressing Pablo who was behind her. I tried to explain that I wasn't fooled. Why didn't she just admit that she found Pablo more interesting? She burbled on, but in my perception all she was saying was 'Tomàs? Tomàs? Here I am.' She was blonde, and her friend – the one talking to Pablo – was brunette. But the blonde in front of me kept transforming into the dark one, like Carroll's baby turning into a pig. I couldn't keep track of who I was talking to.

Pablo leaned around the blonde and tapped me on the arm to say that he and the brunette were going to take a walk along the canal.

"Don't miss the plane," I said.

"If I miss it, I miss it," he shrugged. "They'd rather I wasn't there anyway."

"As long as you and I are there," said the blonde. "Tomàs? Hello?"

"What?" I asked, confused. "You and I?"

She went to the bar, but she still seemed to be talking to me. "You know who I am. Tomàs?"

A few minutes later, Pablo and his girl left. The blonde wandered off too, leaving me a joint, which I smoked down to the roach.

"Let's get a cab," Jacinta murmured, lifting her head from the table. "I have no idea where the train station is."

And that's the last thing I remember until Jacinta woke me up in the hotel saying we had twenty minutes to get to check-in. Pablo wasn't in his room.

"Maybe he's gone straight to the airport," Jacinta said as we tumbled into a taxi.

I'd have disabused her of this optimistic notion but I didn't dare speak. There are few experiences more unpleasant than sitting in the back of a speeding cab on a motorway, suppressing the urge to throw up. Fortunately I felt detached from my body – it was as if I were a yellow balloon on a string tied around my own neck, sucked out of the window of the car and buffeted in the wind, slap-slap-slapping against the panelling as we raced to the airport. It was horrible. I was grasping for self-control like a greased priest.

At the terminal I stood dumbly behind Jacinta for check-in, handing over my passport when asked, trying to stay upright on a floor that seemed to be made of mattresses. I attempted to steady myself against the desk but it dodged and I nearly collapsed to my knees.

"We'd better get some coffee and solid food inside us," Jacinta said when we got to the flightside. "I have an almost feral desire for a sticky pecan Danish."

"Oh, Christ."

I stumbled behind a pillar and vomited. I could still feel the marijuana in my system as I stared down at my puke, wiping my chin on my sleeve. A loop of words was running through my head in a chant. "*The soft hot red. Here I am. Here I am. In the soft hot red.*" My stomach spasmed and I could see it turning and rolling like a bag of blood in the shape of a foetus, almost losing its form, struggling to remain human.

"*As long as you and I are there. Listen.*"

At the departure gate I tried to get a grip. I looked out at the runway, bargaining with myself. If I could quell the nausea until three more planes had taken off, I wouldn't be stoned any more. If the next airliner to come into view was a 747, the mad loop of chatter in my head would stop. If Jacinta didn't say anything for a whole minute, then I'd stop trembling.

"Are you sure you don't want me to get you some water or something?" Jacinta said.

Hello? Tomàs? Listen.

"I'm not listening," I muttered.

"Suit yourself," Jacinta huffed. "Only trying to help."

In the tunnel to the plane, running my hand along the wall to keep myself upright, it seemed as if I was walking down my own oesophagus towards my stomach and the repetitive, unrelenting voice. I paused at the door of the aircraft, scared, and Jacinta bumped into my back.

"What are you doing?" she whispered.

I said nothing. I shrank from the doorway.

"A little nervous?" asked the stewardess, smiling.

Jacinta grabbed my arm "Tom, for God's sake, you're holding up the queue." I felt her hair against my cheek as she leaned over my shoulder, whispering. "You're just stoned, that's all. Get on the plane. Don't show me up." She was using my mother's voice. "What will people think? You don't embarrass the family like this. From Pablo I know this behaviour. But – Tomàs!"

I got on the plane and took my window seat. I buckled up my belt. Merely to distract myself I paid attention for the first time in my life to the safety demonstration and I read the plastic emergency card as instructed. But I still felt panicky, and as we took off I was breathing slowly and deeply in an attempt to control the nausea. I could see the sick bag in the pouch in front of me and I resisted the urge to reach for it. That would be an admission that I was going to puke again and I wanted to delay it indefinitely. The sun threw rays across my lap as we banked into the sky and watching the parallelogram of light slide up my thighs I was still making deals with myself. If I could hold on until the sun was on the other side of the aircraft, I told myself, I'd be all right.

Hello? Tomàs ? Listen. Here I am. In the soft hot red.

My stomach boiled like milk. I put on my earphones, as if that would drown out the repetitive chatter. I found the news channel and turned up the volume.

Property prices may be levelling out. In December the average cost of a home in the UK fell two percent. Tomàs ? It's me – Perdito.

"Oh, Jesus Christ," I whimpered under my breath, dragging the phones from my ears and letting them fall into my lap.

You know me, Tomàs. You know me. It's Perdito. Listen.

"Tom – are you okay?" Jacinta said.

I'm here in the soft hot red. It's all right. I'm real.

I turned to Jacinta, swallowing the saliva that had suddenly filled my mouth. "I'm so stoned," I gulped. "Help me. Oh, God. I'm hearing voices in my head."

It's not the drugs. It's me. I found a way in.

"What sort of voices?"

Sick and crazed though I was, I couldn't tell my sister what I was hallucinating. I wasn't going to open myself up to the impatient ridicule that she directed at Pablo when he invoked Perdito's imaginary ghost.

"I've got to get off the plane," I babbled. "Tell them I'm ill. Appendicitis. Anything." I undid my seat-belt and tried to stand.

"Sit down!" Jacinta hissed. She turned to the middle-aged man in the aisle seat next to her. "He's a bit uncomfortable with flying," she said smiling.

"My wife's the same way," the man said. "She does tantric breathing. Has he tried that?"

I've waited so long to talk to you. Never been able to find a way to get to you. It's so different here.

"Oh, please. Oh, God," I murmured. I scrabbled for the bag but not quickly enough. I was sick all over my legs.

"For fuck's sake, Tom," Jacinta said. She hit the call-button to summon a stewardess. The man in the aisle seat stood up quickly and told Jacinta to get me to the lavatory. She stood too and I stumbled out into the aisle, heading towards the back of the plane. The other passengers looked up to see me approaching, vomit soaking into my jeans, and then they lowered their eyes to their magazines, appalled at the sight of me.

"I'm sorry, I'm sorry." I waved aside a flight attendant as I reached the lavatory. I couldn't get the door open. I yanked at it blindly and I felt my bowels loosen.

"Oh, please God, no."

Standing there with one hand on the door of the lavatory, I soiled myself. The stewardess leaned over my shoulder, pushing the door at the appropriate spot, and it folded in to admit me. I fell forward and turned to close the door and lock it.

For half-an-hour I knelt on the floor of the cramped little lavatory, wretching unproductively into the stainless steel bowl as diarrhoea grew cold and clammy in my underpants. And the voice would not shut up. It babbled in my head like a junkie.

You're so much more like me. I understand. We are twins. Don't ignore me, Tomàs. Don't deny me. Here I am. Back together again. We are complete. We are in the soft hot red. The smell of me is in your hands and in your gut and in your eyes. I can taste your thoughts. It's not the drugs. We're complete.

There must have been something other than cannabis in those joints. Something dangerous. I banged my forehead against the toilet seat between stomach-flipping heaves of nausea and chesty gulps of humiliation – but I couldn't silence the chatter. I knew that foreign chemicals in my brain were firing arbitrary synapses – molecules pinballing around up there, ricocheting and ringing bells and lighting up bumpers, careening randomly from lobe to lobe – but knowing it wasn't enough to stop it. I couldn't think my way out of my own head.

Acknowledge me. You can hear me clear as honey. Please. Speak to me.

No. I would not conduct a conversation with narcotic compounds in my brain. I was stoned, but I wasn't insane. I wasn't Pablo. I may not have kept control of my body, but I'd be damned if I was going to let go of my mind.

Our mind.

No, no. Cunning chemicals, feeding my own thoughts back to me. No, no. I slammed my forehead against the toilet seat again.

I understand about Louise. No one understands like me. I can help.

"Shut the *fuck up*!" I spat, thumping my head down as hard as I could.

The door rattled behind me.

"Tom – are you okay? Let me in."

"I can't," I called to Jacinta. "I can't come out."

"Tom, open the door now."

I struggled to my feet, feeling the revolting wet squelch between my buttocks, and I opened the door a crack. Jacinta was standing there, and a stewardess was behind her.

"Christ, you're bleeding," Jacinta said. "What happened to your head?"

I put my hand to my face and it came away red. I ducked back into the toilet and looked in the mirror. Blood was seeping from a split in the skin of my forehead, dribbling along my eyebrows and down the sides of my face. I wiped my sleeve across my brow and peered out again, beckoning Jacinta close so that the stewardess couldn't hear.

"I've crapped myself," I whispered, flushing with shame. "I can't come out. I'll stay in here till we land and you can get some jeans from my luggage."

"Oh, God, Tom," she said. "Wait there." She pulled the door shut.

I leaned back against the wall, listening. The voice had stopped. I still felt queasy but the nausea too was retreating. I washed my face and cupped some water to my mouth despite the sign saying that it wasn't drinkable.

There was a knock on the door, and I opened it. Jacinta was standing there with a pair of powder-blue trousers in her hand.

"They can't land the plane if you're not in your seat. Clean yourself up and try these. They're the crew's spare pair."

The crew's spare female pair, it turned out. Two inches too small on the waist and a good five short in the leg. I held them up with my belt and wore my shirt untucked to hide the gaping fly that failed to cover my pubic hair. I stuffed my soiled jeans and underpants into the towel-bin and checked my watch. We were still an hour from Barcelona and I didn't intend to emerge until we began our descent.

The walk back to my seat, when it came, was horrendous. Every single passenger on that aeroplane must have known what I'd done. And then, of course, we disembarked and I had to go through passport control to baggage claim with everyone smirking at the powder-blue trousers that ended three inches above my socks, everyone pointing at the seeping wound on my forehead, everyone laughing at me. I wished I had died in the lavatory.

As soon as I'd retrieved my bag from the carousel I went to the gents and changed into a pair of corduroys.

"I am never, ever going to let you smoke dope around me again," Jacinta said as we walked through Customs. "I've never been so embarrassed in my life."

"Don't worry," I said sheepishly. "I'm swearing off the stuff. I'm so sorry. But it's Pablo's fault, hooking us up with those women."

That was twenty years ago, and I've not smoked dope since. I've never taken any kind of drug at all – not so much as cough medicine. And I've drunk alcohol only five or six times – perhaps fewer.

There are things in my head that I never want to let out.

*   *   *   *

I made my first move twenty years ago in Amsterdam, in a bar full of smoke and drums. Both my brothers were unlaced by narcotics and Tom was still skinless and raw after Louise. As they swung towards each other, I let go of one and reached towards the other, like the linkman in a trapeze act. In the moment of stasis between them, touching neither, I was instantaneously shot through with vivid confusion. Hanging there, nowhere, I seemed to be a prism through which was refracted every pulsing emotion of every person in the Melk Weg. I panicked, disorientated – and then I grabbed out. Instantly I was in a new universe.

I was used to Pablo, who saw wheels of colour, mutating shapes; he lived in a place where nothing was fixedly what it appeared. Every object was a happenstance held between states.

When Pablo looked at, say, an oak table, he saw the swirls of its grain; and in the swirls he saw accumulated decades of summer sun and winter snow. The rectangle of the table seemed to him an arbitrary frame imposed on the chance flow of the wood; the whorls and eddies of the rings extended beyond the planed lines of the table, and his mind conjured other tables from the same oak pushed up against this one, remaking the truncated hoops and bifurcated bands of the tree's fingerprint. Pablo's table came from somewhere and it was going somewhere. Just as he felt the antiquity of the tree, he sensed the longevity of the object, and he wondered about dinners that might be eaten around it generations into the future. But he also noticed the loosening of the man-made seams and the cracking of the grain around inherent knots in the wood; he understood that wood, though it pretends to immortality, carries its death within, as does everything.

Pablo never laid all this out before himself. He just knew it. It was his way. And I thought – of course I thought – that's what a table was. I thought everyone saw tables like that. But once I'd jumped, the world came to me through Tomàs, and Tomàs inhabited a world so unlike Pablo's that I couldn't at first comprehend it.

When Tomàs looked at an oak table he saw a thing that wasn't pine. He saw craftsmanship and skill. He saw grain that would need care, but that would reward that care with glow and sheen, reflecting candlelight, catching low winter sun, garnering deserved admiration. Tom saw a piece of furniture to which the entire décor of the room must aspire – the Moroccan carpet, the Georgian sideboard, the dining chairs carefully selected to complement the table without crowding it. Tomàs's table was the occasion of danger. The very sight of it invoked burglars and woodworm, against both of which protection must be arranged. Its sharp corners might easily bruise an unwary thigh. Opening grain might raise splinters. Once in place the table could never be moved – it was too unwieldy, and its legs would gash wallpaper or chip banister rails; its very bulk would slip discs and pull ligaments. Tomàs knew that the valued and impressive table might easily cause damage, as might anything.

I should have understood that. In Amsterdam, watching skaters on the frozen canal, Tom envisaged how the ice might collapse beneath them like toasted sugar on a crème brulée; and then cracks would radiate from that broken place, running jagged, joining up. Huge floes of ice would heave and tip, sliding skaters into the dark water, where they would flail in desperation before disappearing beneath the surface. Tomàs could see such a catastrophe unfolding as clearly as Pablo would have seen squirrels shelter from autumn lightning in the branches of the oak from which a table was made.

My newly conjoined brother anticipated threat everywhere, and had I bided my time, had I nestled behind Tom's eyes for a while, I would have understood. I would have understood because Tom was right – the world is unsafe. It's not malevolent – it just doesn't care about what crawls on it. No single living thing is important to the universe.

So I should have anticipated that Tom would assess even me as dangerous. But I was itchy. I announced myself there in the Amsterdam bar and later, disastrously, on the plane. I pushed too soon, which impatience has cost the Lyne boys twenty years of cagey anguish. I laid low in Tom for months. I watched and I listened. I inhaled and I tasted. I stayed silent. I had lost none of my hunger for the realm of flesh and the material, but I was less rabid, less electrified than I had been with Pablo. Tom's world was not the frenetic carnival of stimuli that I was used to, and I preferred it. But I needed to live, and it was obvious that Tom wasn't ready to allow me that.

When I returned to Pablo, I was immediately caught up again in the harlequin vortex of his perception – but I was waiting for an opportunity to go back to Tom, where I felt I belonged.

It has been a long wait, but now I am back. This time I'll make Tom understand.

*   *   *   *

"How do you feel?" Alice asked.

I was shaking. I reached for a glass of water and I couldn't pick it up without spilling it.

"I swear, I had completely forgotten that all that ever happened," I said. I held my glass steady in both hands and sipped. "How could I forget that?"

"You didn't forget it," Alice said. "You wouldn't have given up drugs and flying if you'd forgotten it, would you?"

I sat in silence for a few minutes, staring blankly at the biscuits all mixed up in the Tupperware. The memory kept playing back to me in swift-cut snippets. The voice. The bar on the canal. The mutating Dutch girls. The voice. The yellow balloon. The puke and the shit. The voice. The voice.

I shuddered. It would have been bad enough – humiliating and unforgivable – had I merely lost control of my body. The vomiting and the incontinence were shameful but at least they were specific to my thoughtless over-indulgence in alcohol and marijuana. But the voice had been in my head, and I was trapped in there with it. You can't escape your own brain. You can't out-think your thoughts. You can throw up the bad chemicals and defecate the foreign substances from your body, but what's in your mind is who you are. It's impossible to get rid of it. The part of my brain that created that voice was still in there, and given the right chemicals to work with, it could stage a comeback.

"Still," I said to Alice, looking up, "now we know why I have a fear of flying." I'd regained my composure – or, at least, I was attempting to appear as if I had, which is much the same thing. My hands were still unsteady and my breathing wasn't quite level, but I didn't want Alice to think I was so weak as to be rendered incapable by a twenty-year-old memory. "So what do we do about it?" I looked at my watch. "Give me the magic word and we could all be out of here by one o'clock."

Alice shrugged. "Well, that's it. Nothing more to be done. Pack your bag and off you go."

I pictured the walkway to the Malaga flight. I saw myself buckling the seatbelt. I heard the engines working themselves up to a hot roar and driving the aeroplane into the sky. My skin prickled with chill dampness and my guts liquefied.

"There's more to do, isn't there?"

"I think so, yes. The flight to Barcelona is very significant, I'm sure. And you do seem to have had other negative experiences associated with flying. The trip to Scotland, for instance. The initial flight to Amsterdam when the plane developed a fault. Maybe there are more."

I rubbed my eyes with my fingertips. "You think it's a Pavlovian association I've developed? I vomit at the chime of the fasten-your-seatbelts bell?"

"I don't think that flying's the problem, actually," she said. "It's an instance of the problem, but it's not the problem itself."

I scarcely contained a weary groan. It was a little past noon by now and Alice was opening up new frontiers that she evidently wanted to explore. I bit back my irritation.

"Alice – I don't want to tell you your job. Honestly. But my problem – my condition, if you like – is very specific and self-contained. Everything else in my life is just fine. I'm happily in control except for this one thing about aeroplanes."

She stretched her arms towards the ceiling, flexing her fingers, and rolled her head from side-to-side. "Let's take a break. I need to look something up on the 'Net and you ought to get some fresh air. Could you pop out and fetch us lunch?" She saw me glancing at my watch again. "Don't worry. Either we've got plenty of time or it's too late already. What's on offer to eat around here? I'm starving."

"I haven't got anything in. I thought I was going away yesterday. I could phone for pizza."

Alice stood, lifting the tea-cups and plates from the table. "I think you should go out for a walk while I use the computer. Is there a decent Chinese nearby?"

The bossiness again. And the assumption that I was happy to go out and let her have the run of the place – which I wasn't. I can't remember the last time I left anyone alone in my apartment, apart from quick trips to the corner shop for when last night's dinner companion was still asleep. I don't even like bringing them back here. I'd much rather go to their hotel or flat. It's easy to leave politely, but much more difficult to get someone to go.

"Listen, why don't you come with me, just for the walk? You can pop into the library and use the internet while I'm waiting for the takeaway."

She shook her head. "I'm supposed to be staying off my feet. Hip problem. Can you show me where the computer is?"

Hip problem. Okay. I reluctantly led the way to the study, getting between Alice and the monitor while I checked that I'd left no private files open.

"Thank you," she said, sitting down "Vegetarian hot and sour soup for me, please."

"Help yourself to tea or whatever," I said. "The cups are to the right of the sink."

"Yes, thanks." She was already concentrating on the screen

I went to the bathroom to comb my hair and splash my face. "I'll be half an hour at the outside," I called. The towels were all askew on the rail and I straightened them before walking back along the corridor to the study. "I said I'll be half an hour at the most."

"Fine, fine." She nodded at the monitor. "I'll need at least that long."

I stood there for a moment watching her scroll through a screenful of text.

"Would you like a glass of water before I go?"

"No, thank you. I'm quite happy. Now off you trot."

Unbelievable. I was being shooed out of my own bloody house.

"Right. I'll be off then."

"Cheerio," she said without looking at me. Then, just as I reached the front door, she called, "Tom? Have you ever heard that voice again since the Barcelona flight?"

"No," I said, tossing my keys in my hand. "If you don't take drugs, you don't hallucinate."

Alice's head appeared around the door of the study. "But you weren't taking drugs when you had your vision on the cliff in Scotland, were you? So what's the common denominator?"

I frowned. "That was different."

"Oh, I see," she said. "Interesting. Incidentally, can you get some prawn crackers too?"

"Certainly."

I picked up the tied rubbish bag that I'd left on the landing, and pulled the front door shut behind me. Going down the stairs I met Barbara coming up.

"Hey," she said. "You got in all right last night then?"

"Yes, thanks," I said. "Sick day?"

"Working on a presentation. Why aren't you in Spain?"

"I'm flying out this evening." Even saying it caused a thrill of nervousness to run up my back.

"Oh – so no chance of a drink later, I guess. Pity."

The woman was shameless. I'd heard her guest leaving at eight that morning – there was much shouting up and down the stairwell about possible meetings at the weekend – and here she was propositioning me while the pillows were still warm. I've never been a subscriber to the hypocritical double-standard concerning female sexual conduct, but – dammit – you expect a certain decorum to be observed.

Then again, if Alice and I could finish our session by, say, two, I'd have a couple of hours to spare. And Barbara was very entertaining company.

"I'll see if I can pop down this afternoon, hm?"

"You do that."

Perfect – my decision. I'd see how the afternoon panned out.

As I walked towards the High Street I tried to imagine what Alice was driving at when she said that flying was an instance of my problem, but not the problem itself. If I could anticipate her analysis it would save a lot of time. I'd simply confess over lunch, allow her to counsel me – and then we could deal with the fear of flying thing and call it a day.

I had to admit that she had risen in my estimation, just a bit. Obviously I wasn't buying all her rubbish about transferred anger – that was bordering on mystical hogwash – but she had managed to lead me to the recall of the Barcelona flight. Now I'd remembered it I was astonished that I'd ever managed to forget it.

Recall is a very strange thing. When something drops from your memory, it doesn't leave a space like a book missing from a shelf. The remaining books shuffle up and close the gap, and you have no way of knowing that the lost volume was ever there. And we must lose more books than we keep, otherwise we'd remember every minute of every day of our lives. This idea that we're shaped by our past is self-evident nonsense. You can't be influenced by books you don't have in your library.

I pushed open the door of the Jade Garden and walked in. The proprietor materialised around his smile in the murk. I asked for a pineapple juice to sip while I looked through the menu, and I mulled. I reckoned that Alice was going to say that I was in denial. Actually, I was sure she was going to say that, because it's just therapy-speak for 'you have a problem'. It's the precise equivalent of a woman's accusation that one isn't prepared to commit – and it would have to be handled in much the same way.

"I don't feel able to carry on with this relationship, Katie," one declares.

"Aha!" Katie says, as if she's uncannily insightful. "You can't commit!"

Well, yes. That's what I said. A synonym is not a diagnosis.

I've noticed, though, that if one uses that terminology in the first place – "I'm sorry but I'm just not able to commit right now" – the Katies are much less liable to fuss. It's as if, having damned oneself out of one's own mouth, one is beyond redemption, and therefore dismissable. "He can't commit. I mean, he actually owned up to that himself."

To keep Alice on track, I needed to employ a similar strategy. If I told her I thought I might be in denial, she'd congratulate herself on having brought me to this moment of self-awareness and then we could get down to the real business. So what, I wondered, was I expected to confess I was denying?

"Ready, Mr Lyne?"

Li had manifested himself again at my side, his pen poised above a notepad. I ordered Alice's soup and various bits and pieces for myself.

"Can I have strong coffee while I wait?" I asked.

It was comfortably dim in the Jade Garden. The quiet gloom and the sound of running water in the fountain were having a soporific effect on me. Not surprising really – it was Thursday afternoon, and what with Barbara Monday night, my homework for Alice on Tuesday night and Wednesday's debacle at Fleet Services, I'd only slept about ten hours since the weekend. But this was not the time to nod off – and anyway I had good reason to be nervous about sleeping. I hadn't been entirely truthful with Alice when she asked me if I'd heard the voice since that flight to Barcelona.

Not *heard*, no. But dreamt – last night, during the few hours' sleep I managed when I eventually got home. To be accurate, it was right on the edge of slumber, when I was in that weightless state of tumbling semi-consciousness like something suspended in fluid, rolling over and over, falling without descending.

"*Tomàs?*"

Warm and drifting, I was aware of the presence of the voice but I didn't register it. It was there just as the pillow was there against my cheek and the darkness was before my eyes.

"*Tomàs – are you ready now? It's Perdito.*"

The name got through to me. I jerked instantly awake and scrabbled to turn on the bedside light. I was scared and I didn't know why. It's not like me to be frightened by what was, in fact, no more than a kind of aural incubus. But sipping coffee in the Jade Garden, it occurred to me that it couldn't just be coincidence that I'd dreamt of the voice the very night before I'd rediscovered the memory of the Barcelona flight. That recall must already have been floating there a little below the surface of my consciousness – in which case, to credit Alice with hauling it out in a net was more than necessarily generous. Something else had dislodged it from the deep.

I wondered about that as I lined up the beer-mats so that their top edges followed the seam between the wood of the bar and the metal of the drip-tray. It wasn't as if I ever thought of Perdito at all. Why would I? He only ever occurred to me when… Aha.

Pablo, of course. In the police station. All that crap about having let our dead brother go – that was what had dredged the memory up. The hours of Alice's professional probing, her condescending coaxing, my astonishment at how she'd got me to uncover that specific lost episode – it was utter hokum. I'd remembered the flight from Amsterdam for the very sane and mechanical reason that Pablo's references to Perdito had reminded me of it. God, how banal.

I was laying out a second row of beer-mats and chuckling to myself when Li put the takeaway food on the bar beside me. I reached into my back pocket to take out my wallet and, before I'd even opened it, I realised that I had no cash and that my back-up credit card was still lying beside the keyboard in my study.

"It's okay, Mr Lyne," Li said. "You pay me next time you come in."

I was quite touched. After the week I'd had, just that small example of human forbearance was a tonic. I thanked him and set off back to the apartment in a cheerful mood for the first time since Tuesday. I ate prawn crackers from the bag as I walked, still wondering what I could humbly confess that I was in denial of. Or 'about' as Alice would undoubtedly and ungrammatically construct the phrase. I was no more than two prawn crackers along the High Street when I realised that the solution was obvious. And having identified it, I merely had to present it in the way she needed to hear it. I rehearsed as I walked.

"You know, Alice," I would say as I forked black-bean chicken straight from the foil container, "I've been wondering whether I might be avoiding something quite fundamental in my life. I mean, something really big." I'd shrug sheepishly and reach for a sesame toast. "I don't know. Maybe it's not up to me to say this – you're the professional, after all. But…"

I'd wait for her encouraging nod. She'd have adopted her 'non-directing' face, but she'd be silently willing me to take a seven-league stride forward on my life-journey.

"Well, it concerns Pablo. I think you're right. I am closer to him than I admit." A pause here. A bitten lip. "He's very important to me and I don't know why I insist on denying it."

I'd expect a hand-clapping *bravo!* at this point. But I'd press on.

"Thing is, I can't see how that relates to the problem with planes." My eyes, which, if I could possibly manage it, would be brimful of supplicant tears, would meet hers. "None of it seems to make sense, Alice."

From there it'd be an easy ride. I'd suggest that this knotty fraternal problem demanded resolution through months of pricey counselling. Alice, actually or metaphorically, would pat my wan hand. And then she'd do whatever was necessary to enable me to get on the plane to Malaga.

All the principles I'd long applied in my professional and personal relationships were smoothly appropriate here. In pursuit of my inheritance, I'd already steered Angus to where I needed him and now I'd do much the same to Alice. Achieving your objectives is all about taking control.

"Brilliant," I told myself as I bounded up the steps to the front door of my building.

*   *   *   *

On the landing outside my flat I put the key into the lock, pushed – and the door jarred to a stop only two inches open. Alice had put the bloody security chain on.

"Alice?" I called through the crack. I could hear the scrape of furniture being moved across the floor. "What's happening?"

"Can you wait a few minutes, please?" Alice said breathlessly. "I'm not quite ready for you."

"What?"

"It's very interesting, seeing your flat." She was panting a little. "You're the first single man I've ever met who has such a perfectly coordinated set of coffee-mugs. Most guys have a mismatched collection that's come together over years. But yours are all the same design, six in pale green and six in white."

"What are you talking about? The food's getting cold out here."

"And they're arranged in two rows – a green row and a white row. All upside down with the handles aligned to the left." She chuckled. "When you were taking glasses from the cupboard this morning, I moved a mug so that the handle was fractionally awry. You immediately restored it to its proper position. I don't think you even realised you were doing it."

I may well have done. I like things to be tidy. But it wasn't something I wanted to discuss through a barely-open front door. I twisted my head against the crack, trying to work out what she was up to. All I could see, just inside the apartment, was a patch of wood laminate – which was worrying, because there ought to have been an oak occasional table on that spot.

"Are you rearranging my furniture?"

"Yes. Don't worry – we can put it back later."

I slammed my palm against the door. "I don't want it moved at all! What are you playing at?"

I heard the chink of glass being set down. It was probably my art-deco vase, which quite properly belonged in the bedroom. I wasn't some slovenly bachelor who just allowed the layout and design of his apartment to evolve. It was all considered and planned – and there was Alice blithely rejigging it all, presumably to her own taste.

"It's an experiment that I think will help you," I heard her say. Her voice was coming from further back in the flat – perhaps from the study. For God's sake, if she messed up my books, I'd kill her. "What do you think about me moving things around?"

"I think it's a bloody cheek, as anyone would," I snapped.

"Ah, well, that's not actually true." She was back in the living room. "Some people would find it exciting. Others might find it liberating. There are lots of possible reactions."

Again I slammed my hand against the door. "Let me in! You can't lock me out of my own place!"

"You sound angry, Tom."

"Is that what you're trying to do? Make me angry?" I took a deep breath. "Okay – you've succeeded. Well done. Now open the bloody door."

"In a moment. I'm looking for something to use as a blindfold. Do you have a scarf in your wardrobe?"

"What?"

"Back in a sec."

I could hear her footsteps retreating down the corridor to the bedroom. I slipped my hand through and tried to undo the security chain but I couldn't close the door far enough to give myself sufficient play to move it.

"Bloody woman," I breathed. She was coming back.

"When Louise left you, you felt as if you didn't exist, didn't you? I've got your e-mail here." Paper rustled. "You say, 'everywhere was nowhere now.' And earlier, when you're talking about being in the relationship, you mention being no more than a place-holder for yourself."

I leaned my forehead against the door, fists clenched. "Yes. So what?"

"These are expressions of powerlessness, Tom. When one loses one's identity, one has no influence on the world. It must have been very frightening for you."

"I got over it. Now will you please let me in? We're wasting time here."

"I don't think you got over it. You just made very sure that it wouldn't happen again."

In the circumstances – locked out of my own apartment, clutching a bag of congealed Chinese food – that kind of condescending platitude was just about all I needed.

"So that's your diagnosis, is it?" I said. "I must be screwed up because I avoid getting screwed up?" I took a step back and kicked the base of the door. "Let me into my fucking flat!"

"What's going on?"

I turned and there was Barbara coming up the stairs.

"Locked out again?" she asked, smirking.

Alice was still burbling on the far side of the door. "You won't go on the Underground. You won't board an aeroplane. You don't drink alcohol. You resist travelling to foreign countries. You don't permit yourself to be angry – in fact, you do your best to steer clear of any real emotional expression at all. Your whole life is set up to avoid situations you can't control."

"Who's that in there?" Barbara asked as she reached the top of the stairs. "Sounds like one intense chick."

"She's insane," I muttered, standing back to look at the door. If I could land a kick directly behind the chain-lock, it might snap off. Long shot, though – I'd spent a fortune making my home secure and I'm sure I demanded a door that wouldn't cave in to a hefty boot.

"It's a very effective strategy. But for the fear of flying, you're completely and happily in control. You use the phrase over and over again – you have everything under control. That's what matters most to you."

I was squaring up to deliver the kick when Barbara stepped in front of me and leaned towards the crack.

"I don't know who you are in there," she said, "but you're right on the money. He's a total control nut."

I gaped. "What do you know about it? You've only just met me, for God's sake."

"Who's that?" asked Alice.

Barbara turned and looked at me. "Honey, we've fucked a coupla times – and take my word, I know. It's a power thing with you." She grinned. "Which is fine. I like it."

Mother of God, there were two of them at it now – deconstructing me, presuming to explain me away, dissecting me like a laboratory frog pinned out and helpless beneath the descending scalpel. I wasn't going to lie there and allow my innards to be arranged on a dish for their merry amusement. Alice was constructing some absurd, half-baked psychodrama when all I wanted was to be given a simple technique – a way to persuade myself to step through the oval door of the 727 and sit there relatively panic-free all the way to Malaga. As I stood outside my apartment, I considered simply walking out and hailing a cab to the airport. Perhaps I could just force myself onto the plane and suffer the sweating and the shaking, the treacherous bowels, the two hours of terrified, shameful vomiting. But it wasn't a practical option even if I could convince myself it was achievable. My credit card was still in my study, or wherever the hell Alice had moved the desk. I had to get into the flat before I could go anywhere.

I took a deep breath, relaxed my shoulders and swallowed my fury. "All right, Alice," I said, cool and even. "What do you want me to do?"

Cloak it in any negative jargon you like, the fact is I'm extraordinarily good at putting my immediate emotions to one side and concentrating on real goals. People like Alice – and Pablo, actually – seem to think that that's somehow reprehensible or neurotic, but if the choice is between, on the one hand, making a self-indulgent scene and, on the other, achieving something worthwhile, I know which course looks to me the more resourceful and mature.

Alice's face appeared at the crack of the door, and she ran her eyes over Barbara.

"I'm sorry, but who are you?" she said. "Therapy is not a spectator sport, I'm afraid."

"She's fine," I said quickly. I could see another valuable half-hour slipping away while the two of them circled each other. "Let's just get on with it."

Alice considered for a moment. "All right. This is all pretty unorthodox anyway."

"That's the way I like it," Barbara said cheerfully. She sat down, her legs stretched across the top stair, and pulled the Chinese food towards her.

Alice looked at me. "What you have to do, Tom…" she said.

I interrupted. "Can't we have this conversation inside? Talking to a two-inch column of your face isn't exactly helping me engage."

"Not until you agree to my proposal, no. May I go on?"

Despite my frustration, I smiled pleasantly and I nodded. "Just a humble suggestion."

"What you need to do is give yourself permission to relinquish control – just a little and just for while. You'll discover that no harm comes to you. It'll be like having an inoculation – uncomfortable but brief and beneficial. At least, that's the theory. It's the best we can do in the time we have."

I nodded again. Alice liked lots of nodding. It was a positive affirmation of something or other. "Okay," I said. "Listen – you go ahead and move my furniture around. I completely relinquish control over it. I'll even come in and watch."

"Not exactly electric-shock treatment, is it?" Barbara said, picking pieces of chicken out of the black bean sauce and popping them in her mouth.

Alice twisted her head in the crack of the door so that she could see Barbara. "I really must ask you not to speak, please." She returned to me. "I've already rearranged your furniture. I know that makes you uncomfortable."

It didn't. I wasn't in the least uncomfortable, just bloody annoyed. But I was itchy with impatience and I wanted to get on with whatever charade Alice had planned.

"Yes, it does," I said.

"So, in that sense, it's now an unfamiliar space, and yet a safe one, being your home," she explained in her infuriating, calm voice. "What I propose is that I blindfold you and tie your hands – and then lead you in here. I'll guide you around. You'll have to trust me. That's all. Just allow yourself to be led around your own flat."

Between mouthfuls of spring roll Barbara did a very bad job of suppressing a flippant snort. I said nothing.

"Do you understand, Tom?" Alice asked.

Oh, I understood all right. She was asking me to put myself completely in her power – a woman who had locked me out of my own place, who'd disrupted all my things. She wanted me blind, bound and helpless. I'd proved difficult to treat. I'd exposed the charlatan nature of her profession. I'd even teased her about it a little. Yes, I could see why she'd love to have me at a disadvantage. God knows what she might do.

"Oh, go ahead," Barbara urged. "Dammit – I get myself tied up and blindfolded practically weekly. It's a lot of fun."

I glanced at her. I knew that she harboured unusual predilections in precisely this area. What with her perverse leanings and Alice's resentment towards me, there was no imagining what the two of them were capable of. I'd be an idiot to agree to such inescapable vulnerability.

"Tom, I know how hard this is for you. It's because it's so hard that I'm asking you to do it. You came to me for a radical solution and I believe this is your best chance. Please try."

I could tell from her tone that she was desperate to lure me in. She obviously had some utterly appalling humiliation planned. I wasn't going to fall for it. But I had to play along just far enough to get into the flat and grab the credit card.

"Not the hands," I said. "Just the blindfold."

Alice shook her head. "You'll simply pull the blindfold off and I wouldn't be able to stop you. It's important here that you trust me completely, that you allow me to be totally in control."

"Sounds great," Barbara chuckled, licking her fingers. "If he won't go for it, I'm on deck."

"Shut up!" I said. I was trying to think, but – I don't know – it must have been the exhaustion catching up with me. I couldn't keep things straight. And the smell of the lukewarm Chinese food was making me nauseous and clammy.

"Believe me, Tom" Alice said, still peering through the crack of the door, "I realise how frightening this is for you."

"I'm not frightened! Stop saying I'm frightened!" I tried to pace my breathing which was coming short and hard. I had to remember the goal. The two million. I'd had a plan. Yes. "Alice – you're wrong. It's about Pablo. That's my problem. I'm in denial about Pablo."

"Yes, I think you are. You can't accept that your brother's experience of Perdito is a symptom of mental illness because you have those symptoms too. That would be the ultimate loss of control."

"For Christ's sake," I yelled. "I've told you – he's not fucking ill!" I was trembling with the effort of keeping myself focussed.

"Man, you look really sick," Barbara said. "You'd better sit down."

If I could get the credit card, I'd be self-sufficient and I'd figure something out. I'd buy drugs or something. I'd think of a solution. I just had to get into the flat.

"Alice," I shouted. "For the last time, let me in!"

"Tom – you came to me for…"

"Let me in!" I jumped at the door, kicking it hard directly behind the security chain. Alice disappeared, but the chain held. "Dammit!" I staggered back against the banister, shaking.

Barbara scrambled across the landing from the top stair, knocking Chinese food all over the carpet. On her hands and knees, she peered through the crack.

"Jesus," she said, looking over her shoulder at me. "She's out cold. She's bleeding everywhere."

"Oh, great." I dragged my palms down my sweating face and wiped them on my shirt. "Fucking great. Now what am I going to do?"

* * * *

"You know you're going to break your stupid neck, don't you?"

Barbara and I were standing on the patio looking up at the open window of my study.

"Can't see any alternative," I muttered. I grabbed and shook one twisting branch of the wisteria. "I've got to get into the flat."

"I guess," Barbara said. "Alice looks pretty beat up in there."

"Was she bleeding on the carpet or on the laminate?" I asked as I lifted one foot onto the wisteria. "Blood's a bugger to get out of carpet." I reached for a sturdy branch, and pulled myself up so that my trailing foot left the paving. The whole wisteria lurched outward, and I put my foot back down. "Okay – the individual branches can take my weight but the whole thing's not attached firmly enough to the wall." I considered for a moment. "Can you get a chair from Jeremy's kitchen?"

Georgian architects were very keen on impressive proportions. It was about twenty feet from the crazy paving to my study window, which is a dangerous height to clamber – but, for me, the climb worked out at about a hundred thousand pounds per foot. The assessment of risk is all about the ratio to reward.

Barbara came back with a pine chair and I pushed it against the wisteria. "Right. You're going to have to stand on the chair and press the branches against the wall. If I keep my weight close to the vertical, I should be able to get high enough to grab the window sill."

"Can't we just call the police or something?"

Wonderful idea. Man locked out of his own apartment; haemorrhaging counsellor sprawled on the floor inside; furniture in disarray; Chinese food splattered across the landing. Obviously I'd just explain everything to the officer and he – a sympathetic and accommodating sort of chap – would smile understandingly and send me on my cheery way.

"Just do as I say – all right?"

With Barbara standing on the chair and reaching as high as possible to hold the wisteria to the wall, I once again lifted a foot, grasped with a hand, and hauled myself from the ground. Keeping my body pressed in, I edged up to the next branch, and then the next. The wisteria creaked and swayed outwards.

"Put your weight against it!" I told Barbara. A couple more feet and most of my weight would be further up the wisteria than she could reach – she wouldn't be able to hold the branches to the wall.

"I can't push too hard or the chair'll tip backwards," she said. "I can feel it wanting to go already."

I looked up. The window sill was still ten feet above me. I'd never make it before the entire plant ripped away from the wall.

"Dammit." I dropped back to the patio. "This isn't going to work."

"How about if we threw a jug of water through the crack in the door to bring Alice round?" Barbara suggested as she hopped off the chair "Or, like, a soda siphon?"

"Indeed. I'm sure that, once revived, she'd be delighted to help me in any way she could."

Barbara grinned. "I love when you're sarcastic."

Five minutes later we were negotiating Jeremy's kitchen-table through the back door.

"When I planned an afternoon of sweaty humping, this isn't what I had in mind," she said breathlessly.

I like a woman with a sense of humour but Barbara's indefatigable chirpiness was beginning to grate more than a touch. I wished she'd just shut up and do as I said without contributing inane patter.

"Can you go and get a broom from inside?" I asked as I positioned the table a few feet from the wall.

"Are you going to fly up there?"

"Just get it."

I made her stand on the table and lean forward to press the brush-end of the broom against the wisteria as high as she could reach – which was about five feet short of the window sill.

"Right – now keep the pressure on." I said, untying my laces and kicking off my shoes. "Pin the wisteria to the wall. For God's sake don't let it slip, okay?"

I started to climb again, slowly. The wisteria sagged downwards and outwards but it held me. I pressed myself close to the brickwork, exploring with my toes to find the next strong branch on which to put my weight. Twigs scratched my face and kept snagging on my shirt. But within a couple of minutes I felt the back of my head bump against the angled broomhandle.

"Don't move it," I panted. "Just keep it there and I'll go around it."

"It looks a lot higher when you see someone actually up there," Barbara said. "You're almost within reach though."

I pulled myself up another notch so that the broom's bristles were close to my cheek, and then snaked my right arm under and around to grasp a branch that was no more than two feet short of the study window. It gave a little but held against the wall.

"All right," I gasped, surveying the tangled wood above me. "I'm going to have to do this very quickly." I eyed a good thick branch to the left. My right foot sought out a solid hold beneath me and I rested my sole there, not putting any weight on it yet. "I'm going to hoist myself up and then go for the sill with my right hand. You'll have to yank the broom away so I have room to move – okay?" I shifted my weight a little. "On the count of three."

"I have to tell you," Barbara said, "I am so turned on right now."

I grimaced. "Just concentrate on yanking the broomhandle."

"That's exactly what I'm concentrating on, believe me."

I checked the distance to the branch and then to the windowsill. I took a deep breath and tried to flex some blood into my biceps.

"On three," I said, swallowing. "One. Two. Three!"

Pushing my right foot down hard, I grabbed the strong branch with my left hand. Bristles scraped my hip as Barbara pulled the broom away – and at the same moment I felt the whole vine of the wisteria fall back. Scrabbling with both feet, I reached for the window sill and caught it, immediately pulling my knees up to take my weight off the branches below me. I hung there by my fingertips for a second and then threw my other hand across and hooked onto the sill. Pedalling, I found places for my feet, just to gain balance. I gripped there, static.

I rested my forehead against the brickwork. Do not give me fucking lectures about avoidance and control, I thought. Look at me. I'm hanging from a sill twenty feet above concrete crazy-paving. I'm risking my neck. You think I'm a coward? Try this.

I circled a foot around, looking for a firm branch. Pushing myself up, I hefted an elbow onto the sill. The paint flaked as I worked my forearm across, and I levered against the concrete, swinging my other hand up and gripping the far side of the window frame.

"Yay!" Barbara shrieked.

I was there. Safe now. I'd pull myself in through the window and find my card. I'd go to the nearest chemist and buy sleeping pills of which I'd take five times the recommended dose. I'd stupefy myself and stagger onto the plane and fall unconscious as soon as I hit the seat. Just this once, I'd chance drugs. Two million pounds. Worth the risk.

Sweat was running into my eyes and I wiped my face across my shoulder. God, I was tired.

"Climb in! Climb in! You made it!"

Yes, climb in. That's what I had to do next. Grunting, I hauled myself up, my head clearing the sill. And a ghoul was waiting.

"Tom?"

"Jesus!"

Alice's face was an animated bruise, forehead split, nose bent. Her blouse was wet with blood and her hand, as she held it out to me, was slick and crimson. Her glazed eyes drifted for a moment and then settled on me.

"I just want to help you," she murmured, reaching unsteadily for my wrist. "That's all."

I recoiled from her offered fingers, leaning back – and the wisteria snapped beneath my feet. My arm slipped from the sill and my chin cracked against its edge.

I fell.

*   *   *   *

I remember lying on the patio and looking at my leg. My foot seemed to be on backwards. There was a lot of screaming, which might well have been Barbara but could just as easily have been me. Up above I could see Alice's busted face peering out of the window. As I looked at her she collapsed into a dot like a television being turned off. Much less screaming went on in the dark.

Soon there was a lot of business with lights and sirens. And movement. Movement was a very bad thing – plenty of screaming again. I felt my sleeve being ripped apart from cuff to bicep, and a deep barb of pain running into my arm.

And everything slowed down. I was warm and soft as a fresh-baked muffin. People around me were talking in sing-song trills like doves. I wanted to snuggle somewhere and dream about sleeping. I didn't care about the silly plane any more. I was happy just drifting with the lights above me and the doves coo-cooing. Drifting alone and warm and happy.

Tomàs. Listen.

Ah, there. It's you again. Would you mind terribly just going away?

I understand now. I understand that you don't understand.

Yes. No. One or the other.

You need to understand, Tomàs. I need you to understand.

I'm in denial. Haven't you heard? Please leave me be.

I'm sorry.

Suddenly the warmth was ripped from me like a duvet, and pain howled along my leg, spiked through my chest, lifted me upright. I was in a hospital room. My foot was on backwards. Shocked faces turned to look at me.

"I told you to give him a sedative."

"I did! He should be out for hours!"

Tomàs. Concentrate.

"Oh, God. Oh, Christ – make it stop!"

You have to listen to me. You have to do what I ask.

"I will! I'll do anything! Make it stop!"

The warmth descended on me once more and I fell backwards, tumbling over and over, falling without descending in the snuggled comfort and the cooing of the distant doves.

Tomàs.

Yes, I'm listening. I am.

You have to understand. It all has to be explained to you.

Okay. Explain.

No, not me. I can't explain it.

Fine. I'm happy here.

You can't stay here. You have to help.

No problem with that. I was happy to help. I was a very helpful chap. Warm, comfortable, drifting, helpful chap. And the mad voice wasn't so bad after all. As long as I kept agreeing with it, everything was fine. Easy. I'd just keep agreeing.

Tomàs ?

I felt the warm duvet being lifted just a little, and the pain in my leg flared like a threat.

You have to find him, Tomàs.

Okay, okay. Find whom?

The duvet settled again and the pain span away into the tumbling softness.

Find Pablo.

Chapter Fifteen
All That Made-up Crap

At breakfast I munched toast as Pablo sorted my mail.

"Okay – you've got an account statement from Harrod's."

"Admin pile for later in the week."

"Yep. A handwritten envelope postmarked Sunderland."

"One of my authors. Business pile for this evening."

"And an official-looking envelope from Worcester."

"Ah – open that one."

Pablo tore open the envelope.

"There's a receipt and a photocopy of a death certificate."

"Read it to me."

The document gave Patti's married name as Ragnall. Her last address was recorded.

"Could you bring me the phone?" I said.

Pablo didn't move.

"Pablo, the phone, if you'd be so kind."

"I've hidden it in the garden. You'll have to find it."

"Pablo."

"Jesus – all right." Chair legs scraped. He brought me the phone. "I've put Enquiries on speed-dial three. And I just want to say… Oh, forget it. I'm going to deadhead the roses."

"Thank you."

He left, and I dialled. I gave the surname and the address and they put me through. The phone was answered immediately.

"Is that Ed Ragnall?" I said.

"Yes – who is this?"

Faced with the question I didn't think it would be a good idea to announce myself as his adopted son's uncle.

"My name's Stephen. I'm a friend of George Sandham'."

"Oh. What can I do for you?"

"I'm afraid I have to tell you that George has passed away. A heart attack."

"I see. That's a shame."

I didn't know what to say next.

"He didn't suffer," I offered rather lamely. "It was quick."

"Yes, well. That's a blessing."

"Indeed. Yes. You might like to pass that on to Jonathan."

Again, silence. I could hear the school-clock ticking on the wall above the dishwasher. A tap was dripping – Pablo hadn't turned it off properly. He never did.

"Anyway," Ed Ragnall said, "thank you for letting me know. Thank you."

"It was the least I could do."

"Very thoughtful. Goodbye."

"Just before you go," I said quickly.

"Yes?"

"I was sorry to hear about Patti."

"Oh. Did you know her?"

"A long time ago, yes."

"Stephen. Stephen Richmond?"

"Yes," I said.

"How did you get this number?"

"I…"

"Please don't call again, all right?"

"Mr Ragnall – believe me – I don't mean to cause any trouble. But I would really like to get in touch with Jonathan."

"That's not possible. Now I have to hang up."

"Please. All I'm asking…"

"I'm hanging up now. Please don't call again."

The line went dead. I put the receiver on the table. I'd made a mess of it.

"Didn't go well, eh?"

I turned my head.

"I thought you were pruning roses."

I heard Pablo walk to the counter and fill the kettle.

"Was that Patti's husband?" he asked. "He didn't embrace you to the bosom of the family, I take it?"

"No. But I won't give up. It's not for the adoptive father to decide what Jonathan should know or not know."

"Of course not. That's up to you. Coffee?"

"What am I to do, then, Pablo? Keep the truth from my nephew?"

"Why not?" he said. "Everything is exactly as it was a month or two ago, and as it has been for forty years." A teaspoon chinked against china. "The only difference is that you know now. The information is in your head. Why do you want to put it in other people's?"

"Because it's only fair. It's just. The truth is important."

"Well, jolly lucky George died then. What a fortunate break that his assistant's niece was getting married. Damn good thing you knocked over the lamp in George's office."

"You're being facetious."

I heard the fridge open.

"Semi-skimmed all right?"

"I'll take it black."

He brought the mug over to me, and lifted my hand to it.

"If not for those happenstances," he went on, "George's loyal discretion and Patti's responsible choices and her husband's devotion to Jonathan would all have been the supports of a terrible injustice." He slurped his coffee. "Now, thank God, you can do the right thing."

I said nothing. Had I been able to see, I would have had trouble meeting Pablo's eye. As it was, I simply sipped my drink and remained silent.

"Right – I'm going out to do the roses now," Pablo said. "When Mary arrives, tell her I'll give lunch a miss."

He was halfway along the hall when I called him back.

"Yes?" he said.

"If it was mere chance that I found out about this, isn't anything that I do now a consequence of that dumb luck?"

He laughed. "Why are you trying to justify this in my terms? Don't yours work?"

"I was just trying to explain," I said, bristling. "My intentions are perfectly considered – and I need justify them to no one but myself."

"Yeah? Sounds like a chicken-wire teapot to me."

We didn't speak again until dinner. Over phoned-in Thai, I said, "I want you to call Mr Ragnall and wheedle out of him some information about Jonathan."

"And how would I do that?"

"I don't know – but I'm sure you could."

"And *why* would I do that?"

"Because I've asked you to."

I heard him put down his cutlery and light a cigarette. He was going to lecture me.

"Do you understand why I'm so against you getting in contact with Jonathan?"

"It doesn't matter – it's not your business."

"Maybe not. But I'm taking advantage of your powerlessness, you incapacitated old curmudgeon."

I too stopped eating and reached to find a napkin. "Very well. Why do you disapprove?"

He clucked his tongue, thinking. "Take my case," he said. "I've lived most of my life feeling responsible for my brother. Everything I've done, I've done in respect of him. A lot of it has been very enjoyable and worthwhile – but very little of it was just for me. I wasn't actually living my own life. I was living ours."

"Can we take the parallels as read?" I said impatiently. "I recognised them when I first met you, and that's the reason we're here together now."

"Our tracks might be parallel, but I'm further along than you. I've reached a destination."

"Well, perhaps getting in touch with Jonathan will bring me to my journey's end."

"Or perhaps you'll just change gauge and continue along similar lines."

I tutted. "Could you pour me some wine?" He did so, and I took a sip. "This reminds me of conversations I use to have with George. Because he'd come out as gay, he used to insist that I should do the same. No matter that I'm not homosexual – it had made him happy and it might make me happy too."

"Aren't you gay? I mean, the thought had occurred to me."

"No, I'm not. Would you like the telephone numbers of my old flames?"

"Just never found the right girl, huh?"

"Pablo – you're bordering on the impudent now. As you ask, I did find the right girl once, but it didn't work out."

"What happened?"

This was a typical Pablovian tangent, and although reluctant to dwell on my private life, I was relieved that Pablo had been distracted from browbeating me about Jonathan.

"Her name was Vivienne Belitho-Fitzwarren."

I've always thought that my romance with Vivienne just petered out through lack of attention. Lack of *my* attention, that is. But as I spoke to Pablo about the relationship, I remembered a specific moment that was crucial.

Vivienne and I were driving back to London from Twyborough Cross having spent the weekend with my dying mother. I remarked on how well the garden had looked.

"It's just stunning in the spring. Did you go down to the orchard? The blossom on the fruit trees is utterly beautiful."

"The place is breathtaking. It has bags of potential," Vivienne said.

"It requires a lot of upkeep. I noticed that the lawn needs a trim."

"Well, yes. There's so much of it. It could do with some rosebeds, just to add interest to that vast flat expanse of green."

I didn't respond to the suggestion, not then or ever, but at that precise moment I disengaged myself from Vivienne – because her implied scheme for the lawn was entirely reasonable. When we married, as we planned to, she would become the lady of the house and she would want to make changes – beds set into the lawn, a new design for the kitchen, the conversion of the walk-in closet to an *en suite*. It was only right that she should make such plans. I understood that and I couldn't permit it. It wasn't my house. Not mine alone.

"It was Leo's," Pablo said. "Still is."

"Yes."

"And it will become Jonathan's."

"Of course."

"You'll have lived here your entire life, and you'll die here, and you won't have left any mark on it at all. You even denied yourself a wife and family in order to make sure of that. Did you love her?"

"More impertinence." I pushed my chair back and got to my feet. "I need to be excused. Would you take me to the door?"

"Find your own way," Pablo said. "You could do it with your eyes shut."

*   *   *   *

Later, out on the terrace, Pablo read me his final section – the destruction of the blood-baby sculpture and playing the arcade game on Wardour Street.

"That's the lot," he said when he'd finished. "Seems like a good place to stop, given the character-arc and the issue-resolution and all that made-up crap."

"You've been doing your homework."

"I want a gold star from the teacher."

"Well, tomorrow we'll start revising. You can read me everything I edited before it became impossible for me to work, and then we'll try to slot in the newer material. But I think there's something there. Well done."

"Thanks. Shall I open another bottle?"

"No, I'm off to bed now. Thank you for making dinner."

"Your pyjamas are on your pillow."

Before I fell asleep, I mulled over the evening's conversation. Pablo was wrong. Sally was his catalyst for his decision to claim his life back from

Perdito, that was obvious. But mine was Jonathan. To put it in terms of Pablo's 'made-up crap', Jonathan would be the resolution for me.

"I'm grateful for your concern, Pablo," I said the following morning, "but I want to press ahead with the search."

"Yeah, I know."

"So you'll make the phone call?"

"No need. I've found him."

"I beg your pardon?"

"Well, I'm pretty sure I have. I looked him up on the Web."

Perhaps it's my age, but I view the internet as a tiresome professional necessity. Authors and editors consider one a fossil if one can't offer an e-mail address, so I'd had the necessary wires installed. Before I lost my sight I checked my mailbox every fortnight or so and never really explored further.

Pablo, of course, was aware of the possibilities of the technology. After I'd gone to bed the previous night, he'd searched for the name Jonathan Ragnall, which is easy to do apparently. There were very few candidates, and he soon narrowed it down to one, whose personal details were given as part of the marketing material of a civil engineering company in California. Pablo read me the print-out.

Jonathan Ragnall – Operations Director, 36. Jon's our tame Brit! Educated at Worcester Grammar School and Newcastle University, Jon came to the US after graduation 'just to look around'. He wound up in Monterey where...

"That must be him," I said. "It must be. Does it give a phone number for the company office? Dammit – it's the middle of the night in California."

"There's an e-mail address for him. Please – write, don't phone. Give the poor bastard time to think. Start a correspondence and get to the revelation gradually."

"Oh – so engage him in a professional dialogue about road-bridges and then, once he's got to know me, slip in the fact that I'm his uncle?"

Pablo chuckled. "You're lousy at sarcasm. It's not in your nature."

Despite my eagerness to make contact with Jonathan, I saw the sense in what Pablo said. We went upstairs to the computer in the study and I dictated a letter.

"Dearest Jonathan…"

"Much too familiar. *Dear Jonathan*."

"Yes, you're right. *Dear Jonathan*."

It took two hours of argument and negotiation. As I couldn't write the thing without Pablo's help – I've never been able to touch-type – I had no choice but to consider his advice, of which there was plenty.

Dear Jonathan,

My name won't be familiar to you, but yours is familiar to me. I was good friends with George Sandham, who I believe you met at least once – in fact, on the sad occasion of your mother's funeral.

I too was close to Patti during the Sixties. Unfortunately circumstances were such that she and I were unable to keep in touch after she moved back to the Midlands. But I've thought of her often and fondly.

I'd very much like the opportunity to talk to you about her. I'm sure you'd be interested in her life before you were born, and I'd be pleased to answer any questions you might have.

I look forward to hearing from you.

Yours truly,

Stephen Richmond.

Pablo read it back to me.

"It doesn't sound as if I had an affair with her, does it?" I asked.

"I suppose it could. But if you make it plain you didn't it'll give the impression you did. Shall I hit 'Send'?"

I hesitated. "Read it one more time."

"Stephen – you know it by heart. Do you want me to send it or not?"

"Oh, Lord," I said. "Yes. Send it. Yes."

He tapped a key. "There. It's sent."

I slumped in the chair, exhausted. A thought occurred to me. "Is there a photograph of him alongside his details?"

"No. Just the text."

I found myself relieved at that. To have a picture of my nephew available and not to be able to see it would have frustrated me beyond endurance.

However, the idea gave me something with which to occupy myself. Between almost-hourly demands that Pablo check for a reply, I tried to envisage what Jonathan would look like. It was a futile endeavour, given that all I had to go on for the distaff side was my memory of Patti at twenty-six. Perhaps that's why, however I combined my parent's features and my extrapolations of Patti's, my confected image of Jonathan always came out resembling Leo. He bore absolutely no resemblance to me at all – and why should he?

*   *   *   *

Two days passed. Three. Four.

Pablo was working in the garden constantly, because I was much too distracted to concentrate on the revisions of his manuscript. I had calculated at what time in England the working day started in California and the moment I heard the hall clock chime, I felt my way to the terrace.

"Pablo!"

"Yep?" It sounded as if he were on the lawn.

"Do you think you could take a break to check the mail?"

"For God's sake, Stephen – I'm trying to get some work done out here. I'll see if anything's pinged in when I stop for a drink."

"Pinged?"

"Yes – if the computer's turned on, it pings when mail arrives."

"Really? I've never been sitting there when mail arrived."

I made him turn up the volume and leave the study door open. I kept the radio off and I wouldn't let Mary use the vacuum cleaner. I found reasons to stay in my bedroom, which is next to the study, also with the door open.

And eventually, as I was dozing on my bed after lunch on the fifth day, it came – ping! – just as Pablo had said. I rolled over and found the floor with my feet. I extended my arms and went to the open window.

"Pablo!" I shouted. "Pablo! Mail!"

I listened – God, how I wished I could see – but there was no answering cry. I stumbled out to the landing and gripped the newel-post at the top of the stairs.

"Pablo! Where are you?"

"I'm here. I was in the kitchen."

"We have some e-mail."

He was speaking on the phone as he came up the stairs. "Listen – when does it become okay for me to call you? I mean, I just sit around waiting. It's a bit one-sided." He walked straight past me on the landing and I had to follow him, feeling my way. "Good. I'll call you tonight – about eight? Yeah. Dress casual. Bye, darling."

"Yeah," he said when we'd sat down, "it's from him."

"Read it to me."

He was silent for a few moments. "Tell you what – I'll print it out and we can take it downstairs and read it over a glass of wine."

"No – just read it."

"It's printing. Just a tick."

He lifted one, two, three sheets from the printer behind me. A long letter then.

"Okay," Pablo said. "Fancy a nice Bardolino?"

*　　　　*　　　　*　　　　*

Dear Stephen,

I'm sorry I've taken a while to reply. I had to get my head straight on some issues.

When you wrote that you'd known my mother, first thing I did was phone my dad and ask if he'd heard of you. He was real upset. He wanted me to promise I wouldn't contact you, so please keep this to yourself.

Just to get past the I-know-that-you-know-that-I-know thing – yeah, I've been aware since I was a kid that Ed Ragnall isn't my birth-father. But he is my dad. You only get one, right? He's mine and I love him to bits. Want that to be clear.

He's always been kind of jumpy about me learning who my 'real' dad is. I don't know why. It's not like I'm secretly heir to the throne or anything. Maybe I should tell him what I just told you, about loving him. It's not the kind of thing you think about until you get mail from someone who actually knew your mum and your genetic dad before you were born.

Because that's why you wrote me, isn't it? To tell me about my birth-father. It's okay. I already know about him. Surprised? Ed sure would be.

Every birthday I used to get a present from someone who never sent anything to my sisters. It started when I was too young to know the difference, but by the time I was paying attention the sender was known in our house as 'Jonny's Uncle London'. Dad wasn't totally happy about these presents. He always hurried me up when I was opening them. But Mum made a fuss over them and said how beautiful they were. And I was cool with it because it was the only present I didn't have to write a thank-you letter for.

When Mum died, I came back to England for the funeral. I was introduced to George, who Dad said was a friend of Mum's from way back. George told me how fond he'd been of my mother and what great times they had when they were young.

He got pretty drunk at the wake and he was all on his own at a table, so I sat down with him and put the question I'd been wanting to ask since we talked outside the church.

"Were you my Uncle London?"

"Ah! The pseudonym was Patti's idea," he said. Well, he slurred really. "Yes – guilty as charged. Forgive me the appallingly hackneyed turn of phrase, but I always thought of you as the son I never had." He put his hand on mine. "I've become a terribly sentimental old sod in my dotage."

I looked at this guy. He was pretty thick-set. Wavy gray hair. Green eyes. A slight stoop, tall as he was.

And – what do you know? – I'm pretty thick-set. My hair's dark brown but it's going gray fast. I have green eyes. I'm six-three and I have a stoop.

It clicked.

Yeah – I figured it out but I didn't say a word. I've often wished I would have. I had a list of questions as long as your arm, and not all of them were unjudgmental. But right then I couldn't see what good it would do to bring it out in the open. Certainly not at Mum's funeral, and not any time since either.

Thing is, I'm glad I saw him that once, but it wouldn't have made any difference if I hadn't. I didn't want anything from him, apart from to ask questions. And to be honest it was the asking that mattered. I never really cared about the answers. Whenever I've lain awake at night wondering whether I should track George Sandham down, I've thought, "Yeah – and then what?" Nothing. All it would achieve is to upset Ed. Even if my real father had been the king and I really was the secret heir to the throne, I wouldn't have made that call. I harbor no animosity – not any longer – and less curiosity. I have a pretty keen idea why it didn't work out with George and my mum. I guess she knew what she was doing when she married Ed, and I'm not going to defy her at this stage.

Though that's beside the point now, isn't it? When I asked dad how he knew you, he said you'd called to say that George Sandham had died. That was a shock. I guess I felt my options would always be open even if I didn't want to exercise them.

My condolences to you as George's friend. If you were close to him this must be a hard time for you. I've lost many close friends over the years and all I can say is that the grief does pass.

For me, it ends a chapter. Thank you for finding me. Your mail prompted me to write this letter, which has been a closure thing. I've never talked to anyone but my partner about it, and getting it down like this really ties up some loose ones.

Now I'm going to get on with my life. I hope you can do the same.

Take care,

Jon R

PS I don't know if this is appropriate, but I can't resist it. When I was a kid, I honestly did fantasise about my real dad being a king. It was pretty obvious that George was – haha – quite the opposite, despite having had his moments with my mum. That at least is a good thing for Ed Ragnall. It lets him off the macho hook with regard to my own sexual orientation.

Apparently it's hereditary – who knew?

*   *   *   *

I have never been a depressive sort of chap. I was brought up believing that to wallow in misery was impolite. I know that my father regarded Leo's wretchedness as an inexcusable self-indulgence. A fellow's supposed to stiffen the spine and just get on with things.

But the letter from my nephew caused a wave of misery to engulf me like slurry – clogging my mouth, constricting my chest, rendering me immobile. I felt utterly cut off from anything that made sense to me. It was worse than the blindness. I was buried in a place that was not merely black, but also silent, intangible, without form or feature. I was an irrelevance to Leo's son. I wasn't unwanted or rejected – I was simply beside the point. Even if he had known the truth about his parentage – and in the darkness I bayed at the injustice of his misapprehension – he wouldn't have needed anything I could give him.

...if my real father had been the king and I really was the secret heir to the throne, I wouldn't have made that call. I harbor no animosity and less curiosity.

I had planned to present Jonathan with a history he could cherish. I had myths to unfold before him – treasures of memory, songs of a sacred past. I had intended to give him this house and I had anticipated his delight – not at the monetary value of the place, but at what it means to our family.

"Your father grew up here," I would have said. "He played in this garden. He slept in this room. He ate at this table."

I would have made Leo come alive for his son. That act of resurrection would have been my resolution.

Now, there would be none. Nothing resolved or absolved. Nothing to look forward to but the darkness.

*   *   *   *

A couple of things have been bugging me. A bug for each brother, in fact.

First – I want to know how Tom found my place on the canal in Amsterdam. I believe Stephen when he says it's not down to him, but no one else knew where I was.

Second – although I'm happy that Perdito's gone, I can't help wondering where. I imagine him floating around Soho like Tinkerbell's glow, looking for somewhere to settle. I've constructed ghoulish fantasies about him alighting on the still-warm corpse of an expired drunk and reanimating it – tottering along Lexington Street, flexing the fingers and rolling the head, getting a feel for his new body.

I knocked out a short story along those lines. Once you get into the habit of writing, it's difficult to stop. I've been staying up after Stephen goes to bed, scribbling away – stories, poems, sketches. Reams of the stuff.

Not that Stephen cares at the moment. Since he received the mail from Jonathan, he's scarcely come out of his room. I leave sandwiches for him on the landing and I ask him to join me for a drink in the evenings, but he's not very responsive. The sandwiches reappear half-eaten. The wine remains untouched.

Weeks ago, soon after I came back here from Amsterdam, I commandeered the Bentley and went to talk to Stephen's neuro-psychologist.

"Are you sure that Stephen isn't really – I mean non-hysterically – blind?" I asked him.

"I can't discuss a specific case with you, Mr Lyne."

"What if I offered you a huge amount of money?"

He laughed. "Let me ask you this. How does Mr Richmond get around the house?"

"Pretty well actually. He's lived there a long time. He knows it inside out."

"Okay – that might be it. But often the hysterically blind can negotiate a room perfectly – even rooms they don't know. The visual information is getting through, and it's being processed. They can see."

"Believe me – Stephen can't see."

"Such a person doesn't know he can see. He's not lying to us. His brain is lying to him."

An easily-tested proposition, and I tested it as soon as I got back to Twyborough. There's a small table outside Stephen's room, which I moved to the centre of the landing. He walked around it all afternoon. Never touched it. But at midnight, in the dark, he bumped into it.

"What's the cure?" I asked the doctor.

He clasped his hands. "The subconscious mind is clever and powerful, but rarely subtle. It deals in pretty trite metaphors. When it prevents a person from seeing the outside world, it's usually because there's something in the inside world that it doesn't want to look at."

"So what do I do to help?"

"A cognitive shift can sometimes trigger a spontaneous reactivation of the affected sense. In other words, if the person stands somewhere else, he sees things from a different angle. The problem is to shift him."

I've thought about that a lot. There was a time when everyone believed that the Universe was driven by clockwork. People constructed working models that replicated the movements of the planets and stars. Every time a new piece of astronomical information came along, they improved the clockwork models to fit the observable facts. These mechanisms became absurdly complex and increasingly inaccurate. Saturn wouldn't do what it was supposed to. Comets threw the entire machine. But people clung to the belief that Creation was a vast wind-up toy because the alternative was to ditch the entire model and come up with something else.

Jonathan is a blazing comet that's appeared in the sky of Stephen's clockwork cosmos. Stephen planned to incorporate him by reconstructing the mechanisms around him. Same components, differently geared. But

Jonathan's letter has made it clear that he has no interest in being the central widget in anyone's apparatus, and now Stephen is upstairs trying to work out what to do about that. I hope he comes to the conclusion that he's going to have to break up the entire convoluted contraption.

Personally, I think that Jonathan's reply was the best thing that could have happened to Stephen. Jonathan's obviously a level-headed guy and even though he made a mistaken assumption about the identity of his father, it's apparent that he doesn't need to be corrected. He doesn't need anything at all. And as if to spare Stephen any soul-searching about further descendants, he also implied he's gay. All in all, if you were attempting to force Stephen to embark on the painful process he's now going through, you could hardly have drafted a more perfect e-mail.

Which is why I wrote it like that.

*   *   *   *

As autumn passed and Christmas approached, I lay inert, immersed in the sticky morass of melancholy. I would come out of my room only at Pablo's indefatigable insistence, and he'd cajole me into activity and conversation.

"I've swept up all the leaves into piles along the path. Come and kick them."

"I have no desire to kick leaves, thank you."

"Oh, come on – how else is an old blind bloke going to experience trees? Get your coat on and we'll go for a walk."

He led me down the steps from the terrace. The air was sharp with frost and pungent with bonfire smoke.

"Stay off the lawn. I've just spread a feed on it. Come round towards the folly."

We kicked through piles of fallen leaves – him enthusiastically, me grudgingly – and then we sat in the folly, the stone seat cold on the backs of my thighs even through my heavy coat.

"I have a thermos of soup and some bread," Pablo said. "I hope you like oxtail." He guided my hands – one to the mug and the other to a hunk of bread. "There's pepper here if you want it."

"No. It's fine."

"So – listen. It's November 28th. Sally called this morning to tell me her decree absolute has come through."

"Ah. You'll be leaving then."

"For a few days, yes. But Mary'll still be here."

I sipped the soup. "You go, Pablo. To use Jonathan's phrase – get on with your life. I can't expect you to look after me forever."

"I don't intend to. But you and I had a deal. I wrote my story for you, and you have to get it in a fit state to publish."

"I thought you didn't care whether it was published."

"I've changed my mind. It's bloody good. So I'll be back on Monday, and we're going to start work."

The prospect of working on Pablo's manuscript hung over me all weekend. I was wearied by the very thought of having to concentrate on anything other than my own despondency. But at the same time I looked forward to Pablo's return. He had been gone only a few hours before I realised that my bleak, dark days were bleaker and darker yet without his facetious concern for me. On the Monday morning I sat in the kitchen while Mary bustled about and I listened for the Bentley's wheels on the gravel like a child straining towards sleigh-bells in the snow. When I heard the scrunch, I made my way to the front door which I opened just as two car-doors slammed. Perhaps Pablo had brought Sally with him.

"You're early," I said.

"Hello again," said a woman's voice. "I told you I'd be back."

Chapter Sixteen
In the Soft Hot Red

"Tomás? Pay attention."

"I'm in hospital. I've done something terrible to my ankle. I'm on powerful painkillers."

"Tomàs!"

"Hence the voice. I'm dreaming a voice. I'm in the thrall of narcotics."

"Tomàs – I have to make you listen to me."

Concentrating hard, I lifted Tom's consciousness up through the fog of the morphine, as you might lift one end of a garden shed to sweep out from under it. He screamed, suddenly awake. I held him there for a few seconds, then let him drop back into the drug.

"No," he said, gasping. "That proves nothing. That's exactly what I'd imagine. It's not real."

"Then listen to your dream. Where's the harm in that?"

"I'm not going to conduct a conversation with a figment of my imagination. I'm not insane."

"You can talk in a dream, surely?"

I felt him give a little, but he was still terrified of me. I didn't understand why.

"I don't know how I come to be in the world, Tomàs," I said. "All I know is that I'm here – but at one remove. I can only connect with the world through you and Pablo."

"Not through me. I don't want you leeching off my life."

I stayed calm. Although I was aware, I wasn't foaming at the mouth, needled by stimulation as I would have been in Pablo. I found ways to think in Tom that made sense to me. I was sensitive. I was sensible.

"There were three of us in the womb. Any of us could have been smothered. It could have been you."

"No – it could have been Pablo maybe. You and he were all mixed up. But it's nothing to do with me."
"I'm your brother. One unlucky twist in the amniotic fluid and I'm denied a life – do you think that's fair?"

He focused and tightened in the opiate cloud. "Is it what?"

"Is it fair?"

Tom seemed to rise up in a rush. "What's not fair is being the one who's fine, the one who doesn't need care. What's not fair is being the one who'll be able to amuse himself, the one who'll cope." Tom's memories sparked and lit up all around me, flashing like the torches of a search party looking for a lost boy in the dark. "Pablo was first, indulged and fussed over because he was damaged. You came second, you sacred chimera, because you were the source of sorrow and guilt. And I was last – the first-born, cheated even of that distinction, taken as read and told to be grown-up about it. Is that fucking fair?"

"No, it's not," I said. I was astonished, but now I understood why he resented me, if not why he was afraid. "But you're alive."

"And you're not. So go back and haunt your murderer. You're nothing to do with me."

I moved in the mist of the morphine, trying to get closer to him. "I am. I feel it."

"That's rubbish." I heard something there. Something uncertain. "You're just a fraternal twin to me – just a brother. If..." He paused.

"What?"

"...if you existed at all, which you don't, the two of you would have to deal with it. You're his twin – so you're his responsibility. I'm no more liable than Jacinta."

I rummaged through the years – Dad in Orlando telling Pablo and Tomàs about the circumstances of their birth; Pablo in his bunk bed sharing the secret of me with contemptuous Tom – right back to imprinted but undeciphered memories from the hospital in Samoa when the surgeon prompted a gardener to explain my miserable fate to our stranded and uncomprehending mother. I turned every page and I scanned every image, all the way back to my big brother's first squalling breath. And I found nothing to explain Tom's fearful hesitancy.

"Tomàs..."

"I'm going to wake up now. I'm hungry."

"Tomàs, we have to find Pablo. The three of us must be together."

"To use a phrase of my friend Barbara's," Tom said, "dream on."

Pushing me away, he blew into the morphine fog, which parted and began to clear.

"Tom – you can't pretend I'm not here," I insisted.

"Dream off," he said, and woke up.

* * * *

Tom was obliged to stay in hospital, his leg strapped and his ankle in plaster. As soon as the pain was manageable they stopped giving him morphine and his mind settled, but I didn't permit him to convince himself that I had been an addled dream. I didn't speak – I didn't need to. He could feel me there.

Barbara visited and he asked to use her mobile phone, on which he called Angus Jakes.

"Well, that was an almighty fuck up, wasn't it?" Jakes said. "You might have called."

"I was unconscious for three days, Angus. But – yes – it was a mess. Get me the number and I'll do the meeting by phone tomorrow."

"Where the fuck do you think I am now? Fucking Malaga! I'm going to have to pull this one out of the fire myself."

"But what about buying the shares?"

"I dunno. Listen – we'll leave it a few months and revisit, okay? Incidentally, do you have income insurance? Because we're going to stop paying you from the twenty-first."

Tom handed the phone back to Barbara.

"How you feeling?" she said. "You look like shit."

"What you see is what you get."

"That lady whose nose you broke? Alice? Well, she's not going to sue you. You want my opinion, she's crazy."

"As I'm sure you told her."

"Her angle is she shouldn't have put you in that position. Unethical and unprofessional, she says. On the other hand, she doesn't want to see you again."

"It's mutual." Tom shifted the pillow behind his head. "And what are you doing here? I mean, nice though it is to have a visitor, not really within the terms of our relationship, is it?"

Barbara slipped a hand under the sheets. "I have a kinda thing about casts."

"No, no, no," Tom said, slapping her away. "Christ. You're sick."

Barbara shrugged. "It's a hospital."

*   *   *   *

Tom ignored me as he lay there in bed with nothing to do but read pulp novels and take calls from the Condesa ("When your leg is better, you must find Pablo, Tomàs. I'm really worried about him this time. How soon will you be on your feet?"), but something deep inside him was chafing at a long-protected sore – and it wasn't me doing the rubbing. Despite all that had happened, nothing had changed, except for the worse. Pablo had evicted me. Tom did not accept me. I was still denied any connection with the world.

"Hello, again. You've been in the wars, haven't you?"

Tom looked up from his newspaper as his visitor took a seat. It was Detective Inspector Ruth Pontin.

"Oh, great. Alice has decided to prosecute, has she?"

"Who's Alice? No idea what you mean."

"What are you doing here, then? And how did you know I was here at all?"

Ruth Pontin laughed. "I'm a copper. It's my job." She took an envelope from the inside pocket of her leather jacket. "A perplexed pathologist has suffered many late nights thanks to your brother."

"Tell him there's a long-established support group."

Two days earlier DI Pontin had taken a phone call from the technician who had analysed Pablo's blood and matched it to the blood in which he'd been covered when he was arrested. The technician was concerned that his hurried first analysis had not been a hundred percent conclusive so, being a thorough chap, he'd gone back the following day to verify his results. What he found was distressing. The test was not clean. He realised that he must have contaminated Pablo's sample somehow. He tested the blood taken from Pablo's clothes – but that was contaminated too. The DNA in the samples – that from Pablo's swab and that from the clothes – matched, but they both carried another identifiably distinct strand of DNA. There was another blood in there.

"He went back to the sealed back-up," Ruth Pontin told Tom. "And he was most astonished to find the same problem – two sets of DNA in the sample. So he phoned me to say that all bets were off. The samples were so dirty that they proved nothing."

Tom shrugged. "Does it matter, given that no crime was committed?"

"Well, no. Except I hate a conundrum. We've never, in all the time I've been in the job, had three samples contaminated in exactly the same way at exactly the same time. The most likely explanation was that they were all messed up at source. So I did some research into absorbed foetuses."

I had been dozing, but I started to pay attention.

"And it's happened before. There are cases of the child who did the smothering carrying the DNA of the dead foetus in his blood."

"Which, I suppose, is entirely possible," Tom said.

I could see where this was going. And Tom could have seen it too, had he wanted to.

"It is possible, yes," said Ruth Pontin. "But if Pablo and the dead foetus were identical twins, they'd have identical DNA."

I remembered my struggle with Pablo in the art gallery – the feeling I had of being pulled from one and hugged by another.

"Either the three of you were fraternal triplets," Ruth Pontin said. "Or the dead foetus wasn't Pablo's identical twin – he was yours, Tom. The rogue DNA in Pablo's blood is the lost baby's – but it's also yours." She shrugged. "You'd have to give me a sample to find out for certain."

But I knew she was right, and so did Tomàs. Looking for the connection that Tom instinctively understood, I hadn't gone far enough back. I had stopped searching when I reached the door to the world. Had I continued the search into the ante-room of life, I'd have discovered Tom's memory of being parted from me. Flesh retains everything, though it remembers so little. Tomàs and I were one – we were the same soft hot red.

My brother was silent, staring at Ruth Pontin. She hadn't told him the truth, exactly. She'd only awoken the truth that had been sleeping in him for forty years.

I spoke softly in Tom's ear and in Tom's own voice.

"You're his twin – so you're his responsibility."

* * * *

When he could walk again, Tom and I began the search for Pablo. I was certain he'd have fled to the apartment in Amsterdam, but we watched the place for a week and didn't see him.

"We have to go and see Natalie," *I told Tom on the ferry home.*

"I'm still considering whether or not I'm sane," *he said,* "but that suggestion inclines me towards the negative."

Because the world seemed so altered in Tomàs, I was interested to discover whether Natalie would look different to me. For twenty years she had been the only constant in the fractured and refractive collage of my experience. Not only did she accept me, she liked me, separately from Pablo, and as well as him. Though not without him, apparently, which had been a painful surprise. Perhaps my new perception of Natalie would be more like Tom's – and he wasn't particularly keen on her.

She didn't seem to have anything against him though.

"Tom!" *she said, smiling as she opened the front door. Almost immediately her face fell.* "Has something happened to Pablo?"

"I wouldn't be in the least surprised," Tom said. "When did you last see him?"

Ten minutes later we were on our way to Buckinghamshire.

"Nice car. Smells new," Natalie said.

"It's hired. Pablo stole mine."

I lurked behind Tom's curt antipathy and studied Natalie. I could still sense in her the propensity to perceive realities higher than the material. The leaning was there, but it was hidden by Tom's dismissive scepticism, which obscured the compelling parts of her like clumps of reeds and the branches of willows might censor a skinnydipper in a Sixties sex comedy. I wanted to see more. She intrigued me – but she no longer attracted me.

"Pablo says that Perdito has gone," Natalie said.

"So I hear," Tom said.

"Really? I thought you said you hadn't been in contact with him."

"He told me at the police station."

"Oh." She gazed out of the window at the city going past. "I don't get that at all. Where would he go? How would he go?"

Tom and I had agreed that we wouldn't tell Natalie where I was. From my point of view it was an issue only between the three Lyne boys; and Tom was not yet sufficiently comfortable with the truth of my existence to want to talk about it to anyone, least of all Nat.

"I have no more idea than you, but I'm sure you're happy to speculate."

"Well, it depends what you think Perdito is. I mean, we're all part of the same life-energy, but the way it's projected through each of us is unique – like sunlight through a stained-glass window. Same source of energy, different colours – you know?"

"Very lucid."

"So I think that he survived in the womb as an individual long enough to take on his own unique and colourful design in a human sense. And he just clung on there after his body became, like, non-viable."

Tom glanced at Natalie and winced as she took out a cigarette and opened the passenger window. "

"All Perdito wants is the chance to live his life in his own time independent of anyone else's permission or interference," Natalie said, cupping her hand around the flame of the lighter.

"Well, we have that in common, then," Tom said, accelerating onto the dual carriageway.

Wherever he might have run in the meantime, Pablo was back where Natalie had last seen him. He was staying in a beautifully-restored white Georgian house set in grounds that were simultaneously sumptuous and understated. As we approached along the gravel drive Tomàs shook his head.

"How does he do it?" he muttered. "How does he always land on his feet like this?"

Natalie shrugged. "He doesn't care."

"That's what makes it so galling. He attracts all this good fortune and he doesn't care."

"Not 'and'. 'Because'."

Pablo's host was a well-spoken and well-groomed blind man in his sixties who, having introduced himself at the door, ushered us through to the drawing room. He couldn't have been sightless very long because his house was full of books. It was practically built of books. Had the walls crumbled behind the bookshelves it might be centuries before anyone noticed.

Stephen Richmond denied that Pablo was staying at the house, but within minutes my missing brother walked through the front door.

"What do you want?" he asked.

Tom glanced at Natalie, and then back at Pablo. "Just to talk – lives may depend on it."

"Whose lives?"

"Pick any two of three."

"Pablo," Natalie said, "don't you even care what's happened to Perdito?"

Pablo looked at Tom. "Do you?"

Tom was reluctant to answer that in front of strangers.

"Tell him you want your car back," I said.

"I want to know what you've done with my Alfa," Tom said. As he said it I leapt – just for a moment – and Pablo felt me. His eyes met Tom's. He appeared confused, and then he got it. Or at least, he suspected.

"Everyone needs a vehicle to get around in," he said thoughtfully.

Tom nodded slightly.

Pablo cogitated as he tapped out a cigarette which he lodged in the corner of his mouth. "Okay, let's go outside," he said. He walked towards the doors to the garden and Tom followed.

Stephen Richmond turned towards where he estimated Natalie to be standing. "Please help yourself to a drink," he said.

Pablo led the way around the vast lawn to a pseudo-classical gazebo overlooking a lake. He sat down on a bench, and Tomàs sat beside him. The litter of cigarette ends on the floor suggested that Pablo spent considerable time there.

"You must be in shock," Pablo said. "It's very difficult not to say 'I told you so.'"

"It could be simply that I'm as insane as you," Tom said. He shrugged. "No – okay. Whatever he is, he's something."

Pablo took the last drag of his cigarette and flicked the burning stub of it towards the steps of the gazebo. It bounced off a pillar and rolled back. He ground it out beneath the toe of his high-top. His face seemed to age when he was thinking – as if, unanimated, his features gave the years time to settle. I hung back behind Tomàs's eyes, silent, waiting to hear what he proposed.

"What he wants is connection; direct experience," Pablo said. "You understand that now – yeah? That's justice for him."

"He's very keen on things being fair," Tom agreed.

"Me too," Pablo said. "I've carried him for forty years. Now it's your turn. Only fair."

"You're palming him off on me?"

"Just allow him some time. Natalie can teach you the technique for letting him take control."

If Pablo had intended to utter a sentence guaranteed to put Tom off the idea, that would be the one to choose.

"Wait, wait, wait," Tom said. "Unlike you, I already have commitments. Ten hours a day at a proper job, for a start. The only reason I stay in my bloody awful job is to buy time for myself. I'm not donating that to the cause, brother."

Pablo tapped out another cigarette and looked out at the bare trees, branches dark against the bright winter sky. "You're in the wrong business, you know. You ought to be in the car-valeting line."

"What?"

"It's where the money is. I, for instance, might employ a car cleaner, if one were available."

"What the hell are you talking about? I didn't think you had a car – apart from the one you stole from me."

"I don't. But I'd want a valet anyway, just in case I ever bought a car that needed valeting."

Tom rubbed his eyes with his fingertips. "Are you out of your mind? What has this got to do with anything?"

"I'm thinking an annual retainer of, say, a hundred grand – all documented and properly payrolled," Pablo said, standing up.

Tom stopped massaging his eyes and looked at Pablo. "Where would you get a hundred grand?"

"Do you care?"

I was a bit slow in understanding the significance of this exchange, but as Tom thought through the mechanisms, it clicked. Pablo would pay Tom a huge salary for an imaginary job. Tom would present evidence of his income to the trustees who would release the millions he was due. Suddenly all Tom's time would be his own and his end of the bargain was that he'd give some of it to me.

"Think about it," Pablo said. "Get Natalie to show you what to do."

"What to do? Do what?"

Pablo lit his cigarette. "Practice having him drive. If you go for this, you need to know what you're letting yourself in for."

"Is that what you did with him? Allow him to take over your body?"

"Yeah, it takes a few months to get right." Pablo exhaled a stream of smoke. "And I have some stuff of my own to sort out. Listen – I'll meet you in the tea-room of the Ritz at noon on the fifteenth of April."

"If you think I'm letting you out of my sight again," Tom said, "you're very mistaken. I wouldn't trust you as far as I could throw you tied to a piano."

"Don't worry," Pablo said. "I'll be there."

"Your record for reliability doesn't inspire…"

"I swear on Dad's letter."

Tom sat back and nodded. "Okay. Twelve o'clock, April fifteenth at the Ritz."

Which would be the anniversary of our father's death.

* * * *

"Of course, of course. I should have guessed," Natalie said. She turned off the hot tap and checked the temperature of the water, sloshing the scented bubbles around a little. "Where else would he go? Of course he's occupied you."

"It all seems so obvious in retrospect," Tom deadpanned, emerging from his bedroom in a robe. "It's almost banal."

"Do you have candles?"

"There are some in the sideboard. Just plain white ones. Not perfumed or anything."

"I'll fetch them. Get in the bath."

Tom followed her through to the living room. "Is the bath really necessary? I mean, can't I lie on the couch or something?"

"We have to get you totally relaxed," Natalie said. "You won't drink a glass of wine. You won't smoke a joint. All I have to play with is warm water and half-light." She opened the centre drawer of the sideboard. "Get in the bath."

"I'm really not comfortable with this."

"Look – you're simply going to allow him to take control for half an hour. You're in your own home. You can stop at any time. It's perfectly safe." She rummaged in the drawer. *"Do you have any candle holders to put these in?"*

"Underneath in the cupboard."

Tom went back to the bathroom and shucked the robe. He wiped condensation from the mirror and looked himself in the eye. I looked him in the eye too. He was scared.

"Is there any music you find particularly relaxing?" Natalie called.

"Not really, no."

He stepped into the bath and lay down, careful to shoosh the bubbles modestly over his penis. Natalie came in and placed lit candles around the room; she turned out the overhead light.

"Close your eyes," she said.

"Why?"

"To help you drift."

"What are you going to do?"

"Nothing. Just talk."

"You're not going to touch me or anything?"

"I promise I won't."

Tom closed his eyes and tried to release the fearful tension in his limbs.

"You're grinding your teeth," Natalie murmured.

I felt my way forward, silent – and I realised that in Tom I had become more and more silent. I didn't cajole or carp. I watched and I moved lightly.

Tom was trying not to think about the only thing he couldn't stop thinking about – the flight from Amsterdam, and what that loss of control had cost him. From that memory flowed thoughts of how he hated Pablo's eccentricity, and how he despised me for being the reason his brother was indulged.

"I want you to imagine a warm, dark place," Natalie said. "Somewhere safe and quiet."

Tom shifted in the water. "Quiet but for the muffled pulse beyond the rippling uterine walls, presumably," he said.

"Shh. Don't think. Feel."

I sidled forward as if I were not moving at all, like a commuter anticipating where the door of the crowded train would come to rest.

"Perdito is there with you in the warm, safe place. Can you feel him there, even with your eyes shut?"

"This is ridiculous. We were plankton – not even recognisable foetuses – when Perdito was with me." Tom crossed his arms across his chest in the water, eyes still closed. "And the womb wasn't very safe for *him*, was it?"

I felt his arms intertwine. I felt his scrotum loosening in the warmth. The tickle of bubbles was on his lips as he slid down a little, and I was aware of it.

"Time and independence," Tom murmured. "Dead or alive, apparently we all want the same thing."

"Just let him take control. Let go, and let him in."

"I can't feel a thing. I think he's asleep."

"Perdito?" Natalie said. "He'll let you if you ask. Just like Pablo."

"I'm nothing like Pablo," Tom said.

Natalie burbled on and Tom lay back, rolling his head lazily from side to side in the steam. I could feel the muscles in his neck, the shifting light of candles on his eyelids.

"There's nothing to fear," Natalie crooned. "It's warm and safe here."

In the silence a clock ticked, a tap dripped, a car cruised past on the road outside. I pushed very gently, but I was pushing against a warm draft. There was nothing there to lean on.

Tom scratched his thigh. "Look, forget it," he said drowsily. "Go and make some tea. I'll be out in a minute."

"Nothing?" Natalie wrinkled her nose. She sighed and shook her head. "Yeah – all right. It's obviously not working. Are you going to be okay in here?"

"Give me five minutes to lie here and soak," Tom murmured. "I don't feel like moving."

And with that, he got to his feet, naked, bubbles sliding off him.

"Oh. Do you want a towel?" Natalie said.

"It's me," I said to Tom. "I wanted to stand up. And you stood up."

He was startled. "Is this it?" he said out loud.

I reached for the towel that Natalie offered and wrapped it around my waist.

"Yeah. I'm driving," I said – and I was speaking aloud too. Perplexed, I stepped out of the bath.

"Perdito?" Natalie said. "Is that you?"

Tom spoke in my head. "I just feel slightly removed – as if I had a heavy cold and a bit of a temperature. Is that all there is to it?"

I tested around. White bath. Whirring extractor fan. Tree-mint shampoo. The world was as it had been a moment before, but turned up a little. The contrast was a bit sharper; the colour a tad richer; the stereo a touch better defined.

"Yeah. It seems to be just this. This is all there is."

"What's the big deal then?"

I shook my head. Tom's head. There was a head and it shook.

"I don't know," I said. "I honestly don't know."

*   *   *   *

Over the following few weeks, Tom gave me control frequently, sometimes for hours at a time. I went to the cinema and the supermarket; I surfed the internet; I was in the driving seat on two or three dates with women, and I retained control even through the sex.

Natalie called in every so often. She was fascinated by the experiment.

"How does it feel when you let go?" she asked Tom one Sunday afternoon. "Does it change your perceptions?"

"It doesn't make that much difference, to be honest," Tom said. "It's a bit like cooking dinner when you're distracted by the television. You peel the potatoes and season the steak without making a conscious effort to do so, and later you barely remember eating the meal although there's an empty plate on the tray by the sofa."

It didn't make that much difference to me either. Driving Pablo I had been hyperstimulated– electrified, crackling with sensation – but when I was driving Tom's body, I was no more than aware. There was no dry friction between us – no static build-up while I was dormant and no spectacular discharge when I touched the wheel. This was how Tom experienced reality, and I recognised it. I had been here before.

A month earlier in Springheeled Jack's, I'd woken up to a universe where the lights on the pinball machine were merely something to look at, and the taste of brandy was all in the mouth and nose. I embarked on a five-day orgy – drugs, women, alcohol – thinking that it would all be so much more immediate without Pablo in the way. But it wasn't. It was pale and tiring. The more I racked up the stimulus – more coke, more girls, more brandy, faster, harder, louder – the less exhilarating the effect. Eventually, enraged and frustrated by the refusal of the universe to excite me, I pushed a commuter into the path of a train – and all I got was momentary adrenalin spike and a throbbing headache of guilt. I nearly killed a man, just to feel alive.

But I was alive. This, apparently, was what life should feel like to me.

"You know, when Perdito was part of Pablo," Natalie said, "I could always tell which was in control. Pablo was energetic; Perdito was fidgety. Perdito was fervent; Pablo was enthusiastic; Pablo was wry; Perdito was sarky. Even their faces were different somehow. I don't get that with Perdito and you." She looked at Tom as he poured hot water in to the tea mugs. "Even now, I'm not sure who's in there."

I wasn't sure either. Passenger or driver, the trip felt about the same. For thirty years I had protested that I just wanted to be myself, to experience the world directly, to live my own life – and now, at last, I'd been given that chance and it turned out that being myself was boring, my experience of the world was dull and my life was barely worth living.

Tom brought the tea to the table. As he put a mug in front of Natalie, she reached for her cigarettes and their hands touched. Natalie looked up, directly into Tom's eyes.

"Perdito?" she asked, suddenly eager.

"No," Tom said immediately. "Absolutely not."

Natalie flushed. "I didn't mean... You know. But Perdito and I..."

"I know." He smiled. "It's nothing personal. There are still aspects of this that are deeply weird, and I'm not yet certain where my boundaries are."

"I know, I know. I'm sorry."

Tom couldn't see it, but it was obvious to me that Natalie was barely holding herself in one piece. She felt cheated and abandoned. Pablo had moved on, and I had lost interest in her as a girlfriend now that I didn't see her through the prism of Pablo's perceptions. But as I looked at her, glued together by no more than pride and nicotine, I suspected that she was experiencing the world a lot more vividly than I.

I remembered Pablo dragging me along Old Compton Street, and how I had picked up the murmurs of other realities from passers-by, all crowding around me, each distinct and completely unique, and all of them intelligible to me. There in the kitchen, I pushed back from Tom, like a novice swimmer in the deep end, just keeping my hand on the rail. I lifted my fingers and floated out a little, still attached by the thin red cord that had connected all three Lyne boys for forty years. And the second I relinquished that fingertip touch, I could hear the whisper of Natalie's perceptions, like a voice carried across water.

She was unhappy, but not surprised. She didn't expect the world to be fair – she had always distrusted it. The foster families, the care workers, the priests and the teachers – they all said the right things, but nothing had ever come of their assurances. Natalie knew that she could rely on nothing but her own ability to learn, understand and anticipate. Everything you're told is a lie. You have to find the truth on your own.

I could hear this whisper, and I could taste the scent of it – and I wondered what it must be like to be Natalie, to look out from behind her eyes as I had looked out from behind Pablo's and Tom's. I wanted to know how Natalie perceived an oak table, how she would react to Amsterdammers skating in the dark on a frozen canal.

I moved towards her, wanting to press against her, into her, like a kid crawling under the canvas of the circus tent. There was gap, and perhaps I could slip through it. Perhaps I could nestle in the soft hot red of Natalie, silent and unsuspected, a spectator in an unimagined world. But

I was tethered still to Tom, and I could hear, behind me, the slushy white noise of the endless rain on the dark highway. If I freed myself from Tom, there was no knowing what would happen. It might be that I would be gusted away, out of the light, back to the eternal spray-spattered darkness of the eternal blacktop. Yet again, I might die before I had ever lived.

I couldn't let go. I didn't dare. I melted into Tom, and looked out at Natalie as she sipped her tea and stared fixedly at the tabletop.

Chapter Seventeen
A Walk in the Garden

We worked all through the winter on Pablo's manuscript. I had been dreading it but in the event I found that it helped my state of mind. It requires intense concentration to edit and refine a manuscript that one can't see, and one has no time to mope. Pablo split his time between Twyborough Cross and Sally's place, and when he was away I played back tapes of him reading versions of his manuscript, making notes on a little voice-recorder he'd bought me.

As Christmas loomed I found myself becoming anxious at the prospect of a week alone, but again Pablo intervened. He brought Sally and her eleven-year-old son to Twyborough, and between them they kept me occupied. As spring approached they became regular weekend visitors, and I looked forward to their arrival on Friday evenings. Sally and Pablo would cook while I sat in the kitchen with a glass of wine, chatting. Or I'd help Josh with his homework, directing him to reference books – "Top of the stairs, second or third shelf up, red spine with gold lettering" – and having him read his essays to me.

Two or three times a week, whatever the weather, Pablo and I would walk around the grounds. Pablo insisted that we take the same route every time because – as he said – "one day I'm going to shove you out here on your own and the hell with the consequences". So we'd follow the path from the terrace clockwise around the lawn to the knot garden. We'd go past the oaks and down to the orchard, then along the far side of the lake to the folly where we'd sit for a while and discuss that day's work. Finally we'd stroll along the path through the shrubbery on the west side of the lawn and back to the house.

Spring came. On the Sunday morning that the clocks went forward, I was in the kitchen alone when Josh came downstairs.

"Are Mum and Pablo still asleep?"

"Yes – we had rather a late night celebrating. Pablo's book is finished."

"Okay. I'm making tea. Do you want some?"

"Thank you. Tell me – what's the weather doing?"

"Sunny."

"I should like to go for a walk in the garden. I'll ask Pablo when he gets up."

"I'll take you," Josh said. "Wait while I put my shoes on."

He led me down the steps of the terrace to the gravel path. I pictured the garden before me. Sunlight coming from behind the chimneys; shadows of beech across the lawn; the folly shining white; the lake glinting and still.

"Is there still dew?" I asked Josh.

"Yes, lots of it."

I kicked off my slippers. "Let's walk straight across to the folly."

"Won't we step on the flowers?"

"No – I mean, let's go across the lawn. I'd like to feel the grass beneath my feet."

"Yes, I know. We'll step on the flowers."

I tried to envisage what Josh was seeing. I couldn't understand his hesitation.

"Show me," I said.

He led me forward a few steps and I bent to touch the grass. My hand made contact with leaves when I was only halfway down. I took another step, and another – onto the lawn now – and I could feel foliage against my shins. I fell to my knees, flailing an arm about me. The lawn was gone. My hand found only wet leaves, wide and pointed. They brushed against my face as I crawled in my dressing gown and pyjamas.

"Pablo!" I shouted "Pablo – what have you done?"

I heard a window open.

"Just tea and toast for us," Pablo called.

"What have you done, Pablo? What's happened to my lawn?"

"If you look, you'll see."

"Don't mock me!" I knelt amongst the leaves in the dark, dew soaking through the knees of my pyjama. "Tell me what you've done to my lawn."

"I've changed it. Look."

"Changed it? You had no right!" I turned on my hands and knees, rage welling in my chest. "How dare you? Get out of my house! Get out!"

"Josh – come inside. It's time for us to go."

"But what about Stephen?" Josh said.

"He'll find his own way. Come on – we're going."

I heard the boy run up the steps and into the drawing room.

"Yes – go!" I shouted. "Vandal! My God – what have you done?" I reached sightlessly for handfuls of the hateful leaves and I yanked them from the ground. "How dare you! How dare you do this to my garden!"

The front door slammed and I heard the wheels of Sally's car swooshing away down the gravel drive. Then there was silence.

I knelt there blind on my desecrated lawn and I wept. I couldn't imagine what it must look like, but merely from feeling around me I could tell that it wasn't as it should be. The view from the house – the planned, balanced view that my father had restored to its original splendour – had been ruined. The smooth green lawn – across which Leo and I had run and tumbled and rolled – was violated. All my care, all my devotion and respect – disregarded.

I stood and waded through the thick leaves back to the steps. With one hand on the balustrade I made my way to the terrace and into the drawing room. I went upstairs to my room and crawled onto my bed where I curled tight, shaking with fury. If only I could see what Pablo had done I would know how to remedy it. But I was powerless to make things right – like a man scorned without knowing the cause.

After a few minutes I got up and went to the window. I pressed my forehead against the pane.

"See," I urged myself. "See!"

I threw my dark glasses aside. I gritted my teeth and tried to focus all my concentration on looking, as if to see were a conscious action. I imagined light hitting my retinas and impulses travelling to my brain – synapses firing, images being decoded. But still I was smothered in blackness. With my hands on the sill and my forehead to the glass, I wept tears of frustration, loneliness and self-pity.

And, oh, how I pitied myself – a blind old man alone in an empty house, unwanted and unappreciated; a shadow who haunted his childhood home, mourning the loss of all those he'd loved; a pathetic creature who had failed his only brother. What an unfortunate wretch I was.

Leo would have done better. Had the circumstances been reversed, had I died, Leo would have mourned me and carried on. He would have married and brought his wife here, happy to allow the place to change. But me – no. As Pablo had so unflinchingly remarked, I drove Vivienne away rather than risk this shrine being despoiled.

"Leo," I said aloud. "What should I have done?"

The crucial moment in my life occurred on the outskirts of Cambridge when I was twenty years old. I had always believed that my story thereafter was rooted in that terrible brief event. My plot and my character sprang from that misfortune. It was my structure.

All this crap about structure and narrative flow just makes it look like there's some kind of sense to what happens. There ain't.

For months I'd been listening to Pablo's voice on tape. I had dreamt it nightly. I could hear it in my head just as Pablo heard Perdito.

Life's simply a series of random events that happen to be studded across time like peanuts in a chocolate bar.

My relationship with Vivienne had nothing to do with Leo's accident. Meeting her was just luck. Dumb luck. But I was the author of my own plot, and I edited her out.

A lightning flash of intense white seared across my vision.

Now, when luck had brought me a friend, when this house was home to a family for at least some of the time, I had rejected that good fortune. My narrative structures had been threatened. Pablo had tried to revise to me, and I had driven him away too.

One penny pushes against another, and something happens, or it doesn't.

There were colours now – primary blobs blossoming and fading in the dark.

In the churchyard of St Dominic's I had told Leo how much he'd have liked Pablo. But to protect my brother's shrine – this house full of furniture that Leo touched, the garden preserved as Leo knew it – I had banished a friend with whom Leo would have laughed on the terrace over a bottle of wine. I had made myself lonely in homage to a man who revelled in companionship.

We each live in a firework display of personal meaning, deafened by thumping retorts of memory and blinded by the starburst rockets of our own incendiary past.

Pablo's voice. But behind his, I heard my brother's. That night in Cambridge – Leo as I always remembered him, smiling, handsome, optimistic and confident, lifting my hands from the suitcase and leading me to the door.

"Your high-minded conscientiousness is no good to me. I plan to live vicariously through you, so shuck that abominable tie and we'll be about our proper business."

"I tried, Leo. I tried."

I had meant to give Leo a life through me – but I'd completely mistaken my efforts. I had died vicariously through him.

Now the colours were sticking to the flat canvas of my vision – thousands of tiny fragments shifting and refracting. And if I dared, as I pressed my forehead to the glass of the window, I could almost convince myself that the blob of white to the right was the folly and the stripe of stippled blue was the lake. I wanted to lift my hands and rub my eyes, but I was terrified that I might erase the kaleidoscopic motley that pulsed before me.

"Forgive me, Leo," I said, sinking to my knees at the window. All my life I had craved Leo's forgiveness for my failure to save him. I wanted absolution for having let him die. I was wrong. I had refused to let him die, and for that I now needed his pardon. "Forgive me. I see now."

"He can't do it, Stephen." Pablo's voice again – behind me in the bedroom. "He's dead."

"I know." Leo was dead. Then, in that moment, I allowed it. "I understand." I struggled to my feet, my eyes fixed on the shimmer of a million colours that filled my vision. I swallowed my tears and steadied my breath.

"I forgive myself," I said.

And the colours shifted, coagulated, fell into their true perspectives. The folly solidified and became whole. The lake flattened and spread to the familiar trees, which hardened and gathered their spring leaves around them. And I saw the lawn. From the steps of the terrace below me to the water's edge in the distance, from the knot-garden's arch to the shrubbery around the temple, it was a jumbled, random mosaic of pink and yellow, scarlet and purple, white and orange – thousands of unruly tulips shifting in the morning sunlight, incongruous and ill-considered and utterly unabashed.

I gazed at the vista of radiant colour, chaotic and haphazard, joyous, signifying nothing but itself. I had never seen anything as beautiful.

Pablo walked up behind me as I looked out, blubbering, at the field of tulips, tears streaming from my eyes.

"I'm afraid I also replanted the saplings in the pasture," he said, "and I don't care what you say, you curmudgeonly old bastard, I'm not digging the bloody things up again."

Chapter Eighteen
Are You Staying with Us Today?

Throughout the winter I shared Tom's flesh. I sampled the life that I'd fought for – and it didn't seem enough.

The night before the meeting at the Ritz, while Tom slept, I rummaged in his memory.

New Year's Day, 1965. The babysitter came down with 'flu, so Dad and the Condesa bundled the kids into the car and set off. When they pulled up outside Pelham Grange, Grandad was already there, unlocking the gates. He came over to the car as Dad was strapping the boys into the pushchair and Mum was buttoning up Jacinta's coat.

"I'll take Jazzie for a walk down to the maze," Grandad said. "See you back here in an hour or so."

Inside the grounds of the Grange, Dad pushed the buggy along frost-starred paths, and Mum walked beside, her arm linked through his. Halfway up a gentle hill, beside jumbled rocks from which a spring gurgled forth, there was a bench facing the gardens. Mum and Dad stopped there and looked at the inscription carved into the wood.

…you shall not kiss him; at least not now…

My mother put her hand to her mouth, and my Dad slipped his arm around her shoulders. After a few moments he said, "Let's sit down."

He turned the buggy around so that the boys could see the view, but Pablo had dozed off and Tomàs was drowsy too. Mum and Dad sat in silence, looking out at the denuded winter garden and listening to the trickle of icy water close by.

"I often wonder what he would have been like," *my father said. He tapped a cigarette from the pack.* "Very like Pablo, I suppose."

"Perhaps," *the Condesa said.* "But he might have been very different. People always say Pablo and Tomàs are so alike, but we know how different they are already."

"True. Utterly individual personalities."

Mum smiled. "I think he would have been different again. I think he would have been a very special and unique little boy."

My Dad took my mother's hand, and they sat there in the bright cold afternoon, thinking of their lost son and imagining who he might have been had they ever been able to kiss him.

*   *   *   *

The table at the Ritz was booked in Pablo's name, but he was late. Tomàs was precisely on time, accompanied by Natalie, who had insisted on attending.

"Why tea at the Ritz, of all things?" *Tom asked, tightening the knot of his tie as they took their places at the linen-dressed table.* "It's so pretentious." *He glanced at Natalie.* "Thanks for making the effort. With the dress, I mean." *She was wearing a sober long-sleeved black number and a cropped pink jacket that picked up the cerise highlights in her newly-black hair.* "Christ alone knows what Pablo will come as."

"He'll come as his extraordinary self," *Natalie said – and I could see admiration for Pablo rising off her like steam.* "It's all he can do."

"Speaking of what he can do – do you really think he can raise a hundred grand?"

"What would be the point of saying it if he couldn't?"

White Christmas lights twinkled behind her head. There was a tree in the corner clothed in glittering frost-blue and icicle-silver. Boughs of evergreen framed the door and gave off a scent of winter. From where I looked out, from behind Tom's eyes, all that input was attenuated and controlled. It was backdrop.

Pablo sauntered in, spotted us and strolled over. He was wearing his usual canvas shoes and an ankle-length black cashmere coat buttoned all the way up and down.

"I suppose it could be worse," Tom said.

Pablo took a set of car keys from his pocket as sat down. "Here," he said, pushing them across the table to Tom. "Ask for Michael at the concierge's desk. He'll fetch it for you. I've had it serviced."

"It's here?"

The waiter came to the table. "Ah, Mr Lyne – how lovely to see you again! Are you staying with us today?"

"Hello, Edward," Pablo said. "Yeah, got in last night. Had some business in town."

"Splendid. Can I take your coat?"

"Better not. I've only got my pyjamas on underneath."

Edward chortled merrily. "Full afternoon tea for three?"

"Yes, please. Demonstrate a bias towards the salmon sandwiches. I like those."

Tom was staggered, but he remained straight-faced. Natalie was delighted.

"Pablo," she said, "do you remember when we came here before Alex's show in Hoxton?"

"Can't say I do," Pablo said.

But I could. I could remember the derangement of living in Pablo. Sitting here amongst all this intoxicating splendour, I had begged him to let me drive and later I took Natalie fast and coarse against a wall in an alley off Shoreditch. Back then I span in the vortex of Pablo's perceptions. Now I was impassive on the ice-floe of Tom's.

"So how has it been going?" Pablo asked, looking from Natalie to Tom and back again. "Successfully?"

"Unspectacularly," Natalie said.

"I don't know what all the fuss is about," Tom said. "It's a piece of cake."

I recalled the moment I became aware – the afternoon Pablo got an electric shock from the Christmas lights. That chaos of sensation caused me almost to swoon – but it was Pablo's sensation plugged into me. It wasn't mine directly and that had always been my complaint.

"So do we have a deal?" From the inside pocket of his coat Pablo took two pieces of paper, which he flattened on the table. One was a banker's draft for a hundred thousand pounds and one penny. The other was a payslip showing that amount as earnings. "The cherries all line up," he said, grinning.

Tom tipped his head to one side, looking at the fortune on the Irish linen. Then he surveyed the room, thinking. And when he looked at the Christmas tree in the corner, it didn't overwhelm me. It was pushed back and controlled – not because I processed it that way, but because Tomàs did. His way of being and mine were similar – so similar that when I occupied his senses neither of us felt much change at all – but still, the attitudes and the experience through which the world was interpreted were Tomàs's, not Perdito's.

"Not sure, eh?" Pablo said.

"Actually, I'm waiting for Perdito. He hasn't said a word for days."

Pablo nodded. "Sometimes he sleeps for weeks at a time. You should bear that in mind."

"No," Tom said. "He's there. He's just not saying anything."

Tom knew I was listening to all this. *I'll do it,* he said to me alone. *And not just for the money. It's my turn.*

Very reasonable, I thought. But then I was thinking like Tom because I was using Tom's thinking. I had no way of knowing my own mind. I didn't know what Perdito thought.

I detached and drifted up, still tethered to Tom by the red cord that connected all three of us. Immediately I was aware of the flesh in the room – dozens of people, each living in a universe of their own making, each striving to convey a sense of that universe to everyone around them. Their whispers sussurated about me, and I could tune in to any of them and listen. I could understand – as no living flesh could ever understand – what it meant to inhabit a universe in which each unique whisper made sense.

I'd always said I wanted a life of my own, but I could never live a life using Tom's body, any more than I could using Pablo's. I had built no unique universe. I had merely occupied those of my brothers.

"It's what he wants, Tom," Pablo said. "You know it is."

Tom nodded. "Okay." He picked up the draft and the payslip.

I could hear my mother's voice, in the cold at Pelham Grange on what was not my birthday. "I think he would have been very special and unique little boy."

I could do something unique. I could be special. I could live in the world of flesh as no one ever had, visiting and understanding a thousand universes. I could set up a temporary home in the world of the waiter who was bringing my brothers their sandwiches; of the rich old woman at the next table feeding salmon to her chihuahua; of the taxi driver hovering in the doorway; of the policeman standing on the corner outside the window; of the small boy gazing at him from the top deck of a passing bus. In my life I could live a thousand lives and that mosaic life would be mine, uniquely.

I looked at my brothers – Pablo fiddling with an unlit cigarette as he dialled Sally on his phone, Tomàs saying that he thought he'd be okay now to take a plane to our sister's wedding. I looked around at all the other living flesh taking tea, serving at table, standing in line at the door. I listened to whispers of worlds unimaginable to me, each of them sustained in the unblinding light of sense and meaning that's just an instant's sane hiatus in the eternal, dark, relentless rain.

I know what it is not to be alive. And one day I'll emerge again into that endless downpour and I will have to drive in formless thrum and slushy white-noise forever. But until then I shall make my own way.

Goodbye, Tomàs. Goodbye Pablo. I'm scared and I'm naked, and I'm going alone into the world, as we all do, not knowing whether I shall survive even the first minute. Thank you for sustaining me and carrying me so long. I shall miss you, but I have to cut the cord now. Goodbye.

It's time to be born.

Printed in Poland
by Amazon Fulfillment
Poland Sp. z o.o., Wrocław